John Worth is a British writer and artist whose work explores identity, memory, and the search for belonging. His debut novel, *The Many Truths of Josef Batten*, brings together themes of exile, friendship, and healing across generations.

Born in Sussex in 1961, he left school at sixteen and spent a decade travelling and working in film and television before studying photography at the University for the Creative Arts. He later founded a pioneering digital media agency, and his background in visual storytelling continues to shape his writing.

Alongside his literary work, John is a practising artist. He has exhibited widely in the UK, with paintings, prints, and photography. He lives and works in Lewes, East Sussex.

John shares reflections on art, literature, and creative life through Substack **@johnworth01** and on Instagram **@johnworth.artist**, where he connects with readers and fellow creatives.

Find out more at **johnworth.co.uk**

The Many Truths of Josef Batten

John Worth

To Susanne, enjoy!

Copyright © 2025 John Worth

John Worth has asserted his right under the Copyright, Designs and Patents Act 1988 to be identified as the author of this work.

All rights reserved. No part of this book may be reproduced, distributed, or transmitted in any form or by any means, including photocopying, recording, or other electronic or mechanical methods, without the prior written permission of the author, except in the case of brief quotations for the purposes of criticism, review, or other non-commercial uses permitted by copyright law.

Author's Note:
This is a work of fiction. Though it draws upon real places and echoes certain moments in history, all characters and events have been imagined or reshaped for narrative purposes. Where familiar institutions are mentioned, they are used with creative licence and without claim to accuracy or affiliation. Any resemblance to real persons, living or deceased, is entirely coincidental.

References to song titles and artists — including Tom Jones, Van Morrison, John Martyn, Leonard Cohen, Bob Marley & The Wailers, Nick Drake, Stevie Wonder, Neil Young, Joni Mitchell, James Taylor, Simon & Garfunkel, John Denver, The Carpenters, Leon Russell, Kenny Rogers & Dolly Parton — appear in this work. No song lyrics are reproduced except where permitted by law. All rights remain with the original songwriters and publishers.

https://johnworth.co.uk

ISBN: 978-1-0682779-0-0

CONTENTS

ACT 1: JOSEF BATTEN   7

1. Dog Gone   9
2. Nullarbor Running   23
3. Home, Not Home   34
4. Not Much Of A Fisherman   41
5. You Just Take Your Pictures And Leave!   50
6. Still A Boy In Many Ways   65

ACT 2: ADAM LAIDLAW   77

7. Gone Bush   79
8. The Green Green Grass Of Home   99
9. Practicalities And Arrangements   113
10. Regarding The Pain Of Others   126
11. Cathy   136
12. For The Ones Who Did Not Turn Away   150
13. Comes A Time   156
14. What If We Built A House That Breathed?   169
15. Secret O' Life   209

ACT 3: ELIZABETH CHANDLER 227

16. Let Us Not Romanticise His Trauma 229

17. Uncomfortably Yours 251

18. A Mausoleum To Silence 288

19. A Certain Kind of Fury 304

20. Reframing The Ashes 318

21. Jimmy 334

Epilogue 361

The Josef Batten Trust 364

Index of Music 366

Act 1: Josef Batten

1. Dog Gone

South Australia, October 1986

My life changed forever the day my dog was shot dead.

I was there at the Carrieton Rodeo on an assignment, though not for any publication or news agency. I had no editor's brief or deadline to meet. I went of my own free will, drawn by some intuition that this annual gathering in the South Australian outback might hold significance.

Since adopting her ten months before, my dog Theo had remained faithfully by my side. She possessed the precise blend of intelligence and self-sufficiency to suit my life as a working photographer travelling with his four-legged mate.

By the time I arrived, the rodeo was underway, and the arena was teeming with dust, movement, and noise. I began with a wide shot: ochre earth being churned by boots and hooves; the Flinders Ranges rising in the background; in the foreground a canvas beer tent flapping in the breeze.

I worked instinctively, moving through the crowd as invisibly as I could. A young rider caught my eye, his moleskins stained with dust, one hand steadying a restless brumby, the other tightening the saddle. His face was set, unreadable, and the horse's coat still carried traces of its wild roots.

Around the arena's edge, I found the fragments of character and story I was looking for. A woman watching from the far side of the ring, her gaze amused, with a generous smile; a dusty-faced boy on a fence rail, lit up with wonder as a bull thundered past; an older stockman surrounded by younger men, his stories drawing out laughter and admiration in their faces.

I sought the unscripted and in-between moments. Years behind the lens in all types of situations had taught me how to wait for them and to see when someone forgot to perform.

An elderly couple beneath a gum tree welcomed my lens without performance or pretence offering me the simple evidence of their shared life.

More for spectacle than anything else, I watched and waited for riders in flight. Cowboys preparing with stoic focus, then capturing their bodies suspended against the sky before being thumped onto the red dusty earth.

"You're the photographer, aren't you?" a man said as I leaned against the white railings.

I lifted my camera slightly in response. He nodded and turned toward the light. He was rugged and unsmiling, and I caught his stubble and the loose threads of his top button, the fraying hole in the crease of his felt Akubra hat — tiny details, yet powerful evidence of an outback existence.

The day wound down, but the moments kept presenting themselves. A young woman comforting her partner after a rough ride; a child asleep on her father's shoulders, rodeo programme clutched in her small fist. Each scene was a story, and each frame a potential truth.

Through my viewfinder, I tracked Theo's adventures across the rodeo grounds. Her mottled coat caught the afternoon light as she trotted between groups of spectators, her tail wagging in perpetual motion. Every few minutes, she'd pause and glance my way, ears pricking at the sound of my camera's shutter.

A group of children spotted her near the food stalls, and within moments she was surrounded by small hands offering bits of sausage roll and meat pie, her gentle nature shining through as she accepted their treats with delicate care, then rolled onto her back for belly rubs.

Small brilliant white clouds skidded above the foothills, casting moving shadows on bare red earth. The temperature was perfect — warm enough for comfort but cool enough for Theo to maintain her explorations. She sought out a pair of fellow cattle dogs resting in the shade of a gum tree, and they exchanged careful sniffs before settling into a companionable silence.

A stockman called her over, recognising the working dog heritage in her build. She sat attentively as he spoke to her, then followed him to help round up a stray calf that had wandered from its pen. I caught the sequence through my lens — her focused expression and fluid movements as she guided the calf back to safety.

Between my shots of riders and crowd, I'd catch glimpses of her making her rounds, always with one ear turned towards me, ready for my signal. As the afternoon wound down, I packed away my cameras. One sharp whistle and she appeared at my side, pressing against my leg affectionately. Her coat was dusty from her adventures and her eyes sparkled with contentment as we headed back to the Land Cruiser.

*

Whether I found Theo, or she found me is a question for debate. Perhaps it's best to say I 'encountered' her in November 1985, on a desolate stretch of The Great Northern Highway between Meekathara and Newman. She was sitting bolt upright on the roadside as though she were hitch-hiking or waiting for a convenient bus, her coat so caked in reddish ochre dust she blended perfectly with the rusty rubble strip marking the highway's edge.

The scene struck me: that flat expanse of land, some scrubby green-olive vegetation stretching beyond the red verges, the road gently cambering right on the horizon. Four white lines divided the landscape — one on each edge, two running centre, whilst the sky graduated from pale, almost white at the horizon to deep azure above my windscreen — and this image of a lone, very still dog, as though she were a feature in the opening scene of a western. She remained motionless, staring ahead as I pulled up across to the opposite side of the road from her. I stepped out, leaving the door open, and crossed the empty road.

"Hello boy," I called softly.

After a long pause, I offered water but received no reaction. We stood in that peculiar stand-off — me watching her, her watching nothing — until I turned to leave.

As I walked back across the road, she bolted past me, leapt up into the cab, scrambled over the driver's seat and assumed that same upright pose on the passenger side and, just like that, we became travelling companions.

Theo was a red cattle dog, compact and muscular with a thick neck and broad chest. Her coat, once cleaned of the outback dust, revealed itself as a rich ginger-red, flecked with darker spots across her back and haunches. One ear stood permanently alert while the other flopped at the tip, giving her a perpetually quizzical expression.

Her eyes struck me most. They were amber-coloured and intelligent, and they held a depth I'd rarely seen in animals or humans.

Over our first weeks together, Theo's personality emerged. She moved with the precise, measured gait of a working dog, every movement calculated and purposeful. Yet in moments of joy, she'd transform — bounding across the landscape with an explosive energy, only to snap back to my side the moment she sensed my camera raising.

She never barked. Not once. Instead, she communicated through subtle shifts in posture and those extraordinary eyes. A slight tilt of her head might have meant she'd spotted something worth photographing. A gentle paw on my knee warned me of approaching vehicles long before I heard them.

At night, she'd curl into a tight ball beside my swag, and after a while together I noticed her nose would always point north when she slept as though guided by some internal compass. By day, she'd sit for hours watching the horizon, tracking the movement of clouds, birds, and distant cattle with an unwavering focus.

The vet in Newman reckoned she was about three years old, healthy despite her abandonment. I named her Theo, though it wasn't until the vet pointed it out that I realised my mistake about her gender. By then, the name had stuck. She had no collar marks and no signs of previous ownership. She, whom I'd thought was a he, was just a strange, magnificent creature who'd materialised from the desert and chosen me as her human.

For nearly a year, we traversed the sprawling landmass, my companion retaining her graceful demeanour whilst I documented the raw, untamed beauty of Australia's remote wilderness and its inhabitants with my camera.

*

I returned home to Australia from Lebanon in June 1985, driven by a need to reclaim my spirit and find solace through my lens.

I had spent weeks confined in that stinking room, the air heavy with the reek of sweat, rust, and stale urine. My right wrist was shackled to a radiator by a short chain, my body aching from the unyielding cement floor, muscles wasted away from lack of movement. I counted twenty-two days in the flickering light of a single, bare bulb.

Others were held in similar rooms across the city — journalists, aid workers, professors. Some had been there for months, even years. Whispers circulated before my capture: Terry Anderson of the Associated Press had been taken; British journalist John

McCarthy would be seized later that year. Some would never return. Unlike them, I was still alive. Still whole.

My captors were Hezbollah, a militant Shi'a group that thrived in Lebanon's civil war chaos. Iran-backed and fiercely opposed to Western presence, they saw men like me as bargaining chips. In 1984, they kidnapped CIA station chief William Buckley and tortured him so severely that it took years to confirm his identity after his death. Others like Jeremy Levin were dragged from their homes and beaten mercilessly. I was familiar with their stories; now I had become one of them.

Beirut in 1985 was a city in ruins — once the Paris of the Middle East, now a shattered landscape of bombed-out buildings and burned-out cars. The Green Line divided Christian East Beirut from Muslim West Beirut, a jagged scar lined with sniper nests and sandbag barricades. Movement was dangerous for foreigners, but I always thought I'd been careful. It hadn't been enough.

I'd avoided wearing a 'press' flak jacket that may have marked me out, but they still took me. It was just beyond the Green Line, and I was in a battered taxi heading toward the Commodore Hotel, a known press refuge. The checkpoint was unofficial — a makeshift roadblock manned by masked gunmen. A man in fatigues tapped the car's bonnet with his rifle; the driver raised his hands in surrender. The door yanked open, and a hand gripped my collar, dragging me into the street. My camera shattered on the ground as someone wrenched my arms behind my back. Then the sack came down over my head.

I was shoved into a car thick with the scent of sweat and petrol. No one spoke as we wound through a city I had spent many assignments documenting but could no longer see. Now here I was: three weeks in darkness, waiting. The others — hostages taken before me — were beaten, some starved. Their cries echoed through the walls at night. When my turn came, I expected the worst.

Instead, they unchained me without a word, covered my head again and dragged me into another car. When we stopped, they pulled me onto a deserted street and cut the plastic ties from my wrists before vanishing. By the time I was found outside the Commodore Hotel, slumped and shivering, I was no longer the same man. The isolation and fear I felt in captivity had eroded my sense of self.

*

After Lebanon, Australia called to me like a distant refuge. I needed open spaces to breathe again, a landscape vast enough to absorb my fractured soul, and people whose lives carried on far from war's shadow. So, I set out across this great continent in my handsome cream Toyota Land Cruiser FJ45 with Theo joining me a few months into my journey.

I travelled its length and breadth capturing moments of human resilience amidst nature's stark beauty, the kind that renews rather than destroys. I'd left Perth in September 1985, heading north through mining communities where men's faces were streaked with iron ore dust. My camera caught their exhaustion, their moments of release in local pubs, the massive machinery consuming the earth. The vehicle's reliable suspension easily conquering corrugated roads and river crossings without complaint.

In the Kimberley, the landscape shifted to boab trees and ochre cliffs. In the far north of the Dampier Peninsula at One Arm Point, the Bardi people cautiously allowed me to document their lives — always on their terms and with permission.

Every few weeks, I packed rolls of exposed film and sent them to Anne Delacourt, my photographic agent at *Agence Frontière* in Paris. She supervised their development in professional darkrooms, ensuring the highest standards were maintained. Anne had an exceptional instinct for selecting the most compelling images for syndication to the magazines and newspapers she knew were hungry for fresh documentary work. She had an unerring sense of which frames would resonate with their readers.

Even as my journey continued, she was already in negotiations with a major publisher about producing a high-quality coffee table book to mark its conclusion, after which I was expected to return to war photography. The book was already in development, with a title, *Australia: The Witnessing Eye*, approved and in place.

The wagon held my essential world: camera gear, films, swag, tarpaulins, cooler, jerry cans, and a metal box of dried and non-perishable food. Its long wheelbase proved perfect for this nomadic life, the part-time four-wheel drive handling whatever challenges the outback presented.

From the Kimberley, I'd slowly traced a path through the Northern Territory, down through Queensland's Gulf Country, inland through New South Wales to Broken Hill and into South Australia.

I had fully expected to pick up my international assignments once more, as I had for the past three and a half decades, but that day I had no inkling that my lifelong journey as a photojournalist would eventually conclude at the outback rodeo grounds in Carrieton, South Australia.

*

The late afternoon sun was beginning to cast shadows across the dusty road as Theo and I left Carrieton and we rumbled steadily north heading for Hawker, the wagon's cream paintwork splashed orange in the fading light. Theo sat in her usual position — upright, alert, watching the world through the passenger window. The road stretched ahead through sparse mallee scrub, the ancient peaks of the Flinders Ranges looming closer with each mile. To our right, the slowly setting sun painted the wheat fields golden. A wedge-tailed eagle soared overhead, riding the thermals in lazy circles.

I'd spent my life keeping people at arm's length, viewing the world through my viewfinder rather than engaging with it, but Theo had changed that. She'd slipped past my defences that day on the highway, claiming her spot in my life with such certainty that I hadn't noticed the walls beginning to come down. I often wondered what she saw when she looked at me. A broken man trying to piece himself back together? Or simply someone who'd offered her water and a ride that day in the desert? Perhaps both. Dogs don't judge the way people do.

We passed the turnoff to Wilson, the gravel road disappearing into the gathering dusk, Theo's head tracking something in the scrub — probably a kangaroo — before returning to her vigilant forward gaze. The trust in her eyes whenever she looked at me was absolute, uncomplicated by the baggage humans carry. It was the first real connection I'd allowed myself in decades, possibly ever.

Returning to Hawker, the light was fading as we came to a stop beside the weathered caravan I'd called home for the previous week or so. The air was dry, tinged with eucalyptus and the ghost of distant rain that would never arrive.

My eyes flicked towards the house of its owner, a classic South Australian outback dwelling, single-story, corrugated iron roof, a veranda sagging with age. Peeling paint curled away from the wooden posts and the yard, fenced in rusted corrugated iron, was a graveyard of forgotten machinery: a broken tractor slumped in the corner, an abandoned Holden rusting into the earth, half-swallowed by stubborn weeds, the scruffy caravan permanently pitched on the furthest edge away from the house. Everything here seemed to be waiting, caught in a slow decay.

My host Harry was sitting on his veranda, so I lifted a hand in greeting, expecting the same easy camaraderie we'd shared on his porch days before. But Harry didn't move. His gaze was fixed, unreadable. I hesitated, unsettled by his stillness. Shrugging it off, I pushed open the door. Theo leapt out, stretching herself before trotting toward a patch of scrub on what could only loosely be described as lawn and, as I was moving to the back of the wagon to retrieve my camera bag, a sudden gunshot ripped through the evening air.

The reverberations lingered in a stark quietness, as though time itself had stopped in that instant. I turned.

Theo lay splayed in the dust, lifeless, a dark blood stain already seeping into the parched earth. My breath stilled in my chest, I felt my pulse slowing to a singular, thudding beat in my ears. On the veranda, Harry was clattering down the steps, shotgun gripped tight, his face twisted into something both ancient and raw.

"Fucking dog! Shitting on my lawn!"

I didn't think or speak. I reached instinctively for my camera, already loaded with a fresh roll of Tri-X pan, its weight grounding me as I lifted it to my eye. The world immediately shifted into black and white; into light and shadow, something I could dissect and understand. The familiar click and whirr of the shutter became my only anchor.

I framed Harry: bare feet pounding against the dust, grit collecting on his calloused soles; his jeans were new but had already creased with his shape; a leather belt cinched tight; his white vest damp with sweat. Every muscle in his wiry frame coiled tight with rage, tendons standing out like wires beneath sun-darkened skin.

Harry's face was contorted in fury, his jaw appearing like a broken hinge; his unshaven cheeks peppered with grey stubble; and eyes wild and small like black coals burning in their sockets. His hands gripped the shotgun, knuckles taut; his veins raised; the barrel gleaming cold in the dying light against the heat rolling off his body. His mouth twisted around the words he spat out with venom; his lips cracked from the relentless outback sun; flecks of spittle were flying with every shouted curse; the tendons in his neck standing out like whipcords; his throat bobbing with rage.

I moved silently forward without lowering my camera. I wasn't thinking, I never thought in moments like this. I acted, framed, and captured. It's what I did when violence flared and when people revealed themselves in their most primal state. My camera had seen war zones, refugee camps, and riots and this was no different.

He stumbled, yelling incoherently as his anger consumed him, and he hurled the gun to the ground and stood motionless, his chest heaving. I took one last shot, studying him through the viewfinder for a moment longer. In that instant, his face showed a flicker of calm replacing his anger.

Without a word, Harry turned, picked up his gun and stomped back toward the house, his bare feet scuffing against the ground, kicking up little clouds of dirt until he reached the veranda steps and entered the house, slamming the screen door behind him.

I stood for a moment, the silence pressing in. The sky was beginning to streak purple and orange, darkened at the edges, and as night crept in the air felt thinner.

Without thinking I walked back to the wagon, opened the rear door, and placed the camera back in its bag. I turned toward the caravan, stepped inside and with measured hands, packed my belongings, rolled up my clothes and tucked away the few things I had left in this temporary home, carried the bags outside, and loaded them into the Toyota.

I returned to the caravan and pulled a blanket from the narrow bed and walked back out into the yard to Theo's body where I knelt beside her. As I laid the blanket out, smoothing it against the earth, I could feel that the warmth had already begun to fade from her stocky frame. Gently, I gathered her up and blood darkened the fabric as I wrapped her. Cradling her close against my chest, I opened the rear door of the wagon and laid her wrapped form carefully inside.

Since we'd first pulled into the yard thirteen life-shattering minutes had passed and Theo was gone.

Instead of confronting Harry, yelling, fighting, or demanding answers or retribution, I drove away without purpose or direction, the road beneath me blurring into one long strip of grey.

Heading south the landscape was familiar yet foreign, the pale ochres and reds of the earth and the foothills were softened by dusk's fading light, the sky now a canvas of bruised purples and deepening blues. I couldn't feel anything — no sorrow or rage, only the empty void. The routine hum of tyres on bitumen and the rhythmic flicker of passing white lines became a lullaby of sorts, numbing me further with each passing kilometre; sparse trees silhouetted against a starlit sky, occasional flashes of wildlife darting across the road, and vast open plains stretching into oblivion.

Where was I going? What would I do? These questions drifted through my mind. Control had always been my lifeline, my camera capturing chaos from a safe distance, but now it felt as though it had slipped through my fingers like sand.

Emotion had always been something to observe from behind a lens, never to be expressed. Anger and hurt were strangers to me; feelings were locked away, distant and unreachable.

Alien pain began to surface, a dull ache deep within, that I didn't know how to confront. I kept driving towards uncertainty, an unfamiliar weight pressing down harder with each kilometre.

At a lonely T junction, I turned right where the lights of Port Augusta loomed in the distance. The fuel gauge had dipped dangerously low, and at a truck stop, a neon BP sign flickered wearily. Climbing out of the wagon, I lifted the nozzle to fill up and a harsh fluorescent light exaggerated the emptiness around me. The smell of petrol filled the air, sharp and acrid. I went inside to pay, and the attendant looked up from behind the counter. He was a young man with tired eyes that held a flicker of curiosity.

"G'day," he greeted me.

I reached for my wallet but paused mid-motion. For a moment, I couldn't remember why I was there or what I was supposed to do. My mind went blank, a fog rolling in and obscuring everything. I stood there, staring at nothing.

"Mate? You okay?" His voice broke through my haze.

I blinked, feeling disoriented and out of place. Words failed me; my throat constricted as if speech had become an impossible task. Fumbling with my wallet, I pulled out some cash. The attendant's gaze softened with concern as he counted it quickly before handing back change without another word, his silence a small kindness in a moment of vulnerability.

"Take care," he murmured when I turned to leave.

As I drove back out onto the highway the car's interior felt vast and empty without Theo beside me. After a few hours, I pulled over to the side of an empty stretch of road, cut the engine and sat in the dark silence that was crashing in on me, hands remaining locked on the steering wheel. Something was happening inside me — unfamiliar sensations I couldn't name or understand.

Throughout my career, I'd photographed grief countless times and captured the raw anguish on the faces of mothers who'd lost children, soldiers who'd lost comrades, and survivors who'd lost everything. I'd documented their pain with detached precision, my lens creating a barrier between their emotions and my own carefully constructed emptiness. But this... this was different. The void I'd cultivated for decades was filling with something dark and heavy. My chest felt tight and constricted, each breath shorter than the last. The vast South Australian night was pressing in, and I felt truly alone.

I'd always thought myself above such basic human feelings as loneliness. Emotions were messy, unpredictable things that clouded judgment and compromised objectivity, and I'd prided myself on my ability to remain untouched, unchanged by the horrors I witnessed. Yet here I sat, undone by the absence of a dog. Not just any dog. Theo, my companion. The only living creature I'd allowed close enough to matter. She'd been my wordless friend through countless journeys and encounters with anonymous strangers. In her absence, I was drifting aimlessly, untethered in an empty void.

My throat constricted painfully, and the steering wheel blurred before my eyes. I blinked rapidly, refusing to acknowledge the tears gathering in them. This weakness — this feeling — it was alien, unwanted. I tried to push it away, to reclaim the familiar numbness that had served me so well for so long. Was this what loss felt like? This hollowness that somehow weighed more heavily than anything I'd ever carried.

2. Nullarbor Running

Sometime after midnight, I slowly rolled into Ceduna, a town perched on the edge of the vast Nullarbor Plain. It lay cloaked in a peaceful darkness, and sparse intermittent streetlights were casting eerie shadows across empty roads.

At the outskirts of town, I steered into a vast truck stop, its fluorescent lights casting a glow on a trio of massive Kenworth rigs being prepared to traverse the desolate 1200 kilometre stretch from east to west. I noticed a hitchhiker sitting by the roadside, a red rucksack propped up beside him. His figure was slumped yet watchful, eyes glinting in the artificial glow. A sense of unease settled over me as I hoped he wouldn't ask for a ride.

I parked and stepped out of the wagon, stretching my stiff limbs. As I moved to refuel, his steps were hesitant but determined.

"Excuse me," he called out, "Are you heading west? Could you give me a lift?"

His voice was young and refined — English I thought, or maybe Scottish — and carrying an undertone of midnight weariness. I kept my eyes on the pump, filling up the tank with mechanical precision.

"Anywhere west will do," he added over the sound of the petrol gushing into the tank.

I said nothing, letting silence speak for me. He turned back towards his pack; taking my silence as rudeness or indifference, I assumed.

Once the tank was full, I replaced the nozzle and went to pay. The cool air inside was a stark contrast to the lingering warmth outside. As I approached the counter, I caught sight of a shovel displayed near some camping supplies. On impulse, I grabbed it along with a few basic provisions, water bottles, and some canned food, and placed them on the counter.

The cashier keyed the prices into the till without comment.

"Anything else?" she asked.

I shook my head and handed over cash before heading back to my vehicle.

As I walked out, the hitchhiker was still standing by his red rucksack, hope fading from his eyes. Without acknowledging him further, I climbed into the wagon and started the engine. The neon lights of the truck stop dwindled in my rearview mirror as I sped off into the night, down that long straight stretch of Eyre Highway that seemed to lead into darkness and oblivion.

*

Hours later, where the road met the Great Australian Bight and Great Southern Ocean, the Bunda Cliffs zoomed into view, large and imposing. The vast emptiness of the Nullarbor Plain had splayed out on either side of me, bathed in the ethereal glow of the Milky Way above. My tired eyes had struggled to stay focused on the endless highway stretching before me, and the occasional rumble of my tyres against the road's shoulder was the only thing keeping me alert through the hypnotic journey.

The night sky was a celestial tapestry with the occasional faint streak of a shooting star, a big moon hanging high and full was casting a bright silvery glow over the landscape.

I pulled over near a cliff edge where the precipice fell away, and moonlit cliffs swept around the bay's circumference exposing the daunting scale of the sheer cliff faces. I grabbed the shovel and began excavating a depression in the earth. The stubborn stony ground resisted my efforts, and I could only manage a shallow indent, but it would suffice.

I unwrapped Theo from the blanket and gently laid her alongside it. I smoothed the blanket over the indent and placed her cold limp body on top of it. Her fur still carried the dust of our travels, and I could almost see her ears twitching in sleep as I draped the blanket back over her. I paused for a moment.

"Goodbye, Theo," I whispered. "Thank you."

I slowly stood, my joints stiff from crouching, and scanned the harsh limestone ground for suitable stones to cover her. The edges of the blanket remained loosely draped over her form as I began my solemn task. One by one, I gathered the stones, selecting each with care — some smooth, others jagged, but all of them feeling weighty in my hands. Gently and purposefully, I placed them over her still form, building layer upon layer until I had created a small, neat mound of rocks. In the growing darkness, the pile stood as a silent memorial, barely visible against the vast emptiness of the Nullarbor Plain.

My heart felt like I had buried it with her as I took a flannel shirt from the wagon and made a makeshift sack with which to gather some smaller stones, twisting the fabric into a crude pouch. Slowly, in a trance, I searched the surrounding scrub for the smoothest uniform-sized pieces I could find. When I had collected enough, I crouched back down next to her makeshift grave and set to work spelling 'Theo. The finest friend' arranging each stone with careful precision until the words stood out against the dusty ground.

I stood and walked over to the edge of the cliffs. The ocean below was an inky black expanse, the stark white of arcing and cresting waves crashing softly into sheer cliffs.

As I stood there, listening to their rhythm, another sound reached my ears — the distant cries of whales. Their calls were haunting, echoing through the night like mournful songs. Each exhale sounded like a heavy sigh, followed by low-frequency moans that seemed to vibrate through my very bones; sounds that grew louder and more insistent, filling the air around me — raw and guttural wails that didn't seem to belong to any creature of the sea.

It took me some time to recognise my own cries bellowing out from deep inside my chest. The dam inside me had broken. Years of suppressed grief and pain came flooding out in an unrelenting torrent. My knees buckled, and I collapsed onto the cold ground, sobbing uncontrollably into the night.

The cries of the whales had merged with my own, a symphony of sorrow echoing across the cliffs and out into the vast Southern Ocean. Uncontrollable sobs for everything I'd lost, for the boy I'd been, for the man I'd become, for Theo, who had shown me how to begin to feel. Ten months of companionship and understanding gone in a heartbeat.

*

I rejoined the main road and ahead lay hundreds of kilometres of highway stretching endlessly into the darkness; the vast Nullarbor seeming to mock my solitude, its emptiness a mirror of the void within.

As morning light crept into my rear-view mirrors, I crossed the border into Western Australia, where the highway abruptly expanded and seemed to transform into a more superior quality road surface.

I spotted a marker indicating an abandoned communications outpost, partially concealed by windswept dunes, and a faded sign for *Old Eyre Highway* drew my attention. On impulse, I steered onto the dirt path. The raised suspension and four-wheel drive made easy work of the rutted road as I shuddered and clattered along the rippled ground. A narrower-grown trail meandered through scattered bush vegetation until it emerged at the top of a chalky escarpment.

There, silhouetted against an emerging golden dawn sky, stood the shell of an abandoned roadhouse. Its roof had partially collapsed, and desert winds had piled red dirt against its western wall. The petrol pumps were long gone, leaving only rust-stained concrete islands.

I parked in the building's shadow and killed the engine. The silence pressed in, broken only by the ticking of the cooling engine and the whisper of wind through empty window frames. The front door hung askew on one hinge. Inside, my boots crunched on broken glass and sand. A counter ran along one wall, its surface thick with dust.

A doorway led to what must have once been living quarters. The roof was mostly intact here, and the air felt cooler, and musty, carrying the stale scent of decades-old dust. Pale rectangles on the wall marked where pictures had once hung, their ghostly outlines a testament to memories long forgotten. In one corner, an iron bedstead still stood, springs exposed like ribs, its thin mattress having rotted away to nothing but a few mouldering tatters. A wooden chair lay toppled nearby, one leg missing, whilst cobwebs stretched between the bed frame and the wall like gossamer curtains.

I unrolled my swag against the far wall, where the morning sun wouldn't reach. The blankets smelled of dust and long roads. My body felt heavy, and disconnected, as if I were moving through deep water. I lay down and closed my eyes, with an image of Theo's grave swimming before me in the darkness.

I must have fallen into a deep sleep almost immediately, my body feeling like it had been pulled into the earth, heavy and unyielding. Dreams began to creep in, vivid and disjointed, flashes of lightning on a stormy night:

I found myself underground, crawling through tight spaces that seemed to tighten with each breath I took. The cave walls closed in around me, pressing against my chest, making it increasingly difficult to breathe. My heart pounded in my ears, a relentless drumbeat, as I forced myself through narrow potholes and along dark, winding tunnels. The rocks seemed to constrict, tightening with every inhalation.

"Help!" I screamed, my voice echoing back at me in a mocking whisper that faded into the oppressive silence.

Panic surged through me as the air grew thin and stale. I clawed at the rocks, my fingers scraping against their rough surfaces, desperate to find an opening, a way out. Just as I thought I would suffocate, the tunnel expanded into a vast chamber bathed in golden light, a sanctuary emerging from the darkness.

The beauty of the cave stunned me, momentarily halting my frantic thoughts. Stalactites hung from the ceiling, chandeliers in a forgotten cathedral, their mineral-rich tips glistening in the soft light. Stalagmites rose from the ground, sturdy and majestic, reaching upward, yearning to touch their counterparts above, creating a natural colonnade.

I breathed deeply, feeling a momentary relief wash over me. But I noticed something peculiar. Embedded within each stalactite and stalagmite were photographs; images that felt hauntingly familiar, frozen in time yet painfully vivid.

The first one caught my eye: a South African policeman gripping his rifle while a young black protester hurled a stone. The shadow of a falling body loomed just beyond the frame, a silent witness to the violence.

I stumbled back, gasping, my eyes darting from one formation to the next. My gaze shifted to another formation — a young Congolese soldier with wide, fearful eyes boarding a UN truck while smoke rose from a torched village behind him.

"Why?" I muttered, shaking my head in disbelief.

Each step revealed another horror encased in stone: A German mother screaming through barbed wire as her child cried on the other side; a Cuban teenage militia member cradling an old Soviet rifle; a self-immolated body, still emitting smoke, remained unnervingly upright on the Saigon street while nearby, a young boy's horrified expression was mirrored in a puddle of spilt petrol; an emaciated Biafran child with a distended belly clinging to his skeletal sibling.

The images became more intense, more unbearable. An Israeli tank commander kneeling in the Sinai sand, his tears mixing with dust; rows of empty shoes lining the Mekong River banks as refugees fled; an American soldier cradling dog tags amidst Vietnam's menacing jungle.

The cave spun around me, a whirlpool of chaos and destruction: British soldiers looking away as Catholic children threw stones; Palestinian boys gripping chain-link fences with tears streaking dusty cheeks; a blindfolded American diplomat with an armed militant looming behind him.

My screams mingled with the cacophony of war echoing off the cave walls. The jagged formations became jagged memories piercing through my mind, every photograph forcing me to relive the horror it captured in excruciating detail.

"Wake up!" I yelled desperately, but the nightmare tightened its grip, refusing to release me from its clutches.

I jolted awake. The silence pressed in once more, only this time, it felt like salvation, a reprieve from the relentless torment of my memories.

*

I woke to suffocating heat, the sun having crept across the room to find me. Sweat pooled beneath my clothes, yet a deep chill rattled through my bones. I pushed myself up from the swag, muscles screaming in protest.

The room tilted and swayed. I steadied myself against the wall, its rough surface grounding me. Something was wrong — terribly wrong. My body felt like a mechanical toy wound too tight, springs and gears threatening to burst through my skin. Grief sat like a stone in my throat. I wanted to weep, to let out the pressure building inside me, but the tears wouldn't come.

I stumbled outside. The afternoon heat hit me like a physical blow, yet I couldn't stop shaking. My teeth chattered as if I stood in a blizzard rather than the Australian outback. Water from my canteen splashed over my hands as I tried to drink.

The vastness of the landscape pressed in around me. Too much space. Too much emptiness. Without Theo's steady presence beside me, the world felt unstable and threatening. For the first time in my life, I recognised what was happening — the carefully constructed walls of my mind were crumbling.

I made my way to the Land Cruiser, each step uncertain. The metal door handle burned my palm as I pulled it open. Inside, the steering wheel felt foreign under my hands, like an object from another life. I turned the key, the engine's rumble both familiar and strange, and pointed the vehicle toward the highway.

*

Five hours later, as I approached Norseman, the sun dipped low, spreading shadows that danced across the barren landscape. Nearly twenty-four hours had passed since I had left Hawker and a life that now seemed like a distant memory.

I reached the junction, the first in over a thousand kilometres, where the highway forked left toward Esperance and right toward Kalgoorlie and Perth. Left, or right? The need to decide loomed urgently, demanding an answer I didn't have. My mind was a foggy mess, and any clarity I could muster eluded me like a wisp of smoke before I could decide.

I pulled over and sat in the silence of the cab, dusk settling around me, stars beginning to prick the darkening sky. I shivered despite the warmth of the evening, my body continuing to be bound in a relentless cycle of grief and exhaustion. To my left lay the prospect of Esperance and potentially the continuation of my assignment. To my right lay Kalgoorlie and Perth, the prospect of the home I rarely visited.

The emptiness inside me echoed as I sat there, hoping for some answers, some whispers from above to guide me. But nothing came. The heavens offered no solace or direction. Eventually, I indicated right. The decision came not from reason but from sheer exhaustion.

*

A few hours later the lights of Kalgoorlie pierced the darkness as I approached from the Goldfields Highway. The road widened, transforming from endless outback into civilization marked by scattered streetlamps spreading pools of orange light onto the road.

There was life happening even at this late hour. Mining operations never ceased here — the Super Pit's luminescence resembled a man-made dawn on the skyline. The broad Hannan Street, originally designed for horse-drawn wagons transporting the gold, was now flanked by grand Victorian edifices, testament to a wealthy history.

I pulled up outside a milk bar, fluorescent lights still buzzing. The owner was clearing up to close for the night but waved me in with the weary smile of someone who'd seen every type of person pass through.

"Last pie in the warmer," he said, wrapping it in wax paper, "YMCA's twelve bucks a night. Basic, but clean. Better than kipping in your car."

The pie's warmth seeped through the paper as I sat on a wooden bench outside. Above me, the streetlamp attracted moths dancing in endless circles. The pastry crumbled in my fingers, the meat filling was barely lukewarm, but I couldn't remember when I'd last eaten.

The YMCA was a solid brick building with windows glowing yellow against the night sky. Inside, a corridor stretched past a common room where two men played cards. My footsteps echoed on the linoleum floor as I approached the reception desk. The tiny dorm they put me in was sparse — a single bed and a bunk bed next to a metal-framed window, and a shared bathroom down the hall. The lower bunk looked as if it was available, it didn't look comfortable, but it was clean. A worn armchair sat in the corner, its fabric bearing the ghosts of countless travellers before me.

As I stared into the darkness willing sleep to come the door creaked open. Light from the corridor spilled across the floor and two men stumbled in.

"She's mental, mate. Completely lost it."

The shorter one rattled the bed frame as he clambered up the ladder and collapsed onto the top bunk, his nasal twang was slurred yet bitingly sharp.

"Bitch threw all my fuckin stuff out the window."

The tall one settled into the armchair with an arrogant air, his angular frame casting strange shadows.

"Had my share of fuck'n dramas in Africa." he boomed.

"Africa? What the fuck were you doin' there?"

"Mercenary work."

He leaned forward, voice dropping.

"Saw things. Did things. Village raids. Didn't matter if they were civilians."

The drunk man gave a low whistle.

"Brutal."

"Nothing compared to what I saw in Kings Park last month though." The tall man's voice took on an edge. "Full moon. Group of them in black robes. Had this altar set up near the war memorial. Blood everywhere."

I lay perfectly still, barely breathing, as he described the ritual he claims took place in this massive park near the centre of Perth in disturbing detail. My mind rationalised that he was lying, but in his tone, there was also a potential truth lurking.

"Oi, we've woken someone." The drunk man noticed me stirring below him.

"Hey mate, you awake?"

The tall one's attention shifted to my bunk.

"What's your story then?"

I remained open-eyed, silent and motionless, feeling my heart pounding against my ribs as they continued attempting to prise me, their voices growing more insistent until eventually they gave up and their conversation drifted into mumbles.

At about four in the morning, I silently slipped out of the bunk and gathered my things. Any sleep I'd had was hard won. His disturbing story was still echoing in my mind as I crept past his sleeping figure and out into the empty hallway.

3. Home, Not Home

The streets of Kalgoorlie were deserted, save for the occasional mine worker's ute heading for an early shift, their headlights cutting through the gloom. The wagon was waiting outside, a shadow against the grey pre-dawn light and a comforting presence in my rapidly changing world. Six hundred kilometres stretched between me and Perth, a journey that would span nearly seven hours.

As I pulled onto the Great Eastern Highway, my mind drifted to the old chemist shop with its portrait studio and darkroom. Mo and Belinda Batten had taken me in during those war years, giving me a home when I had none. Their unconditional kindness was something I recognised but probably never truly understood.

The weathered facade of the terraced shop had stood unchanged on Oxford Street since 1971 when they'd both died within months of each other. Its shabby Victorian frontage stubbornly ignored the signs of the gentrification very slowly developing around it.

When Mo died, I'd been in Cambodia and only heard the news after his funeral. I was there a further two months when I heard about Belinda and just managed to return in time once her funeral had been arranged with only hours to spare. Within days I flew away again, Bangladesh this time. The grief must have been inside me somewhere, on a slow burn, their deaths a reminder of the human connections I could sense but had always kept at arm's length.

The shop and house remained mine now, preserved like a time capsule. The front room's glass cabinets still displayed relics of bottles of tonics and medicines, thick with dust and the echoes of a bygone era. The portrait studio in the back held Mo's large format camera, draped in a sheet that had yellowed with age. Even the darkroom chemicals sat crystallised in their bottles, untouched for decades, a silent testament to the passage of time.

Over the years I'd occasionally stopped by in between assignments, managing the archive of my prints I kept there and sleeping in my old room upstairs but never staying long enough to call it home. The rooms remained dark, furniture draped in sheets, photos fading on the walls. It was a place frozen in time, holding memories I'd never fully embraced, a sanctuary and a mausoleum all at once.

The sun crept over the horizon as I drove west toward Perth. The road ahead was long, but the journey was a familiar one, a bridge between the man I was and the boy who had once found refuge in a chemist shop on Oxford Street in the Perth suburb of Leederville.

Since Theo's death two days before, I'd become a quaking mess. My face felt stretched and swollen, my insides leaden. I could feel myself shaking, at times almost violently. I'd begun to realise the magnitude and full extent of my implosion and was aware I was experiencing a full mental breakdown. My thoughts were fragments, pieces that wouldn't fit together. I didn't know what I was doing, where I was going, or what I wanted.

For the first time in my life, my camera felt like a useless weight — the desire to capture moments, to document life through images, had evaporated — the mask it provided had slipped off, leaving me exposed to the raw reality of my existence. There was no buffer, no lens to distance myself from the pain inside me.

I struggled to keep the wagon steady on the road. Every jolt and bump seemed amplified by my state of nervousness. By the time I limped into Oxford Street in Leederville, I felt like an absolute wreck. The familiar buildings loomed around me — silent witnesses to my disintegration. I pulled up outside the old shop front, the place that had once been my sanctuary. The sight of it — unchanged and stoic — brought a flood of memories crashing down on me, Mo and Belinda's faces flickering in my mind's eye, their kindness a distant echo.

It all became too much. The weight of Theo's loss, the unravelling of my own identity, and the crushing realisation of my vulnerability broke through my fragile composure. Tears streamed down my face uncontrollably. I could feel myself weeping, sobbing — lost to myself, lost to the world.

As I switched off the engine waves of grief surged through me. Each sob wracked my body with an intensity that left me gasping for breath. In that moment, everything felt unbearably real — every suppressed emotion and unspoken truth bobbing up to the surface. The old shop front stood as lifeless and shuttered as ever, offering no comfort or solace. My tears blurred its outline into a hazy spectre of my past life.

I cried for Theo and for myself — for every moment lost behind a camera lens and for every emotion I had buried deep within me over decades of witnessing human suffering from behind a lens that had now become meaningless.

*

Oxford Street buzzed with vitality — cafés, boutiques, and young professionals rushing along the pavements, their lives starkly different from the peaceful, neighbourly existence of Mo and Belinda's era and the delicate war years and post-war recovery of my youth. The hustle and bustle, the crowds, the traffic, and the noise were all foreign to me, and I was dreading the inevitable interactions required to get by while I was there. I had always been adept at blending into the background on assignments, avoiding contact when it suited me. But now, I could feel myself slipping into a paranoid state of mind, and it was becoming increasingly difficult to conceal this deterioration. I knew I could scarcely hide my anguished spirit and that I needed to escape as quickly as possible.

I set about preparing to leave and spent the following two days in Leederville in a frightened state of overwhelm. At the post office, I dispatched the most recent set of film rolls to Anne in Paris, including the Tri-X Pan with the shots of Harry moments after he killed Theo. I didn't intentionally send that roll, and if I'd considered it, I might have withheld it due to its personal significance.

The next task was sorting out the housekeeping affairs. I dropped the Land Cruiser off at Joe's Garage for a service and walked a further block to the ANZ Bank to settle outstanding matters and to ensure the regular bills to do with the property would be taken care of during my next long absence. The bank clerk recognised me immediately, a flicker of familiarity crossing his face as he efficiently handed over the renewed debit orders. These were essential to ensure that all necessary payments would be taken care of. He proceeded to count out a substantial amount of cash, the sound of the notes crisp and methodical as they were stacked into neat bundles. Each bundle was carefully placed into a cloth sack, which he handed to me with a nod. I took the sack and tucked it away securely in my satchel, away from prying eyes.

I headed to Dick Edwards' estate agency on the corner of the block. The building had a fresh coat of paint, a stark contrast to my dilapidated shop front. Dick greeted me with his usual charismatic smile, though there was an undertone of concern in his eyes when he saw the state of me.

"Dick," I began, feeling the weight of my request, "I need you to carry out any maintenance on the shop for at least another few years. That includes windows, leaks, boiler checks, and all that. Don't forget the yard and make sure any weeding is taken care of."

He nodded slowly, leaning back in his chair. "Still holding onto that place, eh? You know it's prime real estate now. You could get a good price."

He could see I was in no place to respond. "Just keep an eye on it for me, will you?" I said, handing him a cheque. "This should cover it."

Dick raised an eyebrow, surprised by the amount. "If you need more or if I'm not back before it runs out, I'll send…" My words trailed off as I turned to leave in a heightened daze, the weight of the unspoken lingering in the air. I couldn't bring myself to finish the sentence, the confusion and uncertainty gnawing away at me.

Dick was accustomed to this type of request; he had always been more than an estate agent. For decades, he had been Mo and Belinda's key-holder, even when they were alive, entrusted with the care of their property. Our connection went back to our school days, we were never close friends, but we had been familiar faces in each other's lives for as long as I could remember. It was an unspoken bond, a shared history that made these interactions seamless, if not entirely comfortable.

I opened the door to depart and felt a terrifying moment of panic set in.

"Please keep taking care of it," I said as I exited.

*

The sun had barely risen as I walked to Joe's Garage the following morning to collect the wagon. Joe had sourced the Toyota FJ43 for me the previous year, and with his characteristic enthusiasm prepared it for my long and arduous subsequent adventure. I trusted him implicitly.

He emerged from the shadows of his workshop, blinking against the early morning sun while wiping his grease-stained hands on a rag, the familiar scent of oil and metal hanging in the air.

"She's all set," he said, his voice carrying a note of satisfaction as he handed back my keys along with the bill.

"If you ask me, you got off lightly although she needed a new alternator and new discs all round. But she's had a full service, and I've tightened her up too so there should be less of a rattle and hum on your travels now."

His words, thorough and reassuring, were a testament to his meticulous care and attention, the very qualities that made me trust him with the Land Cruiser.

"Cheers, Joe," I responded, a spark of gratitude breaking through my inner turmoil. I looked at the amount on the invoice, counted out a large wad of cash from my wallet, and handed it to him.

"Blimey mate," he remarked, "if I'd known you were paying cash, I would've knocked a bit off for you."

"No worries, Joe," I said, appreciating his thorough work.

"Only glad you could sort her out so quickly."

As I walked over to the vehicle, I noticed the wagon gleaming in the early morning sun, looking almost brand new. I ran my hand along the smooth surface, feeling the cool, freshly polished metal.

I drove straight to the Army Surplus on Newcastle Street. The store was crammed with gear: rows of heavy-duty tents, camping stoves, and weather-resistant clothing lined the shelves. The air smelled of canvas and rubber, an odd but not unpleasant mix.

I selected a sturdy canvas tent large enough to stand up in. I added a couple of sleeping bags variously rated for temperature, a new portable stove and billy cans, enough cooking utensils and water purification tablets to make off-grid cooking manageable for a very long time, extra fuel canisters and more tarpaulins to cover my gear in case of rain. At the last moment, I threw in a fishing tackle kit as well, which was an odd choice for someone who had never fished in his life — perhaps for a means of survival or maybe a semblance of peace.

At Coles supermarket, I filled a trolley with non-perishable food items, canned beans, porridge, sugar, packets of rice and pasta and dried fruits. Each item felt like another brick in the wall I was building between myself and civilisation.

In the afternoon I fuelled up the wagon and the spare fuel canisters then set to work packing and organising it. The tent was secured tightly on the roof pallet along with the fuel strapped down for stability.

As evening descended upon Leederville, the lampposts blinked to life beside Mo and Belinda's timeworn shop windows, bathing the aged windowpanes in soft illumination. I had packed to leave the place countless times before, but this time it held an air of permanence. I was feeling compelled to vanish, sensing that my sole path to healing from my inner chaos lay in disappearing altogether.

Overnight the vehicle stood ready, loaded for one more finite expedition while I collapsed for some much-needed sleep. At around 2 am, I jolted awake, the stillness of the night surrounding me. With a last look around to confirm everything was in order, I locked up the house and ventured out onto the deserted street.

4. Not Much Of A Fisherman

As I trundled north through Perth's sleeping suburbs, traffic lights blinked a spectral green and red, casting ghostly glows on deserted intersections. Each stop felt silently surreal, almost an echo from a forgotten world, or a world that would soon wake up in my absence.

The suburbs passed by in a blur of indistinguishable houses, their windows dark and lifeless. In Stirling, where the suburban sprawl began to thin out, the houses grew larger and farther apart. Here, the air smelled faintly of eucalyptus and salt, a hint of the ocean not far away, the vehicle's headlights illuminating the occasional possum darting across the road or a lone cat prowling the kerb.

By the time I reached Balcatta, Perth's city lights had begun to fade behind me as I merged onto Mitchell Freeway still heading north. The highway was an unspooling ribbon, leading me away from everything familiar. The fast-developing suburb of Joondalup comprised a smattering of construction sites and newly built housing and beyond it was nothing but open stretches of single-lane highway until the road narrowed into Indian Ocean Drive, winding its way up the coast with glimpses of water flashing in moonlight.

*

The turn-off came unexpectedly, a barely visible track between dense scrub. I almost missed it in the growing light. The wheels crunched over loose limestone as I guided the wagon off the road, the vehicle's suspension groaning at the change in terrain along a sandy track winding through coastal heath, branches scraping against the freshly waxed bodywork.

Theo's absence in the passenger seat felt like a physical wound. No alert ears pricked at the sound of birds stirring in the pre-dawn. No watchful eyes scanning the bush for kangaroos.

I stopped to deflate the tyres to accommodate the increasingly sandy terrain, the hiss of escaping air matching the rhythm of the waves I could now hear in the distance.

The track eventually opened onto the beach, pale almost white sand stretching north and south as far as I could see. Small waves lapped at the shore, their white edges glowing in the dim light. I engaged low-range four-wheel-drive and turned north, keeping to the firmer sand near the waterline.

For kilometre after kilometre of empty coastline, no footprints or tyre tracks were marking the sand, no signs of human presence, only the occasional piece of driftwood or cluster of seaweed. The isolation wrapped itself around me and was both comforting and suffocating.

A rocky headland appeared ahead and nearby I found a sheltered spot to park between two larger dunes. The engine's rumble died, leaving only the sound of waves and wind. Dawn was breaking properly now, painting the clouds in shades of pink and gold that seemed obscene in their beauty.

I climbed out of the wagon, the cool morning air bracing against my skin. I stretched, feeling the ache in my back and shoulders from the long drive.

Setting up camp was a familiar routine. I retrieved a tarpaulin and poles from the back of the vehicle, selecting a spot above the high tide line where the sand was still firm. With methodical precision, I drove the poles into the sand, stretching the tarpaulin between them to create a makeshift shelter. It wasn't much, but it would provide shade as the sun climbed higher.

I unpacked the fishing rod. It seemed straightforward enough and was designed for surf fishing: rod, reel, line — all easily assembled correctly as far as I could tell. But what about bait? I'd neglected to bring any with me.

I crouched by the water's edge, searching for any indication of life in the sand. Tiny crabs darted about, vanishing into minuscule holes as I drew near. Could they serve as bait? I had no idea how to catch them or if they were even suitable, which left me feeling disheartened. Here was I, a seasoned veteran of war zones and of documenting human anguish through photography yet perplexed by the basic task of finding fishing bait.

I sank into my camp chair, letting the day unfold around me. The ocean stretched endlessly, a vast expanse of blue meeting blue at the horizon. The rhythmic lull of the waves was hypnotic, pulling me in and out of dozy sleep like the tide itself. I could almost feel the sand beneath me breathing, rising and falling with each surge of water.

My eyes fluttered open to the bright midday sun before closing again, the light casting red shadows through my eyelids. Theo's absence gnawed at me; her unconditional companionship had been a balm to my restless soul. Now, alone, I had nothing to distract me from the ceaseless churn of my thoughts.

The sheer beauty of this place was almost cruel in its intensity. The pale golden sands, the cerulean sea, and the whisper of a breeze, all conspired to highlight my isolation. The emptiness around me mirrored the void within. Yet, in this stark solitude, I felt a peculiar liberation. No eyes watching me, no expectations to meet.

I let my mind drift with the waves, each one pulling memories and emotions from the depths where I'd buried them. Faces of people I'd photographed during their darkest moments surfaced, eyes filled with despair, hope, and resignation. Their silent cries echoed in my mind.

But there were no cameras here, no lens to shield me from the rawness of my own emotions. The familiar knot in my chest tightened as I struggled with a nervous energy that had no outlet. I shifted uncomfortably in my chair, trying to shake off the sense of being trapped within myself.

In the distance, a lone gull cried out, a sharp contrast to the soothing hum of the ocean. It sounded almost like a taunt, a reminder that life went on elsewhere while I remained suspended in this limbo.

That night, I lay in my swag for hours looking up at the night sky. The Milky Way arced gracefully from one horizon to the other, a celestial dance that had been playing out long before any human set eyes upon it. The sheer scale of it all made my worries seem insignificant. My mind churned with ancient questions, those that have plagued humankind for millennia.

Where am I?

The question seemed absurd in its simplicity. Here I was, on a remote beach in Australia, far from everything and everyone. Yet *where* felt more existential than geographical.

Who am I?

A war photographer? A man running from his past? Or a soul adrift in an uncaring universe?

Why am I here? Why are we here? The questions tumbled over each other in my mind. What purpose did any of this serve? The suffering I'd seen, the lives I'd documented, did any of it matter in the grand scheme of things?

What is the truth of all this?

I felt a deep ache inside, a yearning for answers that seemed perpetually out of reach. I stared up at the stars until they blurred into an indistinct haze. Eventually, exhaustion claimed me, and I drifted into a fitful sleep. But even in my slumber, those questions must have been gnawing at my subconscious. Hours later, I woke with a start. The sky had shifted; constellations now stood where others had been before, and the tide had ebbed out by a few metres.

The night remained silent except for the whisper of waves meeting sand. It felt as though the universe was mocking my search for meaning with its indifferent beauty. Lying there under that extraordinary starlit sky, I continued to seek answers in the cosmic vastness above me, hoping against hope that somehow, somewhere, I might find them.

*

The Congo, 1964

The memory crept into my mind unbidden, like a thief in the night. Four young rebels, mere boys really. Three soldiers, their faces hardened by war and cruelty, slapped and bullied the boys with the butts of their rifles. I stood there, my camera an unfeeling eye, capturing every moment.

The boys were terrified. Their eyes darted around, searching for an escape that didn't exist. They still looked as though they had only recently stepped out of childhood, faces still round and innocent beneath the fear. My heart should have ached for them. But it didn't. My camera clicked away as if detached from the horror it recorded.

I watched through the lens as they were lined up, one by one. The soldiers positioned themselves behind each boy, rifles raised. The first shot rang out — loud, final. The boy crumpled to the ground in a heap of limbs and lifelessness. My finger continued to press the shutter.

The next shot followed swiftly, another life extinguished in an instant. The soldiers glanced at me, seeking some sort of approval or recognition for their brutality. I gave them nothing but the relentless click of my camera.

The third boy fell before his body even realised, he was dead. His face hit the dirt with a soft thud. By the time the fourth shot echoed in that wretched place, I felt nothing but a hollow emptiness where my soul should have been.

The soldiers drove away in their jeep, leaving behind only death and silence. They seemed satisfied with their work, perhaps believing that the images I had captured would cause a stir in newspapers around the world. And they did, those frames of bullying, cowardice, and brutality were splashed across the pages for all to see.

But why? Why had I been able to witness this horror without breaking? Why had it seemed like just another assignment? Why hadn't I intervened? Tried to stop them? Begged for mercy or compassion? What was it in me that allowed me to stand by and document such terror?

The contact sheets from that day remained etched in my mind's eye, frame by frame of life turning into death. Who else bore responsibility? The editors who chose to use those images? The media barons who profited from them? The readers who consumed them with morbid curiosity?

Who?

Why?

The questions twisted within me like knives, each one cutting deeper into my already tormented mind. The faces of those boys haunted me still, their final moments forever captured in stark black and white. No answers came to soothe the agony that memory inflicted upon my soul and so I lay there under that vast starlit sky, grappling with ghosts from a past that refused to let go.

*

I had fallen into a deep sleep, the kind where dreams and reality blur into one. The dawn had come and gone, and the sun was already climbing higher when the sound of an approaching vehicle stirred me. I turned over, bleary-eyed, squinting against the sunlight. A large Nissan four-wheel-drive came into view, rock music blaring from its speakers. Three men were inside; their faces lit with excitement. As they drove past, they shouted greetings.

"G'day mate! Ripper day for some fishing! Let us know if you need anything!"

I said nothing, watching as they stopped about fifty metres to the south. They moved with an almost infectious energy, noisily setting up camp and assembling their fishing rods. Soon they were waist-deep in the sea, casting lines with practised ease. Fish after fish came wriggling out of the water, adding to their growing haul.

Eventually, one of the men broke away from the group and ambled over in my direction, a large Kingfish Whiting dangling from his hand. The fish's scales glistened under the sun, reflecting a spectrum of colours that momentarily distracted me from my thoughts. He laid down the fish on my tarpaulin, and gesturing that it was mine to keep, he flashed a broad grin.

"Mate, there's shoals of them out there!" he exclaimed, enthusiasm brimming in his voice.

"You should be out there with us! It's teeming today." His eyes sparkled with the thrill of the catch, making me momentarily forget my burdens.

I gave a half-smile. "Not much of a fisherman," I admitted. "Besides, I've got no bait."

"Ah, no worries! We've got plenty." He gestured back towards their camp, his hand sweeping in a broad arc.

"I'll give you some bloodworms." His loud twang almost echoed across the beach, carrying a sense of camaraderie and generosity.

"Come and join us when you're ready!" he added, his voice infused with an inviting friendliness that momentarily lifted the weight from my shoulders.

He walked back towards his mates, leaving me with his offering. My mind raced, a swirl of foggy thoughts and emotions. The friendly intrusion had shattered the fragile peace I had briefly found. Hastily, I began packing up my things, shoving gear into bags with a sense of urgency that bordered on desperation. I secured everything in the wagon and without looking in their direction, started the engine, the roar of the motor drowning out the distant laughter and chatter.

*

I drove north up the beach, the vast expanse of shoreline stretched out endlessly before me. The interruption from those fishermen had destabilised me, their boisterous energy and camaraderie were alien to me, foreign concepts only serving to remind me of my isolation. I needed to experience whatever was happening to me on my terms, away from prying eyes and well-meaning gestures.

As I continued driving, a lifeless eye stared up at me, unblinking and vacant, a stark reminder that life could be snatched away without warning. I glanced at the fish resting on a tea towel in the passenger seat — Theo's seat. Its silvery scales glistened under the sunlight filtering through the window, a stark reminder of life and death. Less than half an hour ago, this fish had been swimming freely in the ocean, blissfully unaware of its fate. Its streamlined body sliced through the water with grace, its fins guiding it through currents and tides.

Eventually, I spotted a narrow track to lead me back to the highway, almost concealed by the dunes. With a turn of the wheel, I steered off the beach and onto firmer ground. Before rejoining the main road, I pulled over to re-inflate the tyres, using my foot pump to gradually restore them to their proper pressure. I carefully placed the fish inside my cooler box, ensuring it lay comfortably amongst melting ice packs.

As I merged back onto the highway, a seed of an idea began to form as to where I might achieve the sanctuary I so craved. During the last rainy season, Theo and I had permission from the people at the Aboriginal Corporation to stay on their land in the far north beyond Broome for a few weeks. They had been kind but firm in their boundaries. My camera was only welcome when they allowed it, always with their permission and always under their watchful eyes.

The communities there held a deep connection to their land and sea and were beginning to reclaim what was theirs. There was talk of them turning parts of their ancestral land into a space for sustainable tourism, but not yet a consensus on how they might do that. They had welcomed me cautiously at first but had grown to trust me as I respected their rules. Mornings had been serene; the tranquillity of the place offered me a solace I hadn't known in years. After my harrowing experiences in Lebanon, moments of capturing peaceful scenes were profoundly healing. Each sunrise brought a new sense of calm, a stark contrast to the chaos I'd documented through my lens in war-torn regions.

As Theo and I drove away from the community for what would be our last time together there, they had bid us farewell with genuine warmth, mutual trust and respect. Perhaps they would allow me to return once more; maybe there would be solace into which I could disappear along those familiar shores.

For now, though, to be alone in my wagon on this long trip northward, the driving offered me a solitude in which to surrender myself to my inner turmoil, free from interruption or intrusion.

5. You Just Take Your Pictures And Leave!

The scenery shifted subtly from the flat, scrubby vegetation of Breton Bay to the more rugged terrain of the Midwest. After about four hours, I approached Geraldton. The early afternoon sun hung high, bathing everything in a harsh stark light.

I pulled into a truck stop on the outskirts of town. It was a typical Australian roadhouse, a sprawling area with fuel pumps, a diner, and a few scattered picnic tables under rusting metal awnings. Big rigs lined up like sleeping giants, their drivers resting or refuelling before continuing their journeys. The air smelled of diesel and frying food.

The roadhouse had seen better days. Its weathered facade bore the marks of countless seasons, paint peeling off in patches and signs faded by relentless sun and wind. After fuelling up, I wandered into the diner. The smell of hot chips and burgers wafted through the air. Behind the counter, an elderly woman with kind eyes and deep laugh lines took orders with practised ease.

I looked around as I sipped a coffee: truck drivers in worn flannel shirts and wide-brimmed hats, families taking a break from their road trip adventures. Each one had their story; each one carried their burdens and joys along these dusty roads. As I stepped back into the glaring sunlight, the heat assaulted my senses. Squinting, I made my way to the wagon. Out of nowhere, a thick-set man with rough, calloused hands approached me.

"You got any work?" His accent was heavy, and his English was limited. "Not trouble, only work."

I tried to ignore him, pushing past towards my vehicle.

"I go north, ship boat," he persisted, his tone edging on aggressive.

I kept walking. This wasn't my problem. The last thing I needed was another stranger disrupting my fragile equilibrium.

"Ride, you give me ride," he demanded again.

I shook my head, continuing to ignore him.

"Ty chamie!" he swore after me. "Spierdalaj!"

I stopped dead in my tracks and turned around. "Na czym polega Twój problem? Jadę tylko kilka kilometrów w górę drogi" The Polish words flowed out almost instinctively. What is your problem? I am only going a few kilometres up the road.

His eyes widened in surprise, a flicker of recognition crossing his face. It seemed he'd never expected anyone here to speak his native tongue.

"Mówisz po polsku" You speak Polish, he stammered, his tone shifting from aggression to astonishment.

"Tak," I replied curtly. "Choć w dzisiejszych czasach niewiele." Though not much these days.

He stared at me for a moment, then extended his hand tentatively.

"Stanislaw Kowalczyk. Staszek."

"Josef." I took his hand reluctantly but firmly.

"Jesteś Polakiem?" Are you Polish? Staszek's question hung in the air between us, heavy and charged.

I hesitated, caught off guard. Polish? My identity was a tattered idea I rarely considered. Australian? Polish? Both felt like distant concepts, not something to grapple with at this moment.

"Dlaczego to ma znaczenie?" Why does it matter? I muttered, avoiding his gaze as I shifted my weight against the side of the wagon.

Staszek's eyes burned with an intensity that surprised me.

"To ma znaczenie, poniewaz... bo ja tez jestem Polakiem," It matters because... because I am also Polish, he blurted out, words spilling forth like a torrent, urgent and raw. "Uciekłem. Opuściłem statek we Fremantle.." I escaped. I jumped ship in Fremantle.

I clenched my jaw; every syllable was drawing me deeper into his tumultuous past. Staszek's urgency clawed at something within me that longed for solitude but was drawn toward empathy.

"I can't go back," he continued in Polish, his voice barely above a whisper now. "My brother Marek was taken by the secret police after martial law was declared. They were looking for him... for being part of Solidarity." His breath hitched and pain rippled across the features of his face.

The tales of suffering echoed within me, his brother's fight for freedom mirroring my own struggles against silence and despair.

"I was a sailor," Staszek continued in Polish, bitterness creeping into his tone. "Hard work on ships, living for the sea... but I knew I had to run." He gestured wildly toward nothing and everything at once. "In Poland. You are trapped, watching friends disappear."

I neglected to mention that I too had been in Gdansk during the brutal winter of 1981 and that I too had faced imprisonment. However, the differences in our experiences were glaring. I had voluntarily placed myself there, driven by my career as a photographer. When I was eventually arrested, my ordeal lasted only a few days before I was extradited to West Germany. At that moment, the stark reality of my profession, capturing their suffering through my lens, hit me like a runaway train, leaving me grappling with the weight of my own choices.

*

Gdansk, Poland, December 15, 1981

The air was thick with tension, and the image unfolded before me like a slow-motion tragedy.

There, in the foreground, a lone shipyard worker stood wrapped up in a wool scarf and heavy coat. His stance was defiant and unwavering despite the bitter cold and swirling snowflakes that clung to him. He was holding up a makeshift and tattered Solidarity flag crafted hastily from a bed sheet. The red lettering screamed *Solidarnosc — Nie Poddamy Sie,* Solidarity — We Will Not Give Up. The words were blurred under the weight of falling snow.

Behind him, a dark, formidable column of riot police was advancing through the slush-covered street. Their visored helmets and batons transformed them into faceless enforcers of oppression; their breath hung in the freezing air.

The tram tracks beneath the protester's feet seemed to draw an invisible line between him and the encroaching storm of authority. It was as if he were standing on a stage set for an inevitable confrontation, each element perfectly aligned to tell a story of resistance and courage. To the left, civilians peered out from a shattered shop window, faces etched with tension and silent admiration. A woman clutched her child close as she shielded his eyes from the impending violence. An older man watched with a hollow gaze; his cap pulled low over eyes that had seen too many crushed dreams, innocent lives poised on the edge of chaos, the brief stillness before the storm's fury unleashed. I pressed the shutter just as fear and defiance merged into one.

The image I took became more than a photograph; it became a symbol and a rallying cry for those resisting authoritarianism worldwide. Newspapers from Paris to New York carried *Defiance in the Snow* as the headline on their front pages, sparking solidarity and hope among those who yearned for freedom.

Years later, in a 2001 interview, Piotr Kowalczyk, who was identified as the shipyard worker in my photograph, reflected on that pivotal moment with a profound sense of resolve:

"I was afraid, of course. But fear cannot build a future. We had to stand. It was a moment where we had to decide whether to succumb to our fears or to rise above them, and for the sake of our children and the generations to come, we chose to stand firm. We knew that our actions that day would echo through history, forging a path towards the freedom we so desperately sought."

The moment my photograph circulated in the Western media, showcasing the defiance of the Polish people, I knew my presence there would become increasingly dangerous. The photograph had done its job, igniting a flame of resistance and solidarity across continents. Yet, it had also painted a target on my back.

Three days after capturing that moment of defiance, I was arrested as I left my dreary communist-style hotel — shoved into the backseat of a Polski Fiat car; the door slammed shut with an ominous finality. The streets of Gdansk blurred past the window as we sped towards an uncertain destination.

The jail cell was cold, and the icy walls closed in around me. My captors' faces were masked by stern expressions and shadows cast by the flickering overhead light. The interrogation began almost immediately, a barrage of questions, accusations, and thinly veiled threats. They rifled through my belongings with methodical precision, each item examined as if it held some hidden secret.

Two days later the decision to extradite me had been made and it came as a relief. My notoriety had saved me from a potentially far worse fate. The young soldiers who escorted me to the plane wore expressions of forced neutrality. But as we boarded the aircraft bound for Berlin, I caught glimpses of something else.

One soldier hesitated before fastening my seatbelt, his hand lingering for a moment longer than necessary. His eyes met mine briefly, a silent exchange that spoke volumes.

"You're free," he seemed to say without words. "We wish we could be too."

*

Squinting at each other in the harsh sunlight the weight of Staszek's words resonated deeply, twisting my heart with an ache that felt familiar yet foreign. Was it the camaraderie born from shared pain that ignited within me an unwelcome desire to reach out and offer comfort, to let him spill more secrets to me on this desolate road where isolation had been my only companion? Or was it guilt?

A shadow whispered at the back of my mind; any conversation would demand energy I was severely lacking and threatened the fragile barriers I'd erected around myself. Staszek looked at me earnestly now, searching for understanding, or someone to bear witness to his truth amid my silence,

"I'm sorry," he implored, still in Polish. "But can you help me?"

Torn between my need to be alone and respect for another soul seeking refuge from their past, I felt as if fate were steering this vehicle toward uncharted territory where pain mingled with compassion, a crossroads that would define what little remained of my weary heart.

Staszek looked like a relic from another world. His clothing, worn and threadbare, seemed like remnants of a distant, colder land unsuited for the relentless heat of Western Australia. The small canvas knapsack slung over his shoulder bore the unmistakable Soviet design, utilitarian, stark.

"Alright," I muttered, "get in."

He hesitated, then clambered into the passenger seat, his eyes darting nervously around.

As we set off northward, he began talking; a torrent of words in rapid Polish that filled the silence I had so carefully cultivated. He smelled musty and needed a good wash. His voice rose and fell with an urgency I recognised from countless war zones, the cadence of someone desperate to be understood. I gripped the wheel, focusing on the road ahead.

Staszek's voice was relentless, recounting tales of his life at sea, his escape from Poland, and the fate of his brother Marek. Each story was a jagged piece of his shattered existence. After what felt like an eternity, he paused and glanced at me.

"What is your work?" he asked in Polish.

I hesitated before replying.

"I'm a photographer."

His eyes lit up with sudden interest.

"Photographer? Like... weddings?"

"No," I said gently. "War."

His enthusiasm dimmed slightly as he processed this. "War photographer? You take pictures of soldiers?"

"Something like that," I muttered.

He prised from me some scant detail of my long career until eventually recognition slowly dawned on him.

"You... you took pictures in Poland? During martial law?"

I nodded.

"Defiance in the snow," he whispered, eyes widening with realisation. "That was you? Josef Batten?"

"Yes," I admitted reluctantly.

He stared at me with a mix of awe and curiosity.

"Tell me your story."

But I remained silent, my mind a fortress against his increasingly probing questions.

As we pushed on Highway 1 toward Carnarvon, Staszek's initial admiration soured into frustration. He ranted about the suffering of the Polish people, cursing my perceived indifference and privileged life.

"You don't need to care," he spat out angrily in Polish. "You just take your pictures and leave!"

His remarks were biting. Truth laced with a venom that cut deeper than I expected.

An awkward silence sat between us for miles until we neared the Hamelin Pool turn-off. Staszek broke it with a muttered comment about beer cans and rubbish strewn by the roadside.

"Must be the Aborigines," he sneered.

With that, I exploded, my voice harsh and unyielding. "You have no idea!"

A much more tense silence enveloped us as we pulled into Billabong Roadhouse. Staszek disappeared into the restroom, and I brooded while I filled the fuel tank before going inside to pay.

When we met again out in the forecourt I faced him coldly. "I'm turning off up ahead. You'd better find another ride from here." I said in Polish.

Without waiting for his response, I retrieved his knapsack from the back of the wagon and handed it to him. I mustered a reluctant "Good luck", climbed in and drove off. I could see his bewildered face in my mirrors as I left in a cloud of dust and partial regret.

*

Staszek's words echoed in my mind. "You just take your pictures and leave!"

The accusation stung because it carried truth I'd never confronted. For decades, I'd moved through war zones like a ghost, capturing moments of agony and triumph, but never truly engaging with the weight of what I witnessed. I'd prided myself on my invisibility, my ability to slip in and out unnoticed, but now that very skill felt like a curse.

What had I achieved? My photographs had won awards, graced magazine covers, and shocked viewers over their morning coffee. But had they changed anything? Had I been nothing more than a vulture, feeding off others' suffering? The countless faces I'd photographed swam before my eyes — mothers clutching dead children, soldiers with thousand-yard stares, refugees trudging through mud with their lives in plastic bags.

Staszek's fury came from a place of real pain — he'd lived through the events I'd merely documented. His brother had been arrested, his mother harassed, while I'd clicked my shutter and moved on to the next crisis, the next war, the next story. His weathered face and piercing blue eyes had held more truth than any of my carefully composed shots.

A late afternoon sun still beat down mercilessly as I pulled into a large truck stop on the edge of Carnarvon. My hands shook as I pulled over, the engine's rumble fading to silence. The steering wheel was hot to the touch and sweat trickled down my back. I stepped out into the scorching heat, my legs unsteady. For the first time in my life, I had begun a process of feeling the weight of every image I'd ever taken, every story I'd witnessed but never truly told. The realisation crashed over me like a wave — I had been present at some of history's darkest moments, but had I ever really been there at all? The idea of having a camera around my neck, once a comfort, now felt like a millstone.

I slept fitfully in the back of the Land Cruiser, and the vinyl seats stuck to my skin as I tossed and turned, haunted by memories I couldn't shake.

Moments before dawn, I pulled back onto the highway, my mind a carousel of haunting images — faces of the dead, the wounded, the desperate. They'd always been there, locked away behind the viewfinder, but now they demanded attention, clamouring like hungry ghosts.

Who was I without my camera? The thought terrified me more than any war zone ever had.

The North West Coastal Highway sliced up the red earth while in the distance salt flats shimmered like mirages to my left, and scrubland dotted with spinifex grass rolled away to my right. The sun had climbed higher, turning the morning haze into a scorching glare that made me squint despite my sunglasses.

I barely registered passing the turnoff to Coral Bay. At different times, I might have stopped to photograph the pristine waters and the ancient stromatolites, but now such beauty felt hollow. The wagon's engine droned steadily as I pushed north, the kilometres ticking away beneath my wheels.

A wedge-tailed eagle soared overhead, riding thermals with barely a wingbeat. Through force of habit, I reached for my camera bag before catching myself. What was the point? I'd captured thousands of such moments, and preserved them in silver gelatin, but had never truly experienced them for myself.

The landscape changed subtly as I approached Karratha — more rocky outcrops, and deeper reds in the soil. Road trains thundered past in the opposite direction, their multiple trailers swaying like metal serpents.

My mind was lost in a basement in Beirut, in the jungles of Vietnam, in a hundred other places where I'd hidden behind my viewfinder instead of facing the reality before me. Another road train thundered past, its massive bulk shaking the air, and I flinched. Me — who'd stood steady under mortar fire, who'd navigated through active combat zones without breaking stride — now jumping at shadows. The irony wasn't lost on me.

The hollow ache in my stomach reminded me I'd barely eaten in days, surviving on black coffee and stale biscuits. The familiar light-headedness was creeping in again, and I knew from bitter experience that if I didn't eat at least something nutritious I would get weaker. I'd been down this road before, pushing my body to its limits in far worse places than this highway, but age was making me less resilient to such neglect.

*

As I pushed on hard along the Great Northern Highway, I watched violent streaks of orange and red graduate rapidly as the sun sunk beneath the horizon to my left.

The darkness was complete as I pulled into Sandfire. The isolated Roadhouse had closed for the night, and people were setting up in the campground. I chose a spot to park up near the fuel pumps away from the campers in case I needed a quick getaway. I set up the small camping stove next to the vehicle, fumbling with the gas connection twice before getting it right. The Kingfish Whiting was swimming in a pool of melted ice at the bottom of my cooler, buried beneath a few other perishable supplies. I retrieved it carefully, bringing it to my nose — still fresh.

I awoke early as a magnificent golden sun crept over the eastern horizon, painting the desert in hues of amber and crimson. As I pulled out onto the highway steam rose from my coffee cup, nestled in a holder on the dashboard I'd fashioned from an old tin can.

My eyes scanned constantly; a habit ingrained through decades behind the lens. Even without a camera, I couldn't stop seeing the world in frames — the way morning light caught the spinifex grass, how dust devils danced across the plain, and the precise moment when shadow met light on distant rock formations.

This gift — or curse — of perpetual observation had served me well in war zones. I could read the tension in a soldier's jaw before he raised his weapon, spot a sniper's nest from the unusual arrangement of shadows, and sense the moment a crowd would turn violent from subtle shifts in body language. My camera caught what others missed because I saw what others overlooked. But it wasn't only about composition or timing. I'd learned to see beneath surfaces, to catch the fleeting expressions that revealed potential truths behind carefully constructed facades. A mother's grief in the twitch of a finger, defiance in the set of a child's shoulders, desperation in the white-knuckled grip on a refugee's bundle.

Now, without Theo's steady presence beside me, this hyperawareness felt more like a burden. Every detail reminded me of her absence — the empty passenger seat, the way morning light fell across the space where she should be, the silence where her breathing should be.

Before Theo entered my life, I'd wandered the world's battlefields and crisis zones in perfect isolation. I'd grown comfortable in that — locked inside myself, measuring my worth through the images I created. Each photograph was a testament to my ability to remain detached, to observe without participating.

Theo taught me what a real connection felt like. Not the fleeting encounters with subjects I photographed, or the professional relationships I maintained with editors and fellow photographers, but something deeper, raw and honest. Every morning, she'd greet me with those intelligent eyes, full of trust and affection, and each evening she'd settle beside me as I reviewed my day's activities, her warm presence grounding me in the present moment. She didn't need words to communicate her loyalty, understanding, and love.

Now her absence carved a hole in my chest that no image could fill. The pain of losing her was different from anything I'd experienced before — sharper, more personal. It wasn't something I could frame through a viewfinder or capture in black and white. It lived in my bones, in the silence of the Land Cruiser's cabin, and the space beside me where she should be. I'd never sought the companionship of another being, now I was a lost soul without it.

*

The spinifex grass stretched endlessly towards the horizon, a sea of golden stalks against the deep red earth. The highway was empty except for the occasional road train thundering past in a cloud of dust. A weathered sign for LaGrange Mission flashed past, the letters barely legible against the sun-bleached metal. The highway stretched ahead in a perfect line, disappearing into the shimmering heat haze where the sky met Earth.

That's when I spotted it — a tiny flash of bright crimson red amongst the red and ochre earth and olive-green scrub, two hundred and fifty metres to my left. It shouldn't have caught my eye at all, yet it blazed like a beacon against the palette of the landscape. Fresh tyre tracks carved through the spinifex, creating a crude path that meandered away from the highway. I eased off the accelerator. Something about that splash of red tugged at my consciousness. In all my years behind a lens, I'd learned to trust these moments of inexplicable attention, when some detail demanded notice.

Without thought, I pulled onto the shoulder and executed a three-point turn, the wagon's tyres crunching on the loose gravel. I couldn't explain the compulsion that drew me back, not then and not now. In this vast emptiness between Sandfire and Roebuck, where the landscape barely changed for hundreds of kilometres, that tiny red anomaly pulled at me like a magnet.

I steered off the highway, following the fresh tyre tracks through the scrub and bounced over the uneven terrain. The red object grew larger as I approached.

Scattered around it lay the detritus of someone's life — a paperback copy of Steinbeck's *East of Eden*, a handful of cassette tapes glinting in the sun, clothes strewn like confetti, a splayed-out dusty sleeping bag. My stomach knotted as I spotted what looked like a broken Sony Walkman, its yellow plastic casing cracked open, the tape spools exposed.

Then I saw him. A young man's body lay face down in the scrub, curled into himself, completely naked. An ochre dust caked his skin, gathering in the creases of his joints. The backpack — the flash of red that had caught my eye — lay emptied, its contents scattered in a wide arc. I pulled up as close as I could, and the morning heat hit me like a wall as I stepped out crunching on the gritty soil and approached the motionless figure. The air was still, with not even a whisper of wind to disturb the awful scene before me.

With my heart hammering against my ribs, I knelt beside the young man, reaching out to check for any sign of life. I pressed my fingers against his neck and felt the faint flutter of a pulse beneath the dirt-caked skin. His chest rose and fell with shallow breaths.

His sleeping bag was close by and rustled as I straightened it out beside him. With practised hands, I rolled him gently onto the fabric, wincing at the raw grazes that covered his back. His face, though bloodied and grimy, held a youthful softness. Water sloshed in my canteen as I unscrewed the cap and lifted his head, letting a few drops fall onto his cracked lips. His eyelids flickered, a low moan escaping as consciousness slowly crept back. More water dribbled down his chin, and he spluttered, coughing life back into his lungs. My hands moved with the careful precision I usually reserved for adjusting camera settings and, brushing away layers of the ochre dust from his torso, I checked for broken ribs. In his half-conscious state, it was difficult to tell. His arms and legs bore only surface wounds — angry scrapes and forming bruises, but nothing that wouldn't heal.

Around us, his possessions lay scattered. I gathered each piece and placed it in the red rucksack. From my many battlefield experiences, I knew that moving him too quickly and soon might prove critical, possibly even fatal. The body needed time to stabilise after trauma — I'd seen too many casualties worsen from hasty evacuations in war zones across the globe. Best to allow some recovery time and let his system find its equilibrium before attempting to transport him. The desert's harsh conditions weren't helping matters, but at least he was conscious and responsive now.

I returned to the wagon, the heat already building to an oppressive weight. From the back, I pulled out four sturdy poles and a heavy tarpaulin. The ground fought against the poles as I hammered them in, red dust billowing with each strike until they held firm. The tarpaulin stretched taut between them, creating a patch of blessed shade and I draped a towel over his naked body and gently dabbed his facial wounds with a damp flannel and guided the water bottle to his mouth again, enabling a few careful slow sips before his consciousness lapsed again. He lay with his head propped on a folded bundle of clothes.

I didn't attempt to speak to him as we sheltered from the brutal heat around us. I could see from the way he was drifting in and out of consciousness that we should not remain there too long and that he would soon need some medical attention.

Back at the wagon, I unrolled my swag across the rear bench seat, spreading it flat to create a cushioned base. The padded canvas would help absorb the bumps of the rough road ahead. Over this, I laid out my flannel sleeping bag, turning it inside out so the soft lining would be gentle against his raw skin. I manoeuvred the vehicle as near to the shelter as possible and, summoning every ounce of power within me, hoisted him with tremendous effort into the back, cradling his head throughout the transfer. Several pained sounds escaped his lips before his eyelids drooped, and he sank into the improvised bedding.

I quickly took the shelter down and packed everything into the wagon, his red rucksack placed on the front seat.

6. Still A Boy In Many Ways

Two hours later, the Broome District Hospital emerged through the shimmer of heat rising from Robinson Street — a low-set cream building with a red corrugated iron roof, typical of the region's architecture. Palm trees dotted the grounds, their fronds casting fractured shadows across the sun-bleached walls.

I parked the wagon as close to the emergency entrance as possible. The young man hadn't stirred during our journey north, though his breathing remained steady. Through my rear-view mirror, I could see the makeshift bed I'd created had served its purpose well.

The hospital's facade showed its age; paint peeling at the corners, louvred windows collecting red dust from the pindan soil. A weathered wooden sign, its lettering faded by countless wet seasons, hung above the entrance. The grounds were quiet save for the whirring of ceiling fans that spun lazily on the wide veranda.

A couple of Aboriginal families sat on benches beneath the shade, children playing at their feet. Their eyes followed my vehicle as I pulled up, but their expressions remained neutral, accustomed perhaps to the sight of emergency arrivals from the vast outback beyond the town limits. The emergency entrance consisted of simple double doors, their paint chipped and marked from years of trolleys and stretchers passing through. A small garden bed lined the path leading to the doors, filled with hardy local plants that had managed to survive despite minimal care, desert rose and frangipani trees providing splashes of colour against the clinical backdrop.

In the empty waiting room, a nurse looked up from her paperwork, her eyes widening as I explained the situation.

"Where did you find him?" She grabbed a clipboard, already moving towards the entrance.

"About two hours south and around one hundred kilometres north of Sandfire." I followed her outside.

Two orderlies appeared with a stretcher. They moved him carefully from the wagon.

A weathered-looking doctor with greying temples met us in the emergency bay. His hands moved with practised efficiency as he checked vital signs.

"Severe dehydration. Multiple contusions." He lifted each eyelid, shining a penlight. "Possible concussion. Let's get him on fluids immediately."

The nurse inserted an IV line while the doctor continued his examination. They pulled a curtain around him, and I went to the entrance to sit in the waiting area.

Around half an hour later the doctor reappeared.

"Will he be alright?" I asked.

"He's conscious and stable, but..." The doctor paused, his expression carefully neutral. "There are certain indicators that suggest... well, we'll need to do a more thorough examination."

I watched as they wheeled him away, disappearing behind swinging doors. Something in the doctor's tone, in the careful way he'd chosen his words, left me with an uneasy feeling. After what felt like an eternity, the nurse returned with admission forms.

"We'll need some details. Do you have any of his possessions?"

"The young man's rucksack is still in my Land Cruiser." I went out to get it.

"He's managed to tell us his name is Adam," she said, glancing at her notes.

Adam. The name settled in my mind, giving shape to the broken figure I'd found in the desert.

"Where are you staying in Broome?" she asked, "Will you be returning to see him?"

"I hadn't planned to," I replied. "But I can stay on for a while."

Her face softened. "The Roebuck Bay Hotel will have rooms. I can get a message to you there when he's ready for visitors."

"Right then," I said, grateful for the suggestion.

*

The Roebuck Bay Hotel's single-storey structure dominated the corner of Dampier Terrace and Napier Street, white-painted walls glowing in the fierce sunlight, its wide verandas offering blessed shade to the handful of patrons beneath. Through decades of cyclones and development, the Roey had stood firm since 1890, its wooden bones creaking with stories of pearl divers, pastoralists, and wanderers like me.

The pub's front bar beckoned through open doors. In the cool darkness, my eyes adjusted slowly, taking in the worn wooden floorboards, the long bar stretching across one wall, its brass rail polished by generations of elbows.

A gruff-looking barman looked up from polishing glasses.

"What can I get you, mate?"

"Need a room," I said, leaning against the bar.

"Single or double?"

"Single."

I glanced around the room. There were a few regulars nursing their middies of beer and a group of intrepid young travellers gathered in a dark corner, their voices excited and musical. The walls bore testament to Broome's history; sepia toned photographs of pearl luggers, their crews lined up proud on deck, alongside faded newspaper clippings and vintage beer advertisements.

"Hundred and twenty a week," the barman said, reaching beneath the counter for a ledger. "Or twenty-five a night. Name?"

"Josef Batten," I replied, fishing out my wallet. "I'll take it for the week."

*

I hauled my camera bag, some food items and a small suitcase to the motel-style accommodation of the Roey. My room key scraped against the lock, and I stumbled inside.

The bed called to me — a simple single with crisp white sheets. I dropped my bags, kicked off my boots, and collapsed onto the mattress. The ceiling fan whirred overhead, pushing around the thick tropical air. Through the open window came the sounds of Broome — distant laughter from the pub garden, the rumble of passing vehicles, birds calling in the distance.

I drifted in and out of sleep, rising only to use the bathroom. Time blurred — afternoon faded to evening, evening to night. The sounds from outside grew louder then quieter again as the pub emptied. My dreams were fragmented things, full of desert highways and empty spaces. Once I thought I heard Theo's nails clicking on floorboards, but when I opened my eyes, the room was dark and still.

Late the following morning, sunlight was streaming through the window when a soft scratching sound pulled me from sleep. A piece of paper had been slipped under my door. I forced myself up, muscles protesting, and retrieved it. The handwriting was neat and precise:

"Adam is ready for visitors now."

*

I pushed open the door to the hospital ward; a clean open room filled with cooled sunlit air. Adam was propped up in bed, his expression serene despite the bandages and bruises that marked his face.

The room was nearly empty, with a few other patients lying soundlessly in their beds. The nurses moved about with an air of calm efficiency.

"Hello," I greeted him softly, approaching his bedside. "I'm Josef."

Adam's eyes met mine, and he smiled weakly but with genuine warm-heartedness that reached deep into my bones.

"Adam," he replied. "Nice to meet you."

I nodded, finding myself at ease in his presence. There was no need for forced conversation or small talk.

"How are you both doing?" A nurse appeared at my side, "Can I get you anything?".

Adam turned to her.

"Do you have a chess set in the hospital?"

"Yes, I think we do. I'll see if I can find it." She said softly.

As she left, Adam looked at me.

"Do you play?"

"I know the rules," I admitted.

"Well, I can refresh your memory if you'd like to try."

The nurse returned with the chess set and placed it on a tray that she wheeled across Adam's bed. With laboured motions yet deliberate grace, he positioned the chess pieces across the board, handling each one with purposeful attention. I found myself mesmerised by his careful movements.

While we played, casual dialogue flowed effortlessly between us, weaving seamlessly through our turns on the board. Throughout our game, he wove in mentions of his passion for books and art, speaking with an enthusiasm that defied his physical wounds. We didn't need to speak about what had happened or his injuries; an unspoken connection was rapidly building on something deeper, a mutual understanding that felt both comforting and familiar.

The nurse returned with a cup of tea.

"I thought you might like a cuppa." She said as she set it down on the table beside the bed.

I sipped it gratefully as we continued our game. The clinking of chess pieces and the occasional murmur of conversation filled the ward.

In that peaceful hospital room in Broome, surrounded by sunlight and the hum of life outside, I felt an unexpected sense of belonging, some comfort in the presence of this young man, whose body was injured but whose mind seemed to have emerged unscathed.

Over the following three days, I visited Adam each afternoon. We played chess, drank tea, and shared comfortable silences. His bruises began fading from angry purple to softer yellows, and his unobtrusive strength remained constant.

The hospital routine wrapped around us like a cocoon — nurses' rounds, mealtimes, the quiet tick of the clock. Through it all, Adam maintained a calm presence that drew me back each day. Not once did he mention what had brought him here, and I never asked.

When the doctor discharged him, I waited as he gathered his medications and supplies. The nurse provided instructions about changing dressings and watching for infection and Adam nodded, his attention focused and clear despite everything.

"I've got a room for you at the Roebuck," I told him as we left the hospital. "Just along from mine."

He smiled that same warm expression that had first greeted me.

"Thank you."

The short drive to the hotel passed in comfortable silence. I helped him out of the wagon, noticing how he moved with deliberate care but without complaint. His room was sparse but clean — a bed, a chair, a small table by the window.

As I watched him settle in, something struck me. Despite his physical injuries, Adam possessed an inner wholeness I'd lost — or never had. He was carrying both his physical and mental pain with grace, while it was clear to me that mine had become scattered inside me like broken glass.

We sat by the window and neither of us felt the need to fill the silence with explanations or questions. Instead, we simply existed at that moment, two very differently damaged souls finding unexpected anchors in each other's company.

"Fancy a game?" Adam asked, producing a travel chess set from his bag.

I pulled up a chair, and we began to play.

*

Each morning and evening I had driven to a track that led me to an uninhabited part of Cable Beach. The isolation suited my fractured mind. I'd sit beneath my wide-brimmed hat, watching the Indian Ocean's relentless surge while memories I'd suppressed for decades crashed through my defences.

Whereas before I witnessed others' pain through my camera, there on Cable Beach I bore witness to my own, and it was excruciating. Each crashing wave echoed my inner turmoil. In that way, the ocean was conspiring to make me confront every haunting image and sorrowful moment, not as an observer, but as the subject.

Lebanon. The damp basement. Children in Cambodia with vacant eyes. Bodies floating down rivers. The priest in Derry, hands raised, blood seeping through his cassock. Each image that had earned me acclaim now returned to torture me, merging and morphing in my mind until I could no longer separate one horror from another. My camera had allowed me to witness these atrocities without truly seeing them. Now that barrier had crumbled, leaving me exposed to the raw truth of what I'd documented. The faces of the dead continued to haunt my dreams.

I'd kept from Adam what occupied my mornings, concealing my precarious state of mind whilst we spent time together later in the day. He remained oblivious to my identity and profession —

those details I'd deliberately withheld. He was healing well, his physical wounds mending cleanly. Each afternoon I'd visit him, play chess sitting in plastic chairs outside our rooms, share meals, and then retreat to my spot on the beach where I could fall apart again in private. The vast emptiness of sand and sea became my confessional, though I found no absolution there.

"Take me to the beach with you," Adam said one evening as I was preparing to leave his room. I hesitated, my sanctuary threatened. But something in his request made it impossible to refuse.

"Of course," I replied.

I guided him out into the street where I helped him climb into the Land Cruiser.

*

The evening breeze carried the tang of salt as Adam limped across the sand, his movements cautious but determined. His face lit up at the sight of the endless ocean, and I felt a strange sense of compassion watching his childlike wonder. Despite his injuries, there was a lightness to him I envied. The sun hung low, bleeding orange into the horizon. For several minutes we sat in comfortable silence until Adam turned to me.

"Where are you going?" he asked softly.

At first, I didn't quite grasp what he was referring to, but then it dawned on me. He was asking where I had been travelling to when I found him. I kept my eyes on the distant waves.

"Somewhere isolated. Away from people." I traced patterns in the sand with my finger. "I have an idea where, but I'm not certain yet. I need to be alone."

"After your experience in Lebanon, I imagine you need the space to heal."

My finger stopped moving. The pattern in the sand blurred as my vision narrowed to a pinpoint. Adam could sense the confusion I must have instantly felt by my body language and the awkward silence. The waves continued their eternal conversation with the shore. A seabird called overhead, its cry carrying on the wind.

"I know who you are, Josef," he said gently. "I know what happened to you there."

I turned to examine his profile, seeking an explanation. War photographers exist in the margins — we capture the light but seldom step into it — we generally steer clear of recognition or fame. I was known to those with a vested interest, and it didn't surprise me that Staszek figured out who I was, but only a minuscule fraction of people could name me, and an even tinier fraction would recognise me. Yet here, on this secluded beach, this young man recounted my captivity as though he were reading from my memories.

"How?" I whispered, the word barely audible over the crash of waves.

Adam's gaze remained on the horizon. "We encountered each other the night you were in Ceduna filling up with fuel, a few weeks ago."

"I asked for a ride," Adam continued, his voice steady. "You ignored me, but I knew it was you and I understood why you didn't wish to engage with me."

A flash of memory — a fleeting image of Adam with his red rucksack, notable by his polite precise Scottish voice, it made sense now. I had driven off without a second glance, my mind clouded by exhaustion and grief.

I shook my head, bewildered.

"But how did you recognise me?"

"I've followed your work since I was a young boy," Adam admitted. "I've always been interested in world affairs and photojournalism. Your images... they've had a profound impact on me."

He paused as if weighing his words carefully.

"Earlier this year, before I left on my travels, I read about your kidnapping in Lebanon in *The Observer*. The article talked about your ordeal and mentioned your new project photographing the outback and its people."

Of course. Anne Delacourt, my agent at *Agence Frontière*, had insisted on publicising my Australian journey, promoting it as a significant new chapter in my career. She had arranged for an article to be written that juxtaposed my harrowing experiences in Lebanon with my initial, more serene work in the Pilbara minefields. A photo of Theo and me standing in front of the Land Cruiser and taken soon after she found me had accompanied the piece, capturing a rare moment of tranquillity and companionship. The image, showing Theo's expressive eyes and my weathered face, was syndicated widely.

Adam glanced at me then, his eyes reflecting a mix of curiosity and empathy.

"When I saw you at that truck stop at the start of the Nullarbor, I recognised you and your car from the photograph in the paper, and I put two and two together."

I stared at him, astonished by how articulate he was and how much he knew about me. My life, once hidden behind a camera lens, now laid bare before this young man who had been following my work for years.

"Why didn't you say anything then?" I asked.

Adam shrugged slightly. "I don't know… maybe I felt you would not want to be recognised… somehow it didn't feel appropriate."

His words hung between us like an unspoken truth. He had seen through my invisibility and recognised the suffering etched into every line of my face. We sat in a comfortable silence for a long while as the sun dipped below the horizon.

*

Lying on my bed at the Roey that night, my body wracked with violent tremors. The ceiling fan pushed warm air around the room, yet I couldn't stop shaking. My teeth chattered, muscles spasming beyond my control. The conversation with Adam had cracked another layer.

For years I'd stood before carnage, genocide, war. Click. Wind. Click. A mechanical process, as detached as the camera itself. I'd been able to document everything without feeling, to capture horror through an unblinking lens. But now I understood. I hadn't been strong. I'd been frozen, locked in the same state of emotional suspension I'd entered as a child.

The tremors intensified. I hugged myself tightly as waves of sensation crashed through me. This was how it felt to thaw — every nerve-ending awakening at once, raw and exposed.

Lebanon resulted in the first crack in my armour. Now I lay here, my body processing decades of trapped trauma, releasing it in these uncontrollable tremors. My nervous system was desperately trying to regulate itself after years of forced numbness. I recognised the shaking was both terrifying and necessary, like a fever breaking. Each episode left me drained but somehow lighter, as if ancient grief was finding its way out of my bones.

Despite his youth, he couldn't be more than twenty, still a boy in many ways, Adam had seen through my carefully maintained invisibility. His simple act of witnessing, of understanding that evening, had touched something profound in me. I felt seen; for the first time in my life, someone had recognised not only what I did, but who I was behind the lens. In his discreet, intense way, he had understood the weight of all I carried without my having to explain a single thing. It was terrifying and liberating all at once, like stepping out of a darkroom into brilliant sunlight.

Act 2: Adam Laidlaw

7. Gone Bush

Adam Laidlaw, London, September 2014

As I write, I have a photograph of Josef on my desk; a self-portrait from January 2013 — possibly the last photograph he ever took.

He looks into the camera with raw openness, offering you his full, undivided attention. His beautifully creased face bears the lines of a man who smiled often and easily. Crow's feet fan out from his eyes, and his mouth is poised to say something gentle. In that gaze, the viewer cannot escape feeling the sense of being both seen and heard.

I witnessed Josef's transformation and for me, this photograph is symbolic evidence of a person's ability to rewire their inner world and reset their life.

The proof was in his smile.

One day, it unexpectedly arrived and from that moment, it never truly left him. For the latter decades of his life, it clung to his face, softening the sharp lines of his features, a continuous trace of warmth that remained until the final hours before he gently slipped away from us.

Josef Batten lived a life in two halves, the first half marked by an unsmiling silence and a personality remaining in shadow. The second half was altogether different, marked by something lighter as if he had made peace. The turmoil he sought and that defined him had been replaced by a profound serenity, and the embrace of human connection.

It was the smile that stayed with you. It never wavered; was never sad or anxious, and I never saw it touched by anger. Always the same smile, it said that whatever troubled him before had loosened its grip and let him go.

Without trying, he magnetically drew people to him, and this might seem strange for a man who had previously sought to either be invisible or to escape from people. There was an ease about him that made others feel at home in his presence. People were drawn to him, travelling to that remote place to see him, and he accepted their company with grace.

Josef had developed a gift for making people feel as if they were the only person in the room, even when surrounded by others, reading emotions with an almost uncanny precision. He listened more than he spoke, his eyes always alert, taking in every detail.

And then he would photograph them — the people who lived there or visited him in Broome.

Every one of the thousands of the Broome portraits reflect this shift in him, capturing not only faces but the essence of the souls behind them. Josef created a unique sanctuary in the most secluded of locations and welcomed the outside world into it. People would come and go from his life, each feeling a little lighter for having known him.

It seems unimaginable that anyone would have noticed that crimson speck in the scrub, but as I got to know Josef, I understood why he made a U-turn on the highway that morning in 1986.

That I owe my life to him is indisputable.

Since that fateful day, he never left Broome and the Dampier Peninsula. Initially, he disappeared into the wilderness, and perhaps he had a plan never to re-emerge, it's unclear to me, but what I can understand is this: the reason Josef found the serenity and peace he did, was because of his choice to stare into the face of his truth, to stand still and stop running.

This was the defining factor.

He never shunned nor disregarded the wider world beyond Broome; quite the opposite, he remained well-versed in global events and contemporary issues, but I'm convinced it was his commitment to staying rooted in a single location for the remainder of his life that unlocked the tranquillity he discovered.

In the early years of our friendship, Josef disappeared so thoroughly that many believed he'd ended his life in a remote area where his body couldn't be found. Only I, a few of his associates, and an isolated Aboriginal community in the Dampier Peninsula knew the truth and we saw no need to correct this belief.

During his disappearance — a period of profound transformation — Josef shared his story with me. At first, it only came out in tiny, disconnected image fragments, but as time went by, I came to understand that the act of recounting his experiences in this way was an essential part of his healing journey. Each revelation, each fragment of his past, seemed to lighten the burden he carried, and we eventually patched together a narrative for his life that paved the way for his emotional recovery.

Josef and I were constant companions during the latter part of his life, and I wish to share with you what I learned and tell the story of our friendship, collaboration and most of all our profound connection.

*

First, let's get this part of the story out of the way.

He found me naked, bloodied and grit-infested, along with the meagre contents of my rucksack strewn around me some two hundred and fifty metres from the road, amidst the green and red scrub on the desolate verges of the Great Northern Highway.

I had waited for over six hours for a ride out of Port Hedland. It was probably the excesses of boredom that led me into the panel van with two men whom I could instinctively sense were not going to entice me with warm conversation and humility.

I was dumped where they thought I couldn't be seen, where I would at worst die or eventually stagger naked to the road, by which time they would be long gone.

They did it because they could. Up there, who would have cared or believed a Pommy boy. If it's a little-known fact today that a significant proportion of rape victims are male, back then it was implausible, a taboo, a joke and unlikely to be of the slightest interest to the police in Port Hedland or Broome.

Although they took my money, it wasn't a material robbery — otherwise they would have taken my Walkman, passport, and other valuables. What has stayed with me and still matters, is the way they left me wrestling with a shame I didn't deserve and a wound to my sense of self I'm still learning to heal. I was angry and hurt by what those men had done to me and in the years that followed, my recovery didn't take place in a straight line.

*

In those first weeks and months everything felt painfully raw and there were days when I felt like I was existing without skin. I know I could have disappeared into that pain, and it could have broken me. But it didn't. Not entirely. I think there were two reasons for that:

The first was Josef. Sitting with him in the long silences of his grief — listening when he chose to speak and recognising the burden he carried, helped me create some space for my own recovery. His presence gave me a tether and enabled me to look outward, rather than folding in on myself. And in doing that, I had a sense of purpose, and it enabled me to face the world.

The second reason is harder to name, but I think it came from my mother, Maggie. She has never talked much about strength, but she has always carried a spiritual toughness that she instilled in me from my earliest years. My childhood near Jedburgh, a rural town on the Scottish Borders, was a patchwork of experiences she stitched together that gave me the solid foundations to tackle adversity and whatever life had to throw at me.

She was a force of nature, graceful yet unyielding, her eyes always filled with a blend of compassion and intellect that made me feel both comforted and challenged. Our traditional farmhouse was a sanctuary of books, music, and art, and every room had its rhythm, from the classical music playing in the background to the stacks of literature that lined the shelves.

My father, a fifth-generation farmer, took his own life when I was two years old, and Maggie raised me alone. She never spoke much about him, but it was clear his absence left a void, and she refused to allow it to consume us. Instead, she poured her energy into making sure I grew up with a combination of survival skills and a deep appreciation for beauty and knowledge.

After his death she continued to manage the farm, negotiating her share of his estate with his parents and siblings. By the time I was ten, she had taught me all the practical skills I needed like mending dry stone walls and fences, shepherding, caring for livestock — and by the time I was twelve, I was already driving tractors and Land Rovers across the three hundred acres of our land.

Maggie harboured a profound mistrust of the education system so, following my time at primary school, she took it upon herself to educate me at home. From the ages of eleven to sixteen our mornings were devoted to a comprehensive and varied curriculum that encompassed subjects ranging from maths to geography, literature to music, and it even included Latin. It was Maggie who energised me with my profound love for music, from a very young age introducing me to everything from JS Bach to Joni Mitchell and thanks to her dedication, I achieved a high level of proficiency in violin, guitar and piano.

She taught me how to observe beauty and would often take me on long walks through the countryside, pointing out the subtle colours in the changing seasons or the intricate architecture of old stone houses. The walks weren't only about observing; they were also lessons in truly seeing the world around me.

When I was sixteen, Maggie left the farm in the capable hands of her managers and began taking me on tours of the cultural centres of Europe. Paris, Rome, Florence, Vienna, Berlin, Athens, Madrid, Istanbul.

Each city left an indelible mark on me. We explored art galleries and ancient ruins, her enthusiasm guiding me through the depths of European history and culture. Her most memorable phrase being "Art is not only about what you see; it's about what it makes you feel."

These trips were more than an education; they broadened my horizons in ways no classroom ever could. Each time we returned to Jedburgh, I felt as though I had lived several lifetimes in the weeks and months we were away.

As I approached adulthood, Maggie encouraged my independence and when I was nineteen, I decided to travel the world. It was both a blessing and a gentle push out of the nest. So, in early 1986 I left to travel across Asia bound for Australia.

*

The morning after I had disclosed to Josef I was aware of his identity, we checked out of the Roebuck and departed Broome.

We made the decision silently. It was clear Josef was in urgent need of seclusion and, for the time being at least, he wanted me to accompany him. When I placed my rucksack in his car, neither of us discussed our actions or our destination, we both had an instinctive understanding of what we were doing.

We purchased some provisions at Streeter and Male's general store and, heading north out of Broome, the paved road quickly turned into an unsealed pindan track. There were no signposts or indicators of our location, and the barren terrain was an abrupt reminder that we were entering a largely wild and untamed environment.

We crossed over dried creek beds and sandy channels carved into the ground, deep scars from the previous season's rains. In a matter of weeks, this road would likely become impassable for extended periods, and once the heavy rains arrived, we'd have no choice but to remain wherever we ended up.

Josef had driven these tracks the year before when he had been on his assignment and negotiated with the newly created Aboriginal Corporation to photograph some of the communities dotted in the Dampier Peninsula.

He had stayed for nearly three weeks, and together with his dog Theo moved among the communities with a respect for their land and traditions, careful to only photograph people with permission and stay in areas they designated acceptable to them. He captured the essence of their landscapes and the intricate details of their living practices, focusing on their profound relationships with the land and sea.

Josef had enjoyed their hospitality in ways he'd never expected and during that brief period discovered murmurings of a peace within himself he had rarely experienced. When it was time to depart, one of the Elders had expressed that he would always be welcome to return. Therefore, gaining permission for our stay on this occasion proved far less complicated than we had anticipated. The Elders' openness and willingness to accept us was both a surprise and a relief. They immediately understood his need to be undisturbed and trusted we would respect their land and leave it as we had found it. The land they guided us to was in a remote coastal inlet named Nigalya Cove, hidden along the rugged northern Dampier coastline.

For us to be welcomed so readily onto this sacred land was a privilege that demanded our respect and sensitivity. We were expected to tread lightly, to acknowledge the deep spiritual ties that bound these indigenous communities to this coastal landscape.

Their connection had been forged over thousands of years, creating a tapestry of customs, stories, and daily practices that were inseparable from their identity.

When we arrived at Nigalya Cove, the sky was a deep, cloudless blue, the sun blazing high above the jagged cliffs and at first sight, it felt like a secret paradise. Red cliffs guarded a narrow stretch of pristine white sand edging the turquoise waters of the Indian Ocean. To the left was a tranquil lagoon bordered by lush mangroves. In many ways, it felt as though nature had provided a perfect haven for us.

It took us several days to acclimatise before we settled on where to build a semi-permanent camp that would provide the most shelter and shield us from the occasional storms the imminent wet season would inflict on us.

Thankfully, Josef had left Perth with enough tools, rope and canvas tarpaulins to make a practical, strong and secure shelter. We pitched a large canvas tent and constructed a lean-to shelter alongside it, shaping some poles from branches and developing a roof from tarpaulin covered with thick leaves we gathered from the surrounding bushland.

I hadn't expected to find strength in another person's suffering. We had both seen the worst of humanity, and in our shared darkness we found a fragile lifeline.

The act of disappearing wasn't about escaping imagined physical threats; it was about finding a space within which Josef could make sense of his life — and I could regain mine.

Through Josef's mostly silent companionship, I began to recover my dignity and heal from my wounds. He didn't ask for details about what had happened to me; he didn't press for explanations or offer hollow platitudes. His presence alone was enough. In his silence, there was understanding, a recognition of my pain that words could never fully capture.

*

The mystery of why Josef instinctively turned back on the highway that morning, when he saw the crimson speck of my rucksack, unravelled one evening amidst the fractured exchanges we shared around the campfire.

He chose his words carefully when he explained to me how he saw everything in detail. Not only occasional details: the very reason he became a photographer is because he perceived precise details everywhere. Even without his camera, he was watchful of everything before his eyes; every image was processed, memorised, and logged within a second. Every detail became a stimulus. It had always been this way, for as long as he could remember.

He heard details too; in much the same way he saw them. There was no blocking out sound; every crackle, bang, drip, note, and nuance reached him all at once, blending into a cacophonic soundscape where meaning was often lost in an abstract malaise.

For much of his life, he was unaware his experience was unusual, that others did not process sight and sound with the same relentless intensity. He didn't realise this sensory overload made it difficult to form meaningful connections or that his silent presence could often make others feel uncomfortable. Somehow, sheltered by the insularity of his condition, he felt safely locked in.

When Josef told me this there was a vulnerability in his words that struck me deeply. He had spent so much of his life isolated by his heightened perceptions. In that moment, I understood a little more about the world he saw and heard so vividly and how it had shaped him and set him apart from others and led him to this place in his life.

*

During those initial weeks at Nigalya Cove, we discovered a rhythm that felt simultaneously fresh and timeless. A brief stroll from the camp brought us to rocky outcrops brimming with marine life. We would gather a plentiful supply of bait from the lagoon's shallows, where small crabs and shrimp were concealed under the rocks and among the mangroves and I swiftly taught Josef how to fish using his rod as well as with basic lines and hooks.

In the early morning light, we would wade into what were usually tranquil waters where the sand met the rocky outcrops. Casting into the clear blue sea required skill and timing, letting the weight of the line carry the bait out. It would never be long before we had enough fish for a meal or two, mostly Barramundi and Snapper, sometimes a Queenfish or Emperor Fish.

We had gathered enough firewood to last through the wet season and stacked it beneath the lean-to shelter and each evening we would cook over an open fire. In the mornings a humid heat would hang heavy, and in the afternoons the rains would arrive with predictable regularity; sudden, hard, sometimes briefly and at other times unrelenting. Josef moved through our daily routines with intense efficiency. His silences were easy to mistake for calm, but at times his hands would tremor in the middle of a task, and I would notice his gaze fix somewhere beyond the present moment.

When he began to speak of his past he would offer only fragments. There was no embellishment, no attempt to shape the telling. The facts emerged in raw, unfinished pieces. I listened carefully, trying to stitch them into something whole, but the gaps remained. His childhood, especially, seemed to exist only in framed descriptions of images that floated free of context, detached from any coherent narrative. At that time, it seemed there was no fuller story for him to tell, the fragments were all he had. Whatever came before or after these moments was lost or was perhaps never fully understood. And yet, the fragments revealed more than he likely intended. In the spaces between them, I began to piece together a fuller story.

One night, unprompted, he spoke of the journey that had brought him to Australia. He was nine years old when he ran away from Poland in 1939. His voice was steady, almost dispassionate, as though the remarkable adventure he undertook and the telling of it required no emotion. But the facts alone were enough to suggest what it must have taken — courage maybe, or the blind drive of a child who no longer had any choice. Whether it had been ingenuity or a simple survival instinct that led him across the world was unknown. He gave no easy answers to my requests for more details, only more fragments. And yet, each piece seemed to reveal something deeper, not only to me but to himself. I wondered how much of his life had been lived this way, disconnected moments without a clear thread to hold them together.

The work it took to survive in the camp sustained us, but it seemed it was these revelations that anchored him and kept him from drifting into deeper turmoil. Each story, however brief, was an attempt by him to shape the chaos within. As the rains fell and the days bled into one another, I began to believe that the act of speaking, of allowing someone else to bear witness, might have been his way of managing his internalised pain.

*

Katowice, Poland, March 1939

From the age of seven, he had travelled to school alone each day by tram. It was there, in the echoing corridors and shadowed classrooms, that he learned how to disappear, not in the way of magicians or ghosts, but in the practised way of a child who understands that invisibility can be a form of survival.

School did not teach him spelling, trigonometry, or languages. Instead, it taught him how to step back, to observe without being seen, to slip into the spaces where the world blurred into something less sharp, less dangerous. His real education took place in his mind. School was merely the setting for his escape into imagination.

Dreaming was not an indulgence but a necessity.

In a world of rigid discipline and sudden brutality, he found safety in the act of seeing — really seeing. He learned to latch onto fleeting moments, to extract beauty from the smallest fragments of his surroundings. And it was the tramlines that first revealed to him the power of framing and composition, and of the perfect balance between chaos and order.

Each morning and evening, the tramlines were his solace. More than simply steel embedded in stone, they became an ever-changing canvas; fluid yet structured, shifting with the light, bending with the streets, guiding his eye to the vanishing point. He studied the way they caught the rain, how they cut through the grey cobbles like silver threads, how they swirled and looped at the turning points, drawing intricate, unspoken patterns onto the city. The sound of them; the clatter, the metallic hum, the sudden crackle of the rod against the wire, was like a secret rhythm beneath the silence of the streets.

The houses that lined the route stood still, their shuttered facades hiding lives he could not know, struggles he could not see. But the tramlines belonged to no one. They led forward. They suggested motion, possibility, and where they vanished into the horizon, converging into a single thread, he sensed that there had to be something beyond — something other than Katowice.

Each day, the lines and shapes sparked something in him. At first, it was only a feeling, an exhilaration in the act of looking. He did not yet understand that this way of seeing, this instinctive grasp of form and contrast, light and shadow, was the first whisper of something larger, something that would one day shape the course of his life. But already, without knowing why, he let his eyes frame the world as though it were an image waiting to be captured.

*

Jozef Kazimierz Dobrowski was born on 28 January 1930 in Katowice, Silesia, Poland.

His mother died giving birth to him on the table in the dimly lit basement tenement apartment that was their home. In that cramped space, the loss of his mother left behind an emptiness and the last semblances of anything that could have resembled love.

His father was a baker who found solace in the bottle, leaving for work at dawn and returning in the afternoons with the heavy stench of alcohol and despair clinging to him. The sound of his father's boots on the stone stairs to their front door was always a prelude to dread.

Josef's existence in that basement was made up of shadows and silence. His grandmother was a bitter woman with a worn-out spirit who was supposedly living with them to care for him and his sister, Krystyna, who was three years his senior. But in truth, Krystyna was Josef's true guardian, her presence a fragile shield against their father's neglect and rage.

The apartment reeked of boiled cabbage and sorrow. In the front room opposite the kitchen, Josef and Krystyna shared a bed that grew narrower as he grew older. At night, they lay side by side under blankets, their bodies seeking warmth and comfort from each other. The kitchen, next to a tiny windowless room where their grandmother slept, was a place of cold utility. The table on which Josef had been born and his mother died, was surrounded by four mismatched chairs and a stove that rarely held anything more than simple soups or stews.

Krystyna bore the brunt of their father's cruelty. He never laid a hand on Josef, but Krystyna's cries would sometimes pierce the night like shattering glass.

The night before Josef disappeared, her cries had been harrowing. She didn't return to their bed that night. When Josef woke up, she had not resurfaced and ignoring his grandmother he readied himself for school, closed the door behind him and walked to the tram stop, never to return.

*

In late March 1939, Katowice and all of Poland was holding its breath. The threat of war with Nazi Germany loomed. Weeks earlier, they had invaded Czechoslovakia, and it was only a matter of time before Poland was next.

Katowice felt suspended in an uneasy silence, the air thick with anticipation and wrapped in uncertainty. It was a city waiting, knowing that something inevitable and terrible was approaching. The streets, once bustling with the mundane rhythms of daily life, were heavy in that waiting, like the stillness before a thunderclap, when you knew the sky was about to break. People on the tram would speak in hushed tones, their eyes darting about, searching for unseen threats.

And who was he? Simply a bewildered boy trying to make sense of the world.

That morning, Josef walked to the tram stop, his head bowed as always, willing himself to be invisible. The streets were damp, the cobblestones slick with rain. The tram tracks glistened like silver veins; the ones he imagined as pathways to somewhere else, somewhere better.

He often carried with him this notion of 'goodness.' If he could be good — truly good — then nothing bad could happen to him. He would pick a line on the pavement, a crack, a stone, a place where, when he stepped beyond it, he would become good. Maybe then his father wouldn't rage. Maybe then his sister wouldn't suffer. Maybe then the ethnic German thugs who wore brown wouldn't look at him with those cold, dead eyes.

As the tram neared the city centre it would become more crowded, mostly packed with workers in tatty coats clutching their lunch pails. The collars of their thick coats were turned up against the damp, their eyes sunken with worry. Women clutched bags close to their bodies, their hands red from the cold, expressions drawn tight with unspoken fears. The wooden seats were hard, and their slats pressed into his small frame. He would kneel on them, peering through sepia-stained windows, trying to make sense of the increasingly monochrome world outside, a world he knew was changing but didn't yet understand how or why.

On that morning, a man got on the tram carrying a bunch of red flowers. In a city that was turning grey with fear, those petals burned against the gloom like tiny embers of defiance. Josef stared at them, transfixed, framing them into an exotic image as they swayed with the movement of the tram — as fragile as everything around him.

In that moment he saw something else, something that held him still. A man and a woman on the pavement walked toward each other. He in a heavy coat, she with a bag swinging at her side. They met, smiled and kissed — their bodies folding into one another — an extraordinary moment of warmth in a world growing colder by the day.

Josef was mesmerised. He had never witnessed tenderness so freely given. It was a revelation — something apart from the harshness of his home, the brutality of his father, the fearful silence of his grandmother. At that moment he forgot everything, the tram stops, his school, the lessons he was meant to endure. The world outside the window became his whole existence; he let the tram carry him past his stop, past his school, past everything he knew.

When the tram reached its destination, the central station, he got off. The crowds surged around him purposefully, knowing their destinations. But Josef had none. He walked toward the trains, watching them breathe clouds of steam into the air, their doors yawning open and swallowing passengers whole. And without thinking, without a plan, he stepped onto one. The doors shut behind him with a finality he didn't yet comprehend.

He did not look back; he did not know where he was going; he only knew that he could not return. It was the tramlines that had led him away, carrying him toward a future he could not yet name. Long before he had a camera in his hands, they had already taught him how to see.

*

Josef lacked papers, a passport, a ticket, a map, and any comprehension of life outside the soot-covered industrial region of Katowice and its neighbouring towns.

Envisioning a nine-year-old manoeuvring through the turmoil of Europe at that time was challenging, but as he explained his escape through fragmented descriptions of images, it seemed to dawn on him that his journey must have been driven by an instinctive understanding that he had no other option but to keep moving.

As he described these images, he revealed to himself how fortunate his timing had been to flee when Poland was on the verge of the Nazi invasion. A few months later, any escape would have been impossible.

The first part of Josef's journey was to Kraków, and he described to me the stark details of how he sat on wood-slatted benches in the third-class compartment and watched as a conductor approached him.

The details were as vivid as they were astonishing and quite believable. He assuredly told me that the conductor's jacket was navy blue and double-breasted with brass buttons and silver braid epaulettes, that red piping edged the jacket and that his trousers were sharply creased. His hat had a red band, and the stiff black peak was shiny, and it had a badge on it with PKP insignia and a Polish eagle in the centre.

When Josef silently ignored the request to see his ticket, the conductor simply continued down the carriageway without challenging him as though he were a ghost.

The sequence of events that followed was, in the way Josef told them, laced with accidental and unbelievable good fortune.

In Kraków, he wandered around the city aimlessly until an elderly man approached and asked him where he was going. Josef didn't answer.

This man had been a professor of mathematics at Kraków University who happened to be Jewish and was in the process of leaving the city. Somehow over the course of that day, an unlikely friendship emerged. Josef's description of him suggested a photographic memory:

"His study was dimly lit, and a brass lamp sat on a heavy oak desk covered with notebooks and pieces of paper with mathematical symbols. A nearly empty leather suitcase sat open on a worn rug; several books, some clothing, and a silver framed photograph were neatly stacked next to it ready to be packed. The Professor had grey hair and wire-rimmed round glasses perched low on his nose and was leaning over a desk, his dark suit was slightly rumpled, his tie loosened. Bookshelves lined the walls, filled with books with cracked spines. A candelabra with seven arms (a menorah) sat on a nearby shelf."

The following day Josef walked with the Professor and the leather suitcase to Kraków's Central Station.

*

Their passage would have undoubtedly been fraught with danger and uncertainty, and Josef could not describe any of the practical details of how the extraordinary journey took place or why they managed to succeed.

With each fragmented image he offered me I was confounded by the story. He could only give me a verbal sketch of the images he memorised on the journey rather than any comprehensive detail as to how they did it.

It was only through sensitive questioning and a piecing together of the fragments that I was able to map their route. Over many weeks I began plotting it out with notes and descriptions of the images Josef described. Initially, I drew a rough map of Europe from memory in a sketchbook and began to chart the potential route, and as he spoke, I would note down the description he gave, number it and put the number where I thought it could be on the map, each with a question mark.

In Broome many years later when we had maps and were able to research the facts and details on the Internet, Josef and I generated a more accurate picture of the likely journey he took with the Professor:

There is no doubt that in March 1939, travelling across Europe demanded ingenuity and the right connections. It would seem that the Professor possessed both. He must have created a persona for Josef as his grandson whose papers had either been lost or hadn't existed in the first place.

At Kraków station, they likely boarded a train to Nowy Sacz, near the Slovak border. This route was less travelled and would have allowed them to avoid the heavily controlled German zones. From there, they crossed into Slovakia via Piwniczna-Zdrój, a rural post where surveillance was minimal. Bribery and local guides would likely have facilitated this crossing. They would have continued by train from Košice, a major railway hub in Slovakia, to Budapest in Hungary.

Budapest would have been a crucial stop. Here, they would have needed to secure fake papers or bribe officials to continue their journey. The Professor's credentials would have likely played a vital role in maintaining their façade.

Their next destination was Vienna, a perilous leg due to Austria's annexation by Nazi Germany in 1938. However, refugee networks were in place to assist Jews escaping persecution.

From Vienna, they travelled through Innsbruck towards Switzerland by train. Switzerland's neutrality made it a critical haven for refugees, but crossing into it involved some risk and the border guards would have been unpredictable. However, official letters from academic institutions and the professor's reputation may have helped them gain entry.

Once in Switzerland, they took a train to Geneva or Zurich before heading towards France. In March 1939 France remained a sanctuary for Jewish refugees. Organizations such as the Committee for Assistance to Refugees helped arrange temporary visas or exit papers.

Throughout this harrowing journey, the Professor's quick thinking and resourcefulness would have been vital in navigating the complex web of borders and authorities. His standing probably provided just enough leverage for them both to survive the perilous trek across the volatile conditions in Europe. In passing Josef off as his grandson, he was able to garner sympathy as he talked his way through difficult borders and situations and his ingenuity to do so would have been driven by necessity and sheer willpower.

The Professor had already arranged a passage for himself to Australia, intending to board an ocean liner in Toulon bound for Sydney in a several week's time but Josef wasn't sure how long they waited in Toulon before they boarded the ship.

If it was incredible that the Professor reached Australia safely, it was an even greater mystery how he got Josef onto the ship, continuing to maintain the charade of him being his grandson during the long journey. Josef could not recall the names of the ports the ship called into but from his image descriptions, they would most certainly have included Gibraltar, Port Said and the Suez Canal, Colombo in what was then Ceylon and Singapore before crossing the Indian Ocean to Fremantle on the west coast of Australia, on through the Southern Ocean to Melbourne and to Sydney. In all, it would have taken them four to six weeks.

Ironically, it was in Fremantle that the charade unravelled. They disembarked and when they returned to rejoin the ship the Professor was challenged by immigration officials, and they were both hurried into a room where some intense interrogation took place. There was a lot of antisemitic sentiment in Australia at the time, and the officials were not kind in their interrogation, so it was most likely then that the Professor revealed he had used Josef as useful cover to aid his passage across Europe. He would have known that at some stage he needed to hand Josef over to authorities and whether that was in Fremantle or Sydney, it made no difference.

Eventually, the Professor was grudgingly permitted to rejoin the liner, and Josef was taken away and passed into the care of the Child Welfare Department in Perth.

As is now commonly known, neglected or orphaned children in Australia were subjected to some appalling abuses at the government or church-run institutions into whose care they were placed. Had he not been processed by a kindly woman named Dora, assistant to the director at the Child Welfare Department, things could have been quite different for Josef.

Dora was the sister of Belinda Batten, and when she told her about this nine-year-old boy who couldn't speak a word of English and how he'd turned up in Fremantle after a remarkable escape from Poland, they discussed his fate. Belinda, childless herself, sometimes fostered infants or youngsters needing temporary placement at her home, and Dora enquired if she might consider taking Josef while they found him a place in an orphanage.

By an extraordinary stroke of luck, this was how Josef came to encounter the generous-hearted couple Mo and Belinda of Batten's Chemist and Photographic shop in Leederville, Perth. In September 1940 he officially became their adopted son, assigned with the name Josef, with an S rather than Z, Batten.

8. The Green Green Grass Of Home

It was 1987 and the last of the March rains had drained into the earth, leaving behind a season of gentler balminess and the air around the camp was filled with the scent of damp bark and the sound of the cicadas was less insistent.

Josef continued to move through our days in silence and, with his thoughts walled off, he felt both near and distant. When I tried to stir a little humour into the quiet, he responded with a shrug, or else his replies were so dry they crumbled any notion of levity.

One evening he asked how long I intended to stay. The question surprised me. We had never spoken of the future, not in any practical terms. I told him I wanted to stay, but my visa was running out and that I would have to go to Perth to extend it.

This was when he made his proposal.

He didn't know if or when he would be able to surface again, only that he couldn't return to the life he had left behind, yet there were things he wanted me to do for him. He explained what had to be arranged while I was in Perth. As he did so his guardedness eased, and he let me glimpse something of the man who had existed before this self-imposed exile. Perhaps he already knew it would be a long time — many more months, possibly years — before he could return to the outside world, and I was the only person he fully trusted.

We agreed that while I was away, he would keep the Land Cruiser with him for safety. The narrow track to the community was unreliable — in the wet it was an hour's drive at best — and I had been making a weekly journey for small supplies and to maintain our ties with the Elders.

Then came the part I hadn't expected.

Once he confirmed I had an Australian bank account, he placed a cheque for AU$35,000 in my hand, along with a thousand dollars in cash. I was to pay the Elders generously for a ride to Broome, then fly to Perth. Josef had planned everything with meticulous care. He wrote carefully worded letters that he sealed with precision and gave me a list of instructions:

In Perth, I would post a letter to his photographic agent in Paris, then wait a week before calling her. I would take another letter to the Leederville branch of ANZ bank and deposit the cheque into my own ANZ account. Back then, travellers on working holiday visas were encouraged to open Australian bank accounts.

I would meet Dick Edwards at his estate agency, present a letter of introduction, and collect the keys to the chemist shop where he suggested I base myself while in Perth. He also wrote a letter to Joe at the garage requesting he source him a second reliable Land Cruiser, no more than five years old, and I was to return to the camp with it.

From his home, I would retrieve his archives: many boxes of contact sheets and photographs together with Mo and Belinda's papers and memorabilia. Before returning, I would withdraw in cash at the ANZ the remains of the funds he had given me.

I grasped the significance of the responsibility he was placing upon me. He knew then that he would never return to the life he had been living and was making contingency plans for whatever he chose to do next. Rather than finding it strange, I was thrilled by the anticipation of my upcoming task.

*

In the early morning light, Josef drove me in his usual silence. It was the first time he had left our camp in nearly four months. With the improved drier conditions, it took nearly half an hour to navigate the track to the community where we found Albert Warrun, one of the Elders, sitting under a boab tree and asked him for a ride to Broome.

Almost wordlessly, he simply said "Tomorrow."

When we returned the following morning Albert Warrun was already waiting by the tree in a tired Ford Falcon two-door sedan. Its yellow paint had dulled under the relentless sun and was scarred with dents and rust speckles and a deep scrape down the driver's side. Its fastback and the air scoop on the bonnet gave it a mean sporty look, but the worn tyres and sagging rear suspension made me wonder if we would make it to Broome in one piece.

Josef drove off without ceremony and Albert Warrun nodded for me to get in.

We came to know Albert Warrun well in the time Josef was there — he was our liaison while we camped on his land. He was a man of profound wisdom that seemed to be etched into his weathered face and the deep furrows across his brow, his voice was gravelly and deliberate, and his words were carefully measured.

Born in the early 1920s, he had spent his youth working on remote cattle stations before returning to his ancestral lands in the 1970s to advocate for Aboriginal land rights. His father had been a lawman, and Albert Warrun carried his teachings close to his heart. He knew every inch of the coastal landscape, the mangroves, the tides, the hidden trails that wove through the bush.

He had an unspoken authority that commanded respect, but there was also a generosity in him. Later when we had got to know him better, he would visit the camp and we would share stories around the campfire, and he taught us about bush medicine and the significance of different plants and animals.

Albert Warrun had a son who had been killed in Vietnam, and he had a soft spot for those who were lost — physically or emotionally. Perhaps that was why he welcomed Josef so readily. There was an understanding between them, an unspoken recognition of shared burdens. Albert Warrun's presence came to provide a grounding force for Josef, they would often sit together in silence, the crackle of the fire between them speaking volumes without words.

I placed my rucksack in the back of the Falcon and as I climbed into the passenger seat and its V8 fired up with a guttural growl, the seat wobbled precariously, and I was forced to brace myself against the dashboard to keep from leaning back into nothingness.

As we pulled away from the community, Tom Jones' voice filled the car with the *Green Green Grass of Home*. In our four months at the camp, I had not heard any music, only the rhythmic sounds of nature, pounding rain and the movements of the sea. The comedic irony of the song was strangely welcome.

Usually, this unsealed road needed to be negotiated with a four-wheel drive, but Albert Warrun drove with practised ease, slowly navigating the rougher terrain without hesitation. Every so often he would look over at me and chuckle.

"Tom Jones, mate, bloody good yeah!" or "Englebert Humperdinck, bloody good yeah!"

The eight-track player had a thick tape cassette jammed inside it that switched between Tom and Engelbert with a mechanical ka-thunk. For nearly four perilous and slightly nerve-racking hours the tape played on repeat whilst I precariously balanced in a seat that didn't seem to be attached to the floor.

Eventually, I managed to settle and even found myself lulled by the rhythmic throb of the engine, the juddering thuds of the suspension and the alternating voices of Tom and Engelbert singing what sounded like identical songs.

When we pulled up outside the Roebuck Bay Hotel, I thanked Albert Warrun, and we sat together on the veranda. After a long silent while, he wandered off and I sat alone allowing the Green Green Grass earworm to fade a little before I entered the bar.

*

It felt strange yet liberating to step back into the Roebuck Bay Hotel after so many months in isolation and the smell of beer and stale tobacco was mildly comforting. I checked in, dropped my rucksack in the room, and strolled down Dampier Terrace to Broome Travel to arrange a flight to Perth. There was an Ansett flight departing later that afternoon, and although they could have booked me a seat, I chose to allow myself a few days to gently ease back into the outside world before heading to the city.

In Broome, everything seemed to move at its own easy and simplistic pace and amidst the small-town vibe I felt at home and contented in those few days. A warm April breeze made the many hours I spent reading on a wicker chair outside Carla's Café thoroughly enjoyable. I took some long slow evening walks along Cable Beach and saw trains of camels being led along the water's edge; their profiles shadowed against the setting sun.

On my last evening, I went to Sun Pictures, a unique open-air cinema that had been there for decades. The seating comprised deck chairs arranged beneath the stars and while I watched *Good Morning Vietnam* an occasional plane from the nearby airport would whoosh low over the top of the screen making a low rumbling sound amidst the film's soundtrack. A part of me was reluctant to leave so soon, but the following afternoon I checked out of the Roey and walked the short distance to the airport to take the flight to Perth.

*

That evening, I took a bus from the airport to Northbridge and checked into a hostel I'd stayed at previously. The exterior was a mishmash of bright murals and fading paint and inside it was alive with the hum of conversations in various languages.

I claimed a bunk and had a few friendly exchanges with some fellow travellers. I'd stayed in many of these types of places and the conversations invariably revolved around the same questions. Where are you from? Where are you going? Where are the casual jobs? Where were the faulty Telecom Australia phone boxes where you could make unrestricted international calls for 50 cents — and did the Perth branch of the Hare Krishnas provide free meals as they did in Sydney?

I was pleased to be re-entering this world but somehow no longer identified myself with it in the way I once had, it felt strange and no longer relevant.

I left the hostel in the early dawn and stepped out into the refreshing cool air, and as I walked to Leederville the city began stirring; the cool air was replaced with the sharp exhaust fumes of commuter traffic.

Eventually, Oxford Street stretched out before me in a long straight line; contemporary stores stood beside the worn exteriors of older establishments and amongst them, Batten's Chemist looked like an abandoned and neglected artefact. Time had dulled its signage, and I could just about make out the words *Batten's* and *Chemist* and *Photographic* etched into the glass storefront.

A few doors down I sat outside a cafe at a small table and watched the people hurrying by; their faces set in the determined expressions of those with places to be.

From there I could see the door to Dick Edwards Estate Agents on the corner of the same block and watched a man unlock it and enter. When I followed him in a few minutes later he looked up from his paperwork failing to conceal his wariness of a boy with a rucksack. He took the letter and eyed me suspiciously before opening it. He grunted something, folded the letter back up, and went to a cupboard where he pulled out a set of keys, placed them on the desk between us and returned to his paperwork as if our brief interaction had never occurred.

I turned the key in the door to Batten's Chemist with reticence. As soon as I stepped inside, a peculiar sensation washed over me and many of the scattered snapshots of his life he had recounted in the camp began to merge into a more coherent story.

The air smelt musty, and I moved slowly so as not to disturb the ghosts. Most of the furniture was covered with dust sheets but I could see it was sturdy, built for function rather than comfort. There was an overall sense of sparse utilitarianism that provided an insight into Josef's upbringing; practical, no-nonsense, with little room for luxury.

In the photographic studio at the back of the shop, its remnants lay in disarray. The large format camera was a ghostly figure on a large wooden tripod; its frayed black hood had puddled on the floor under a dust sheet.

The darkroom door was ajar, revealing shelves of ageing chemical bottles and film drying racks. I could picture young Josef learning from Mo Batten, absorbing the trade with intense focus, hearing Mo's guidance and seeing Josef's concentrated expression as he mastered the components of studio and darkroom photography.

In the studio, there was a large walk-in storeroom, its shelves reaching from floor to ceiling on both sides, filled with a dense collection of black archival boxes. On the right side of the room were around sixty boxes, each carefully labelled with white tape marking the coded years from JB1947.1 through to JB1985.2 in perfect chronological order. On the left side of the room were hundreds of glass plate negatives and more archive boxes with labels spanning from 1926 to 1964; no doubt historical records of Leederville's inhabitants as photographed by Mo Batten in the studio.

I ran my fingers lightly along the spines of Josef's archive boxes. These weren't merely photographs, they were fragments of a life spent witnessing the world's darkest moments. My hand stopped at 1968. I carefully lifted the heavy box down, placing it on a small table near the door. Opening the lid, I found dozens of 11x14 prints in clear acetate sleeves. I turned them carefully, mindful not to leave fingerprints on the protective coverings.

Some were taken in Vietnam, some in Nigeria, each detailed with their date and a catalogue number with typed captions on the reverse. In one a skeletal Biafran child stared back at me, his ribs pressing against paper-thin skin. The composition was flawless, the black and white tones revealing every devastating detail with unflinching clarity. After a long moment, I carefully returned the print to its sleeve and closed the box, replacing it on the shelf feeling like an intruder in someone else's nightmare.

A door from the studio opened into an enclosed yard that extended about 50 metres, barren and dry except for a lone eucalyptus tree rising from a crack in the concrete, its desiccated, flaky leaves littering the ground.

Upstairs, the living area was humble. A tiny kitchen with an old-fashioned stove and chipped enamel sink hinted at simple meals shared around the pale blue Formica table. The sitting area held an assortment of knick-knacks and family photographs, faded but lovingly displayed. It struck me how little had changed since Josef's childhood; it was as if time had stopped in this place.

In what seemed to be his bedroom, a small area with a slim bed, an old wooden desk, and a wardrobe, I spotted signs of Josef's more recent presence. The bed appeared freshly made though it was covered with a quilt that was old and faded. The bedside table was dust-free and some garments in the wardrobe gave the impression of having been worn years, rather than decades, ago.

I was struck by the absence of books. On a heavy dark shelf unit there were only a few encyclopaedias, an atlas, and some technical photography reference manuals, but otherwise, nothing more. In a house that seemed mostly abandoned and frozen in time, there were merely sporadic traces of Josef's occasional presence, rather than any feeling that it was truly his home.

Josef had wished for me to stay over in the house, yet I intuitively sensed that the place wasn't welcoming to visitors and that its history deserved to be respected and left undisturbed. Despite my keen interest in uncovering more pieces of Josef's life and knowing that the house contained many clues to his story, I chose to stay at the hostel during my time in Perth. I would carry out all of Josef's instructions while there, but I intended to maintain a clear boundary between his life and mine.

*

Josef's instructions were neatly compiled with details of locations and tasks made out in meticulous block capitals, almost as if he were shouting them out.

The Leederville ANZ branch was in a small arcade of shops, a short walk from the chemist shop. As I deposited the cheque, I handed over the letter and waited as the bank clerk perused it. Josef had instructed them to arrange for a significant cash withdrawal via my bank account to facilitate his stay on the Aboriginal reserve. The clerk glanced at me and instructed me to provide three days' notice before departing Perth to ensure the necessary cash was ready for collection at the branch and to bring my passport.

At his garage I met Joe, an amiable laid-back character in his late thirties with bleached blonde hair and the look of a surfy type — I assumed the VW Combi in his yard with boards attached to the roof was his. As he read the letter, his face belied an edge of seriousness, and he said he could tell Josef was shouldering some burden when he last saw him. When I questioned what he meant he said everyone needs to "go bush" sometimes and that he'd honour Josef's wish for him to "keep schtum".

At that point, the penny dropped, and I realised each of the letters — to the bank, to Dick Edwards, to Anne Delacourt — were not only to ensure his affairs were in order, but also to enable him to disappear undisturbed for as long as it took. I agreed to drop by in three or four days to see if he had sourced a Land Cruiser and by midday, I was back in Northbridge where I checked back into the hostel.

The contrast between the hostel and the chemist shop was stark — it was a hive of youthful exuberance. In the courtyard, my senses were awakened by a German boy strumming a guitar and quietly practising *Suzanne* by Leonard Cohen.

*

The walk from the Northbridge hostel to Perth's Central Business District led me through a patchwork of narrow streets, where cafés spilt onto the pavement and street stalls were selling fresh fruit and handmade trinkets.

In Forrest Place, the Beaux-Arts grandeur of the General Post Office was a relic of another era, and the marble floors gleamed beneath its towering dome, reflecting filtered light from the high, arched windows. I posted Josef's letter to Anne Delacourt in Paris.

Along the building's sun-bleached wall stood a row of telephone boxes where I fed fifty-cent coins into the sticky metal slot while I spoke briefly to Maggie. The line crackled, swallowing dollars in seconds as I rushed to tell her I was fine, that she should write to me in Perth and Broome. She didn't ask what had happened in the silence between my calls, and I saw no reason to tell her.

The Department of Immigration and Ethnic Affairs was a monolithic structure of concrete and glass looming over Wellington Street, its reflective surfaces mirroring the relentless Australian sun. A gust of artificially cooled air enveloped me in the cavernous hall with rows of occupied plastic chairs. I took a number from a dispenser, the small slip of paper marking my place in the unyielding queue and prepared for the hours to unfold — the process of a visa extension was probably going to take a while.

Eventually, I was called to a booth, and a clean-cut young man in a crisp white short-sleeved open-neck shirt informed me that extending my visa wasn't straightforward. My only option was a tourist visa, but only if I could provide evidence of sufficient funds to support myself without working. Processing times varied, often taking weeks. He scheduled an interview for two days later, instructing me to bring a bank statement and passport. I was to remain in the country and avoid international travel until a decision was made. The process felt efficient yet ambivalent as if they both wanted and didn't want people to stay in Australia. Either way, I was pleased my bank account would show sufficient funds but concerned they might ask why I had received such a large lump sum so recently.

*

For a few days, I enjoyed a sense of relative normality at the hostel. Young people came and went with carefree abandon, and it thrummed with life. After so long in the wilderness it felt good to experience simple things like going to the launderette, taking the bus to Cottesloe and relaxing on a beach, sharing travelling tales over games of pool, reading in a hammock in the yard and playing games of chess.

Getting my visa extended was easier than expected. The ANZ branch supplied me with a statement, and I attended the immigration appointment and thankfully there were no awkward questions. I was asked to wait and after half an hour my passport was returned to me with a six-month tourist visa added to the two months remaining on my existing visa, but with the stipulation, I was not to work. I felt liberated. And, unusually for me, a rare drinker, I bought a six-pack of tinnies from the bottle shop to celebrate.

That evening, in the courtyard, the German boy sat on the edge of a low wall, singing *Suzanne* once again. This time, he had an audience; Swedish, American, Israeli, and English travellers drawn in from their usual boisterous conversations, lulled into quiet by the warmth of his voice. When he finished, he looked over at me and, without a word, proffered his guitar as an unspoken invitation.

I couldn't resist and, as I took the instrument and gently adjusted the tuning to suit my hands my fingers acted of their own accord, I eased into my version of *Road* by Nick Drake, emulating his intricate fingerpicking style, something I had been perfecting since I was ten. As I settled into the acoustic introduction I hesitated, uncertain my voice would hold steady for the brief, delicate lyrics. At that moment, the German boy came in with the opening line, his timing perfect.

I smiled, letting him take the song alone. When we finished, the courtyard erupted into whoops and claps. I handed the guitar back with a nod of gratitude, a warm glow spreading through me.

How did he know this song? In those days, Nick Drake was an obscurity, a secret passed between a devoted few. Maggie had been one of them. She played all three of his albums from the moment they were released in the early seventies, introducing me to music so rare and delicate, that it felt like a private language. Until now, I had never met another Nick Drake follower and felt I had met a fellow traveller in the truest sense of the word.

*

The following morning, I walked to Joe's Garage. There was a certain comfort in his straightforwardness and no-nonsense approach to work and life. He had lined up a suitable Land Cruiser for AU$14,500. I wrote him a cheque there and then and we agreed I would collect it in two days, so he had a chance to service it and check it over.

I made my way to the chemist shop to consider how to best organise and transport Josef's photographic archive. It comprised a carefully curated catalogue of every photograph that had been published or that he or his editors had chosen for books or exhibitions, and the weight of its value sat heavily with me. Josef had explained to me that with each assignment the negatives remained with his agency in Paris and that he would receive in the post a contact sheet for each roll of film and an 11x14 print of each published image. He always insisted on having the final word on the captions designated to each photograph and would request changes if he felt they didn't accurately reflect the context. Sometimes though, images were published with captions that were inaccurate and there was not much he could do about that, particularly if he was still in the field and unreachable.

Examining his archive, where some years necessitated only a single box and others demanded two, hinting at busier periods, I was eager to explore his earliest work to gain an understanding of how his career began.

I reached for the 1947 box; its cardboard edges slightly frayed from years of handling and began sifting through the contents. The images were taken in Perth and mostly of new immigrants and refugees. Stark yet intimate, they captured moments of raw human emotion; faces of refugees disembarking ships, their expressions a blend of hope and apprehension. Children clutching their parents' hands tightly as they stepped onto foreign soil. The elderly gazing into the distance, their eyes reflecting a lifetime of loss and endurance.

Fremantle was a major entry point for European immigrants arriving in Australia in 1947. Ships carrying refugees and migrants often came via displaced persons camps in Germany, Italy, or Cyprus — and Poland was one of the largest sources of postwar migration to Australia. The archive showed he photographed many Polish refugees, along with those from the Baltic states, Ukraine, and other parts of Eastern and Central Europe and *The West Australian* was the first newspaper to publish Josef's photographs.

I wondered if it was because he spoke Polish that they may have commissioned him to take photographs of them in the hostels and migrant camps that were springing up in and around Perth.

The photographs in the box covering 1948 revealed he had travelled to Adelaide, Melbourne and Sydney and was now a specialist in photographing refugees and migrants and gaining a reputation with *The Melbourne Age* and *Argus*, as well as *The Sydney Morning Herald*.

I fought the urge to explore more boxes and returned them to the shelf. My mission was to collect this archive and deliver it securely to Josef, whose silent solitude at the camp was a vivid image in my mind, but the practicality of storing such a precious archive in the camp was unclear and slightly worrying to me.

9. Practicalities and Arrangements

When Josef first arrived in Leederville as a nine-year-old immigrant, he was like a ghost among the living. The harsh Australian sun bore down relentlessly, which for him was a jarring contrast to the muted greys of Poland. He didn't speak a word of English, and the streets of Perth felt alien and overwhelming. He found the incessant summer heat stifling, constant and inescapable.

Mo and Belinda Batten were warm and nurturing, their kindness a stark contrast to the cold detachment Josef had known. They ran the chemist shop with friendly efficiency and were well-liked in the neighbourhood — a comforting constant in a world that seemed to change by the day. Inside, the shop was a sanctuary, redolent with the sharp tang of medicinal tonics and the faint chemical scent that drifted from the darkroom at the back.

Josef was a quiet and watchful child, his senses attuned to every detail: the creak of the floorboards, the sluggish churn of the ceiling fan against the heat, the soft rustle of pages as customers flipped through magazines as they waited for their prescriptions or to have their portrait taken. He absorbed everything in silence, his mind alert to every nuance of light and sound.

When he was eleven Mo gave him a Brownie box camera which became his refuge. Simple in form, with a waist-level viewfinder and a satisfying click, it didn't require great skill, but for Josef, it became a tool for precision and control. He wandered the sunlit streets of Leederville, framing the world through the lens with painstaking care. In a life that often felt chaotic and uncertain, the camera offered a soothing sense of order.

His photographs were not exuberant or carefree; they were composed and contemplative. He captured the overlooked beauty of the everyday, a row of houses bathed in golden light, children playing by the kerb, and an old man reading on a bench. Each image was infused with an intensity, a sense of stillness.

Mo and Belinda encouraged his passion. Mo taught him how to develop film in the darkroom, a process that struck Josef as almost alchemical. Under the dim red glow of the safelight, he would watch in awe as ghostly images emerged in the trays of developer, proof that something as fragile as a moment could be made permanent.

Josef's growth in their care was not loud or dramatic, but slow and profound. He learned to navigate his new world through the viewfinder, finding comfort in capturing fragments of life frozen in time. The chemist shop became more than a workplace or a home, it became a sanctuary where he could simply be himself, free from judgment.

In those formative years, Josef transformed from a silent observer into a budding artist. His journey was one of resilience and discovery, shaped by Mo and Belinda's steadfast support and his own finely tuned sensitivity.

Leederville State School, however, was less forgiving. Josef had a way of slipping into the background, a skill honed during his early years in Katowice and the long, gruelling journey with the Professor. The other children sensed something different about him. At first, they tried to bully him, but Josef possessed an uncanny ability to disappear and blend into the scenery. He wasn't imposing, but his silent intensity made him unreachable.

Those school years were lonely. He sat at the back of the classroom; his gaze fixed on the blackboard yet always alert to the murmurs and snickers that flared around him. Lunchtimes were solitary, spent in a corner of the playground with his brown paper bag of sandwiches and an apple.

Home was different. Mo and Belinda offered consistency, their daily routines a source of comfort. Evening meals were simple but nourishing, meat pies with mashed potatoes and peas, fresh fish or lamb chops with boiled carrots. Belinda would sometimes make a stew with whatever cuts of meat were available, stretching it with root vegetables and thick gravy.

Life during the war years meant making do. Rationing was a constant. The bread was sometimes stale, milk often came powdered, and fresh produce was rare. Yet Belinda had a gift for turning humble ingredients into satisfying meals. They ate around the small kitchen table upstairs; their conversations filled with a sense of belonging.

Josef often wandered to the library on Oxford Street. It was a dust-scented refuge. While there were few books on photography, he discovered something just as vital — illustrated magazines. Life, Picture Post, and local publications like Pix and Walkabout opened entire worlds through images. He would spend hours turning pages, studying how moments were captured. One issue of Picture Post featured work by a Frenchman named Henri Cartier-Bresson. The way Bresson froze a glance, a gesture, the instant before it vanished — those images struck Josef with uncanny force. There was no need for words. Each photograph spoke directly to his own experience of observing life from the edges.

Through Life magazine, he encountered the stark, compassionate portraits of Dorothea Lange — weathered faces of displaced families in the American Dust Bowl, mothers clutching children in the desert heat. Their stillness reminded him of people he'd seen on the journey from Katowice — proud, enduring. And in Walker Evans' work, he recognised an architectural honesty: tired storefronts, bare interiors, solemn expressions that held entire histories. There was dignity in every frame. He lingered, too, over the urgent wartime photographs of George Rodger and Robert Capa, the steel and smoke of Margaret Bourke-White's industrial scenes, the ghostly flash-lit candour of Weegee's New York nights. He didn't know all their names at first, but he recognised something in their images: a search for truth, for stillness inside chaos.

These photographs became his teachers. They showed him that silence had a language, that stillness could tell a story. With his Brownie box camera slung over his shoulder, Josef began to carry these lessons into the streets of Leederville — watching, waiting, and learning how to see.

On weekends, Mo sometimes took him to the New Oxford Theatre to see newsreels and war films. The flickering images, soldiers marching, cities in ruins, and people's lives transformed by conflict, both haunted and captivated him.

As Leederville changed — new shops opening, old ones fading — Josef's world remained anchored by the chemist shop and his growing love of photography. Each trip to the library or the cinema added depth to his understanding of the world and the art of capturing it.

His teenage years unfolded in a duality: invisibility at school, creativity and exploration at home. It was in this still, internal crucible that Josef's identity as an observer began to solidify. His eyes noticed what others missed, his mind endlessly framed moments, as if behind an invisible lens.

As he grew older, his photographs began to tell stories — not only of others, but of himself. Stories of life, struggle, beauty — and the persistence of a boy who had once arrived in Leederville like a ghost, and slowly learned to exist, to see, and eventually, to be seen.

*

In the years following the Second World War, when nations were struggling to reshape themselves from the wreckage of conflict, Josef emerged as an observer of human displacement.

Perth was becoming a landing point for thousands of war refugees and new immigrants. With a Contax II camera over his shoulder, seventeen-year-old Josef moved among them. He captured images of arrivals on the Fremantle docks where he had taken his first steps onto Australian soil. He then graduated to the makeshift hostels and camps where they awaited an uncertain future, and then to the streets where they began carving out their new lives.

His photographs were many and varied and not simply records; they were raw emotional testaments to survival and longing; to the resilience etched in the faces of men, women, and children who had left behind shattered homelands. They captured the weight of histories carried in battered suitcases; the apprehension of families gazing across unfamiliar landscapes; and the silent determination of hands gripping official documents that promised a future, however unclear.

In numerous respects, his work echoed the photographs captured over ten years earlier by the trailblazing documentary photographers who chronicled the Great Depression in America. Photographers like Dorothea Lange and Walker Evans, both commissioned by the Farm Security Administration, created some of the most iconic images of the twentieth century, including Lange's famous *Migrant Mother* from 1936.

One of Josef's iconic images from this period showed a young girl, no more than six, standing alone on the pier, clutching a ragged doll as the sea wind pulled at her dress. Her parents, to the edge of the frame, were speaking with an immigration officer, their tense postures reflected in the girl's wide, uncertain eyes. Another striking photograph depicted an elderly man seated on a wooden crate beside a heap of luggage, staring into the distance as if searching for something — or someone — who would never arrive. The details of the loose thread on the buttons on his shirt and the creases in his face told a story of loss and endurance, a reflection of so many who had been displaced by war.

More than simply historical records, they were windows into Josef's world and an unspoken narrative.

His work quickly gained recognition. The newspapers were the first to publish his images, but their reach extended further, catching the attention of editors from international magazines hungry for narratives of post-war migration. His compositions, marked by their stark contrasts, and their piercing intimacy, spoke of a universal human experience and it was not long before invitations arrived from other publishers who sought to commission more of his work.

In Melbourne, he wandered the sprawling migrant camps, documenting the same themes of upheaval and reinvention. In Sydney, he stood on the quays at Pyrmont or Woolloomooloo as the ships from Europe disembarked, his lens capturing the first tentative steps of those who would eventually call Australia home.

One particularly poignant image taken in Sydney showed a mother pressing her face against the wire fence of a processing centre, her fingers entwined with those of her son on the other side. The raw desperation in their expressions made it one of the most widely circulated images of the era. His ability to blend into the fabric of these spaces, to remain unseen yet deeply present, became his defining skill.

The recognition of his work continued to build. By 1951, his photographs were no longer confined to Australian publications and were appearing in international journals including *Life* magazine and *Picture Post* and his name found its way into editorial conversations in London and New York.

Then came an unexpected invitation. A telegram arrived from The London-based *Courier Press Agency* who, having followed his growing body of work, offered him a position as a staff photographer. It was a calling he could not ignore. London was at the heart of the press world, a gateway to the types of assignments that could define a career. In late 1951, he once again found himself on a ship, not as an observer of displacement but as a man stepping toward his uncertain future.

The world remained in turmoil, with conflicts simmering in regions that had never truly known peace. Shortly after his arrival, he received his first assignment — exchanging London's typical dreary January, shrouded in pea-soup smog, for British East Africa, where unrest was beginning to stir.

Enter Josef, the photographer of conflict and war.

*

The following afternoon I made my way back to the chemist shop to phone Anne Delacourt at *Agence Frontière* in Paris. I had no inkling of the significant role she would come to play in my life. I was merely following Josef's directions and didn't know what the discussion would entail or where it might lead.

A 1960s Bakelite telephone rested on a dark wooden table in the studio. Surprised it still functioned, I dialled the lengthy international number and when we connected, Anne's voice was astonishingly bright and clear, as though she were in an adjoining room.

Her role at *Agence Frontière* extended far beyond that of a mere agent. Anne oversaw every film roll he sent her from the field. She ensured they were correctly processed, logged and archived, and each was carefully edited, and the prints made their way safely to publications around the globe. This wasn't only logistics; it was about safeguarding the work and vision of the photographers in her charge.

Anne also took charge of Josef's safety. When he ventured into conflict zones, where danger lurked at every turn, she adhered to a strict routine of daily check-ins. She demanded coded telex messages to confirm his safety, providing an additional layer of protection in areas dominated by turmoil. Her attentiveness meant that if Josef were ever captured or in peril, she would immediately mobilise all available resources to secure his release. It was largely due to her swift actions that Josef was freed early when he was abducted in Lebanon; her connections persuaded Hezbollah that his work held more value to them if he were able to continue it.

Interactions between them were marked by an unspoken understanding and mutual respect. Anne negotiated with international publications like *Le Monde* and *The Guardian*, ensuring Josef's images were not just seen but honoured with proper bylines and fair licensing fees. She fought for exclusive distribution deals for high-impact stories and secured additional compensation for image reprints and syndication. But Anne's role wasn't confined to business dealings and safety protocols. She was also a fierce advocate for the ethical usage of Josef's work. In a world where sensationalism often overshadowed truth, she ensured that his images were contextualised accurately, preserving their integrity and dignity.

Josef relied on Anne not only for professional support but also for a semblance of normalcy amidst the chaos. Their relationship was devoid of unnecessary words; it thrived on trust and a shared mission. When Josef returned from assignments, it was Anne who conducted regular debriefs and editorial reviews, offering both emotional support and professional feedback. Anne Delacourt was more than an agent; she was a guardian of Josef's legacy, a steadfast presence who ensured that even in the darkest corners of war, his reputation would shine through.

*

If Josef's initial list of tasks had surprised me, my call with Anne unsettled me even more. What she revealed left me reeling, shaken in a way I hadn't anticipated.

We spoke for over an hour, a conversation filled with revelations, not least the astonishing fact that for the duration of his self-imposed exile, Josef had, by proxy, instructed Anne to grant me power of attorney over his practical affairs. The weight of it landed heavily. I was only twenty, inexperienced, uncertain of what such a responsibility truly entailed, and I told her as much. The idea that I should be entrusted with managing any aspect of Josef's life felt almost absurd.

But Anne was calm and reassuring. She told me I wouldn't be alone in it, that she would guide and support me as we navigated his affairs together, at least until he decided what came next, where he wanted to be, and whether he wanted to return at all. For now, though, it was clear he had no intention of re-emerging, no desire to be found or disturbed. From the contents of his letter, it seemed he understood precisely what was happening to him, recognised the intensity of his unravelling, and accepted that it was something he had to endure alone. He was severing himself from everything familiar, stepping deliberately into a fire he knew he had no choice but to walk through, trusting that if he could withstand it, he would emerge stronger. But the pain of it, he knew, would be excruciating, and any outside interference — even well-meaning — would only make it harder to bear.

Anne and I both understood that no one could have lived the life Josef had — witnessed what he had seen, carried what he had carried, without eventually having to pay a heavy price. She told me she had long expected this moment to come, that it did not surprise her to receive the letter. She explained that if I accepted, my role would be to manage the practical aspects of his life and, in doing so, to support his well-being for as long as he remained in self-imposed exile. It would be a job, a paid responsibility, though it hardly felt like one in the conventional sense.

As we spoke, it became clear that despite his reluctance to discuss finances, Josef had, throughout his career, accumulated a significant fortune, not only from his assignments but from book royalties as well. He had always lived simply, travelling light, rarely spending beyond the bare necessities, and as a result, he had no real need to keep working. He could easily afford to cover both my role and any expenses that came with it. His letter had been precise in its instructions: Anne was to arrange for me to rent a property in Broome, where I would safeguard his archive and establish a routine that included fortnightly visits to the camp. It was, in many ways, a strange and intimate task, a tether between us even in his absence.

We spoke about why Josef had not been able to share these plans with me, and as we talked, I realised the answer had been there all along. He had spent his life controlling every aspect of his world, maintaining the shield he had built around himself, and to sit across from me and formally dismantle it — to speak aloud what he was doing and why — would have been impossible. Our relationship was unlike any he had known, his first true friendship, and trusting me was already an act of letting go. To speak of practicalities and arrangements might have threatened the fragile balance of our unique dynamic, so instead, he had left that to Anne. I understood. So much of what Josef and I had shared existed in the unspoken, in the spaces between words. It was imperative that, whatever formal agreements we put in place, we should protect that dynamic.

At that point in my life there were no concrete plans. I had no intention of returning to Europe, and no desire to pursue higher education. The path ahead was wide open, so Josef's request was acceptable, at least for the time being. Anne and I worked out a plan: a place in Broome would be rented for at least six months, somewhere secure enough to house Josef's photographic archive.

When she asked me if I would need anything during the stay, the answer came without hesitation — music. A guitar, something to play, and a way to listen to music. That was easily arranged; purchases would be made as needed, with receipts provided for everything, including all living costs while in Broome. In this way, a kind of unofficial employment took shape. Within a few months, any formal work would breach the conditions of the visa, so the arrangement remained simple, the cash from the ANZ account would be used to cover rent, expenses, and my day-to-day needs.

The following morning, I walked into Perth's CBD, driven by the urge to find music to take back to Broome. In Pier Street, Dada Records revealed itself like a hidden sanctuary for the musically curious, the shuffling sound of customers flipping through records, and the faint crackle of something obscure playing over the speakers was instantly pleasing. A trove of forgotten treasures, each shelf held the possibility of unearthing something extraordinary. I set myself a goal to purchase thirty second-hand cassettes — a mix of the familiar and the unexpected, spanning genres and eras.

Hours passed browsing the worn cassette cases. A recording of Bach's Violin Concertos surfaced — music that had always brought steadiness. Nearby, tucked between more familiar classical works, was a Sarasate collection, his fiery *Zigeunerweisen*. Some modern classical was also on the list: John Cage's *In a Landscape* and Harold Budd's *The Pearl*, each offering something hypnotic and transportive. Van Morrison's *Astral Weeks* was non-negotiable, as was Miles Davis' *In a Silent Way* — its hushed brilliance perfect for late nights alone.

The longer I spent there, and the higher the stack of tapes grew, the more the sales assistant began to take notice of me. We sparked up a conversation, the kind only those deeply passionate about music tend to have. It began with music, and drifted toward guitars, and when I mentioned an interest in buying one his eyes lit up. He enthusiastically recommended Zenith in Claremont, a place he vouched for as a haven for serious musicians.

Before departing, I also inquired about a portable cassette player to play my tapes on, something beyond a Walkman, equipped with proper speakers capable of filling a room with sound while still being battery-operated. Without a moment's hesitation, he reached behind the counter for a catalogue and showed me the Sony CFS-99. It was a robust stereo boombox, designed for high-quality playback, with clear treble and rich bass that wouldn't distort at higher volumes. Unlike the flimsy plastic models saturating the market, this was something substantial, and would honour my collection, whether I was indulging in Keith Jarrett's quiet piano in *Köln Concert* or the rhythmic beats of Talking Heads' *Remain in Light*.

With a bag heavy with tapes, I headed straight to Alberts Hi-Fi on Murray Street, where the sales assistant confirmed that the Sony was indeed the best option, so I paid for it on the spot in cash. I also bought a new Sony Walkman WM-D6C to replace the one broken during the attack, which promised a far superior listening experience.

*

In the following days, preparations for the return to Broome took shape. A cash withdrawal was ordered at the ANZ. The music player was tested in the chemist shop, and the lively, exquisite sound of Yehudi Menuhin playing violin concertos brought the dead air of the shop to life. It filled the space with joy while I considered the best method for transporting the photographic archive boxes.

At Joe's Garage, the 1984 HJ60 Land Cruiser he had sourced was ready for collection. Its bronze finish was immaculate, paired with a black roo bar at the front it looked sturdy and built for long journeys through the outback. The cargo area was ample and deep, more than sufficient for Josef's archive with extra room to spare.

From there, it was straight to Zenith in Claremont, and I spent nearly an hour moving between six-string acoustic guitars until I eventually settled a Maton CW80/6 that, from the first moment I held it, felt like home. That was the one. So, I bought it along with a hard case, plectrums, and three sets of spare strings.

At the bank, I presented my passport and signed their documents. The teller promptly counted the notes — fresh hundreds and fifties, tallied by machine and then manually verified. Each bundle was neatly wrapped in bands and placed in a cloth ANZ bag. A visit to a removal firm followed to purchase cartons for the archive boxes, five per carton, which I packed up and stacked by the chemist shop entrance.

On the day of my departure, I rose early and, as soon as he opened, I returned the key to Dick Edwards. He was more conversational this time and promised to honour Josef's wish to disappear and keep his location confidential. As I was leaving, he was eager for me to inform Josef there had been several queries as to whether the shop might be put up for sale, and that he could secure an excellent price if he chose to sell.

10. Regarding The Pain Of Others

My journey to Broome was nothing like the hitch-hiking trip five months earlier. Heading north from Perth, the Great Northern Highway carried me inland, into country that felt older, wilder, and far more still. I wanted to experience more than a passage from one place to another — I wanted the road itself to become a kind of symphony, a feast for the senses.

Cassette tapes lay on the seat beside me, each piece of music drawing its own reflection from the land. *Bach's Violin Concertos* by Menuhin, stirred the earth awake. In Sarasate's *Zigeunerweisen*, Perlman's violin slipped through cliffs and ochre ridges, carrying me deeper into the journey. Around Mount Magnet, *Wieniawski's Violin Concerto* cut sharp against the rocks, its urgency echoing the rawness of the horizon. That night, I slept beneath stars, the violin still resonant in the silence.

Further north, John Cage's *In a Landscape* blurred movement into a kind of drifting, the land shimmering to its pulse and rhythm. Harold Budd and Brian Eno's *The Pearl* washed over ghostly plains, while Arvo Pärt's *Tabula Rasa* fell like clear light on cracked earth.

Later, the gorgeousness of Van Morrison's *Astral Weeks* poured a flood of voice and urgency into the wagon, as expansive as the landscape itself. Near Eighty Mile Beach, Neil Young's *Comes a Time* spoke to me as though it were a summing up — simple, spacious and unforced. After two days and nights on the road, it was almost as if the vehicle, music, and land were one.

The final approach felt almost ceremonial. Jarrett's *Köln Concert* deepened the dusk; each piano note was an arrival. Sand replaced stone and the sea pulled the horizon wider, and by the time Broome appeared, Miles Davis's *In a Silent Way* had given itself over to the rhythm of waves. I slept on the sand at Cable Beach with the music still inside me.

*

The sound of the waves crashing against the shore woke me with the soft light of the rising sun spilling over my shoulder and the beach either side of me stretched out, empty and desolate, yet undeniably beautiful.

Brewing tea and cooking eggs, I took my time and sat reading and contemplating my commitment to a new life. Broome had already begun to feel like home. The thought of finding a place to live preoccupied me, but there was also a pull to check in with Josef at the camp. I was unsure how long it would take to find a rental or what the process would even look like, but I found it was much easier than I had anticipated.

Stepping into the modest office of Keith D. Hinton & Associates, the agent behind the desk barely spared me a glance before he gestured for me to sit; a fleeting scepticism in his eyes as he sized me up. When I mentioned I would pay six months' rent up front, plus the bond, his attitude shifted almost imperceptibly. He wasn't used to seeing someone my age so determined and certain.

"There's a place on Darnley Street," he said, his voice neutral. "Three bedrooms. It's a bit rough around the edges, but it might work for you. I'll show you."

The house was on a quiet street, a short drive from the centre of town. When we pulled up, I could immediately tell it wasn't much to look at. It sat back from the road behind a large untended lot, the land overtaken by scrubby grass and scattered debris. The sheer expanse of the space swallowed the house, which sat in the centre of it looking forlorn and abandoned. Its weathered exterior had peeling paint and sagging eaves, and the windows were filthy with grime, and the frames were mouldy.

Inside, the rooms were simple and functional. The furniture was mismatched and there was a musty smell, but it didn't need to be luxurious. It was close enough to town, and it would serve its purpose. The bedrooms were spacious, though bare. The kitchen was fine, though it smelt stale and in desperate need of new life to be breathed into it. The agent mentioned that the owner had recently tried to sell it, but no one had made an offer they were willing to accept. Now, they were hoping to rent it out.

Wandering through the yard, the enormity of the work it would take to make it liveable settled over me. I relished the idea of it. The land, though wild and untended, felt oddly comforting. It was peaceful, the silence punctuated only by the occasional rustle of the wind through the scrub. There was something about it, something in the stillness, that made me feel like I could make this place work. The agent must have sensed my decision before I voiced it. Returning to the office, we signed the lease, and handing him six months' rent and the bond, all paid in advance, the keys were mine.

Back at the house, thoughts had already turned to settling in. I placed the boxes of Josef's archive, along with Mo and Belinda's papers and memorabilia, in one of the bedrooms. That first night, despite the humidity, the house felt strangely cold, like camping in a large, imperfect tent. Foreign and unfamiliar.

I spent the following day cleaning. A trip to the local hardware store provided everything I needed — brushes, buckets, and a selection of detergents. I had a determination to bring some semblance of order to the place and a sense of home.

*

The following morning, I set off for the camp with enough provisions packed for three or four days and as the red dirt road north opened, I carried with me a mix of anticipation and uncertainty.

On a whim, I'd packed my guitar. It was unclear how Josef might respond to music at the camp; the months spent together had passed in near silence. In all that time, the subject of music hadn't surfaced. During the weeks away, questions lingered — how had he managed on his own, and what would be waiting on my return? A resolve formed: the guitar would remain unplayed unless it felt truly welcome.

As the kilometres passed, my thoughts turned to the future of Josef's archive. Should it remain boxed in the bedroom, or be laid out chronologically on temporary shelving? It felt too precious to gather dust, yet without knowing Josef's intentions, any decision felt premature.

Driving into the community, a familiar figure appeared beneath the old boab — Albert Warrun, his gubinge walking stick resting beside him, eyes fixed on the horizon. We exchanged greetings and he looked up, eyes heavy with concern, and wordlessly gestured to sit. He'd visited Josef.

From the way he spoke, it was clear Josef wasn't doing well. He described him plainly but with a deep understanding. He was thinner, paler, his movements sluggish. His body had slowed; his hair hung in straggly strands and his voice was dull. According to Albert Warrun, Josef was retreating. Disconnected. No joy, only sadness in his eyes; distant — a man lost between worlds. Josef had undoubtedly descended further in my absence.

Listening to Albert Warrun, most of it was already familiar, yet hearing it aloud validated what I already knew. He had only ever known the renowned photographer — Josef as he appeared a year ago — and lacked the deeper insight into what might be unfolding. Still, the conversation helped shape expectations for my return to the camp. In those early days at the camp, Josef had carried a gentle, if troubled, authority — an intensity that lingered in the air around him. Before my trip to Perth, that same intensity had begun to turn inward, collapsing in on itself.

*

Albert Warrun's depiction had been spot on; he did appear gaunt, his body shrunken under a baggy shirt, his hair hanging limply around a face that seemed even more reclusive than before, masking the attractive man that lay within. There was an emptiness in his demeanour, and he was only partially present.

I had already decided not to comment and had no impulse to ask how he was or draw him out. That wasn't what he needed or wanted. So, by afternoon, the old rhythm resumed: a peaceful co-existence, side by side but apart, with our conversations limited to practicalities.

Still, a flicker of relief passed over him. He thanked me for agreeing to stay on and provide support from Broome, his tone formal, as if reciting lines committed to memory.

The update I gave him was straightforward: Anne had been contacted, the house in Broome secured — six months, rent paid. The archive and other boxes were safely stored. Joe had sourced the additional Land Cruiser, and after a brief inspection, Josef nodded in approval and said it was mine. The meaning behind that remark remained unclear, and I didn't press him.

Mentioning the guitar and the music felt important, a small offering of something personal. I hoped he might ask to hear me play it. But he didn't. Only a nod, no questions, no sign of curiosity. All he offered was a mumbled "Good" here and there as if mentally checking off a list. Grateful, perhaps, but untouched — nothing in him stirred.

There was no need to press further. Whatever was unfolding inside him required space, not inquiry. What mattered was that he knew his wishes were being followed.

*

As the sun's full strength began to wane, I caught some fish for supper. I settled on a rocky outcrop where waves lapped at the shore. Through the clear water, small fish darted between rocks. Standing on a flat stone, I cast my line and let the quiet take hold.

I prepared three plump Snapper over the fire along with some vegetables and our meal was shared in companionable silence. I was reassured to see Josef eat, sensing he hadn't been fishing much during the absence, which explained his noticeable weight loss.

Once our meal was finished, I asked Josef about the boxes of archives and whether I should lay them out on shelves. For the first time since the return, he began to open up and provide a specific response. He requested the boxes be organised precisely, and that I sequentially bring two or three on each of the fortnightly visits we'd agreed upon. At that moment, his unusually detailed instructions struck me because they contrasted so sharply with his current condition and demeanour.

When I explained about having opened a few of the boxes and seeing the extraordinary images he was again entirely unresponsive. The power of those photographs and the mere fact that one man had produced them and that these boxes contained the output of a whole career was overwhelming to me. But to Josef, the making of those images was connected to the source of his intense internalised pain, and I could only imagine that he intended to use his archive as a tool to aid his recovery.

*

I had been right to surmise that he needed his archive as an anchor; a lifeline to navigate the storm swirling within him. His intention was to confront every image with me present and to confront the implications of it. His instruction for me was to simply be present as he did so.

In the months that followed, every visit saw me return to the camp with a few years' worth of archive boxes, each curated with his specific instructions, as if he were orchestrating the revival of his past.

It became a ritual for us to sit together at the trestle table in the tent, usually in the late afternoon before supper, and go through each box from which he carefully acknowledged each image, and he described the context in which the photographs had occurred.

It normally took more than one sitting to get through a box — a painstaking and emotionally exhausting process for us both. But it was an important component of his self-guided therapy. After each visit, I would return the boxes to the archive in their correct order.

On that first visit after my return from Perth, he barely spoke, yet the words he did share weighed heavily in the air.

Late that evening he described how the flashbacks and nightmares that frequently haunted him had intensified; that the echoes of his experiences were crashing against the walls of his mind with such a ferocity that he feared they might plunge him into a madness from which he might never return.

His moments of delusional turmoil were cataclysmic, rocking the foundations of his psyche and leaving him trapped in a state of dread, unable to function.

He explained that some days were more suffocating than others; he would emerge from intense stormy periods into the fragile light, only to be swallowed back into the darkness days later. It was a pattern he'd come to accept, though acceptance brought no ease.

He likened it to experiencing severe turbulence on an aeroplane — rationally he was aware that it was unlikely to prove fatal, yet he was gripped by the uncertainty of how long the violent shudders and jarring bumps would persist. He knew there was nothing to be done until it subsided, that he had to endure the unease and fear until calm was restored and he could once again see the light filtering through the clouds.

To me, this metaphor resonated fully; it crystallised my understanding without the need for deeper enquiry. By confronting his archive, gazing into the suffering and contextualising it, he could begin to negotiate his crumbling psyche.

There was no doubt in my mind that Josef paid a very high price for his photographing of human suffering and for his seeming ability to act with such indifference, but I was in awe of his strength to sit through the pain it brought him without the use of any pharmaceutical interventions, therapy treatments, narcotics or alcohol. Every interaction we shared revealed a fierce determination within him to traverse the flames unaided.

In his mind, at least, I sensed that my role was primarily to serve as a pillar of practical support. This instinctive understanding came with a heavy weight of responsibility, particularly during those moments when I was preparing to embark on my fortnightly journey from Broome to Nigalya Cove. I was aware of an unspoken dependency that rested on my shoulders — a psychological burden on me that he seemed unaware of.

Yet, despite this heavy consciousness gnawing at me, my time in Broome gifted me with a profound sense of liberation and freedom. I transformed the house on Darnley Street into my sanctuary. Clearing a neglected patch of the yard, I created a small garden retreat where I could lose myself in the embrace of the night, strumming my guitar around a campfire or immersing myself in the pages of a good book.

I purchased some planks from the local timber yard and constructed sturdy makeshift shelves in the spare bedroom, removing the bed and clearing the space entirely, dedicating it solely as an archive room. I set up a trestle table and, with Josef's permission, used it to delve into the archive and map out a chronology of all his assignments throughout his lengthy career.

At that time, Broome was a small town without a library service, so I lacked any books or materials to cross-reference the photos with broader world events or their political context. Depending on the typed captions attached to each photograph, I made notes and reminders to investigate further when I could get to a library. In this manner, my limited understanding of his career could develop into a more coherent narrative.

On each visit to the camp, I made sure not to ask Josef any questions that might help me fill in the blanks — he needed to concentrate on his own method of interpreting each photograph he had produced.

*

It's difficult to fathom the depth of Josef's endurance. Each image we pored over revealed a world in which he was the constant, silent observer of unimaginable suffering. His archives of photographs spanned decades, documenting wars, famines, and natural disasters. Every frame captured the raw emotions — fear, despair, pain — that etched themselves onto the faces of those caught in the chaos.

In each photograph we looked at together, Josef's presence in the image was palpable. His camera acted as a barrier, a shield that allowed him to witness and record without becoming overwhelmed by the horror. It was his way of maintaining control in situations where chaos reigned supreme. For over thirty-five years, he never paused to reflect on the toll it took on him. The camera provided him with a purpose and a means to navigate through the destruction and death that surrounded him.

Yet, now here he was, in self-imposed exile. No cameras hanging from his neck, no shutters clicking away to capture moments frozen in time. Josef had abandoned his shield, and for the first time since he picked up his first camera, he was entirely exposed. Stripped bare of the tool that had given him distance and protection, his emotions were untethered and raw.

During those days I spent with him at the camp, I came to understand how profoundly intense his career had been. Each assignment had chipped away at his humanity until he became almost mechanical in his detachment. But without the lens to mediate between him and the world's suffering, everything he had suppressed over the years came rushing back with brutal force.

11. Cathy

For more than half a year, we continued to adhere to our biweekly schedule. On each visit I spent a few nights there, bringing him supplies. Sometimes, I'd pick up Albert Warrun en route to the camp who would join us for supper and sit mostly silently with us. By dawn, he'd disappear with his gubinge walking stick, presumably heading back to the community, though I was never certain.

In December 1987, as we sat with more boxes of images and the tent flapped noticeably in the rising breezes, signalling the arrival of the wet season, some images emerged that shifted my perception and understanding of the Josef I knew so far.

In June 1967 Josef had been in Israel and the Middle East covering the Six-Day War which was a brief, but pivotal conflict fought between Israel and the neighbouring states of Egypt, Jordan, and Syria. In a swift and decisive military campaign, Israel launched a pre-emptive strike against Egypt and, within six days, captured the Sinai Peninsula, Gaza Strip, West Bank, East Jerusalem, and the Golan Heights. The war dramatically redrew the map of the Middle East and intensified the Israeli Palestinian conflict, the effects of which are still deeply felt today.

The photographs Josef took there unfolded like chapters of a book written in light and shadow:

One image, stark in its simplicity, showed the Western Wall in the days after East Jerusalem was taken — Israeli paratroopers pressed against ancient stone, their heads bowed in prayer. Above them, on the rooftops of the Old City, elderly Arab men watched in silence, their expressions unreadable. In that single frame, Josef had caught the uneasy choreography of conquest — jubilation below, grief above — the wall acting as both a witness and a stage.

Elsewhere, in a haze of dust, a line of Palestinian families moved across the horizon, small against the sweep of land that no longer belonged to them. Faces turned toward the lens, unreadable yet exposed, carrying what they could; a child's blanket, a tarnished kettle, a limp bundle of clothing slung over a grandfather's shoulder. Another frame showed an older woman and a young girl, silhouetted by the desert sun, their shadows long and oddly graceful, as if they belonged to another century.

Every picture seemed incomplete, as though it extended past the edges, and it was fascinating to examine the contact sheets of the negatives from which they had been chosen, looking at them through a magnifying loupe, revealing additional frames that elaborated the narrative.

*

As we reached the bottom of the box labelled JB1967.3, I noticed a shift in the final images, five or six in total. These photographs stood out, markedly different and seemingly out of place among the others. They captured a beautiful young woman in London, her striking features and graceful pose immediately catching my eye.

The first image, in soft grayscale tones, captured her in a moment of introspection. She stood at a simple porcelain sink, her back to the camera, bare shoulders lit by a pale Bloomsbury morning. In the small mirror before her, we can see her face — calm, unguarded — framed by the soft curl of hair and a halo of natural light. Through the window beside her, the silhouettes of Georgian rooftops and chimneys form a layered London backdrop, adding a painterly stillness reminiscent of Lucian Freud's domestic portraits. The image balancing sensuality and solitude without intrusion.

The last photograph in the box moved him; he picked it up and quivered as he described how he took it in very specific detail:

"It was late September in London, and the light in the room was already starting to thin. She'd taken the jumper from the back of a chair, and put it on without a word, arms swallowed in the sleeves like a child dressing up. It was too big for her, but that thick, soft wool, did something to her. Or maybe it revealed something I hadn't seen until then. She was only wearing her knickers underneath, but it wasn't staged, she wasn't trying to be anything. She stood at the window, watching the chimneys across the street as if they were telling her a story. The softness of the jumper blurred the lines; it framed her in innocence and made the moment hover somewhere between childhood and womanhood. She took my breath away."

I couldn't resist asking Josef why those images were there, so out of place and context with the rest of his work. I expected his usual silence and his familiar unresponsive stare. Instead, he paused, and to my surprise, he gave a very precise description of who she was and how the images came about. It was as though he had spent the past twenty years waiting for this very moment to speak about it. His words flowed with an intensity and clarity that made me realise how significant those images must have been to him.

*

London, Early September 1967

He had only recently returned from the heat and dust of the Sinai, and it still clung to him, in the lines around his eyes, in the slight stiffness of his posture.

Josef was a handsome thirty-seven, tanned by war and slightly undone by it, and had been called straight to the offices of *The Sunday Times* upon landing in London.

Charlie Dutton, the editor, all sleeves rolled and empire-building energy, had greeted him like a returning Olympian. There was a performance to the meeting: contact sheets and prints were spread across the desk, the evidence of wars made strangely abstract in that room high above Gray's Inn Road.

Nonetheless, Josef couldn't help but respect Charlie Dutton's commitment. So many editors were content to pander to the immediate, the flashy, the scandalous; but Charlie sought something deeper. This was a man who believed that journalism should, in its pursuit of truth, serve as a beacon of integrity, a call to conscience in the face of chaos. As the newly appointed editor of *The Sunday Times*, he was redefining what it meant to hold power accountable and elevate stories that resonated with authenticity and impact.

That's not to say Charlie didn't harbour some grand aspirations. He spoke in rapid-fire sentences about colour supplements, cultural influence, and photojournalism as an art form. Josef listened, nodded, and contributed very little. He still hadn't had a proper night's sleep since Tel Aviv. The photographs he'd taken there, some raw with the urgency of suffering, others composed with an almost artistic detachment, had already been published.

No, what Charlie was fixated on was releasing an extensive interview with Josef that would feature a collection of his most iconic photographs — he had sensed some potential and aimed to turn Josef into a kind of celebrity.

He pressed a thick envelope of cash into Josef's hand and told him to find a hotel room and get some rest, but added, with a conspiratorial grin, 'I'm going to get you properly socialised into the delights of London.'

That evening, he found himself seated in the back of Charlie's indigo Jaguar Mk 2 3.8, the cityscape blurring past the windows as they sped toward Mayfair. Cathy was already seated in the back as though she were ready for the school run when he got in, with both hands neatly clasped in her lap as if anticipating the start of a lesson. Nineteen, with a serenity that barely masked a deeper unease, her beauty wasn't the sort that announced itself with fanfare; it was the kind that made people go quiet without realising why.

Charlie introduced them with casual brevity.

"Josef, meet Cathy. She's a model."

He shut the door and lit a Dunhill as Daphne, the fashion editor, all lacquered confidence and feline glances, slid into the passenger seat.

Josef glanced at Cathy.

She looked back, almost nervously, "Do you know where we're going?"

He smiled, soft-edged and a little self-conscious.

"I haven't a clue. But I'm very pleased to meet you."

It was nothing. But something happened in that nothingness, a sense of recognition.

The club he took them to was in Berkeley Square, and even before they stepped inside, you could hear the music and laughter and the occasional clink of glass. Inside, the air was thick with performance: men in crushed velvet jackets and women in metallic eye shadow that caught the light like sequins. Smoke hung in layers. The room reverberated to the sounds of The Animals and Otis Redding, everything was both too loud and strangely distant. They followed Charlie and Daphne through the crowd like reluctant children.

The party was curated chaos. There were actors mid-scandal, models barely out of girlhood, painters riding the edge of fame, poets who quoted Rimbaud between lines of cocaine, and East End gangsters in suits tailored with almost comical precision. They were beautiful, brash and drunk on their own relevance.

Charlie floated through the crowd like a host without a name tag, making introductions, fanning egos, and watching it all unfold. Daphne leant against the bar, observing, detached and clinical. Josef, emotionally adrift, was like an intruder at his own wake, and Cathy — Cathy possessed the type of presence that halted conversations mid-sentence. Not because she demanded attention, but because she didn't.

Josef said little, but he watched. Cathy was doing the same. She barely touched the champagne pressed into her hand and ignored the predatory eyes around her with a feigned, delicately awkward, nonchalance. There was something fragile in the way she stood, feeling the heat of every gaze without quite knowing what to do with it.

Eventually, they found a quieter spot, near the edge of the room. A velvet settee, slightly frayed. She spoke of her bedsit in Pimlico, how the curtains never quite closed, how she missed her mother's cooking. Her voice was light but unsteady, the type of voice that didn't often say these things aloud. Josef listened. That was all he did, but it was enough. For Cathy, it was the first time someone had listened.

They didn't stay long, maybe an hour. Charlie vanished into a cluster of television producers and Daphne was deep in conversation with a pop artist, her laughter sharp as broken glass.

Cathy gave Josef a look that needed no translation, and he, without hesitation, said, "Shall we?"

Outside, the square was quiet, the trees unmoving in the stillness. They walked to the corner in silence and hailed a black cab. When it pulled up, he opened the door for her and followed her in. She reached to steady herself as the taxi moved off, and her hand, quite unintentionally, came to rest against his stomach. In that instant, something in him — tight and coiled for years — unwound. The rush was seismic. He didn't speak. Neither did she. But they both felt it.

Later, he would remember that touch more vividly than the photographs, the wars, the parties, and the headlines. That fleeting moment when two lost people found something warm and impossibly tender in one another.

*

For the first time in his life, he no longer wanted to be anywhere else. To Josef, it was all new. It was a feathery warmth. He recalled a feeling so heavenly and sublime, "Your body relaxes and all the stresses and tensions of your life ebb away, giving you a visceral rush so profound you instantly felt at peace with the world and everything around you."

It was the feeling of being touched for the first time by sunlight after years of living in shadow. Not only the shape of the days, but how they felt inside his body. A stillness he hadn't known before. Cathy's presence seemed to soften the edges of everything. Her voice, the way she moved through a room, how she looked at him as if there was nothing in the world she'd rather do than look at him. He wasn't used to being seen like that.

He had never been in love before, not even close. At thirty-seven, he had learned to live without that part of life, to keep things orderly and at a distance. But Cathy was different. She was soft, open, kind and she unwrapped something inside him.

They stayed in a hotel just off The Strand at first. A small room with mismatched furniture and bad curtains. She left her Pimlico bedsit behind without hesitation. He'd wake and watch her sleeping beside him, not quite believing she was real. Whilst she went to work at fashion shoots, he drifted through the city in a haze. After a few weeks, they found a small flat near the British Museum. It was sparse and damp, but it had views of rooftops and patches of sky. They made it theirs without trying.

The early autumn mornings were magical, crisp clear blue skies and the leaves had started to turn. They spent hours in the parks; St James's, Regent's, Hyde Park, walking or lying on the grass, not saying much. Sometimes her head would rest on his shoulder, and he would close his eyes and try to stay in that moment for as long as possible. It was the first time he'd felt truly close to another person. The physical nearness of her, the electric warmth of her touch, it was overwhelming. He didn't think too far ahead. It was enough to wake with her in the morning and fall asleep beside her at night. The feeling of her hand resting on his chest, the sensuousness of her bare feet on the cold kitchen floor, the sound of her brushing her teeth at the sink by the window, humming tunelessly.

He had spent his lifetime learning how not to feel. Now, feeling was all he did. And he let it happen, without question or resistance. He thought about altering his life permanently and never venturing into another war zone again.

*

Many decades later, when Cathy and I had become friends, she explained what it had felt like to her:

"Like it wasn't real — that life was something that had happened to someone else. One moment I was on a bus to Canterbury, as far as I'd ever been in my life, the next I was in London — standing in front of photographers, being told how to tilt my chin, how to move my hips, and how to smile like I meant it."

It hadn't been part of a plan — she hadn't even known there was a plan — but when the scout had stopped her outside the cinema and asked if she'd ever thought about modelling, she'd said yes, even though she hadn't. She didn't talk about Folkestone. Not to Josef, not to anyone.

And she didn't talk about Brian, the boyfriend she'd left behind. It had already started to feel far away. There had been love, yes, but not this freedom or this kind of life.

Josef fascinated her. He was older but didn't make her feel young. Even in his silences, she felt seen. When he looked at her, it was as if he studied something private and beautiful. She had never felt beautiful like that before — not only admired but witnessed. She didn't ask questions, and he shared little about his past. She didn't want to break the spell.

And Charlie Dutton practically bowed to him. That alone had been enough to ignite her curiosity. Charlie had introduced her to people, but he rarely lingered with them and in an instant, his attention could be diverted. But with Josef, he acted like a loyal subject, as though he had done something important, something other people couldn't understand. Cathy didn't understand it either, not entirely. But she understood enough to know she wanted to stay close.

She liked that Josef never asked where she went during the day, and that he didn't mind when she came back tired or moody. She wasn't thinking about next week, let alone next month. She wasn't thinking about love, not yet. What she liked was how it made her feel — held and safe. And she liked how he touched her, gently, as though she might break. There was a respect in him that no one else had ever shown her. It made her feel older than she was. Not grown-up exactly, but significant.

In the early mornings, when she watched him sleep beside her, she sometimes felt a pang of something she couldn't name. He was so still.

She liked the way things were, the peace of it, the drift of their days. She loved their flat near the British Museum, the walks in the parks, the visits to galleries where they barely spoke.

*

They drifted through that winter existing in a hallowed stillness that neither questioned nor required anything more than what they already had. The flat, with its groaning radiators and creaking floorboards, became a world unto itself, a private realm where time bent and blurred, and days melted into one another.

Josef turned down every assignment that came his way, each telegram and call from the picture desk passed over with a shrug or a soft, vague apology. He had no interest in war zones or border towns, not while Cathy was there, sleeping in his bed and filling his lens with the presence he had never known how to hold.

Instead, his days were filled with her: photographing her in the quiet hours of the morning when the light was cold and bluish, or in the golden stillness of late afternoon. And he captured it all — not only her undeniable beauty but something else, something private and unrepeatable: the unfolding of her trust, the way her expression would shift when she thought he wasn't looking, the laughter that rose so easily when she was happy, unguarded, and the sadness that would pass over her face in those stiller moments. It was all there on the contact sheets — frames filled with an unselfconscious intimacy.

By February the spell had begun to wear thin. What shifted things in the end wasn't a quarrel or a moment of crisis, but something far more ordinary and devastating — a newspaper feature, slipped into the colour supplement of *The Sunday Times* one weekend in late January.

Daphne was behind it. She'd stopped by Charlie's office to drop off proofs from a shoot and happened upon some contact sheets Josef had left there. Amongst the dozens of frames, her eye had caught the one by the sink, Cathy in profile, her face turned slightly toward the window and reflected in the mirror, the light falling in such a way that she looked both entirely unguarded and impossibly beautiful. Daphne later said it was the type of photograph that makes you feel like you're intruding on something private, something meant only for the photographer's eyes.

She showed it to Charlie that afternoon with the conviction of an editor who understood the value of a good story. There was, after all, something irresistible about the pairing: the brooding, world-weary war photographer and the nineteen-year-old model with the soft smile and quiet charm. It wasn't hard to pitch, and Charlie had the piece commissioned within the hour.

By the following Sunday, the spread was in print. There were six black and white photographs and a short accompanying article, written with the half-knowing tone that passed for sophistication in those days. It mentioned Josef's acclaim, his reputation for danger, and his haunted silences; it hinted at the unlikely tenderness that had bloomed between them in the peace of their Bloomsbury flat. The photograph by the sink, printed large above the fold, quickly took on a life of its own. Within days, it was being discussed in studio corners, clipped out and pinned up in cafés and art schools. Josef's reputation, already formidable, shifted once again — from witness to the world's pain to a photographer of private truths.

One morning she didn't come back to the flat when he expected her, and when she did return, long after dark, she had been crying. Her makeup had smudged under her eyes, and her coat was damp with rain, and though she tried to pretend nothing had happened, there was a tremor in her voice that gave her away before she even sat down.

*

Until he saw *The Sunday Times* article, Brian had told himself she was still his girl who sent him letters with drawings in the margins, who tucked Polaroids into the envelopes and signed off with x's. He had imagined her modelling as a brief harmless detour, a whim that would lose its appeal and return her safely home and back to him. But the photographs told a different story — of closeness, of affection, of a life that no longer included him. The hurt was immediate and profound. Not only because she was beautiful, but because she looked so happy.

And the photographer — he was everything Brian was not. Older, worldly and famous.

By the following weekend, Brian was in London. He knew where she lived — she had written it in a letter once before the letters stopped — and it wasn't hard to find the building, tucked away on a quiet street in Bloomsbury.

At first, Josef knew none of this. All he witnessed was her quietness, a new silence that stretched out between their conversations. He didn't ask. And she didn't explain. But the contact sheets began to tell the truth. She smiled less and looked away more often. And the flat, once a place of refuge, began to feel like a room waiting for someone to leave.

She didn't say much — not then, and not afterwards — but something shifted in her after that day — a subtle withdrawal. She still curled into him at night, still let him photograph her in the afternoons, but the sense of safety in each other's company had cooled a little. Her smile, when it came, seemed more effortful, and her eyes flickered away from his with increasing frequency, as though she were aware of something fragile between them that might break if they looked too long or too honestly.

Josef, for all his experience, had never learned how to navigate that silence. He recognised pain of course, but the hurt from being inexplicably shut out by someone you love was not something his camera could capture, nor his mind readily process. And so, he waited, helplessly, as the tone of their life together changed — imperceptible at first, like a shift in the weather, but unmistakable all the same.

There were still good days. Walks in the park, impromptu trips to the cinema, the way she'd tuck her cold hands into his coat pockets and rest her head on his shoulder in the dark. But something unspoken had been introduced into their little world, and it had a weight to it that neither of them knew how to name.

*

It was a grey wind-swept morning, the type of March day that felt suspended between seasons — not winter exactly, but not quite welcoming spring.

Cathy had gone out without saying much, only that she needed a walk. Josef, as was his way, didn't press her with questions. After an hour or so of silence, he put on his coat and walked the short distance to the Italian café near the British Museum. It was a modest place, slightly faded, with steamed windows and the smell of coffee. He sat at a small table, ordered a sandwich and coffee, and tried not to think.

But then, outside the window, blurred slightly by condensation, he saw her. She was walking past the café, arm in arm with a young man. They were not speaking but moving in a way that made speech unnecessary. There was an ease and familiarity in the way they moved together. Josef watched them disappear down the street, walking slowly away from him. He felt a rush of nervous sickness in his stomach. In that moment he knew she was walking away from their flat and away from him, as if the entire winter they'd shared had been a soft, passing interruption.

He was not wrong. She didn't return that afternoon. Nor that evening. And when morning came, so did a letter. Folded in two, left on the mat, in handwriting he recognised immediately. She wrote that she was confused, that things in London had begun to feel too fast, too loud. That she had gone to see her parents, to think. There was no mention of Brian.

He didn't try to find her that day. Or the day after. Two mornings later, he hired an Austin Cambridge and drove down through Kent toward Folkestone, unsure of what he would do when he arrived.

Josef never explained to me how he found them, but he described the moment.

"It was cold by the harbour, the wind cutting in from the sea, whipping the water into a pale chop and sending gulls wheeling against the clouded sky. I parked the car and sat for a long time, engine off, my coat still buttoned to the neck. I saw her walking arm in arm with Brian, their bodies folded together against the wind, heads bent in toward each other, they paused beneath the seawall, and she kissed him. Then I understood."

Josef watched them until they passed from sight, turned the key in the ignition and drove straight back to London. The following week he flew to Bangkok, and onto an assignment in Vietnam.

12. For The Ones Who Did Not Turn Away

The following day, after revealing the story about his love affair with Cathy, something in Josef had lifted. He moved more easily and even made a joke as we made coffee over the camping stove. The telling of Cathy, it seemed, had released something, as if the memory, once aired, had settled into a less volatile part of him. We fished together in companionable silence that day.

When it came time for our afternoon ritual in the tent, he reached for the archive box marked JB1968.1. His hand hovered for a moment, and I saw it — a flicker of reluctance and the tightening of the jaw. He opened the lid with care, not curiosity.

The first image was a photograph I recognised immediately. *Rescued from the Ashes.* The woman wearing torn traditional Vietnamese clothing, flanked by two American soldiers, one hand extended toward her like a question. The village behind them was a scorched skeleton, smoke blooming into the sky. I'd seen it reproduced in history books, and at a war photography exhibition in Berlin when I had travelled with my mother Maggie.

I could feel the atmosphere shift, the way you feel the air change before a storm. It wasn't the image that mattered so much as what it was unlocking. The photo was an entry point for Josef.

He had been there — not at the height of the massacre — but, travelling with the 1st Battalion, 20th Infantry Regiment, he'd arrived with his camera just as the smoke began to settle. Not early enough to stop anything and too late to pretend he hadn't seen the awful aftermath of what had occurred. I looked at the photograph again. The woman's face was neither grateful nor afraid but emptied. The soldiers seemed caught in the impossible act of redemption.

Josef had carried this moment for nearly twenty years, and it had become one of his most famous images.

*

My Lai, Vietnam, March 1968

After his fateful visit to Folkestone, he had left London within a week, flying first to Paris, onward to Bangkok and into Saigon. The route was disjointed and exhausting — a mixture of press credentials, forged letters of intent, and unofficial arrangements made through a network of correspondents and photographers. He carried with him only his two Leicas, his rolls of film, and a canvas satchel packed with notebooks and a small first-aid kit.

He arrived in Vietnam on 13 March under the loose protection of a French photojournalist working for Le Monde, who had secured temporary access for him to embed, unofficially, with a mobile U.S. patrol unit. It was a calculated risk. Josef wasn't there on assignment — at least not formally. He was there to bear witness, even though he couldn't yet articulate what he was looking for.

On the morning of 15 March, he was travelling with a detachment of the 1st Battalion, documenting routine patrols near Quảng Ngãi province. The air was heavy with anticipation and rumours had begun to circulate among the men — whispers of a planned operation in a Viet Cong stronghold called My Lai 4. Officers were tight-lipped, but Josef had learned over the years to read the space between words.

On 16 March, Josef and his borrowed unit arrived on the outskirts of My Lai several hours after Charlie Company had already gone in. What he encountered defied even the most brutal logic of war. Smoke clung to the tree line. The stench of charred wood, excrement, and blood hung low in the air. Civilians — dozens, then hundreds — lay scattered like discarded cloth. Children, mothers, babies, the elderly. He did not raise his camera immediately.

It was sometime later, as U.S. reinforcements were moving in, that Josef saw her — the young woman in the photograph — being led away from the ruins by two soldiers who had not been part of the assault. Their faces were pale, drawn. One of them looked barely older than the woman herself. Josef lifted his camera and took the shot, not for beauty, or even for evidence, but because it was the only thing he could do at that moment.

*

It was the photographers who had arrived earlier and walked into the massacre as it was happening and who documented its horror.

Ronald L. Haeberle was the U.S. Army photographer with Charlie Company who was there that morning with two cameras: one military-issued, loaded with black-and-white film, and one private, loaded with colour.

In one frame, a group of women and children huddle in terror, moments before they were gunned down by the US soldiers of Charlie Company. Another shows a dead Vietnamese woman, her body contorted in the dirt, her clothes pulled apart. Yet another depicts the mutilated corpses of villagers tossed into a drainage ditch like rubbish. There is no artistry in these photographs, no attempt at composition — only raw documentation, fragments of unfiltered atrocity.

The photographs did what language could not. When Ronald Haeberle's colour images of My Lai were published in late 1969 they tore away the last shreds of ambiguity. The war was no longer a question of strategy or ideology. It was a field of bodies, a ditch filled with women and children, their faces contorted in final disbelief. These were not combatants. They had no weapons. They had nowhere to run. It was these photos that would eventually shatter the American public's illusions about the war.

The public wanted to believe it was an aberration — that a single unit, Charlie Company — had gone rogue, that a certain Lieutenant Calley was a lone actor in a moment of madness. But the images refused to offer that comfort. They showed not chaos, but method, and not the fog of war, but its grim precision.

Haeberle was not a war photographer in the traditional sense. He had been assigned to document the mission. What he captured instead was an atrocity. And like all those who carry the burden of bearing witness, he would spend the rest of his life haunted by what he had seen, and by what he had not stopped.

Later, investigative journalist Seymour Hersh gave the massacre its voice, but it was Haeberle's photographs that gave it form. Between them, they cracked the silence. And yet, justice remained elusive. Only Lieutenant Calley was convicted. His sentence — life, then house arrest, then release — became a symbol of something deeper: the inability, or unwillingness, of a nation to reckon with its own violence. What toll does it take, this act of seeing? Not only for the survivors, but for those behind the lens? For the ones who did not turn away?

*

Josef never spoke of My Lai in terms of guilt or innocence. He understood the seduction of distance, the ease with which a photograph could be used to redeem or condemn. But he also knew that once you've looked into the eye of atrocity — truly looked — you never leave the frame entirely. You remain there, in the margins, just beyond the light. His black-and-white photograph captures a searing contrast between the brutal devastation of Haeberle's images and the flicker of potential redemption in his own.

At the centre of *Rescued from the Ashes* stands a young Vietnamese woman, barefoot and soot-streaked, her torn áo bà ba clinging to her frame, stained with blood. Her dark hair clumps to her damp face, streaked with sweat, ash, and silent grief. She is flanked by two American soldiers from a unit not involved in the killings — faces grim, movements deliberate. The soldier on her left, helmet pushed back, gazes at her with his arm around her, assisting her as she limps forward. On her right, the second soldier walks half a step behind, one arm slightly outstretched, ready to catch her if she falters. His jaw is clenched jaw and his eyes watchful. Behind them, the village of My Lai burns. Smoke coils above the blackened bones of homes. The charred bodies of civilians, men, women, children and babies lie sprawled across the earth, indistinct among the ash. American soldiers can be seen drifting like ghosts in the haze: some stand still, stunned into silence; others kneel beside the dead, hands helpless, eyes blank with disbelief at what their own comrades — soldiers from Charlie Company, 1st Battalion, 20th Infantry Regiment — have done.

Yet at the heart of the frame, the young woman endures. There is no relief in her expression, only exhaustion, but in the way she holds herself, something lingers — a defiance, a refusal to be erased. Though broken, she is not bowed — she walks with the remnants of dignity still intact. The soldiers at her side carry no weapons but suggest a tentative gesture toward humanity. In that instant, a flicker of frail mercy has been captured within an unspeakable atrocity — a single ember of compassion flickering in the ruins of My Lai.

In the years that followed, Josef rarely spoke of what he saw at My Lai. His photograph was syndicated and published before Haeberle's and for the remainder of 1968 and most of 1969, it told only some of the story — the palatable side.

When Josef and I sat in the tent in Nigalya Cove in 1987 looking at the photograph of the rescue of this defiant young woman what we saw was an image of hope for humanity, a photograph that told a different story to Haeberle's.

Josef's photograph became iconic — in part because it wasn't of the massacre itself but because it expressed forms of redemption. At the time, Josef didn't think of history or headlines, he thought only of Cathy, of the sea at Folkestone, and of how easily one could step from one world into another and never be the same again.

Many years later we came to know the complete tragic story — and a very different truth.

A note:
In 1987 the official caption written on the back of the photograph attempted to record the true description and read:

Rescued from the Ashes
16 March 1968, My Lai, Vietnam.
A young Vietnamese woman is led to safety by two American soldiers from the 1st Battalion, 20th Infantry Regiment, 'Americal'* Division, in the immediate aftermath of the My Lai Massacre.

*'Americal' was the regiment's nickname given to it when it was formed during World War II in New Caledonia, a French territory in the South Pacific, in 1942. So, while the name sounds almost poetic or symbolic, it is now indelibly linked with one of the darkest moments of the Vietnam War.

13. Comes A Time

Western Australia, November 1987

That evening we ate the barramundi we caught earlier in the inlet beyond the mangroves. We steamed it gently, tucked in leaves with wild ginger and fire-charred yams, neither of us saying much.

After supper sitting by the fire, Josef sat across from me cupping his tea like it was some fragile thing. We had spent many exhausting hours with the Vietnam photographs from 1968 — the blackened husk of a village; a child's sandal caught in a fence; a woman's eyes, refusing to close even in death. I couldn't tell if it was pain or something gentler that passed across him afterwards, but I was witnessing something — a softening.

For six months we'd done this. Every two weeks — quiet mornings in the sun, then darker afternoons under canvas with prints spread between us on the trestle table like fragile truths, his stories unravelling in pieces, never in order. But that night, for the first time, he didn't flinch or retreat when I asked a question — he stayed. He looked older, but also more alive and his eyes had a wetness I'd never seen before. Not sadness exactly, something more like relief, and I remember thinking that some part of him was beginning to turn toward the light.

I waited until the fire had died down before I let the question rise. It was something I'd carried with me since we'd met, a curiosity that had grown with the silences between us.

I asked Josef if he enjoyed music.

His response came without hesitation, as plain and unadorned as the question itself. In all his fifty-seven years, he had never truly listened to music. He had never owned a record, never purposefully listened to the radio, never sought out a concert or followed a melody out of interest or joy. Even with Cathy, music had played no part. There were film soundtracks, but they were incidental — background to the images, forgotten the moment the credits rolled. He wasn't curious about music. It didn't touch him. He had spent his life avoiding it, not out of disdain, but because it simply didn't speak to anything inside him. To him, it was simply noise.

Yet, that night, there was a change in the way he spoke, without defensiveness or shame, which made me wonder if something significant was about to shift.

*

On each of my visits to the camp, I had packed my guitar, strapping it in beside the canvas roll and water drums. It had become a ritual of its own — tuning it before I departed, then leaving it untouched. I was waiting for some unspoken permission.

That evening, after our conversation about music, I thought the moment had passed. His answer to my question had landed with a truthful finality and I didn't push further. But to my surprise Josef turned to me and asked if I would play my guitar. There was no ceremony in his voice but the sensation in me was immediate and unmistakable. My body felt light and giddy with the surprise of it. I stood and walked the short distance to my car, retrieved the guitar from its case, and carried it back with both hands as though it were fragile.

Sitting by the fire I tuned the strings carefully, one by one, letting my fingers find a simple rhythm, a few quiet chords to test the night air. I began playing *Comes a Time*, one of those Neil Young songs that feels as though it was written for the fireside. There's a fiddle in the original recording, weaving through the verses, so I replaced it with some tender fingerpicking, letting the tones ring and stretch. I kept my voice low, not trying to impress, only to offer. The notes found their place in the warm dark, echoing gently into the night.

As I played, I watched him sitting opposite me in stillness — he was not rigid or guarded, but open. His posture hadn't changed, but his focused attention told me he was hearing more than sound. When I reached the final chorus and let the last chord settle into silence, I looked directly at him and gently smiled.

Josef's eyes met mine. It wasn't wide or dramatic, but it was a definitive smile. It was an acceptance that lived beneath the surface and, for that moment, let itself be seen. I knew then, without question, that something had begun to thaw in Josef's psyche.

*

I'd slipped into a blissful rhythm in Broome. Between my trips north to the camp, the house on Darnley Street became more than shelter. When I first moved in, it was merely a sagging frame with a leaky roof and flaking paint, but I began nurturing it immediately. I planted desert daisies and marigolds out front, a scruffy bougainvillaea that clung to the porch rail, and kangaroo paw that caught the late light like little flames. I laid out a path from the gate to the front door with red pindan sand, flat stones, and smooth white pebbles I'd gathered on long walks.

I'd signed the lease for a further six months, even though I knew I'd soon have to leave the country for a while to renew my visa. New Zealand was an obvious choice — a brief pause in cooler air before returning to the red dust and the humidity of the Kimberley.

Those days in Broome had a looseness I've rarely known since. I'd play the guitar most mornings, sometimes for hours. I became a regular at Carla's Café. There was always someone passing through

— other travellers, young and sun-creased — and I found myself becoming a welcoming host, even if I hadn't meant to.

Often in the evenings, I'd take people in the car out to the far end of Cable Beach, the stretch where the road dissolves into sand and sky. We'd build fires and play guitars, drink cheap wine from enamel mugs, and sing. We'd sleep there often, curled in blankets and I never had to worry about the next day.

Some afternoons I'd head into town to busk in the grassy patch near the courthouse markets. I'd sit beneath the flame trees and play without expectation. Occasionally, a small crowd would gather and one morning I looked up to see Albert Warrun standing at a distance, resting on his stick, watching. He didn't say anything, he just stood motionless for a while before disappearing the way he always did.

I loved that life. I loved the way people flowed through it — open, unguarded, transient. I let them into my home, offered them fruit and coffee, listened to their stories and sometimes gave them the spare room for a few nights. There was no plan, no pressure. Just space, music and the sea.

*

In December 1987, as the wet season gathered over the Dampier Peninsula, I planned a trip to Auckland to apply for another tourist visa. I expected to be away for three weeks, returning by mid-January.

Before I left, I made my usual visit to Josef. This time, along with my guitar, I brought the portable stereo, fresh packs of batteries, and a handful of tapes, hoping perhaps, to play him some music. As always in the late afternoons, we met beneath the canvas of the tent. The trestle table was cleared, the folding chairs set in place, and together, we laid out the photographs, working slowly through the years 1968 and 1969. After My Lai, Josef had travelled to Nigeria.

The Biafran photographs were stark, haunting images taken during the height of the Nigerian Civil War, often referred to as the Biafran War. Josef captured them over several months in mid to late 1968, during his time embedded with humanitarian convoys and aid workers. He shot entirely in black and white, using natural light, his lens focused on small, unspoken moments: a shared bowl of rice, a glance between siblings, the empty space where someone had once sat. The images exposed the harrowing consequences of starvation and warfare: youngsters with swollen bellies and vacant stares, mothers holding emaciated babies, and queues for food winding along barren roads.

Josef struggled to describe how he had strived to avoid exploitation, aiming to humanise and convey dignity, but the line between witness and voyeur was perilously thin, almost impossible not to cross.

In that struggle, something had profoundly changed. He had never narrated, but he was noticeably more present in the way he talked about voyeurism. There was a renewed honesty, not in an earnest way, but in a raw, exposed way. He didn't only show me the work; he opened to it. There was less resistance, less guardedness, and for the first time, I noticed him watching how I moved between the images, as though my seeing was, in some small way, helping him to let them go — as though he felt my seeing them was an act of forgiveness.

As a rainstorm rolled across the cove and the camp grew dark with shadow we remained under the canvas, I was glad when he gestured for me to play again. This time, I sang *May You Never*, fingerpicking the melody and tapping the rhythm softly on the body of the guitar. I followed this with *Fire and Rain*, the words and music barely audible above the sound of the rain on the canvas.

When I'd finished, he sat utterly still, but not in the way he usually was. There was a softness in his face I hadn't seen before. In that silence, I imagine now seeing him re-entering the world, without ceremony, like someone waking up from a long, cold sleep.

Early the following morning, before I left for Broome, we shared breakfast and tea. I asked Josef if he'd like to hear the original versions of the songs I'd played for him. It was a soft nudge toward something. He amiably liked the idea, so I played him *Comes a Time* by Neil Young, *May You Never* by John Martyn, and *Fire and Rain* by James Taylor, and there was a palpable pleasure in him I'd never witnessed before.

I asked if he'd like me to leave the player with him together with a few tapes to listen to while I was away. To my surprise, he said yes so, I showed him how to use the cassette player on the sound system. He'd never touched one before, and the processes of fast forward and rewind were unknown to him. Neither of us could know whether the music would mean anything, but the tapes I left for him were:

Joni Mitchell – *Court & Spark*
Nick Drake – *Five Leaves Left*
Arvo Pärt – *Tabula Rasa*
Neil Young – *Comes a Time*
John Martyn – *Solid Air*
Bob Marley & The Wailers – *Legend*
Johann Sebastian Bach – *Violin Concertos (BWV 1041–1043)*
James Taylor – *Sweet Baby James*

*

I spent just over three weeks in New Zealand, mostly staying at a small travellers' hostel near the harbour in Auckland. The building had thin walls and a crooked staircase, and my bed was in a shared room on the second floor. The noise from the street drifted in most evenings; voices, music, and the clatter of the Korean restaurant kitchen next door, and I found it oddly comforting after the peace of my house in Broome and the wilderness of the camp.

Christmas came and went with a soft joy. A group of us, people from all over, put together a shared meal and we ate it on the rooftop under a tangle of fairy lights, with the wind rolling in from the harbour and people taking turns to play guitar through a tiny amplifier.

I spoke to Maggie a few times while I was there. We didn't talk long, but the conversations felt good. I told her about the house on Darnley Street, and I hoped she would visit me at some point, and she liked the idea.

I also made my monthly call to Anne Delacourt, something I'd promised to keep up while I was away. I explained about playing the music, how Josef had begun to soften and that I sensed the worst of his process seemed to have passed. He was, I thought, in the early stages of recovery, though I didn't say it quite so plainly. She told me Josef's absence had begun to stir attention further afield. Someone had written a piece in a New York newspaper about his disappearance. The tone, she said, was speculative but not unkind. For the first time, people had begun to wonder aloud if he was still alive. She'd maintained she hadn't heard from him herself, but that it wasn't unusual. He had always vanished and resurfaced on his own terms.

Before we finished the call, she told me something unexpected. A large advertising agency in New York had been in touch with her office. They'd found a series of photographs Josef had taken of Harry, just after Theo was shot, images pulled from the agency's catalogue of Josef's work. Anne hadn't known the context of the images or why they were there, but their drama and impact were palpable, and the advertising agency was interested in using them as part of a campaign for a brand of jeans — they wanted it to be gritty and controversial, and these photographs were highly compelling. Anne sounded both bemused and faintly amused. Her photographers didn't usually produce material for commercial clients, let alone for something as mainstream as denim. Still, the agency had been persistent. She wasn't sure if the enquiry had anything to do with the article about Josef's disappearance. It could have been a coincidence, or something more subtle. Either way, she said, it was unusual.

My brief foray into city life brought unexpected pleasures. I found Replay Records on O'Connell Street. The store's wooden bins were a treasure trove of memories, each cassette a portal to a time long past. I found James Taylor's *JT* and Simon & Garfunkel's and John Denver's *Greatest Hits*. These were the melodies that had often filled our farmhouse, songs my mother, Maggie, would play and I still hold romantic images of hearing them with the sunlight streaming through the kitchen window. They were the foundation of my musical journey, pieces I had taught myself and formed the staples for my busking sessions. On *A Song for You* by the Carpenters; the title track's soulful saxophone had once inspired me to pick up the instrument at fourteen, though my proficiency never quite matched that of the guitar, violin, or piano. So, I bought them all and they formed a collection of songs that had shaped me and were ready to be rediscovered.

On many afternoons, I would take my guitar into the centre and play near the ferry terminal, not with any real intention of busking, but simply because it felt good to be part of something living. I particularly enjoyed singing my own acoustic version of the Carpenter's *Top of the World*, one of the first songs I learned as a child, and still, somehow, the most generous. There was a simple and open-hearted sweetness in it that children seemed to enjoy as they watched my fingers speedily pick out the notes in a perky country style. I'd throw in a small shake of the head; a comical gesture that made them laugh. I loved the smoothness of Karen Carpenter's caramel voice and would try and emulate it, but of course never quite reached it. People stopped to listen, and somehow everything, the salt-tinged air, the shifting light on the water, seemed to gather around the song. Some came back, their faces becoming familiar, and I earned more from that song than any other; but what mattered most was the feeling it left behind — lightness, connection, a sense that something good was still possible.

I visited the Australian High Commission on Queen Street to renew my visa, carrying with me everything they might ask for: an onward ticket to Singapore, proof of funds, and my return address in Broome. Before I'd left, Josef had handed me a cheque for five thousand dollars enough to secure my visa extension for a further six months without complication.

I had first met the German boy, Lukas, months earlier at the young traveller's hostel in Perth, where we'd played a Nick Drake song together. Hostel life meant travellers' paths often crossed, so it was a welcome surprise to see him again. A few days after Christmas, I set off north with him and his English girlfriend, Claire.

Lukas was tall, with cropped blonde hair, a single silver earring, and a soft-spoken, dry humour that put you at ease. Claire was quieter still and quick-witted, with a laugh that lit up her whole face. For their travels in New Zealand, they'd bought a beautifully rusted, sun-faded 1970 Holden Kingswood station wagon.

We drove together to the Bay of Islands, where the air warmed and the sea turned an unfamiliar shade of translucent blue-green. The town of Paihia felt slow and small, suspended in its own rhythm and we stayed in a hostel behind the dunes. At night, you could hear the sea through the wooden slats, constant and near. The building was painted a pale yellow, its paint flaking at the edges. A long veranda ran along the front, strung with washing lines, where towels stirred like flags in the salt-heavy air. We stayed four or five days, doing very little. Swimming in the mornings, reading and cooking in the evenings, walking along the beach without any need to talk. We played guitar most nights, sitting on the steps of the veranda as the light drained slowly from the sky.

After three weeks in New Zealand, I flew back to Perth, then straight to Broome. The thick and familiar humidity hit me as I stepped out onto the tarmac.

*

By the time I left Broome for the camp the following afternoon, the sky was thick with heavy northern rain — the kind that falls without hurry, but with absolute intention. It pressed down over the land, dense and full.

It was the longest I'd been away from the camp, and I left town with the car loaded to the gills with supplies. I was looking forward to listening to the tapes I'd picked up from Replay Records, curious to hear how they might sound out here, so far from the setting in which I'd first grown to love them.

As I drove out of town, I was conscious that 1988 had arrived in Australia not only with celebration for the bicentenary but with a shadowy weight. The radio in Broome spoke of commemorations, of events planned in the capitals, of speeches rehearsed in Canberra. But on the fringes, where the truth lives closer to the surface, the bicentennial year meant something else entirely. I knew that Albert Warrun's community would be watching the country watch itself.

The track north was washed out in places, and the bush was thick with new growth. The pindan was dark, bleeding red at the edges of the road, and the heat hung low and oppressive — slow as if the land itself were holding its breath.

Around ninety kilometres in, the road disappeared beneath floodwater, which didn't come as a surprise. I slowed, tested the edges, and pressed on, hoping it would hold, but it didn't. The vehicle sank gradually and stubbornly into thick red mud, until the wheels lost all grip. With the rain tapping heavily on the roof, I switched off the ignition. Outside, the bush was hushed, silvered with water and a long silence followed, broken only by the occasional flick of movement in the grass. I wasn't sure, even if I was rescued, whether I should turn back to Broome.

Eventually, an hour or so later, the rain eased and a Toyota Hilux with impossibly high suspension appeared. Its tyres were huge, like pontoons, and two men I didn't know climbed out. Without hesitation, they assessed the situation, hauled chains from the back, and, saying nothing, towed me free of the mud with the effortless generosity I've only ever encountered in places too remote for ceremony.

When they were gone, I let the engine run for a while and decided to push on toward the camp. I pressed play on the tape deck and *Top of the World* came through, full and clear, the opening line unexpectedly luminous and comical. The way Karen Carpenter's voice rose into the humid air, there was something naïve and unapologetic about it, like a bright flag in a storm — a small offering to the moment.

When I turned off the main road onto the track into the community, the dirt firmed under the tyres. The rains had passed, and the sun was high, sharp and bright. Up ahead, near the edge of the settlement, a tall flagpole stood beside the rusted frame of an old windmill. A newly hung and enormous Aboriginal flag flew there — black above red, with the yellow sun burning in the centre — shimmering in the strong breeze, steady and unmistakable. Strung between two trees, a hand-painted banner read:

NOTHING TO CELEBRATE 200 YEARS OF RESISTANCE

Some children were happily playing cricket with a broken bat in the wet dirt nearby, but the poignancy and importance of the scene spoke to me. The paint was faded in parts and the letters uneven, but they were certain. Along the bottom edge, ochre and white handprints had been stencilled. The message was loud — this wasn't a celebration; it was a reckoning.

I'd hoped to see Albert Warrun and check in but there was no sign of him, so I kept going, heading straight for the camp and Josef.

*

Nothing could have prepared me for what I found when I arrived, or rather, what I heard.

The moment I opened the door of the car, it was *One Love,* by Bob Marley and the Wailers, clear and bold and utterly incongruous. I stood there, stunned. Josef, who never listened to music, who barely knew anything about it, who said it meant nothing to him, was playing Bob Marley and the Wailers. Very loudly.

The canvas shelter fluttered in the wind, and a pot sat next to the fire's remnants, with the player teetering on an overturned crate, its speakers directed towards the beach. He couldn't have offered me a more precious gift than to experience and observe this moment.

In the distance, out in the shallows of the inlet, I saw him, a figure casting a line. He was shirtless, calf-deep in the turquoise water, moving with an ease I'd never seen in him. He didn't see me watching him. The music was drifting out across the cove, and he must have set it going before he walked down to fish, knowing it would carry. It wasn't only the surprise of it that I felt, but the depth and pure joy of the reggae beat. And there he was standing in saltwater, fishing to Bob Marley, letting music fill the space around. I stood by the car, listening, smiling, letting it sink in.

I made my way down from the camp and sat on a drifted log, pulling off my Blundstones and socks before stepping onto the sand. Josef must have seen me because he turned, and the smile that spread across his face was soft, almost shy, but unmistakably real. It held none of his usual guardedness and no irony or detachment, only warmth. He reeled in his line and stepped out of the water with bare, deliberate feet, setting the rod down gently on the sand. Without a word, he started towards me. He paused for the briefest second and leaned forward and placed his arms around me.

It was tentative at first, uncertain as if the very idea of a hug was unfamiliar to him, the motion unpractised, but then, slowly, something in him gave way. He allowed himself to settle into the space between us, to be held. I kept my arms around him, feeling the subtle surrender in his shoulders. A body so often wound tight and guarded was beginning to soften and trust.

Behind us, *One Love* was fading out, and the unmistakable opening of the following song rose up — *I Shot the Sheriff… but I didn't shoot no deputy… oh no no.* The timing was absurd and perfect, and I began to cry — not a quiet tear or two, but a sudden, unstoppable flood — blubbering, unfiltered emotion spilling out as though my body had been waiting for this moment.

Later, I wondered if that had been the first time he'd ever embraced anyone — I mean truly embraced them and let himself be that close. And I wondered, too, about what it had cost him to come this far — to the very edge of himself — and choose, even for a moment, to surface from his silence.

14. What If We Built A House That Breathed?

I can't say with certainty what it was that woke Josef from his lifelong silence, and I don't believe it was simply the music that opened him up, but perhaps it was the catalyst.

What I saw in him that day was someone who had slowly laid down his burden and a guilt too heavy to carry anymore. Maybe he'd been born with the grief, and it was threaded into his blood and bones — a deep imprint from his mother's death as she gave birth to him. Who can say, and what does it matter?

He had spent decades behind the lens, bearing witness to unspeakable things. It was his means of survival and perhaps that detachment had served him, but it had also exiled him from himself and others and now it was time to let that all go.

As the following months unfolded, so did a change in our relationship, subtle at first, and then all at once undeniable. Josef began to meet me when I arrived for my twice-monthly visits. He would hear the car long before he saw it, and by the time I pulled into the clearing he'd often be there, waiting at the edge the hint of a smile on his face.

We fell into a different pattern, shaped by simple rituals: cooking, walking the shoreline, and sitting in peaceful shade during the heat of the day. We didn't always talk, but the silences between us no longer felt like an absence, more like the pauses in music that held everything together.

We continued the late-afternoon ritual of slowly working our way through the years of his career. We were deep into assignments in Bangladesh, Cambodia and Northern Ireland and I sensed a difference in the photographs. They were rawer somehow, less composed. There was one photograph that I could barely bring myself to look at, taken in Bangladesh, in 1971, in the final weeks of the war.

You could feel the heat in it, the dust rising in waves off a racetrack, and the thick blur of humanity pressing forward. In the foreground, four men lay face down on the dirt, their hands bound behind their backs, their shirts dark with sweat and blood. One of them had lifted his head slightly, enough that the lens had caught his expression — part agony, part disbelief, part desperate plea. It was this man's face that held me, and I could not look away. Behind them stood the fighters of Mukti Bahini, their youth visible even in shadow. One boy held a bayonet poised above his shoulder, his jaw clenched in resolve. Around them, the crowd surged, mouths open, hands raised, caught in the confusion of witnessing what should never be seen. When I turned the photograph over, the typewritten caption was barely legible: *Dacca, December 1971. After the surrender. Four alleged collaborators. No trial.*

What struck me most was not the brutality, but the depth of the layers in the image; the terrible stillness just before the killing; the moment before innocence or guilt ceases to matter; the man who lifted his head; the boy with the bayonet. And behind it all, Josef, standing there with his camera, unaware he was absorbing a memory that would never leave him. I asked him once if it ever became too much. He looked at me, not startled, but thoughtful, as though no one had asked him this before.

"It always was," he said. "But I didn't know it then. Or maybe I did. I didn't know what to do with it."

The photographs from Cambodia were darker — not only in tone, but in atmosphere. He didn't say much about those at first, and I didn't press, but on one afternoon, as he lingered over a shot of a temple courtyard, the bodies of monks lying just beyond the colonnade.

"I stayed too long," he murmured. "In all of it. I stayed too long."

We sat with that in peaceful silence for some time. The wind moved through the casuarina trees; a gull called once and was gone.

There was something sacred in those afternoons. We weren't excavating pain from the photographs for its own sake, we were making sense of it, frame by frame. And in our renewed ritual, music often played low in the background. Sometimes jazz — Mingus or Davis or Coltrane — sometimes Fairport Convention or Aretha Franklin. I'd slip a tape into the deck before we unpacked the prints, and it became our language of sorts. I'd watch him close his eyes when a phrase or chord moved him, and later he'd ask me what it was, or request to hear it again.

Music and photographs were two ways of catching something as it passed; two ways of remembering without being overwhelmed. We were building something between us — not a shared past, but a shared present, and maybe even a shared future, though neither of us would have said so aloud.

Our silences changed. They became companionable and less defensive, and the music became something more than background. After the first unexpected blast of Bob Marley, I started bringing up a few new cassettes each week together with some fresh TDK C60 blank tapes, and I would use a double tape player to make recordings so we both had copies in Broome and the camp.

Music was a language we began to share. Josef was tentative at first, as if uncertain whether he was permitted to enjoy it, and gradually his curiosity deepened. He asked questions and he listened closely. He liked Coltrane, something in the searching, unresolved notes, I think, echoed the map of his mind. He was intrigued by Nina Simone's voice, by its command and defiance. He asked me about Nick Drake, Leonard Cohen and Billie Holiday.

He listened to Satie's *Gymnopédies* one afternoon with his eyes closed, and when it finished, he whispered,

"Again."

I had always thought of music as something expansive, a world to explore, but for Josef, it seemed to do something more intimate, it touched something buried — something he'd kept sealed away.

And in that undoing, I saw a different man emerging; still with shadows but no longer ruled by them. Our conversations changed too. He began to ask about my life, my childhood and family and my hopes, though never directly. His questions came sideways, wrapped in anecdotes or framed in abstract terms, but they were questions all the same. And in turn, he began to speak of light — in fragments at first: a meal he once ate in Aleppo, the colours of dawn in Chad, the smell of wet earth in Cambodia after the rains, of the beauty he had noticed, even when the world around him was filled with brutality and sadness.

In some strange way, we were each other's teachers: I brought the youthful pulse, the hunger for meaning, the music and the questions; he brought stillness, discernment, and the weight of experience distilled down to something clean and spare.

We met in that wilderness not as teacher and student, or father and son, but as something else entirely — two men, separated by decades, living side-by-side in the presence of each other's honesty.

*

By early May 1988, the thick heat that had cloaked the peninsula for months began to loosen its grip. The air grew lighter, and the evenings were edged with a quiet that only arrived once the rains had gone, and the earth began to breathe again. In the gentler climate of the dry season, the shift brought with it a subtle pressure, an awareness that time was moving on and once again my visa was running out.

I'd made a life for myself in Broome, I enjoyed the lack of expectations and obligations, of being an accidental host to other travellers, the way the town opened itself just enough and never too much and I wasn't ready to let it go.

I brought the subject up with Josef, although not all at once. I didn't want him to feel responsible for my constraint, but I needed to speak it aloud. The question, of what to do, where to go, hovered between us for a time, unspoken. Gradually, it found its way into our conversations. He listened, as he always did, with attentiveness.

He said he wasn't ready to leave the camp, not yet, but that when the time came, he imagined he might enjoy living in Broome too; the pace of it, the peculiar coastal beauty and the feeling of being tucked far enough away from the world.

The night before I was due to leave for Broome he made his suggestion, in that same offhand way he often delivered things that mattered: maybe we should buy the house on Darnley Street.

It caught me off guard. Not because I hadn't thought of it — I had, many times — but because hearing it from him made the thought feel somehow more possible, more real. I told him it was a lovely idea, but that the house was barely standing. Years of storms and wet seasons had taken their toll, and the termites too.

Gently and without hesitation he said, "Maybe we could tear it down and start again."

The we in it all stayed with me. I wasn't sure what it meant. Was he imagining that I might still be around when he eventually left the camp? Or was he offering the idea of something shared — a project, a home, a future, however uncertain? In any event, it was a door opening and a gesture not only toward staying but toward belonging.

Later, long after the fire had burned out and Josef had gone to his bed, I sat alone beneath the stars, letting the thought settle in me. The house on Darnley Street — half-ruin, half-relic — might yet become something new. Something we could shape with our own hands. A place to return to and perhaps begin again.

*

As I was packing up the following morning for the drive back to Broome, Josef joined me by the car.

The light was soft through the trees, and the day seemed to begin without urgency. He spoke with that calm clarity he reserved for things that mattered, without fanfare or hesitation. He asked me to get in touch with Dick Edwards when I got back, tell him to put the chemist shop on the market. He wanted it done cleanly, with no fuss, and for the best price. There was no nostalgia in the request, only a quiet resolve.

He asked me to inform Anne Delacourt that he would not be returning to the field or taking on assignments. She likely expected this, but the message would still be significant — a definitive end. Anne, always reliable, would continue overseeing his archive and business. Yet, this felt like a final closure.

And, almost in passing, he wondered if I might investigate what would be needed for me to stay, whether there was a way to apply for a visa that might allow it. He suggested I speak to a solicitor in Broome, someone who could guide me through it. He didn't present it as a plan or a request, but a wondering out loud — one of those thoughts he released into the world without trying to shape the outcome. But I heard it for what it was: an invitation and a gesture towards the future.

*

Bach's Violin Concerto No. 2 in E Major drifted from the speakers, its opening bright and unhurried, as I eased the Land Cruiser back onto the red track to head south. The road was empty and familiar, and the music moved with me, string by string, weaving something hopeful through the quiet.

My mind turned to Darnley Street and the generous plot of land the house was sitting on. I imagined a new structure rising from the ground, timber, air and light everywhere; a shaded courtyard at the centre acting almost like a campus quad with an internal veranda all around. Sliding glass doors, high ceilings, and the soft pull of a breeze in every corner. A place where music lived, not only played, but lived. A space for others to come, to stay, to breathe. A hostelry, of sorts, though the word felt too heavy for what I was conjuring in mind. This was something lighter. A place for people to arrive and gently come undone. Big Jarrah wood tables, peaceful rooms, the smell of bread cooling. Music drifting from a corner, sometimes recorded, sometimes played. The whole house humming with the stillness that only comes when something has been built with care.

And in that imagined space, I saw Josef — barefoot, moving slowly, placing a tray of coffee on a wide wooden bench, or showing someone a photograph. There was a looseness in him, a joy. It wasn't the man I'd known, not quite, but it was a version that seemed possible. The shape of who he might become if peace were allowed to linger.

The concerto rose and carried me with it, the red road unfurled ahead, and the house stayed vivid in my mind, as though it had always existed and was simply waiting for us to find it.

*

Back in Broome, I walked to the post office in the afternoon sun and, with a bag of coins, stepped into a phone box that reeked of stale cigarette smoke. I called Dick Edwards, who answered with estate agents' polish and ease.

I kept it simple — Josef wanted the chemist shop placed on the market. Dick didn't hesitate and said he'd list it immediately but would need a signed letter of instruction from Josef before being able to entertain any offers. He expected quick interest, given the building's commercial value and history and he asked me to check in every few days for updates. Before ending the call, I reminded him to keep Josef's location and plans private, and Dick agreed without question.

Later, as the sun began scorching my back outside Carla's Café I glanced at my watch, calculating the time difference between Broome and Paris. Eventually, I made my way back to the phone box and fed it copious coins while dialling Anne's number. The connection crackled as it reached across continents. Anne's voice carried through the static, calm and composed as always. I explained that Josef had no intention of returning to any more assignments and she expressed relief rather than surprise. She asked about my plans and her question hung in the air as I fumbled for an answer, coins slipping through my fingers into the machine.

Then she dropped the bombshell about Josef's photograph, the one of Harry dressed in jeans with rage etched into his face, gun discarded beside him which, she explained, was now gracing billboards and magazines across America and Europe. A six-figure sum from the advertising agency had come Josef's way and the image had become iconic, a key part of an Italian clothing brand's intention to reshape how people viewed advertisements — no longer glossy fantasies but controversial and gritty slices of reality.

I listened in stunned silence as she described its impact, how the image was illuminated on screens in Times Square, and how it had sparked widespread curiosity about Josef's whereabouts. The irony was somewhat twisted because the photograph was taken moments after Theo's death at Harry's hands. My thoughts swirled in a maelstrom of concern for Josef. How would he react? Would this recognition drag him back into darkness or propel him forward? Anne couldn't provide answers but mentioned that stories about Josef's disappearance were now global news. Rumours placed him everywhere from Rio de Janeiro to the Namibian Desert. I thanked Anne and hung up, leaning against the glass of the phone box, heart pounding as I grappled with what this meant for Josef and our secluded life.

*

The following morning, Carla at the café recommended a solicitor to see, someone who didn't waste time but wouldn't steamroll me either.

Munro & Finch, Solicitors & Conveyancers, was set back in a shaded courtyard beside an old bakery on Dampier Terrace, the type of place you'd miss if you weren't looking.

As I entered, Miriam Finch rose from her desk to greet me. I didn't know then that she'd spent a decade in Perth courtrooms before trading the city's noise for a quieter life. She wasn't brisk, nor did she affect any surface cordiality, but she had that rare quality of listening with her whole attention, as though she were tuning in beneath the words I managed to string together.

Miriam asked careful questions and took notes in longhand and her handwriting was elegant, upright and unhurried. I told her, in outline only, that I was considering buying a property in Broome with an Australian sponsor, someone who preferred, for now, to remain unnamed. I also mentioned, almost as an afterthought, that I had a one-way ticket out of Perth in June, and perhaps I could leave and re-enter on another tourist visa if need be, but I wasn't certain. When I'd finished, she explained how she worked, and outlined her hourly rates. I told her I could pay for as much time as was needed to get the application properly dealt with. She said she'd begin gathering all the options; make calls to Perth or Canberra and track down whatever information wasn't available locally. Things would need to move quickly, she said, but that was fine.

Miriam looked to be in her late thirties and carried herself with an understated resilience. She was tall and fine-boned, an elegance born of stillness rather than style. Her grey eyes held a watchful kindness that was hard to read but easy to trust. I liked that she took on cases from the surrounding communities and that many of her clients were Aboriginal. There was something grounding in the knowledge that the person helping me chose to stand with people whose lives weren't always easily seen by the system. There was a friendliness in her professionalism and as I walked back towards Darnley Street, I had the feeling Miriam and I might become friends. There was something in her measured speech, her understated wit and her unwavering calm. She had the integrity of someone who had seen both sides of life and chosen, without fanfare, to stand on the right one.

Walking up the path I'd made to the house, I understood how the silence around the plot was vast but not empty, and there was room here for something real and I felt a tremendous sense of excitement.

That afternoon I called Dick Edwards who already had three serious expressions of interest in the chemist shop. Nothing formal yet, but enough to suggest a bidding war if things moved fast. He sounded pleased, optimistic even, though he was clear that nothing could happen until he had Josef's letter of formal instruction. I told him I'd drive up to Josef the following morning and expected to be back in touch within three days.

*

I left Darnley Street sometime before 4am and by the time I turned off the red road and the scrub began to thin the light had settled into that milky stillness that comes just after dawn. I'd spent much of the drive rehearsing what I might say, trying to shape the news into something manageable, something that wouldn't unsettle him, but nothing had quite landed. And, as the camp came into view, I heard the music I'd become used to hearing; this time the celebratory sound of Stevie Wonder and the unmistakable opening bars of *As*, floating on the air.

Songs in the Key of Life had become one of Josef's favourite tapes, so I wasn't surprised to hear it. He was by the stove when I pulled in, his back to me, a coffee mug in one hand, and for a moment he didn't seem to notice the car, and I watched him there in the morning light, his frame relaxed and at ease. When he turned, he looked pleasantly surprised, and a soft smile broke across his face. Without hesitation, he walked toward me and folded me into an embrace.

It was a beautiful welcome, but the reason for my return so soon sat between us, waiting its turn. I'd spoken to Dick the day before. He'd already found three serious buyers, each of them prepared to move quickly, and the only thing standing between them and the next step was Josef's letter of instruction. I didn't tell him about the photograph straight away.

We stood for a while by the fire pit, mugs in hand, the music still curling through the air behind us. There was a steadiness in the camp that morning, as though nothing urgent could touch it.

And so I waited a moment. Then, as we sat in the shade, I told him everything Anne had said, about the campaign, about the photograph of Harry and the reaction it had sparked. I explained how it had found its way onto billboards, into magazines, illuminated onto the giant screens in Times Square, how the image had become a central part of a gritty, controversial and unsettling international advertising campaign, and how people were being moved by its rawness. I also told him that his disappearance was now international news and that there were imaginary sightings of him in remote places around the world.

At first, Josef looked puzzled. He squinted slightly as if trying to recall a dream half-remembered, shook his head lightly and said, almost to himself,

"I'd forgotten I even sent that roll."

I realised I'd never told him that Anne had discussed the potential of it with me months earlier, after the first tentative enquiry from the advertising agency. When I told him the campaign had already paid him a six-figure sum, with more still coming, his eyes widened and slowly, almost shyly, a grin began to spread across his face. It wasn't only delight it was disbelief tipping into joy.

And then he laughed — something I'd never seen him do — a full, open laugh that came from deep in his chest and seemed to catch him by surprise. It burst out of him just as the beat of Stevie Wonder's *Another Star* rose behind us, loud and jubilant, echoing across the camp. I started laughing too, grinning like an idiot, the weight lifting off my shoulders and in one effortless sweep we were on our feet, hugging again, arms tight around each other, rocking in rhythm to the beat. The joy was so sudden, so pure, it overwhelmed us. I felt it in my chest, in my throat, rising in tears, not of sadness, not at all, but of something vast and luminous. Love, I think. Life, undiminished and fully felt.

We held each other there, two grown men swaying in the middle of the bush, tears slipping down our faces, with laughter rising through them. And the song played on, its bright rhythm carrying across the wilderness as if it knew the shape of our joy.

After the laughter and tears, we let a meditative stillness take us, and the jubilance of the morning softened into something steadier. Arvo Pärt's *Für Alina* drifted out into the bush in delicate fragments, barely more than breath. Delicate piano chords hung in the air like light on water, dissolving into silence between each phrase. We sat with the gentleness of it all and I watched the trees leaning ever so slightly with the breeze, thinking about the potential of the house we might build in Darnley Street.

Eventually, in that hush, I heard Josef unzip the battered canvas camera bag that had sat unopened since I'd met him. I heard the soft clicks and the light metallic shuffle of him assembling the camera. When I looked over, he was fitting a lens, his movements unhurried. He looked up and there was a question in his eyes.

"Do you mind?" he asked.

I nodded. I didn't mind at all.

And so, he photographed me. He made no demands and gave no direction; he simply followed me attentively capturing the unspoken movements of the day. I felt him behind me as I cast my line into the still water down at the inlet and I let myself be seen.

In that new configuration: Josef the photographer, me the subject, something tender was passing between us. It wasn't about art or documentation, it had more to do with trust and connection, the allowing of another person to witness you without defence.

*

That evening we ate by the fire, the warm air folding gently around us as the light retreated from the land. I'd caught a mangrove jack earlier that afternoon, plump, sweet-fleshed, its skin crisped over the flames with a little salt and lemon. We shared it in easy silence with oily fingers picking through the bones.

I told Josef about the vision I'd had of us building a house as a haven and how it had come to me on my journey back to Broome. I saw it clearly: a place open to the sky but sheltered from the world, filled with music, laughter, and light, a place where people came and stayed and made something of their time together. I described the internal courtyard as a garden turned inward, where the wind could pass but the world could not intrude. A veranda that ran the inside perimeter, an architectural gesture of both welcome and protection. I imagined big communal spaces softened by shadows and the scent of frangipani, rooms where sound could echo gently, where the light was filtered through timber and slatted screens.

It had felt abstract before, but now, sitting beside Josef in the hush of evening, it felt possible, maybe even real. He took it in with the intensity I'd come to know and for the first time since we met, he asked me what I wanted, what I longed for, what shape my life might take if I allowed myself to dream.

I told him how much I loved making things. Not simply designs or drawings or songs, but spaces, atmospheres, and moments. I said I wanted to bring all of it together somehow and to create something beautiful and lasting. A collaboration, a home and a work of art that could be lived in. I told him I'd like to do it with him. When I turned to him, I saw that his face was alight with a kind-heartedness that rose from within. We sat for a long while sketching out possibilities, speaking of solar angles and wind paths, of old materials and new ways of living. We weren't only planning we were forming a dream out loud.

By morning a solid plan had taken form, what began as a dream was already pressing its feet into the earth. Over breakfast of grilled damper and the last of the gubinge compote he'd made the week before, Josef laid it out in simple, steady terms.

The sale of the chemist shop in Perth would more than cover the purchase of the Darnley Street house, with enough left over to build something substantial. The unexpected windfall from the photograph would cushion everything else. He spoke plainly, without ceremony, as though this future had always existed, and we were only now stepping into it.

There was something deeply moving in the way he spoke, with a generosity I hadn't expected. He told me he would do everything he could to support me with permanent residency. He wrote the letter to Dick Edwards, instructing him to proceed with the sale, and another to Anne Delacourt, giving her a fuller sense of where he stood now. He asked me to take photographs of the Darnley Street plot and the house, to pick up a disposable camera in town and bring back whatever I could. He wanted details, shadows, lines, and possibilities. He said I should speak to Miriam too, to see what she made of it all. Whether there were any caveats, any local knowledge about planning issues or environmental constraints that we might have missed.

We spent the rest of the morning in an unstated momentum. There was laughter, sketches in the sand, and hands moving to describe walls, windows, and angles of light. By early afternoon, I felt the pull to leave, not out of impatience, but purpose. The longer I stayed, the longer those plans would remain abstract. I said I should get back to Broome to set the wheels in motion and Josef didn't delay me. He smiled, something steady and luminous in his eyes, and pressed the envelopes into my hand.

*

In the weeks and months that followed, everything began to move with urgency. As her role had deepened, I told Miriam who Josef was, and she became his solicitor too. She took the news with a subdued delight. Not in any showy or self-congratulatory way, but with a spark that suggested her life and work had opened a little with the subterfuge behind his disappearance. The fact of Josef, his name, and his history seemed to lift something in her.

With her guidance, we agreed on a figure and submitted an offer through Keith D. Hinton & Associates on the old house in Darnley Street. The acceptance came through almost at once. It felt, somehow, as though the place had been waiting for us all along. Josef and I had already named it in our conversations beneath the stars at the camp: *The Stopover*. A shared home, a place to build together; somewhere to welcome others with perhaps seven guest suites, maybe more, woven around a central space that belonged to no one and everyone. A house shaped by light, music, silence and slow arrivals.

Back in Perth, Dick sold the chemist shop in Leederville for almost a third more than expected. The market had surged, and the place went quickly. From that moment, the liaison between us took on a strange, frenzied energy. Josef stayed in the wilderness of course, and it fell to me to carry documents, updates, and questions. Miriam acted for him on the conveyancing, while I became the middleman between it all; between Broome, the city and the camp, between the past and the future we were building.

I found myself travelling the long road from Broome to the camp every three or four days. I didn't mind, life was in motion, and I was lucky enough to feel it humming through me. I carried letters and contracts and bank papers, sketches and plans, but what I looked forward to most was sitting with Josef again, beneath the canvas of sky, sharing sketches and stories, drawing the house in our minds. Josef's smile that once appeared like a flash of light now lingered and had found a home on his face.

*

With my permanent residency application, Miriam became more than my solicitor, she was an anchor in a process seemingly designed to make the applicant feel adrift. She moved through the bureaucracy with the ease of someone who had long since stopped fearing it, interpreting forms and deadlines not as obstacles, but as a map, without performance, only a clear-eyed certainty. She suggested that if I could demonstrate the financial capacity to start a business and develop the Darnley Street property, there was a chance to fast-track the process. It was a window, she said, not a promise. Time, as ever, was a pressure. My tourist visa was still valid, just, and the application would need to be lodged before it lapsed. If we got it right, a bridging visa would catch the moment, slip in silently and take its place, letting me remain in the country while the application moved through the slow interior of the system. I couldn't leave the country, not without undoing it all.

Josef didn't offer commentary or caution. He simply pressed an envelope into my hand, dust-marked and warm from his pocket, its edges slightly curled. Inside was a cheque for one hundred thousand dollars, written in his unmistakable, blockish handwriting. It was the only way he could move money from the camp, and something about it felt ceremonial, less a transaction, more an offering. An act of faith passed from one life to another.

Before I banked it, Miriam photocopied the cheque in silence, clipped it neatly to the file, and wrote a short, firm note about supporting documentation. She didn't remark on the amount, but I caught a shift in her posture, a recalibration. It wasn't only that it was a large sum, it was the solidity of it and the signal it sent — one of commitment. And so, the process began.

*

One afternoon, late in June, Lukas made an unannounced appearance in Broome. I hadn't seen him since Auckland.

Claire had flown back to the UK, their parting amicable, and Lukas now travelled alone. He'd sold the car they'd shared in New Zealand, returned to Australia and was living out of a bright green Ford Falcon panel van, its long body dust-streaked and sun-bleached, the type of vehicle that made its own introduction wherever it parked.

He was much the same, lean, tanned, with that easy, sideways grin. His clothes were lighter, looser, and he looked more lived-in than before, as if the road had worn him in rather than worn him down. His family were industrialists from the Ruhr Valley, and he had the air of wealth that seemed to hover around him, like a scent he never mentioned. But it was Lukas's curiosity that set him apart. He cared deeply about materials, about form and function, particularly glass. Its transparency, its strength, the way it captured and bent light.

Without revealing who Josef was, I told him about The Stopover and the plans we were shaping, especially the use of internal windows and open spaces. For Lukas, something clicked into place, and it was he who first suggested we go further and reimagine the internal structure so that nearly every wall was glass. He talked about light as if it were a guest we ought to invite in, not keep out. He imagined a building that would look, from the outside, modest despite its size, and familiar, its verandas facing the street like any other house in town. But once inside, it would unfold like a secret, the architecture airy, modern, glowing with natural light.

Lukas stayed on, becoming part of the build and the fabric of my days. Over time, he became more than a friend, he was an ally, a sounding board, someone whose presence lent clarity when the decisions grew dense in the uncharted territory of house design.

Years later, he would go on to become one of the best-known glass designers in Europe. But when I think of him, it's still in those early days of dusty boots and sun-glinted mornings, his van parked under a flame tree, the two of us shaping something out of light and ambition, neither of us quite knowing what it would come to mean.

*

In early July, the bridging visa came through, and a week later the exchange and completion date on the chemist shop arrived. At that stage, Lukas was still unaware of Josef's identity, and he went off travelling into the Kimberley while I drove south with purposeful urgency, eating up the long stretch of road between here and there in record time.

The building on Oxford Street still held the stories of other people's lives. It had been Mo and Belinda's home, their livelihood, the place Josef had come to inhabit in their absence. I moved through the rooms carefully, the way you might through a museum after hours, aware of echoes. There wasn't much to pack, but what remained mattered. Josef had asked that I box everything, even the smallest items. He wanted Mo's cameras, the remains of his darkroom equipment, and a few key pieces of furniture sent up to Broome, most notably the old Formica kitchen table, its surface worn to a soft patina by time and tea mugs. The rest I was to give away where I could. I discarded anything broken or beyond use. The removal company came and went with instructions to deliver to the house in Darnley Street.

When the removals were completed, I allowed myself time to look forward. I walked the city with a list in my back pocket —

architects, timber yards, builders' merchants. I sat for hours in Perth city library, flipping through back issues of *Architecture Australia*, marking pages with pieces of paper torn from a notebook. I took out a subscription and arranged for it to be sent to Broome. I was searching for ideas, materials, and names. I wanted to learn from lines and elevations, to gather up all I could before heading north again.

When I returned to Broome, Lukas had already made it back before me. The car rolled into Darnley Street, dust rising behind me, and there it was, the house waiting, the shape of things beginning to settle into place. Inside the sitting room had transformed. Everything from Perth had been delivered and left in careful, crowded piles, boxes marked in my handwriting, the Formica table propped on its side, a curled rug resting against the wall. It wasn't so much chaos as a welcome clutter that was temporary and full of promise. Lukas had opened the shutters and light was pouring in, catching the edges of old photo frames and the dusty glass of Mo's enlarger.

*

The following day I introduced Lukas to Josef.

The road north was as rough as ever and Lukas sat quietly beside me, sensing the shift in the atmosphere the closer we got to the camp. He hadn't asked questions. He listened when I'd explained what Josef's exile meant to him, and what the meeting would require of both of us.

I'd had to delicately introduce the idea of introducing Lukas to Josef; I took time in explaining who he was and how his ideas had taken root in the sketches of The Stopover, and how his way of seeing space might align with ours. But even then, it wasn't something Josef agreed to lightly. He granted permission, not with enthusiasm, but a dignified resolve, a small step back into the outside world. His exit from the camp would come eventually of course, but it needed to be done at Josef's pace and only when he was ready.

We arrived just after midday. The sun was high and flat, the air humming with the stillness that only happens far from everything else. Josef didn't rise to greet us, he was seated beneath some shade in his usual canvas chair, the coastline stretching silently behind him.

He smiled as I introduced Lukas, and I stepped back. They spoke only briefly, measured words, a few glances exchanged, the air between them taut but not unfriendly. Lukas, to his credit, didn't press. He offered the bare shape of our design conversations, the idea of light moving through glass walls, of a house that held openness within the structure. Josef listened, hands resting on his knees, eyes steady on the horizon behind Lukas as though testing whether the voice matched the man. He didn't offer praise or criticism. We didn't need words to be understood.

Lukas was permitted and our circle had widened.

We stayed only that night, cooking simply, the three of us eating in a triangle by the fire. No stories or reminiscing, only the sounds of the cove, the occasional call of a bird, and the distant wash of tide. In the morning, Lukas and I packed the car and turned south again. Josef stood at the edge of the trees as we left, his figure held still against a rising heat.

*

A few days later Lukas and I flew to Perth with all our sketches rolled up and placed in the overhead locker. Alongside them, a notebook swollen with ideas: photographs of the Darnley Street lot, torn pages from old architecture magazines, scribbled lines from our conversations. The kind that began with a tentative *What if...* and ended with Josef and I staring into the dark as if the shape of the house might reveal itself between the stars.

Perth was cool and draped in rain when we arrived and Lukas and I checked into a budget hotel just outside the CBD, where the carpet held onto damp and the lights buzzed faintly even when switched off. We spent the first two days in a hired Holden, navigating the city's grid, meeting with architects we hoped might understand what we were trying to build — people who thought in heat maps and airflow, who listened when we spoke about silence, and verandas that wrapped inwards. We told them what we were working toward: a house that breathed. A place that would be alive, open to the sky, shaped by the wind, where light could pour through glass without losing its softness.

Lukas focused his attention on the specifics of the glass we needed for the internal structure, partitions and walls that would reflect and carry light through the whole house. They wouldn't just be windows, but architectural elements in themselves. That became our real task: to find someone who could create the bespoke pieces. It quickly became clear we wouldn't find what we needed in Perth and that Sydney or Melbourne would likely be where that part of the build would take shape.

Some of the architects listened. Fewer understood. We left behind photocopies of our sketches, a photo of the site at sunset and pages of notes about the land, its weather, and its shifting light.

Before leaving, Lukas and I met again with an architect who seemed to understand us best. We handed over the site survey, notes on orientation and weather, and Josef's annotated floor plans. We asked her to imagine a place where people might live simply and without apology. A house that held the horizon and opened itself to the wind. Shade, eaves, and a central courtyard that breathed like a lung. We agreed on a fee and commissioned some initial drawings, and she said she'd be in touch within a month.

On the flight back to Broome, I watched the land unfurl below — ochre flats, salt pans, and mangroves tracing out their slow stories into the sea. I thought about what it meant to build something that might outlast us, something rooted and not just practical.

*

By Christmas 1988, my permanent residency had come through, and I had flown back to Jedburgh for the first time in over three years. Seeing Maggie again after so long was strange and familiar all at once. In being there, I felt the shift in myself and a certainty that my life had moved elsewhere. Broome was home now; the project, the people, the light, all of it had taken root in me.

I packed a crate to ship back to Australia, carefully chosen items I didn't want to leave behind: my saxophone, guitars and violin, a selection of books that were important to me, family photographs and a few other valued possessions. Maggie helped me wrap and label each item. She agreed to come out to Broome once the house was finished, a promise I held onto tightly. I told her we'd have a celebration, that she'd meet everyone who had helped bring The Stopover to life, and about Josef, at least the parts that could be told, his skill, his presence and the deep connection we'd formed.

But I didn't mention how and why he found me on the highway south of Broome. There was no need. It didn't belong to the story I wanted her to see, not because it was shameful, but because what mattered now was everything that had come after.

The making of The Stopover was a story in itself — a journey that unfolded over two intense and devoted years. Every decision had been deliberate, each material and detail argued, imagined, and refined. Lukas and I had worked closely with the architect in Perth, blending her ideas into a vision that was both deeply personal and utterly original.

It was Lukas who insisted on the masterful use of glass within the internal walls, tall glass panels, translucent screens, and hidden clerestories — creating a subtle interplay of light and shadow throughout the day. His skill allowed the house to breathe with natural light, to feel at once enclosed and endlessly open. The structure rose slowly from the ground, shaped by many hands, built with a devotion that honoured its purpose: not merely to shelter, but to inspire and heal.

The first steps to develop The Stopover took shape during the sodden months at the end of 1988 when the wet season hemmed us in, and we were left with nothing to do but plan. Most evenings, Lukas and I would sit together, thick notebooks open between us, listening to thunder roll over the mangroves while we debated proportions and possibilities.

We knew timing would be everything. The wet season was for the planning and preparation; the real work, the heavy lifting, the laying of foundations, and the raising of walls would need to be perfectly timed with the coming dry season of 1989. We had one shot to get it right. Miss it, and we risked being stalled for another year or more.

The first act was demolition. In the early weeks of 1989 after I had returned from my short visit home, under rain-heavy skies, we stripped the old place back to its bones. Every scrap of usable timber was salvaged, sorted, and stacked under tarpaulins; whatever couldn't be saved was broken down or burned. As we made way for what could be, it felt like a ritual, a way of honouring what had been.

Life during the build was rough and makeshift. We bought two sturdy caravans and parked them side by side beneath the biggest old eucalyptus, rigging up outdoor kitchens, and showers fed by rainwater tanks, and cramming our belongings, tools, and salvaged materials into a trio of shipping containers. Days were long, muddy, and loud with insects. The heat and exhaustion wore us thin, but we kept pulling together.

We weren't alone for long. Miriam, who had a skill in bringing people together, introduced us to Marguerite, a sharp-eyed, well-organised project manager in her early forties. She had a way of cutting through problems like a surgeon slicing cleanly to the heart of things. Very quickly, she sorted out the chaos, drawing up schedules, sourcing materials, negotiating with contractors, and keeping the flood of decisions from drowning us. She also had a gift for handling mine and Lukas's perfectionism, and her bawdy humour made fast friends of the two of us.

Under Marguerite's fierce guidance, we assembled a team that could turn our visions into reality. Local builders, used to the demands of the Top End climate, took on the groundwork and structure. For the finer details, the hand-built timber screens, the intricate glasswork, the stone showers and courtyards, we brought in craftspeople from Perth, Adelaide, and even Melbourne. The house became a magnet for masters: a stonemason who could lay a path as if it had grown there; a joiner who could coax curves from jarrah and blackbutt; a glazier who understood Lukas's obsession with bending light.

The logistics were staggering. Flights, materials, accommodation, and every moving part had to align or risk throwing the schedule off. Yet somehow, under Marguerite's steady hand and Lukas's and my relentless attention to detail, we kept the machine moving.

And through it all, Josef remained a constant force in the background. It seemed he had bottomless reserves of money beyond the proceeds from the sale of the Leederville property, enough to absorb the costs without ever showing strain. At his insistence, we didn't have to compromise. We chose the best materials, paid fair wages, and allowed ourselves to dream as boldly as we dared.

As the dry season of 1989 stretched into its full, blazing brilliance, the skeleton of the new house began to rise. Slabs were poured and frames climbed into the sky. The vastness of the courtyard we'd imagined became a real, walkable space.

In April 1990, the glass walls arrived from Sydney. By then, we were deep into the guts of the build, the phase where everything felt precarious, so much already achieved, but much that could still go wrong.

The design and manufacture of the glass had been a long, complicated labour. Lukas had designed it together with our architect, and once they signed off, the panels were custom manufactured in a specialist factory tucked away near Sydney's Airport in Mascot. Lukas had insisted on a level of precision that most people would have shrugged off as impossible and he flew to Sydney a few times to liaise with the manufacturers. When ordering glass pieces at that scale, they were irreplaceable if damaged and the real terror wasn't the making, it was the transport.

One enormous rig, loaded with our future walls carved through thousands of kilometres across the continent to reach us. We were all holding our breath until that truck rolled in. And when it did, just after dawn, the whole camp shifted. Marguerite called an impromptu site meeting, running through the unloading procedure like a battlefield general. We'd hired a specialist crane operator from Darwin, and even he looked rattled when he saw the rig inching its way down Darnley Street, straining under the precious, precarious cargo.

The unloading was a choreography that was slow, exacting and terrifying. Each panel was eased off the truck, slung with padded straps, and lifted one by one onto padded frames we'd built ourselves to cradle them. Nobody spoke unless necessary and Lukas stood out of the way, arms crossed, face set like stone, barely blinking as he tracked every movement. It took most of the day, but by late afternoon, the panels were all safely stowed, each one intact, gleaming faintly under the last of the sun. Only then did Lukas relax, sagging onto a stack of timber offcuts with a grunt that might have been a laugh, or a prayer.

That night, we lit a fire and opened a very good bottle of whisky we'd been saving. We sat around the flames, exhausted and giddy with relief, talking about what came next.

*

When I reflect on how The Stopover was built, I know one thing for certain: it couldn't have happened without Marguerite.

She was solid and strong; her presence would fill the room before she even said a word. She had broad shoulders and hands that bore the calluses of a woman who was unafraid of hard work. Her skin was a rich, sun-warmed bronze, and her thick black hair was worn tied back in a no-nonsense plait or messy bun. Her eyes were sharp, dark, and quick to narrow when something, or someone, displeased her. In her work boots, shorts and a battered wide-brimmed hat shoved on her head with sunglasses perpetually perched atop it, she was the force that kept it all moving; the schedules, the money, the stubborn builders who thought they knew better.

Josef and I had the vision, but Marguerite turned it into reality. She didn't only manage the project; she owned it, and no one dared argue for long. She was always in a type of calm and efficient control, except if provoked when she became fierce and foul-mouthed. No one, not even the most hardened builder dared cross her twice. She had an instinct for reading people, sensing bullshit before a word was spoken.

Yet beneath the bark and bite was a woman with a deep, unwavering loyalty to those she respected. Once in Marguerite's good books, she would fight for you harder than anyone. She laughed loudly, swore with joyful invention, and had a wicked, sometimes scandalous sense of humour.

I loved Marguerite and despite her tough exterior, she was not closed off emotionally, she made it very clear that she chose when and how to be vulnerable. Her sharp tongue made her formidable and there was a toughness in her that was shaped by where she came from. Broome's history ran in her blood, and she carried it with her, a weight you could feel the moment she walked into a room.

Her great-grandfather had arrived from Japan in 1898, barely more than a boy himself, drawn by the glittering promise of pearl shell fortunes. What he found instead was a brutal, exploitative industry built on the backs of the young and expendable. He toiled on the decks in blistering heat, hauling tangled lines slick with salt and blood, breathing the sharp tang of brine and sweat until his lungs gave out.

Pearling made Broome rich, but never the divers. Aboriginal men were forced into service, and it was the young Japanese and Malay boys who were sent to the depths again and again, barely trained, often underage, wearing heavy lead-weighted canvas suits that pressed down on their small frames. If they surfaced too fast, they were bent double in agony, crippled or killed by the bends, their bodies twisted by nitrogen bubbles bursting in their veins. Others drowned or were pulled up lifeless by tangled lines. Some simply disappeared. The sea took them without ceremony, and the industry marched on, indifferent to the toll.

Her great-grandfather survived. He married a Yawuru woman whose ancestors had fished these waters for thousands of years. Their daughter, Marguerite's grandmother, grew up between worlds, speaking three languages, belonging fully to none of them.

On 3 March 1942, Broome was bombed by Japanese fighter planes. The town was shredded in a few terrifying minutes; flying boats burned in Roebuck Bay, and some Dutch refugees died in the surf. Marguerite's family lost cousins, friends, and neighbours. Her mother was still a child when she learned that death could fall from the sky without warning.

After the war, the Japanese community, once a part of Broome's lifeblood, was erased or scattered. Marguerite's mother came of age in a town trying to forget its past, raising her daughter with stories that carried both grief and pride. Marguerite's father, a French surveyor who passed briefly through Broome in the late 1940s, was gone soon after she was born. She never knew him. He left no mark but a surname and sharp cheekbones. His absence became part of her inheritance too, and one more burden she had to learn to carry.

Marguerite grew up hearing the stories no one else wanted to tell; of brothers lost at sea, homes burned, promises broken. She came from the in-between, from ocean and desert, from bloodlines that didn't always sit comfortably beside each other, and she learned early that survival meant never forgetting where you came from and never letting anyone else forget either.

She brought skills and leadership to our project, and an energetic defiance. When Marguerite stood on a building site shouting orders, boots in the dirt, she carried a hundred years of survival with her. And somehow, she wove that fierce, stubborn spirit into the bones of the house we built.

*

Our imagining of The Stopover had been a powerful process for Josef. I could see it in him each time I went north, which had become increasingly frequent at the start of the building project. I would bring sketches of the house, lists of materials, and small choices that needed his blessing. It mattered to him to be involved, and it mattered to me that, despite his absence, he felt the project was truly his.

We kept up our late afternoon ritual, steadily working through his photographs. By early 1989, we had covered his entire archive, and the slow process of healing felt almost complete. I was certain it wouldn't be long before he thought about leaving the camp and returning to Broome.

Even so, it took longer than I expected. It wasn't until one morning in August that everything shifted.

I was on Darnley Street, where the frame of the house already stood. Builders were moving around me in dust-covered boots, and the air was filled with the rhythmic thud of hammers and the whine of saws when I noticed two men standing awkwardly on the red dirt path wearing impossibly clean shoes and neatly pressed clothes that didn't belong to the worksite.

They walked toward me, and I knew before they spoke that they'd come a long way. In their New York accents, they asked for me by name, but it was Josef they were really looking for.

I tried to send them on their way and told them there was no one here by that name, but they were prepared. Deeds, planning applications, they had evidence that tied Josef to the house, to this life he had tried so hard to stay hidden from. They said the story had gone global and that they weren't leaving Broome without speaking to him, or rather their editors had told them they were not leaving Broome before speaking to him. One was a tabloid journalist, the other broadsheet, and they both worked for the same proprietor. I watched them walk back down the path, the dust catching at their heels, and felt a terrible knot tighten in my chest.

That afternoon, I made the four-hour drive north. The sun had dropped low as I reached the camp, the sky bruised and heavy with the coming dusk. I found Josef by the fireside, his silhouette bent over the embers and explained everything; the journalists, the evidence, the way the world had somehow found him again.

He sat silently for a moment and smiled and looked around the camp, at the trees, and the ashes in the fire, and said, simply, that it was time. He had been there long enough, and he would leave with me.

I barely slept that night, and in the morning, we set to work taking the camp apart piece by piece, folding, packing and lifting with a great deal of care. Every scrap was cleared, every ash buried. The remaining fire logs were loaded into the two Land Cruisers. By early afternoon, the area where the camp had been looked untouched as if we had never been there at all.

As we reached the community, the old baob stood where it always had, and Albert Warrun was sitting silently beneath its shade. We parked and as we greeted him Josef smiled — a wide, beautiful smile — and without too many words, we gave our thanks. Albert Warrun stood slowly, looking at us both with solemnity. His voice was low and steady when he spoke, the words settling deep into the earth between us.

"You have been part of this place now. You leave with its spirit in you. When your house is ready, I will visit."

He placed a hand briefly over his heart and turned back to his tree.

We stood for a long moment before climbing into our cars and driving south.

*

In Broome, we went straight to the Roebuck Bay Hotel where Josef booked a room without hesitation, moving into the saloon bar with a certainty that felt entirely new. It was as though the decision to face the world had already taken root inside him, and now he was simply following its pull.

Not long after, we found the journalists and arranged a meeting. Before we met with them, Josef asked if it would be all right to involve me in the telling of his story, the years he had spent away, and the part I had played. I nodded without hesitation.

That evening, we sat together at a table in the quietest corner of the bar we could find.

For over an hour, the journalists asked their questions. Josef answered them openly, without defensiveness or apology. It was as if he had decided that, if he was to step back into the world, he would do so without hiding any part of himself.

They asked, cautiously, if he would ever take photographs professionally again.

Josef offered a smile and said he would very much like to begin again, by photographing the people who came to Broome. And then he added, almost as an afterthought, that he would like to start with them, the two journalists. That they would be his first subjects, tomorrow if they were willing. For a moment, the table was silent, and a wonder passed between them, an understanding that they had been offered something rare.

The story of Josef's disappearance; his return; of Theo and Harry; the camp; and The Stopover, was syndicated worldwide within weeks. It captured the imagination of people everywhere, a story they hadn't even realised they were longing for. Josef had been careful not to name the Aboriginal community that had sheltered him, or to reveal the location of the camp.

In the years after we moved into The Stopover, people came to Broome to see him, at first those already travelling through Australia, young and old alike, and then slowly, they came from all over the world for the chance to visit this extraordinary house and to sit before Josef's lens. Celebrities, movie stars, travellers, and ordinary people, all came to be seen by him.

That night at the Roey, we had no idea what was about to unfold. We only knew that something had shifted.

The long silence Josef had lived inside was giving way to something entirely new. His re-emergence marked a new way of seeing. He no longer recorded endings, instead he began to capture warm connections and bright beginnings.

*

The following morning arrived clean and bright, the air still holding its coolness before the sun climbed high. I was already on site when Josef walked up Darnley Street, his silhouette clear against the pale sky. He wore a loose shirt, tucked neatly, his sleeves pushed back, and his step had something steady in it.

He paused near the boundary of the lot, eyes scanning the frame of the house, the movement of the builders, the rising dust and stepped forward to see our project for the very first time. The change I noticed in him was immediate and extraordinary, his shoulders were back, his gaze lifted, and there was something very alive in his face.

I brought him over to where Marguerite was checking the cut timber beside the front corner post. She looked up and, with barely a pause, shook his hand and launched straight into showing him what was happening without any ceremony or small talk.

She walked him through what had been done, the posts and bearers, the roofline, the way the floors would be laid, pointing as she spoke with her other hand resting on her hip. She told him which materials had come late, which ones had been better than expected, how the Broome blokes were good, but the Darwin joiners were slower than promised. She showed him where the tank stand would go, where the electrics would run in, and what still needed ordering.

Josef followed beside her, listening carefully, asking the odd question, practical, respectful things, and I hung back a few paces, watching. It was a beautiful scene. This man, who had vanished into the bush like a shadow, was now walking among hammers and scaffolds and voices, nodding, taking it all in with focused intent. He didn't pretend to understand it all, he let Marguerite lead, but there was no distance in him, no trace of retreat.

Once Marguerite had walked him through every corner of the lot, she gave a short nod and went off to chase a delivery that hadn't arrived. The sound of drills and banter filled the air again, but Josef stayed where he was, standing near the back corner of the building site where the frame caught the sun.

I walked over and stood beside him. For a while, neither of us said anything. His eyes moved slowly across the skeleton of the rooms, resting on thresholds, on timber lines that hinted at walls and windows yet to come.

"It's good," he said eventually. "You've done well."

I didn't answer straight away. I looked at him, at the ease in his posture, the way his hands rested lightly in his pockets. He wasn't holding himself together anymore, he simply was. I hugged him. A long lingering warm embrace.

He walked off down the street, back toward the hotel, the sunlight catching in the creases of his shirt as he went.

*

The way Josef had changed was not in the superficial sense, not a reinvention or a new persona, but something deeper and more fundamental.

When we first met, he was closed off. Not unfriendly, just unreachable. Decades of running had made him hard to access, even to himself.

By the time we entered the camp together, he was carrying the full weight of a life he'd never really stopped to examine, the chaos of his early years in Poland, the escape, and the thirty-five years spent on the frontlines of other people's wars and suffering. Always moving, always documenting.

And when his dog was shot, something in him broke and he stopped. It wasn't the countless atrocities he'd witnessed that brought him to a halt, but something far more personal.

In the stillness that followed, he faced it all, not with therapy, medication, or distraction, but with time, solitude, and a brutal honesty. He walked back through the darkness without losing himself in it, and without narrating the process. But I could see it unfold each time I visited, the slow, steady peeling back of layer after layer, like the finest skins of an onion.

Even though I was there with him, his transformation still carried a mythic quality. It was as if he'd stumbled, almost unknowingly, into a hero's journey. There was no single turning point, only relentless, quiet inner work.

To sit with that much pain, over that many years, and not flinch, or attempt to escape, is something I still struggle to comprehend; how he returned, again and again, to look at those photographs, those moments of suffering he'd captured, and not look away. But he did it, bit by bit, he stripped everything back and somewhere in that long, private excavation, something shifted.

He had emerged unrecognisable from how he was in the camp. When I watched him walk away from The Stopover back to the Roebuck that morning, he was a completely different man, open in a way I could never have imagined. Kind, curious and light, he listened, he laughed and there was joy in him.

And that's what stays with me, even now that he's gone from our lives. Not only that he survived, but that he came out the other side with his heart intact. No bitterness, no bravado, but a 59-year-old man starting over, fully, and on his own terms.

*

I wanted to see what came of the photo shoot.

I wanted to see what came of the photo shoot so a little later that morning I left the building site and drove to join Josef for his appointment with the journalists outside the Roebuck.

When I pulled up, he'd already chosen the spot against a faded timber wall out front, shaded just enough to keep the glare off their faces. He spoke gently, asking about their families, their journeys to Broome, what they'd thought when they first heard rumours that Josef Batten was alive and well, which he said with an ironic smile.

At first, they were guarded, still wearing their professional postures: arms folded, stance squared, eyes sharp, but Josef kept talking. Not at them, but with them. He listened and laughed, and without fanfare, he stepped back and raised the camera.

"Stay like that," he said gently.

He didn't direct them in the usual sense. Instead, he moved around them, pausing to ask another question, capturing whatever shifted in their expressions when they answered. When he lowered the camera, the men didn't leave right away. They lingered, a little dazed, like they'd surfaced from a dark room and weren't quite ready for the light.

This was how Josef began his new life as a photographer of people and presence. And he was a natural at it. He wasted no time settling into the role and for a whole year, he lived in a modest boxy room at the Roebuck Bay Hotel and became a familiar presence, in the bar, on the benches out front, at Carla's café, and of course, at the build of The Stopover.

His quiet charm won over just about everyone. He'd sit in the bar most evenings, chatting with whoever happened to be nearby, nursing his regular Angostura Bitters and soda.

He photographed nearly everyone he spoke to. Often outside, in the soft late light, sometimes inside the Roebuck. Now and then, if the mood felt right, he'd drive them down to Cable Beach and catch them there, unposed, at ease, lit by the sea and sky.

Each morning, he walked the short distance down to The Stopover site, always early, before the heat set in. Throughout the build, he managed to photograph all the workers, from the engineers to the boys on clean-up duty — even Marguerite, eventually. The photograph of her half-smiling, windblown, a pencil tucked behind one ear, standing barefoot in the half-framed kitchen became a classic.

By mid-1990, it was hard to find anyone in Broome, resident or traveller, who hadn't been photographed by Josef Batten. He bought his film stock by mail order mostly from Camera Electronic in Perth — Kodak Tri-X Pan for its grain and tonal range, and Agfa for its richer blacks. For prints, he preferred Agfa Record-Rapid paper, a warm-tone, fibre-based paper with deep velvety blacks and a subtle sepia warmth that suited his new way of seeing people: earthy, honest and timeless.

He had the negatives developed and printed at Atkins Photo Lab in Adelaide. Every few weeks, he'd receive contact sheets in the post. He'd sit by the window of his room at the Roebuck, poring over the tiny images with a loupe, circling frames and making notes with his chinagraph pencil. Then he'd post his selections back to them, and a week or so later, a heavy box of 11x14s would arrive, the smell of darkroom chemicals still on the tissue-wrapped prints.

In July 1990, an exhibition of his Broome portraits was hung at the Broome Civic Centre, a simple, white-walled space in the heart of town. The opening night drew a crowd: locals, tourists, journalists, even a few who'd come up from Perth. There was laughter and pointing and curious contemplation. The people of Broome were moved, not only by the work, but by how Josef had seen them. He had made them visible to each other.

The weekend after the opening, *The West Australian* ran a feature on the exhibition. The headline read: *"From War Zones to the Heart of Broome: Josef Batten's New Lens"*. It included a large photograph of Josef standing in front of the exhibition wall, surrounded by his portraits of the faces of Broome: weathered, laughing, sunlit, unguarded.

The article told a condensed version of his story, enough to feed the legend that was already forming around him. The war zones, the disappearance, the reappearance, and now, his reinvention. It was respectful, if a little breathless. But what mattered most was that Broome saw itself in print, its people and its life, reflected on them with dignity and depth.

That morning, copies of the paper were passed around at Carla's Café, read out loud on the benches outside the Roebuck, and pinned to the wall behind the bar. Josef had become a local celebrity — not in a loud or performative way, but with the affectionate curiosity people reserve for someone who's both mysterious and familiar.

The exhibition stirred more than local interest. Within days, the story spread beyond Broome. *The West Australian* had already run its feature, but then ABC Radio Perth called, wanting an interview for their morning programme. Then *Today Tonight*, Channel Seven's magazine show in Perth, sent up a producer to see if they could film a segment.

Josef agreed to a few of these early interviews, cautiously. He appeared on ABC Radio, his voice quiet, and measured, with long pauses between thoughts. On television, he stood out, lean, grey-haired, eyes clear, speaking gently about the power of bearing witness and why he had turned his camera away from conflict to focus on people simply as they are.

The segment aired on *Today Tonight* the following week. It showed footage from the exhibition, clips of Josef walking through Broome, talking with locals, and taking photographs. The response was immediate. Letters arrived at the Civic Centre. Tourists began asking for him by name. The myth, that he had disappeared and reemerged in Broome, only added to the fascination. Josef Batten became, almost despite himself, a sought-after figure.

For a while, he went along with it and did a few more interviews, including a short feature on ABC's Stateline. But then he began turning them down.

"I've said what I have to say," he told me once. "Everything else is repetition."

*

In June 1990, with the glass walls in place and the interior spaces beginning to breathe with light, the shape of the house was fully realised. We knew then we were on track for completion by the end of August, and with that came the certainty it was time to plan a celebratory opening.

We chose the weekend of 22-23 September, soon after the winter dry would start to soften and before the build-up heat returned. It felt like the right moment, the house would be finished, the courtyard fully planted, and everyone who had been part of it could come together to mark what we'd built.

The preparations began almost immediately. The outer land, still rough from the years of construction had to be cleared of debris and levelled out, piles of timber, scraps of metal, leftover bricks, all of it sorted and moved. We kept the caravans in place and made plans to set up tents and hire a couple of marquees for managing the catering — we wanted it to spill outwards, to draw people in. The bare earth around the house, though not yet planted, would be good ground for pitching, and it seemed right that the celebration would unfold out there.

We made a list of people we wished to attend. Maggie, of course, who would see it all for herself, and Anne Delacourt, who was delighted to be invited and immediately agreed to it. I looked forward to meeting the person who had been instrumental in our lives and whom I had come to know so well over a crackly phone line.

We invited Albert Warrun and his fellow Elders from the community too. Special guests like them would stay in the newly completed guest suites that still smelled of timber and fresh limewash.

The closer we got, the more the anticipation took hold for the moment the place would truly come alive. Marguerite took charge with certainty — she pulled things together as if she'd been waiting for this moment all along. There was no fuss about it, within a day or two, she'd sketched out the shape of it all in her notebook.

The food was never going to be fancy, but it had to be right, generous, and locally produced. There'd be grilled barramundi from Marguerite's cousin's boat, cooked over open flames. Chicken satays with homemade peanut sauce, thanks to Mrs Tan and her daughters. Big pots of beef curry, vegetable laksa, and kangaroo stew with bush tomatoes, promised by Auntie May and her nieces. Pumpkin roasted with wattleseed. Damper baked on coals. Mangoes in everything, mousse, pavlova, Lamingtons of course and watermelon chilled in eskies. Jugs of iced bush tea. Kegs of beer and chilled white wine served in plastic cups.

The town got wind of it, and people started volunteering to help. The Uniting Church ladies offered their kitchen for pre-prepping and serving on the day. The Filipino community promised decorations. Teenagers from the high school signed up to serve the food, and even old Mr Ng arrived one morning with a bundle of bunting and a roll of cable ties, smiling and nodding before prematurely setting to work stringing it between the gum trees.

For the music, Lukas and I put together a set to rehearse and play — nothing elaborate, but honest songs that meant something to us all and that would carry the mood. After we'd done a few practice sessions, we agreed we needed rhythm, someone to tap out a beat on bongos or a small drum kit.

It was Marguerite who found him for us. "You need rhythm?" she said, "Then you need Kai."

She took me to meet him in a rusted shack near the mangroves. He was sitting cross-legged in the dust, shirtless, tapping out something hypnotic on a pair of old bongos. Skin like ochre clay, hair tied back with fishing twine, eyes half-closed like he was dreaming in syncopation.

"Adam," Marguerite said. "Meet my second cousin."

Kai grinned. "That's Broome for you."

His bongo playing aside, Kai Fernando was a muted presence in Broome. At twenty-three, his skin was weathered by the harsh sun, the colour of red earth after rain. His dark hair, usually tied back, was untamed, he had gold-flecked half-closed eyes, and he always seemed to be listening to something below the surface.

Raised by his Yawuru mother from Lombadina and his Portuguese-Irish father, Kai's mixed heritage had made him feel out of place at times. Broome was a town where cultures collided, and people like him often slipped through the cracks. But Kai wasn't one to talk about it. He was a natural when it came to music — and he played with an ease that suggested he'd never needed to learn. The rhythms were inside him, as natural as breathing.

The guest list needed careful thought. We couldn't invite the whole of Broome, so we drew the line where it mattered, everyone who had worked on the build, and those contributing to the catering and decorations. Volunteers, tradespeople and supporters, those who gave time, equipment, and advice. We started drawing up names, adding them as they surfaced in memory.

By late July it was more than a party we were planning, it was a festival of joy and a celebration of community.

15. Secret O' Life

By the beginning of August 1990, as the jacarandas began to haze the streets in violet, the house was finished. We emptied the caravans and unpacked the containers. The hand-built furniture started arriving, piece by piece, and found its places and the gardens were planted and water features installed. It had been conjured from mud and dreams and now it stood radiantly holding its breath, waiting for the lives that were about to unfold within its walls.

The Stopover on Darnley Street had become something far more than simply a place to live, it was a world of its own, tucked behind a façade of tradition. From the street, it looked like an enormous, single-storey Australian homestead, with wide verandas wrapped protectively around every side. The timber cladding in jarrah, blackbutt and spotted gum gave the house soul, a sense of history; but its exterior gave no hint of the life it held inside.

Crossing the threshold was like stepping into another reality. Behind the front door, the house opened into a large welcoming hallway that in turn led into a vast light-filled courtyard garden, twenty metres wide, thirty-six metres in length, enclosed completely by the building itself. Running around the inner sanctum of the courtyard, Lukas had designed a continuous wall of folding glass, panel after panel, so that from almost anywhere inside, you could look out into the courtyard garden. Only the storerooms, the laundry, and a few service spaces broke that ring of transparency, kept private by solid walls. Elsewhere, discreet timber screens gave enough privacy where it was needed without stealing the light.

A wide, shaded veranda traced the entire inner perimeter at three metres deep, creating a cool, generous walkway where stone pots planted with soft grasses and delicate maples sat beside low chairs and benches; sculptures in stone and iron caught the changing light; small, beautiful artworks invited you to pause and notice. It was a place that slowed you down before you even realised.

At the heart of the courtyard, set on a broad wooden platform, was the communal kitchen and dining space, open to the sky, roofed only by a delicate lattice of slatted timber that softened the harshness of the sun. Everything about it encouraged slow movement, conversation, and reflection. This was the space for our evenings and celebrations.

In the middle of the communal platform, right at the heart of the courtyard garden, stood a hand-crafted outdoor chess set, sturdy and weatherproof, made from ironbark and jarrah, its pieces were weighty and sculptural. Josef and I had commissioned it during the early days of the build, imagining it as both a focal point and a meeting place. We played often, sometimes in long stretches that lasted the better part of a day.

The house exuded peaceful influences from Japanese design — deep low eaves, sliding timber shutters, and garden views from every angle. The materials were simple but carefully chosen western red cedar beams, hand-polished blackbutt and spotted gum floors, and recycled teak in the furniture and details. They were chosen for their beauty and strength and for how they would age, the way time would add to the house rather than take anything away.

Although the house's footprint was almost perfectly rectangular, it never felt strict. There were no long corridors or harsh divisions, but a series of natural transitions, spaces flowing gently one into the next.

At the eastern end was Josef's domain. His studio rose high under a vaulted ceiling, lit by clerestory windows and hidden skylights that shifted with the day. The tall glass-panelled wall was concertinaed so the studio could be entirely open to the veranda, allowing him to move seamlessly between inside and out. Hidden behind a discreet door at one end was his darkroom, and within that was a secret door to a light, airy room where he kept the story of his life: negatives, prints, notebooks, letters. This was Josef's private sanctuary where he could retreat from visitors when the mood took him.

His most prized possessions were the legacy of Mo Batten's life and craft, his vintage large format cameras and darkroom equipment, including the enlarger he had generously taught the young Josef to print with.

They were carefully preserved and using them connected him to Mo with each click of the shutter and every print that emerged from the developing trays. He didn't spend a great deal of time printing himself, but when he did it was for the pure joy of it. He would often listen to Mozart's piano concertos in the darkroom as he worked.

Tucked into a purpose-built space on the far wall of his studio stood a hand-crafted wooden cot on silent wheels, allowing him to sleep wherever the mood took him, under the soaring beams, beneath the veranda's shelter, or out in the open courtyard under the stars. We would often find Josef asleep in his bed, hidden in an area of the courtyard where he could lie under the night sky.

His studio was no cold workspace; it was a living place, filled with a small kitchen, well-worn chairs, sturdy tables, and shelves full of books. It was a private world of creation and retreat, echoing the spirit of Mo and the profound artistry of photography.

At the western end, I shaped a simpler space. My rooms were minimal, designed to house the few rare art pieces I had collected and those I intended to collect in time, with space so each could have room to breathe. Like Josef, I had my own kitchen, bathroom, and private storage, but the spirit of my side was different, a place pared back to the essentials.

Running between us and on either edge of the house were seven guest suites, each unique in size and theme, four to the north and three together with the entrance hall to the south, all crafted with the same careful hand. Every room housed low platform beds in the style of Japanese futons, bespoke pieces made with stone and wood joinery; there were walk-in stone showers with rainwater heads hidden discreetly above, and wide glass fronts shaded by sliding timber screens. Each room opened onto the courtyard and carried the scents of wood, earth, and growing things.

The courtyard was a garden of peace. We planted delicate maples, flowering plums, small pines, and low, mossy groundcovers, creating a soft, shifting tapestry of green. Smooth, slatted timber paths threaded through the islands of planting, designed to shed rain yet remain firm and silent under the wheels of Josef's bed or anything else that needed to move across them. The layout wasn't made for display but for peaceful reflection. Here and there, a stone lantern or a delicate water feature murmured of Japan, but really, the spirit of the place was entirely its own.

The communal entrance hall welcomed guests gently, without grandeur, its walls adorned with small, thoughtful artefacts: a hand-thrown ceramic bowl, a carved wooden bench, and a series of mesmerising works by Marinda Yoolany, a Goolarabooloo artist from the Dampier Peninsula. Her paintings, rendered in delicate monochrome, ochres faded to soft greys, charcoal strokes etched against pale canvas, seemed less like images and more like the echoes of land and time, traced patiently by hand.

Behind the scenes, generous larders and a discreetly hidden laundry kept the workings of the house invisible, leaving only the hush of space and light. We wired the whole building with a discreet hi-fi and speaker system, so if the mood took us music could be heard through the different spaces, not with the intention to play it loudly, though occasionally we did, but only enough to shape the atmosphere, like a shared pulse running underneath the place.

Josef and I had gone back and forth about the idea of putting a grand piano out on the community platform in the courtyard garden. There was something appealing about the image — solid, permanent, unapologetically beautiful. But it didn't take long to realise it was wishful thinking. The humidity alone would ruin it, and come the rainy season, it would be little more than a warped ornament. Instead, we decided an electronic keyboard that would emulate the sound of a grand would be a suitable compromise and something we could easily pack away. We wanted one that felt serious, with weighted keys and a sound that carried gravity.

I called Zenith in Claremont and after discussing the options, we settled on the Roland RD-1000 — nothing extravagant, but powerful enough to let the sound breathe and drift through the courtyard.

When it all arrived, we set it up on the platform and ran power from the nearest block. The first time I played it with a slow, open A minor chord it filled the entire courtyard with a sound that was unexpectedly rich.

Inside, the house was a sanctuary of air, light and silence. Visitors often fell into a hush without realising it. Long before I knew the word wabi-sabi, I understood it there, the sacred beauty of imperfection, of age and nature's passing.

It wasn't a house built to be admired from a distance, but to be lived in, to be felt and inhabited; a place to remember what it meant to be fully alive.

*

In the last days of August, Josef and I moved into our new home. After everything, it felt almost surreal to carry in our possessions and place them down on the beautiful floors for the first time.

Lukas joined us, taking up temporary residence in one of the guest rooms although it was already clear that his time in Broome was coming to a close.

Maggie, my mother, arrived on the first day of September. I met her at the airport, and she was tired from the long flight but standing tall, suitcase in hand. At The Stopover her eyes swept the courtyard garden with awe. She didn't say much at first but mused as if she were matching what she could see with the fragments I'd written about in my letters. The look in her eyes was pride, or maybe relief.

She slipped easily into the daily life of the place. She took on tasks like folding linens, rearranging chairs, and making sure there was enough shade for the guests who'd be arriving. It wasn't until later when she'd walked the garden paths and leaned against the warm veranda rail in the evenings, that I understood how much it all mattered to her. Not the house itself, but the life I'd made inside it — she didn't need to say it.

Marguerite, who for years had met the world with fierce intelligence and a restless, almost combustible drive to make things happen, began to soften too. She couldn't stay away. She lingered longer in the evenings, her sleeves rolled up, her laugh a little easier. There was still her usual dry wit and sharp eye, but a tenderness had emerged. She and Maggie got along as if they were simply picking up a conversation they'd paused years ago. I often found them talking at the edge of the garden beds or bent over the same clipboard discussing seating arrangements like it was a tactical operation, Maggie bringing the love, Marguerite her sense of structure.

Evenings on the communal deck became something we all looked forward to. Lukas played one of my guitars, and I brought out the violin, and we eased into the songs we were practising for the party. One night, we were playing one of Josef's favourites *Comes a Time*, Lukas picking out the chords, me weaving the fiddle line, when Josef began to sing.

It started like a whisper, almost as if he didn't realise he was doing it. His voice was rough, but steady and soulful. Lukas and I kept playing, Maggie sat still, one hand resting against her cheek, and Marguerite smiled and watched. When the song ended, we let the silence stretch out a little longer and Maggie wiped a tear from her eye, hoping no one would notice.

Those were beautiful days, and a feeling was growing between us, not a pretend family thing, but something genuine and earned. We were all so different, drawn together from different corners of the world, and yet here we were, in this isolated little town, eating together, laughing, putting up lights and sharing songs amidst the delicate foliage of the courtyard.

And then there was the thing unfolding between Maggie and Josef which wasn't romantic exactly, but it was charged with something rare. A curiosity and mutual respect that ran deep. They talked more and more as the days went on, often off to one side, sharing a pot of tea, or working side by side. I saw how he looked at her, and I saw her relax around him in a way that was trusting and steady. There was affection there, tenderness even.

Josef asked if he could take her portrait one afternoon, and I watched, heart swelling, as she stepped in front of his lens. She didn't pose, she stood there, comfortable, ready, and he looked at her like she was the most important person in the world. Watching them together, my mother and this man who had once been all shadow, I felt I belonged — we all did.

*

We'd already sent out our invitations and were planning to rely on ourselves — our little trio of Lukas, Kai, and me — for the entertainment at the opening celebration, when late one afternoon, Albert Warrun showed up at The Stopover. It was his first time, and he arrived without warning, as always.

From inside the courtyard, I could hear the low rumble of his V8 and the throaty exhaust of his Falcon. When I got up to see, I found him standing silently at the threshold of the reception hall, backlit by the sky.

"Thought it was time," he said. "Brought someone."

Beside him stood a tall man, slim and long-limbed, wearing a faded shirt and threadbare canvas trousers.

"Liam Karri," he said with a smile. His voice was low and unhurried. "Been meaning to meet Josef."

I warmly welcomed them both and Albert Warrun stepped slowly inside with his walking stick — he always called it *Burru*, the name of a stingray ancestor from his grandfather's stories. He paused in the open reception hall, and, without speaking, moved out into the courtyard with the certainty of someone who walks not to inspect, but to listen.

Liam and I followed as Albert Warrun made his way across the garden and into the communal space before sitting down cross-legged on the wooden floor, placing his hat on his knee. Josef and Maggie were already seated at the long table.

Josef read the moment for what it was and simply said, "Welcome, Albert Warrun."

They smiled, and the three of them nodded without ceremony. The silence that followed held its shape. For a while, Albert Warrun didn't speak but his stillness was never passive — it was presence.

Liam Karri had been away for much of the last few years, working between Beagle Bay, Cape York, and parts of Southeast Asia. He was involved in cultural repatriation, youth mentorship, and sea country protections. He moved easily between boardrooms and bush tracks with the same grounded authority. People listened when he spoke but because he didn't waste words.

A few years younger than Josef, he was both an academic and a fellow Elder, known and respected across the Dampier Peninsula, especially in Beagle Bay and Djarindjin, where his family roots ran deep. His father's country was Bardi–Jawi, and his mother's Nyul Nyul. For years, he'd focused on bringing home old stories and images — films, photographs, recordings — ensuring they returned with context and care.

That's how he first heard about Josef Batten.

Josef had prepared an edited selection of photographs taken when he had first visited the communities on his yearlong assignment and he had presented a portfolio of prints to Albert Warrun's community six months earlier, photographs from 1985, carefully wrapped, names handwritten, Elders consulted.

Liam had heard about this photographer, not through the media, but through stories passed between communities; about a whitefella who had returned and camped rough and offered back what he'd taken. He had been curious, but with so much on his plate, he hadn't made it to Broome until now. When Albert Warrun told him it was time, he came. Not to assess, but to witness who Josef was for himself.

A natural ease quickly developed between them, and later, as we sat to share a meal, Josef raised the topic of how we could honour the surrounding communities during the opening celebration, emphasising the need for something meaningful and rooted, rather than mere tokenism.

Liam didn't answer straight away. He let silence breathe a while and said there was a music group up near Beagle Bay we might want to talk to.

The Djilawurr Band. Mostly Nyul Nyul singers, a few Bardi cousins, and a Torres Strait Islander guitarist who'd married into the community. They'd been playing together for years — for festivals, family gatherings, ceremonies. Their sound, Liam said, wove old songlines into tide rhythms, vocals layered over desert reggae. Deep harmonies in Bardi and Nyul Nyul carried stories of country, storms, loss, and return. It wasn't performance, exactly — more like lived experience, carried in the breath and bones of the players.

Liam didn't press the point. He simply said they might be open to it if approached with care.

We all agreed that if they were willing, they would be part of it and there would be no schedule or centre stage, only a space made for them, extended with respect. It felt right.

With this connection we wanted to generate a sense of purpose for The Stopover; a sense that we weren't beginning something, but that we were entering into something ongoing. And music, more than anything, could hold that truth and carry it forward.

*

Three days before our celebratory weekend, Josef and I took the short trip to Broome airport to collect Anne Delacourt, navigating a rain-soaked and pindan-streaked road, rare for that time of year.

When Anne emerged in the tiny arrivals hall, she exuded a poised elegance, even after such a long series of flights from Paris. Her eyes were sharp and observant as she walked towards us with a confidence that was both intimidating and welcoming.

She greeted Josef warmly, her charming Parisian accent filling the air as she marvelled at how much he had changed over the past four years.

At The Stopover, her reaction was immediate and genuine. Her eyes widened with delight as she took in the house, sweeping the courtyard with amazement. Her approval was validating, confirming our hard work was worthwhile and her genuine impression filled me with unexpected pride and accomplishment.

Over the following few days, she immersed herself in discussions with Josef about his new career as a portrait photographer. She was meticulous in her questions about his past work's ethical implications and the legacy he would leave behind. Josef was entirely at ease talking to her and discussing business in a way I hadn't witnessed before.

Anne brought up the matter of the planned book *Australia: The Witnessing Eye* that had been a dormant prospect since Josef's disappearance. The original publishers were still eager, but now there were additional parties interested due to Josef's re-booted fame and notoriety. It was evident that Anne needed Josef to decide on the publisher and the timing of its release, but despite the growing pressure, Josef remained steadfast in his refusal to embark on a book tour. He was adamant about not leaving Broome, so any contract agreed upon could not include a tour. His determination to stay there was unwavering, a fact that both frustrated and impressed Anne.

Throughout these discussions, I observed Anne's ability to navigate complex negotiations with grace and determination. Her presence brought a new energy to The Stopover — a sense that what we had built was not a sanctuary but a place of significance that reached far beyond its physical boundaries.

Anne's visit left me reflecting on the power of Josef's work and the importance of preserving its integrity amidst external pressures. Her belief in what we had created bolstered my resolve to protect it fiercely.

*

The morning of the celebration dawned calmly, the air still holding a crispness that promised a warm day ahead.

People began appearing outside the house soon after 8am, bringing with them pre-prepared food. The atmosphere came alive with the sounds of laughter and chatter as they set up bain-maries to keep their dishes warm in the marquees.

The Djilawurr Band arrived around 10am, exuding a calm yet electric energy. They made their way towards the trees by the marquees, consulted with each other, and gathered beneath an age-old gum where they set themselves up for their performance.

Marguerite was out in the street, orchestrating everything like the battle commander she was. Her voice cut through the air, giving directions with a mix of authority and humour that left no room for argument. People moved briskly at her command, setting up tables and chairs, arranging decorations, and ensuring everything was in place.

By late morning, The Stopover was transformed into a hive of activity. The scent of various dishes wafted through the air, roasts and curries, freshly baked bread, and sweet desserts, all contributed by the community.

The courtyard felt like an oasis of calm, awaiting our guests. Tables on the inner veranda had simple, thoughtful decorations — native flowers in small vases, napkins folded neatly. The outer veranda mirrored this setup, inviting people to relax with food and drink. The communal kitchen and deck in the courtyard's centre were reserved for the small group of Elders, which would include Liam and Albert Warrun, then there were Marguerite, Maggie, Anne Delacourt, Miriam, Josef, Lukas, Kai and me. It was from here we'd sing our set of songs.

At midday the Djilawurr Band took their places beneath the ancient gum tree and as they began, a hush fell over the crowd, anticipation palpable. The opening notes floated through the air, intertwining with the rhythms of the land. The Nyul Nyul singers' voices resonated like echoes from the past, each harmony imbued with the weight of ancient stories waiting to be told. The beats pulsed in synchrony with the earth, creating a musical tapestry that connected the present moment to timeless traditions.

This celebration was a testament to our collective effort and shared history, a moment where past and present converged beautifully under the Kimberley sun.

*

Lukas, Kai, and I had endlessly rehearsed our set of songs. Every chord and beat and the order we would play them was embedded in our minds. After most of the food had been enjoyed, I made my way to the microphone at the centre of the courtyard. The place settled into a respectful quiet hum.

I welcomed and thanked everyone for coming, listing the people who had given so much.

"Welcome to Josef Batten's house," I continued.

"It isn't my place to talk about who Josef is or tell you about his remarkable journey. You can read that in the newspapers, and besides, most of you already know him well."

I glanced at Josef. His eyes met mine briefly before he looked down.

"The songs we're going to sing for you today have a special meaning for us and seeing you all here — they fit perfectly with the love and gratitude around."

I took a breath.

We played *Secret O' Life* by James Taylor. Kai joined in beside me, his bongos like a tender heartbeat.

The guests settled into a hushed murmur and people began filling the space, leaning against the veranda rails, forming a loose circle until nearly everyone had gathered.

"This one's for Josef, too."

I picked up my violin and launched into the lively fiddle intro to *Comes a Time*. I played it with fervour, leading with my voice when I could manage both, and Lukas filled in the vocals when my bow needed both hands. Halfway through, Maggie surprised me by stepping up beside us at the microphone. She slipped easily into the harmony, her voice warm and tender. It was a moment that transcended any rehearsal — a spontaneous gift for Josef and everyone gathered. Maggie's harmony seemed to light something in Josef. He rose from his seat and began to dance — a modest, joyful shuffle that sent smiles rippling through the circle. His movements were small, but the celebration in them was enormous.

Taking a breath, I spoke into the mic.

"I'd like to take a moment to thank Albert Warrun and all the Elders for welcoming us to their land. Your generosity and openness in sharing this place means more than words can say."

Albert Warrun nodded slightly, his quiet authority filling the space more powerfully than any speech.

"This one's for you, Albert Warrun."

My fingers found the first chords of *The Green, Green Grass of Home*. I changed the words in my mind as I went, swapping the familiar oak tree for a boab. Albert Warrun's eyes never left mine. Around him, the other Elders smiled knowingly.

I readjusted the mic again, careful not to make a sound, and stood to sing Simon & Garfunkel's *Kathy's Song*. Josef and I had listened to this song countless times together. We never once acknowledged the poignancy of its title or spoke of his Cathy in connection with it. But it was clear the words struck a chord deep within him.

The next song was for me and Maggie. It was Leon Russell's *A Song for You*. That song had always held a special place in our hearts, particularly the Carpenter's version. Leon Russell's original version is raw and haunting, his voice gravelly and filled with an aching sincerity that seemed to speak directly to the listener's heart. I decided to create a hybrid of both for our performance — a blend of Russell's raw emotion and the Carpenters' polished smoothness. For the instrumental break I picked up my saxophone letting it carry the same melancholy that made the Carpenters' version so tender.

With a quick signal to Lukas, I started the familiar country twang of *Top of the World*. My fingers danced over the guitar strings, finding that infectious rhythm. Lukas and I exchanged grins as if we'd been transported into some joyous, confected version of ourselves. The guests responded almost immediately. As we moved into the second verse, voices from all corners of the courtyard began to join in. It started tentatively but quickly swelled and filled the air with exuberance. The last note hung in the air like a sweet echo. We let it linger for a moment before finishing with our little country guitar flourish and twang. The courtyard erupted in applause and cheers, with a sea of happy faces surrounding us.

I stepped up to the microphone and began singing the first verse of *Islands in the Stream*. My voice carried across the courtyard, threading through the jubilant murmur of our guests. As I sang, I caught sight of Marguerite standing up from her seat. We had been rehearsing our Dolly Parton and Kenny Rogers act in secret for weeks. Her expression was one of determination as she walked towards me taking the second microphone and joined in, her voice strong and clear, blending perfectly with mine. The surprise on our guests' faces was palpable, their astonishment turning into pure joy. Marguerite's voice soared through the notes. It was a side of her few had ever seen, certainly not in Broome, where everyone knew her, but no one knew she could sing like this. As we reached the closing lines, the courtyard erupted once more in cheers and whoops. The energy was electric, each clap and cheer resonating with genuine appreciation.

The opening chords of *Take Me Home, Country Roads* filled the air, instantly recognisable and met with a cheer from our guests. I could hear the murmurs of recognition from the crowd as they prepared to join in. I watched as Marguerite left the platform and ushered the members of The Djilawurr Band to come up and join us and they willingly took to the stage beside us. The atmosphere was electric and as we reached the chorus, our guests didn't need any encouragement. Their voices rose in unison, a joyful cacophony that echoed beyond the courtyard into the skies over Broome. The volume swelled until it felt like we were sending our voices across miles of landscape, straight to Perth.

We sang the final chorus for what felt like the hundredth time but still, it wasn't enough.

With the last echoes of our song fading into the late afternoon, the applause and cheers settled into a murmur and Josef stood up and took a microphone. With a drink in his hand and his presence commanding attention, he cleared his throat, and when he spoke, his voice carried a weight that drew everyone in.

"I never expected to end up here," he began, looking around at all of us. "When I arrived, I carried the weight of a long road, across oceans, years, and the things I've seen but never wanted to speak of again."

The courtyard was silent; every ear tuned to Josef's words.

"I came to Broome as a man looking for somewhere to disappear," he continued. "Instead, I found people who looked me in the eye, called me by my name and made space for me at the table."

He paused for a moment, his gaze softening as it swept over the crowd.

"This place, it doesn't ask you to be anything but true. And in that truth, I've found something I thought I'd never have: a sense of belonging, of peace, of music in the silence."

His words resonated deeply with me and everyone else.

"So tonight," he said, raising his drink higher, "I raise a toast not just to The Stopover, but to all the stops we make, some chosen, some accidental, that bring us home in unexpected ways. Thank you, Broome. You've given me more than I ever hoped for."

With that, he held his drink high in a toast. The rest of us followed suit almost instinctively.

"To Broome!" someone called out.

"To Broome!" we echoed back in unison.

As we drank to Josef's heartfelt words, I felt a glow spread through me from the sense of community that had been so vividly reinforced. The moment hung in the air like an unspoken promise: we were all part of something bigger than ourselves here in Broome — a place where anyone could find their way home.

I caught Josef's eye across the courtyard and gave him a small bow of acknowledgement. His eyes softened in response. This was what connection felt like; this was what it meant to truly belong.

Act 3: Elizabeth Chandler

16. Let Us Not Romanticise His Trauma

Elizabeth Chandler, San Francisco, 2014

When I arrived in Broome in June 2008, I was an Associate Professor of Historical and Transitional Justice Studies at Stanford University. The town greeted me with a soft heat and a sky so vast it seemed to dissolve the boundaries of self, daring me to find a place beneath it.

My life's work had always focused on what history leaves out — the hidden stories and the silence between the official facts. I was drawn to the cracks in memory, where trauma and truth sit side by side, and where forgotten voices might still be heard if you really listen.

And yet, as I sit here now, years later and half a world away, I realise how little I understood then of the story I was walking into — my own included.

I went to Broome carrying more than academic curiosity. I was preoccupied, obsessed even, with a man whose name had shadowed my career and the corridors of my past: Josef Batten. A war photographer whose iconic images had shaped the global conscience in ways that few others had, and whose absence from public life had only deepened the mystery surrounding him.

His photographs haunted me — vivid, intimate, unflinching. They revealed, in equal measure, the worst and best of what it means to be human. But it wasn't only the images that gripped me, it was him, the man behind the lens.

Who was he really? What did he carry? Was he seeking to enlighten the world? Or simply bearing witness to the unspeakable?

I arrived at The Stopover with my questions sharpened like swords. I was not naïve, but I was not entirely honest with myself either. It was no coincidence that I had chosen Broome for my field study — it was a legitimate academic pursuit — but it was also something more personal, and urgent.

I went there with a restless heart and a mind full of preconceptions. I left with something else entirely.

*

Broome, 2008

The Roebuck Bay Hotel — The Roey, as the locals called it — stood with a weary dignity, its façade bearing witness to generations of drift and return, of arrivals like mine. I checked in eager to retreat into the dim coolness of my assigned room.

Inside, I unpacked with deliberation. Each item placed was an act of reclamation, a small assertion of order in unfamiliar territory. My clothes were hung neatly, and my books on historical memory, land rights, and cultural restitution, were stacked beside the bed like talismans. A framed photograph of my birth mother, wrapped in tissue at the bottom of my suitcase, remained untouched. I wasn't yet ready to place her into this landscape.

By the time Liam Karri arrived, I had already mapped the room in my mind as if preparing not for collaboration, but for confrontation. His knock was firm, assured. I opened the door to find a much older man than I had imagined, shaped by the land itself — sun-browned, deliberate, with a gaze that missed little.

"Doctor Elizabeth Chandler," he said confidently, extending a hand. His grip was strong and grounding for a man of seventy— four.

"Liam Karri," I replied, meeting his eyes with a studied neutrality.

We took our seats in two worn armchairs near the window. Outside, Broome murmured with the late—afternoon rumbles of everyday life. Liam spoke first. His voice carried the weight of experience but not ego. He outlined our work: archival visits, interviews with Elders, and the gathering of stories consigned for too long to the margins. He spoke not just of methodology, but of meaning — how history must be held with care, how memory lives not in documents but in people.

I listened closely. There was no performance in his manner. He was measured, and attentive. It was clear this project was not simply professional for him — it was personal. It mattered in a way I hadn't yet dared to admit it might for me too.

I felt a familiar friction rising, impatience, sharpened by jet lag and the residue of San Francisco's chaos. I wanted momentum, answers, movement. And yet there was something in Liam's unhurried pace that spoke of integrity, of doing things the right way rather than the quick way. That, too, commanded respect.

We moved through logistics — dates, contacts, permissions — with the necessary economy of professionals. Yet beneath the pragmatic exchange was the pulse of something deeper: an acknowledgement of the terrain we were about to enter. The red earth of the Kimberley, and the unsettled ground of history, identity, and grief.

When Liam rose to leave, there were no ceremonial goodbyes. He simply said, "Tomorrow then," as he stepped into the hallway.

"Tomorrow," I echoed and closed the door.

Left alone once more in the hush of my room at The Roey I stood motionless, staring at the door that had closed behind Liam. The silence that followed was thick and absorbing and a sharp pang of frustration rose in me. I had travelled halfway around the world to begin this work — serious, demanding work — and yet he hadn't thought to offer even the most basic gesture of welcome.

No invitation to dinner, no suggestion of where I might find a meal in this town that still felt more imagined than real.

I turned slowly, letting my gaze settle on the room. Its walls were bare, its furnishings spare and functional, like a motel room. The bed, though neatly made, held no promise of rest. The desk was already colonised by my papers and books — familiarity that looked pitiful in its effort to domesticate the space. But it wasn't enough. The emptiness here was not metaphorical; it pressed in from all sides, an insistent pressure in my chest.

Maybe I had been naïve to think this place would offer clarity or some peace. San Francisco was in ruins behind me — my marriage, my past, and any sense of certainty — all fractured. And now here I was, in a town that held no context for me, about to begin a project whose scope already felt immeasurable.

My stomach reminded me of more immediate concerns. I hadn't eaten since the aeroplane. With a sigh, I pulled myself from the window and reached for my bag. If Liam wouldn't shepherd me through this first night, then I would have to find my own way.

*

Liam collected me the following morning in his Mitsubishi, a sturdy four-wheel drive that spoke of years navigating the Kimberley's rugged terrains. The drive through Broome was swift, the town stirring to life in the soft morning light. Liam's house, close to Town Beach, appeared modest from the outside, with weathered timber and corrugated iron blending with the landscape.

As we stepped inside, I was immediately struck by the scent — subtle yet enveloping. It wasn't unpleasant but rather a unique blend of earthiness with a faint hint of spice that seemed to linger in the air like a whisper of places travelled and lives intertwined.

Liam's home was an oasis of academic sophistication, finely curated yet unpretentious. Bookshelves lined the walls, filled with texts on Indigenous rights, historical memory, and cultural anthropology. Each volume seemed to hold stories of struggle and resilience, carefully chosen for their relevance and depth. There were no idle decorations here; every object had its place and purpose.

Artwork adorned the walls — pieces that resonated with a deep cultural connectedness. Intricately woven baskets sat atop shelves alongside carvings and artefacts that spoke of heritage and identity. A large canvas painting dominated one wall, its vibrant colours depicting ancestral stories and sacred landscapes. The room felt alive with history, a testament to Liam's commitment to his people and their narratives.

The kitchen opened into the living space, where a long wooden table bore signs of frequent use — a gathering place for conversations over meals shared. A kettle sat on the stove, its hum mingling with the distant sounds of morning birdsong through an open window.

"You live alone?" I asked, though it was more observation than question.

"For now," Liam responded with a slight smile. "Work keeps me occupied enough."

If Liam had his preference, he said, he would still have been residing in his community. He relocated here from Beagle Bay almost ten years before as his reputation and work demands had grown, necessitating easier access to the airport for his travels to universities across the nation and abroad. He never anticipated he would take to urban living; it wasn't his style. However, his bond with Josef Batten was strong, and he cherished the moments they shared at The Stopover. At the mention of Josef Batten, I couldn't help but bristle.

I felt a pang of envy that Liam's professional life appeared to have melded with ease into his personal space. This home wasn't merely a retreat; it was an extension of who he was — steeped in tradition yet embracing new ideas and collaborations. As he led me through the house, pointing out various items of significance, I realised how much there was to learn from him — about balancing passion with responsibility.

We settled at his dining table with cups of strong tea, ready to outline our plans for the days and weeks ahead. The scent in the air seemed even more pronounced now — a reminder that every place carries its history, its own secrets waiting to be uncovered.

As we sipped our tea, the weight of the project began to settle over me. I had to find a way to navigate this vast, complex terrain with both respect and rigour. *Woven Histories: Reclaiming Visual Memory in Post-Colonial Australia* was a commitment to unearth and reassemble fragments of memory, visual and otherwise, that had been scattered by colonialism and time.

"Where do you think we should begin?" I asked Liam, hoping he'd sense the urgency beneath my calm exterior.

Liam leaned back in his chair, eyes narrowing thoughtfully.

"The archives," he said after a moment. "There's a collection at the Broome Historical Society that might hold what you're looking for. Photos, maps, documents — all tied to Indigenous experiences during and after colonisation."

"And what about community engagement?" I said, "We need stories from the people themselves, not just documents."

"Of course," Liam agreed. "I'll introduce you to some key figures in the communities scattered across the peninsula — Elders who can speak to their lived experiences and visual memory."

He paused, then added, "But remember, this isn't only about gathering data. It's about building trust."

I felt a twinge of impatience at what felt like a patronising statement but pushed it aside.

"Understood," I replied, trying to match his measured tone.

We finished our tea in silence, each of us lost in thought. Liam stood and gestured towards the door.

"Shall we?" he asked.

The Broome Historical Society occupied a modest structure close to the old courthouse. Upon entering, the cool air and musty aroma of aged paper greeted us, immersing us in a realm straddling the past and present. Rows of filing cabinets lined one wall, while shelves groaned under the weight of bound volumes and loose papers. Photographs — sepia-toned and faded — hung from every available space, each one a silent witness to moments long gone but not forgotten.

Liam introduced me to Alice, the curator, who possessed an encyclopaedic knowledge of Broome's history. Her warm smile did little to disguise the shrewd curiosity behind her eyes as she took my hand in greeting.

"I'm looking forward to supporting you with this project," she said.

"Thank you," I replied. "We're looking for anything that can help us understand Indigenous visual memory in post-colonial Australia."

"You've come to the right place," she said. "Let's start with the photographic archives."

As she led us deeper into the room, I felt a flicker of something close to hope. This was where our journey would begin — amidst these images and stories that had waited so long for someone to truly see them. And so, surrounded by echoes of the past, I prepared to unravel the project thread by thread.

*

Stanford University had been my sanctuary and my proving ground. It was there I carved out a niche in historical and transitional justice, bridging disciplines that rarely spoke to each other with the urgency I felt every day. My research had always been deeply personal, even when it wasn't overtly so. I built my career on the conviction that history isn't simply a series of events but a living, breathing entity shaped by those who remember and those who choose to forget.

My recent years at Stanford had been marked by a growing sense of restlessness. I had poured myself into my work, driven by a need to uncover and reclaim stories buried by violence and time. But something was missing — a direct engagement with the very histories I sought to illuminate.

My recent divorce from Tyler McCoy only intensified this feeling. Our four-year marriage had crumbled under the weight of unspoken desires and diverging paths. He never understood why I needed a child so desperately; his indifference broke something fundamental in me. In the aftermath, I felt both liberated and lost — a paradox that only deepened my resolve.

The decision to come to Broome wasn't merely an academic pursuit; it was a lifeline. The Woven Histories project was an opportunity for personal redemption, a chance to confront the ghosts that had haunted me since childhood. Growing up with an adoptive family in California had given me love and stability, but it also left questions unanswered, and narratives incomplete. And Tyler McCoy had no grasp or understanding of any of it and how important it was to me.

I told myself that Broome wasn't an escape; it was where things would begin anew. This project had to succeed, because it felt like the culmination of everything I'd worked towards and everything I still needed to understand about myself.

Every step I took in Broome, every photograph I studied, and every story I heard, was a thread woven into the fabric of my quest for identity and justice. It was about making sense of my fragmented past while helping others do the same.

As I stood in the Broome Historical Society, surrounded by sepia-toned photographs and the weight of unspoken histories, I knew this project was my chance to reconcile with parts of myself that had long been obscured by silence.

The project, at its core, was about reclaiming visual memory in post-colonial Australia. It aimed to investigate how Indigenous communities remembered and represented their histories through photographs and other visual media. For too long, these communities had their stories told by outsiders — often inaccurately or incompletely. Our mission was to return agency to the people whose lives and cultures were depicted in these images.

Our research would focus on photographic archives scattered across Broome and the wider Kimberley region. We would delve into the visual records of land, cultural practices, and significant historical events, piecing together a narrative that honoured the voices of Indigenous Australians. It was about building relationships with the people who owned these stories and ensuring their perspectives were at the forefront.

The relevance of this project couldn't be overstated. In a world where historical narratives often serve those in power, it is crucial to uncover and amplify the voices that have been marginalised. By doing so, we not only correct historical inaccuracies but also foster a deeper understanding of cultural sovereignty and resilience. This work had the potential to reshape how we viewed history — not as a monolithic account but as a tapestry woven from diverse experiences and memories.

I knew that writing it up would be no small feat. It would take at least a year of immersive fieldwork, followed by months of meticulous analysis and documentation. I intended to produce a comprehensive report that not only detailed our findings but also reflected the ethical considerations and collaborative efforts that underpinned our research.

Given the scope of it, I couldn't simply commute back and forth from Stanford. I needed to find somewhere suitable to live in Broome — a place that would allow me to immerse myself fully in the work without the distractions of my old life. This wasn't only about convenience but honouring the commitment I had made to this project and myself.

Finding the right place to stay was crucial. I needed a space where I could write, reflect, and connect with the community. A place where I could find some semblance of peace amidst the emotional and intellectual challenges ahead.

As I looked around Broome, with its blend of old-world charm and emerging modernity, I felt a flicker of anticipation. This town held stories waiting to be told and that would become an integral part of my journey toward understanding and healing.

*

Liam looked at me thoughtfully as we stood amidst the archives, his gaze penetrating but kind.

"Would you like to join me for supper at my place this evening?" he asked, his voice carrying an easy warmth. "I can collect you later."

I hesitated for a moment, the prospect of sharing a meal with him stirring a mix of anticipation and unease within me.

"Yes, that would be nice," I replied, managing a smile.

He nodded, satisfied. "Great. I'll pick you up around seven."

As I left the Broome Historical Society, the early afternoon sun had climbed higher and the town buzzed with a light energy, people going about their day with an unhurried pace that contrasted sharply with my whirlwind of thoughts.

I walked back to the Roebuck, my mind racing. The thought of supper with Liam was both exciting and daunting. He was one of the only people alive who understood the depth of my work and the personal stakes involved. But there was also a dread gnawing at the edges of my psyche — a fear of being seen too closely, of my vulnerabilities laid bare.

I entered my room and dropped my bag by the door, feeling exhaustion settle over me like a heavy blanket. The bed called to me with an irresistible pull. I collapsed onto it without even bothering to undress. The moment my head hit the pillow, sleep claimed me in its grasp, jet lag and emotional fatigue converging into a deep slumber.

Dreams flickered at the edges of my consciousness — fragments of memories and imagined futures merging into a disjointed narrative. My mother's face appeared briefly, her eyes filled with sorrow and strength. Then it shifted to images from the archives — sepia-toned photographs that whispered stories waiting to be uncovered.

But soon even those faded into oblivion as sleep deepened its hold on me, offering a brief respite from the tangled web of emotions that awaited upon waking. For now, in this suspended state between consciousness and dreams, there was peace — a silence where anticipation, excitement, and dread could not reach me.

I woke with a start, my heart racing, the residue of a dream clinging stubbornly to my mind. I had been on a bus, as both driver and passenger, yet the door was missing, the side of the vehicle open to the street. No matter how tightly I gripped the wheel, I found myself ejected with my luggage, standing on the pavement, watching it pull away. Over and over. The logic bent back on itself: I wanted to stay on, and yet I kept slipping off. I was not only steering the vehicle but also the one keeping myself from reboarding. A closed loop. Self-sabotage disguised as circumstance.

I lay still, letting the shadows settle around me, trying to decipher meaning from the dream's strange geometry. Maybe it was nothing — my mind simply recycling tension in metaphor. Or perhaps it was a message I wasn't ready to receive.

The clock read nearly six. Dusk blurred the edges of the room, lending the air a dim, violet tinge. I must have slept through the afternoon. The steady whir of an old air conditioner hummed in the background. The room, though familiar, seemed temporarily estranged, as if it belonged to someone else just moments ago.

The thought of supper with Liam surfaced an uneasy flutter in my chest. Something about him unsettled me, not in any obvious way, but in the depth of his gentleness and the deliberateness with which he held himself. We shared a certain reserve, an instinct to withhold. It made our connection feel precarious.

I splashed cold water on my face in the narrow bathroom. The shock of it cleared the haze but did little to still the murmur of thought beneath. Dressing felt mechanical and I chose a plain dress that felt neutral enough. The mirror offered back an image I barely recognised. Composed, yes. But the eyes told a different story — restless, shadowed, too alert. When the knock came, I was already halfway to the door.

As we drove through Broome's evening streets, the dream came back again. A reminder that the greatest barriers are often the ones we don't recognise as our own.

*

The drive to Liam's house was shorter than I remembered, or it was my thoughts that shortened the journey. I could feel the weight of unspoken words between us, a tension that was neither uncomfortable nor entirely comfortable.

At his house, the aroma of freshly prepared food greeted us — a mix of the earthy and briny. The kitchen was well-organised, each item in its place.

"I hope you're hungry," Liam remarked with a smile.

He served up grilled barramundi with a practised ease, seasoned with native herbs that I couldn't quite place but which added depth to the flavour. Accompanying it were roasted vegetables — sweet potato, pumpkin, and wild greens that had an almost nutty taste.

Liam poured us each a glass of cool water infused with slices of lemon myrtle.

"This looks incredible," I said, appreciatively. The simplicity of the meal belied its complexity — a careful balancing act between cultures.

"It's something my grandmother used to make." He replied.

We settled at one end of his long table and as we ate, the conversation flowed easily at first — work, shared interests in visual memory and cultural preservation. Liam watched me carefully as I savoured each bite.

"You're not used to this type of food?"

"It's... different," I admitted. "But in a good way."

"I believe food is like history; it carries stories." He replied.

"Stories worth telling," I added softly. "Tell me something about your upbringing and the place you're from."

Liam paused, his fork hovering over the last piece of barramundi on his plate. He set it down gently and leaned back in his chair, eyes narrowing slightly as if sifting through memories.

"My lineage is Bardi-Jawi from my father's side, and Nyul Nyul from my mother's. Both lines have deep roots in this land — generations of stories, traditions, and knowledge passed down through time."

I nodded, absorbing his words. His voice carried a weight that made me feel like I was stepping into something sacred.

"My upbringing," he continued, "was a mix of the old ways and the imposed structures of the Catholic missions. My parents balanced our cultural teachings with what they called 'whitefella ways.' It was like living in two worlds, constantly navigating between them."

He paused again, choosing his words with care.

"One memory stands out," he said. "It was when I was about eight years old. My grandfather took me out to the country — proper country — away from the missions and the towns."

I leaned forward, intrigued by the shift in his tone.

"We walked for hours, just him and me. No talking, only listening to the land. Every rustle of leaves, every bird call — it all had meaning. My grandfather showed me how to read the signs nature gives us. How to find water, track animals, understand the seasons."

His eyes softened as he spoke, the memory vivid. "There was this moment when we reached a high ridge overlooking the ocean.

He told me to sit down and be still. 'Feel the land,' he said. 'Let it speak to you.'"

Liam looked at me, a small smile playing at the corners of his mouth. "And it did. Not in words, but in a way that settled deep inside me. It was like being part of something vast and ancient."

I felt a pang of envy at his connection to place — a connection I had always longed for but never quite grasped.

"That's beautiful," I said softly.

"It is," he agreed. "But it's also a responsibility — to remember and pass on what's been given."

The room fell silent for a moment as I digested his story. It was clear that every element of his upbringing had shaped him into the man sitting before me — a man deeply rooted in his heritage yet open to sharing it with those willing to listen.

"Thank you for sharing that with me," I said, meaning every word.

Liam nodded, and his eyes settled on me with curiosity.

"And what about your heritage, Elizabeth? Your background?"

His question floored me. The issues surrounding my birth mother and my origins were buried deep, shrouded in a silence I wasn't ready to break.

"I'm Amerasian," I said, the words tumbling out too quickly. "I was adopted by the Chandlers in my first year."

The Chandlers. They were my safe haven in San Francisco, a place I could describe without revealing too much of myself.

"The Chandlers couldn't have children of their own when they adopted me," I continued, my voice gaining steadiness. "They were overjoyed when they had their own kids — two boys when I was ten and twelve."

"Our home was in Pacific Heights," I said, visualising the tree-lined streets and stately Victorian houses. "It's a beautiful neighbourhood, grand homes with bay windows and gardens that bloom year-round."

I could see Liam listening intently, but his eyes held that same probing that made me want to guard my heart.

"My parents, Robert and Margaret Chandler, are both academics. They taught me the value of education and hard work. They're incredibly supportive people." The words came easier now, a well-worn path I'd walked many times before.

"I went to private schools," I continued, trying to distract him further. "Stuart Hall for Girls first, then later Convent of the Sacred Heart High School. They're rigorous academically but nurturing environments."

My voice took on an almost rehearsed quality as I talked about school plays, science fairs, and the occasional rebellious streak.

"Having siblings much younger than me meant I was almost like a third parent to them," I added with a forced laugh. "Michael and Daniel — they're great kids. Michael's studying medicine now, and Daniel's into environmental science."

I felt myself rambling, trying to fill the space with anything but the truth about my origins.

"My family life was stable, boring even." A weak smile tugged at my lips.

Liam listened without interrupting, but I could sense his curiosity hadn't been entirely satisfied. The weight of his gaze lingered, probing gently at the edges of my guarded heart. I shifted the conversation away from myself, asking how he had come to know Josef Batten.

He spoke of Albert Warrun first — a Bardi Elder who had played a pivotal role in his life. Albert Warrun, Liam said, had the rare gift of seeing through people's facades, understanding them at their core. He was a bridge between the old ways and the encroaching modern world, a lawman who carried ancestral knowledge with authority and ensured it was passed down with care.

Albert Warrun had introduced Liam to Josef not long after The Stopover was completed. I could almost picture him through

Liam's recollections: weathered skin, smile lines etched by decades of sun and wisdom, a steady presence whose influence radiated far beyond his physical life. When Albert Warrun died in 1998, the loss reverberated through the community.

The bond between Josef and Albert Warrun had been immediate and unusual, two men from vastly different worlds, drawn together in shared silence and unspoken understanding. Through evenings together in the wilderness of his camp, Albert Warrun had helped Josef listen to the earth.

"It wasn't about sound," Liam said, "But about rhythm, presence, and respect. The land spoke in ways that demanded stillness. In amongst that stillness, Josef had healed himself."

The name Josef Batten sat in the back of my mind like an unwelcome guest. I was very familiar with his war photography and, as an undergraduate, had engaged with the work of all the war photographers from mid-century onwards, from Capa to McCullin to Nachtwey and I'd contextualised their work with the critical theories of thinkers like Barthes, Sontag, Baudrillard and Edward Said. But Batten stood out; he seemed to have covered more conflicts than all the others, and the sheer breadth of his work was staggering. Now, his reputation for portrait work had almost overshadowed that of his war photography.

I encountered his later work, specifically *The Broome Portraits* exhibition in San Francisco. The photographs were undeniably compelling. They captured something raw and unfiltered, drawing me into the eyes of each subject with an almost magnetic force. But the mythology surrounding him — this enigmatic war photographer turned intimate portraitist — irritated me to no end.

As I sat with Liam, listening to him speak about Albert Warrun and the connection between Josef and the Elder, I felt a familiar knot tighten. The stories about Josef always painted him as this haunted genius, a man who had seen too much and felt too deeply. It was infuriating how people romanticised his trauma as if it somehow sanctified his work.

Liam's voice brought me back to the present, but my thoughts kept circling Josef. His name conjured a complex web of emotions: curiosity tinged with resentment; fascination mixed with scepticism. I wanted to meet him, to see the man behind the lens that had captured such powerful images. Yet I desperately did not want to like him. I didn't want to fall into the trap of viewing him as some tortured artist whose pain made his work profound. My academic training urged me to dissect and analyse, to see beyond the surface and question everything. And yet, part of me couldn't help but be drawn in by the sheer intensity of his portraits — the way they seemed to capture not just faces but souls.

"Elizabeth?" Liam's voice cut through my reverie.

"Sorry," I replied quickly, realising I had been lost in thought. "You were saying?"

He studied me for a moment before continuing, as if sensing the internal conflict I was grappling with.

"I'd like to meet him," I said, trying to keep my emotions in check, my voice steadier than I felt inside.

Liam's eyes held mine for a moment longer. "I think that can be arranged."

As we finished our meal in silence, the heft of what lay ahead settled over me. Meeting Josef Batten wasn't about professional curiosity — it was about confronting a part of history that was deeply personal and unresolved. And as much as I tried to steel myself against it, I knew this encounter would stir up something more than academic interest.

*

The Broome Portraits. The memory of them hung in my mind like an echo, haunting and vivid. I first encountered Josef Batten's portrait work in 1997, during my PhD years. The exhibition had been initiated at The Photographers Gallery in London and transferred to the Larkin Light Gallery in San Francisco, a space known for pushing boundaries and showcasing experimental photographic work. Walking into that gallery felt like stepping into another world — one where time was suspended, and each image demanded more than a passing glance.

The portraits were unlike anything I had seen before. Batten had employed two radically different cameras in the same sittings with his subjects: a large-format 10x8 plate camera and a square-format Hasselblad. The duality between these formats was striking. The large-format plates offered a haunting depth that seemed to pull the viewer into another realm entirely, almost spectral as if the subjects were halfway between the living and the dead. They reminded me of Sally Mann's work, but with a rawness that was uniquely Batten's.

In contrast, the square Hasselblad images were crisp, capturing the subjects in tactile, immediate moments. The juxtaposition of these two formats side by side created a powerful dialogue between memory and presence, between the ephemeral and the concrete. It was as though Batten had managed to capture their very essence — their vulnerabilities, their defiance and their humanity.

The subjects themselves were a vivid cross-section of Broome's community — local people, nomads, artists, musicians, and a scattering of celebrities and film stars who had passed through. What struck me most was the intimacy and presence Batten drew from them. Each portrait felt unguarded — he had managed to strip away all pretence and capture the person beneath.

One portrait in particular — a young Aboriginal woman with eyes that seemed to hold the weight of generations. Her gaze was direct yet distant — she was looking through me into something beyond my understanding. It was unsettling and deeply moving.

The exhibition was about capturing something profoundly human. The critic's words echoed in my mind: "a conversation between memory and immediacy, between the soul and the skin." It summed up perfectly what I felt when I saw them.

At that time, I couldn't help but be drawn into Batten's world — one that resonated with my scholarly pursuits of memory, trauma, and cultural identity. Yet there was also a part of me that resisted — the part that questioned the romanticisation of his trauma as if it somehow sanctified his work.

The Broome Portraits had left an indelible mark on me, intertwining my academic interests with a personal quest for understanding — a quest that now led me to this moment in Broome, preparing to meet the man behind those haunting images.

*

My irritation still simmered, so I steered the conversation toward something more practical — my living arrangements and how I would get around. Liam seemed to catch the shift without protest.

He mentioned an annexe at the back of his house was available to rent, accessible through a side gate.

The idea of staying close to Liam had its advantages. He was well-connected in the local community, and his presence might help ease my transition into unfamiliar surroundings. I welcomed the suggestion with genuine relief.

He also offered the use of an old Honda Civic parked out front — originally bought for a nephew who had since returned to his community. Though the car was battered, its rust spots and dents visible, it would enable me to get around Broome on my terms.

The offer of both a place to stay and transport was generous, and I felt a noticeable lifting of the stress that had been pressing on me. Liam rose and gestured for me to follow him outside.

The annexe sat slightly apart from the main house, partially shrouded in evening shadows. Inside, the space was compact but thoughtfully arranged. A well-worn sofa and small coffee table anchored the living area with a desk under the window, while a kitchenette offered enough to prepare simple meals — a two-burner stove, a compact fridge, and a few essential utensils. Down a narrow hallway, a snug bedroom with a single bed and wardrobe led to a clean, functional bathroom. It wasn't luxurious, but it was enough, and it was a minute's walk from Town Beach.

Standing together in the quiet of the evening, my irritation had subsided, and a sense of optimism washed over me.

*

Over the following few days, things began to shift for me. My jet lag subsided, and I began to feel more human, and perhaps a little nicer to be with. I moved into the annexe behind Liam's place. In the daylight, it was a squat, self-contained structure with louvre windows and enough shade to keep the worst of the heat out. It felt like quarters for someone in transit. Books went onto the narrow shelf. I carefully placed the framed photograph of my birth mother beside the bed. A lacquered turtle from Vietnam sat on the windowsill together with some other sentimental objects that functioned as emotional ballast.

By nightfall, the annexe felt less temporary and more like something I could tolerate.

That evening, Liam took me across the road to Town Beach.

"You should see this," was all he said.

We walked without conversation. A crowd had already gathered — locals, a few tourists, families with eskies and beach chairs. I stayed close but slightly behind, the way I always did when entering unfamiliar spaces. It wasn't about fear. It was about control.

The moon was rising — huge, low, and red — lifting itself slowly above the horizon. The tide had gone out, leaving behind a gleaming stretch of exposed mudflats. As the moonlight struck the surface, the illusion emerged: a perfect shimmering staircase climbing into the sky. It wasn't beautiful in the conventional sense but stark, strange and almost unsettling. It was old and elemental as if the land and sky had conspired to remind us how small we were.

Around us, people fell quiet, and a few pulled out cameras. A couple next to us stood barefoot, holding hands.

Liam didn't say anything, and neither did I. I wanted to exist without being observed, without having to explain what I felt. Ultimately, I felt like an alien and the pain of home and loss was still pressing down on me in uncomfortable waves. That and my simmering anger.

The following morning, we were up early. I made coffee and drank it standing up. At nine, Liam appeared at the door for our first trip north along the pindan tracks to the first community we would visit.

We drove out beyond Broome in his four-wheel drive that was typically caked in the red dust of the Kimberly, leaving the bitumen behind, the tyres shuddering over the iron-rich corrugated earth that looked like it had bled from the ground itself. Acacia scrub flicked past the windows and wallabies scattered ahead of us. The air shimmered with heat.

The track ran north for over an hour, cutting through country that felt at once indifferent and eternal. Eventually, we reached a small settlement — clustered houses, corrugated iron roofs, kids kicking a ball in the dust..

I wandered through the community quietly, observing everything intently, feeling like an uncomfortable stranger. Liam walked beside me, his aura calm and steady. I dared a glance at him, hoping to gauge his thoughts. A cluster of women chatted beneath a tarp strung between trees, laughter punctuating the heat. As I passed, a man in a battered hat acknowledged me, his gaze appraising yet welcoming. The rhythm of life here caught me off guard. People moved with intent. Their existence wasn't a display; it was lived, tangible, engrained into the land.

"Do you see it?" I ventured awkwardly, gesturing toward the women, their voices a soft hum against the backdrop of the wind. "Their history is so present here — feels like it's in the laughter, the way they talk to one another."

Liam looked at me thoughtfully before a pensive look crossed his face.

"Yes, but each story they carry is buried under layers of silence. The fabric of memory here is complex."

I felt a pang of frustration at his cautiousness.

"But that's why we're here, isn't it? To observe and stitch together those narratives — to help reclaim them?"

At that, he turned to face me, a hint of challenge in his eyes.

"It's not only about reclaiming. It's about how we approach those stories, Elizabeth. They need to be told with care, not as an outsider dipping into a well of pain."

His words hung between us, thick with meaning. I was about to respond when an Elder of the community approached, drawn by our conversation. Her features were lined with age and wisdom, and she offered a warm smile before inviting us to join them. The transition from our tense exchange to her embrace of the moment eased the atmosphere. As we sat in the shade and shared laughter under the tarp, the initial awkwardness of the conversation faded. It was here, enveloped in their stories, that I realised the richness of what could be uncovered, but only if I allowed myself to listen — and share.

On our return journey, we exchanged few words. The quiet felt natural, not uneasy. I glanced sideways at Liam, his expression contemplative as if he were wrestling with the shadows of history, the unspoken layers unfolding in his mind.

Something had begun to loosen inside me. It felt like the project was properly starting and the sharp edges of San Francisco — the noise, the wreckage of my marriage, the corners of painful memory — began to blur.

I wasn't quite ready to heal. I was still too angry. But it was a start.

17. Uncomfortably Yours

A few days later Liam and I visited The Stopover. As we approached, I felt a mixture of trepidation, intrigue and a buried bitterness. I had seen photographs of Batten's house online, but being there in person was altogether something different and extraordinary.

The driveway leading into it was neatly maintained, with neat pindan-coloured gravel flanked by native flora with parking spaces hidden out of the way behind mature Banksia trees. With their serrated leaves, they blocked the view of the house from the road. Kangaroo paws and grevilleas added bursts of red and yellow among the green, creating a vibrant tapestry that contrasted sharply with the dry scrubby plots that sat on either side of The Stopover.

As we approached the house, its grandeur became more apparent. The structure was sprawling, with a wide veranda wrapping around it. Enormous clay pots lined the walkways, filled with exquisite plants — agave, frangipani, and jade spilling over the edges in lush abundance. Each pot seemed carefully chosen and placed, reflecting attention to detail that resonated with the classical feel of the colonial era style of the house.

I was expecting Liam to knock on the door, but when he pulled out a key and unlocked the front door I was dumbstruck. Just how close were they? The ease with which he let us into the house suggested a bond deeper than a casual acquaintance.

Walking through the entrance hall, my breath caught in my throat. The transition from the exterior's colonial charm to the inner sanctum was startling. What had seemed a large homestead from the outside opened into a world that felt both boundless and intimately crafted. Light poured in from all angles, bouncing off polished wooden floors and glass panels, creating a kaleidoscope of warm reflections.

Liam led me further inside, his movements unhurried. I followed out onto the veranda that circled the inner courtyard and seemed to fill the circumference. My steps faltered as I took in the scene before me.

The internal space was an Eden. Mature trees spread their branches overhead, dappling the ground with intricate patterns of light and shadow. Delicate maples stood beside flowering plums, their leaves rustling gently in the soft breeze. Low pines hugged the earth, creating a green tapestry underfoot, interspersed with stone sculptures that seemed to grow naturally from the ground. Tiny water features whispered in corners, adding to the sense of tranquillity.

Silence reigned here, broken only by the sounds of nature at work, a peaceful hush that felt almost sacred. It was as if the courtyard itself breathed contentedly. The air smelled of earth, a scent that brought an unexpected and unique sense of calm over me, one that I had been longing to feel for what felt like forever.

Liam walked with purpose towards the communal dining area set on what seemed to be a broad wooden platform at the heart of this hidden paradise. A delicate lattice of timber slats above softened the sun's rays, casting a glow over everything below. The space was inviting; tables and chairs were arranged thoughtfully around a beautiful natural wood chess set. The kitchen area was surrounded by well-worn sofas and a sturdy jarrah wood table and chairs, exuding a sense of both functionality and artisan craftsmanship. Everything here spoke of careful attention to detail. It was so obviously a place designed for slow living and meaningful interaction.

I glanced around but saw no sign of Josef or any guests. We seemed to have this sanctuary entirely to ourselves.

Liam moved with ease as if he belonged here entirely. He opened a sleek fridge embedded within one of the timber counters and pulled out a chilled jug of water and gestured towards one of the sofas.

"Sit," he said simply, his voice blending seamlessly into the peaceful ambience.

I sank into the cushioned moulding of the sofa, which felt like it had been designed to perfectly fit my form. There amidst such serenity, I felt an unexpected but welcome sense of peace begin to settle over me.

We sat in a comfortable silence that felt more like a shared understanding than an absence of words. As I sipped the water, I let my gaze wander over the courtyard. It felt like a space that invited you to breathe deeply and let go of the world outside its borders.

Eventually the quiet was pierced by the first sweet notes of a violin. The sound was exquisite; each note clear and pure as it floated through the air. I turned towards Liam, my eyebrows raised in silent question.

He met my gaze with a slight smile and gestured behind him with a nod of his head.

"That's Adam," he said simply. "His living quarters are beyond those trees. He practices most days."

The melody swelled, filling the courtyard with its haunting beauty. A section of Bach's *Violin Partita No 2 in D Minor* danced in the air, each phrase played with such grace and emotion that it seemed to reach into my very soul.

"It's a privilege to sit and listen," Liam added softly.

I turned back to face the direction of the music, letting it wash over me. Each movement was played with an intimacy that made it feel as though the violinist was sharing something deeply personal with anyone fortunate enough to listen. I closed my eyes and allowed myself to be carried away, feeling it resonate within me. The complexities of my own life seemed to fade into the background, replaced by the purity of this moment.

With Liam beside me and Adam's violin filling the air, I felt an unexpected sense of belonging. Damn it. Deep down, I didn't want to like the house, or being there.

*

The violin's last notes had dissolved into the air, leaving behind a stillness that now felt almost oppressive. I glanced at Liam, who seemed perfectly at ease, sipping his water with an infuriating calmness.

"Is Josef expecting us?" I asked, trying to keep my voice even.

Liam's eyes twinkled with amusement as he met my gaze.

"No," he replied simply, setting his glass down with a soft clink. "He's probably off in his studio or out in the bush somewhere."

I fought the urge to roll my eyes. So much for orchestrated encounters and planned confrontations. Here I was, in the heart of this crafted paradise, and Josef Batten had no idea I existed.

"You're irritated," Liam observed, not unkindly.

I exhaled slowly, willing myself to relax into the moment. "I guess I expected... something more formal."

"That's not how things work here," he said with a small smile. "You'll get used to it."

As I was about to respond, a movement caught my eye along one of the wooden paths leading from beyond the trees. A man in his early forties stepped out, and something about him caught my attention.

Adam moved with an effortless grace, his bare-footed steps unhurried yet purposeful. His fine-boned face was softened by expressive eyes that seemed to hold a subtle depth of understanding. He exuded a wholesome goodness so rare it almost felt mythical. I was instantly drawn in — a magnetic pull that went beyond mere physical attraction. It was as if he carried with him an unspoken promise of kindness and strength, a safe harbour in an often chaotic and cruel world.

He reached us and offered a warm smile that touched his eyes and made them sparkle with an inner light.

"Liam," he greeted softly, before turning his compelling eyes towards me.

"Adam," Liam responded, gesturing towards me. "This is Elizabeth Chandler."

"Elizabeth," Adam repeated my name as if tasting its syllables for the first time. "Welcome to The Stopover."

His voice was rich and melodic, with a lilting soft Scottish accent, each word imbued with ease.

"Thank you," I replied, hoping my voice didn't betray how disarmed I felt by his presence.

Adam glanced back at Liam. "Shall we sit?"

We all moved towards the communal seating area once more. As Adam settled beside us, I couldn't help but steal glances at him from the corner of my eye. Every movement he made seemed infused with purpose and grace. Meeting Josef could wait a little longer. For now, being here was enough.

Liam leaned back, his eyes narrowing slightly in thought before turning to Adam. His voice, when it came, was calm and measured.

"Elizabeth's leading a research project," he said. "It explores the meeting points of memory, history, and image and how colonisation has shaped and overwritten Indigenous ways of seeing and remembering. She's working with community-held stories, both in the communities themselves and those tucked away in colonial archives."

Adam turned to me, his gaze warmer, more intent. "And you wanted to meet Josef?"

I nodded; there was more to it than I could name aloud yet.

He smiled, a little crookedly, like someone delivering a punchline and a warning all at once.

"If you want to see Josef, you'd better be willing to be photographed," he said with a light laugh. "People come to Broome for that. It's almost become... a ritual."

Liam smiled in agreement. "People pay to stay at The Stopover," he said, "but only if they agree to be photographed by Josef. That's always been part of it. Not a rule, exactly — more of a pact."

Adam leaned in slightly, elbows on the table.

"It's not really a guesthouse or the type of place you book," he said. "The rooms are kept for those who arrive alone without an itinerary. Couples only stay if we personally invite them."

His voice softened. "We keep it that way for a reason. Solo travellers carry a different presence. They may arrive feeling they are closeted by their solitude, but they nearly always have the potential to open up, even if they don't know it yet. If they're willing to be seen, Josef will find them, and it will be reflected in the photography."

He let the words settle, unhurried.

"It's not a retreat," he added, "but it is a place people seem to come to when they need to come undone a little. Or be witnessed. Or both."

I let the words rest in me. I wasn't sure whether the idea of being photographed without control was transgressive or brilliant. Perhaps it was both and what lent Josef's portraits their power was that unguarded moment when the mask slipped, and something else slipped through.

"I've seen his portrait work," I said, my voice low. "I'd heard about the tradition."

The conversation began to flow more easily after this, and I found myself leaning in, drawn to Adam's presence.

I tried to learn more about him, but Adam, perceptive and amused by my curiosity, deftly turned the conversation away from himself. Instead, he focused on the project and the cultural intricacies of Broome. I felt both frustrated and fascinated by his evasiveness.

Eventually, Liam rose from his seat, breaking my reverie. "I've got a few errands to run," he said, glancing at me. "You alright to make your own way home?"

I nodded, barely registering his words. My mind was already preoccupied with Adam's enigmatic charm. Liam gave me a knowing look before leaving us alone.

As soon as he departed, my thoughts of Josef dissipated.

Adam began resetting the large chess pieces on the board a few metres away, his body and hands moving with a practised grace that mesmerised me. I watched him intently, noting the care with which he positioned each piece, an almost ceremonial act.

"Can I play?" I asked, surprising myself with the sudden boldness of my request.

He looked up, eyes meeting mine with a mixture of amusement and curiosity.

"Sure" he responded simply.

As he finished arranging the pieces, I found myself drawn deeper into the calm yet charged atmosphere that surrounded us. The game began in silence, our focus shifting between the board and each other's expressions. Every move felt like an unspoken conversation and in those moments, I was reminded how much I yearned for connection — for someone who could understand my academic pursuits as well as the tangled emotions that drove them. Adam's presence offered a promise of that understanding.

How easily I drifted into Adam's orbit. My thoughts — usually so composed — fluttered with an adolescent lightness around him. Each encounter sparked a flicker of anticipation I couldn't quite control. In a place as distant and strange as Broome, Adam carried a gravity — an attention rare and disarming. He seemed to glow faintly at the edges, like something lit from within.

And it was that glow that made everything else feel more bearable. The strangeness of the place, the distance from home, the pressure of the work I had come to do — all of it softened in his company. In hindsight, it was my enchantment with him that helped me find my feet there.

"You should come back tomorrow," he said as we rapidly concluded our game as if it were the most ordinary thing in the world.

I blinked, surprised by the ease of the offer. "Really?"

"If there's no answer at the door, Larissa will let you in. She's our housekeeper and lives across the drive."

The thought of returning, of simply walking into their communal world, as though I belonged, felt disorienting, almost dreamlike. I hesitated, a part of me resisting out of old instincts, propriety, and caution. But the deeper part, the part that was tired of keeping its distance, took over.

"Can I bring my laptop? My work?" I asked, unsure why I needed permission.

"Of course," he said, without a moment's pause.

It felt like something more than an invitation — as if he was offering not just space, but permission to be there, fully. I walked back to Liam's annexe flushed with a thrill, but also with the creeping embarrassment of recognising my transparency.

∗

That evening, I took the Honda out to Cable Beach as the sun began to lower, casting a warm, amber light across the twenty-two-kilometre length of its vast white sand.

Clusters of tourists lined the shore, their babble and laughter drifting across the beach. A train of camels moved slowly along the tideline, their shapes silhouetted against the sky's deepening orange. The scene was undeniably beautiful. And yet, there was a dissonance — the logo-covered T-shirts and board shorts, the branded water bottles, and the soft click of cameras capturing curated sunsets. I felt oddly detached, as though I'd arrived too late to something quite sacred.

I wandered down to the water's edge, letting the cool surf lap at my feet, and allowed my thoughts to scatter. I'd come a long way, geographically and otherwise. Meeting Josef wasn't simply a line on an itinerary — it had never been that simple. It wasn't just academic. And Adam… well, Adam had unsettled me, and I felt vulnerable at the thought of him.

There was light where the ocean met the sky, and in that brightness, I caught a sense of my confusion. Part of me wanted to dismantle the myth around Josef, to get to the man behind it. But maybe the myth served a purpose too — something to hold onto while the truth unfolded at its own pace.

The following morning, as I pulled into the driveway at The Stopover, a woman I instinctively knew was Larissa walked towards me, all brightness and momentum.

"You must be Elizabeth! So good to see you," she called, already motioning me inside. "Adam's told me all about you."

There was a natural warmth to her, generous and unfiltered. She led me across the veranda and into the lush, light-filled courtyard.

"Hungry? There's plenty in the communal kitchen," she said, gesturing toward a beautifully arranged spread of fruit and fresh bread. Noticing my laptop, she handed me a small card with a password on it.

"The wi-fi can be patchy out here so it's best to go to the veranda when you need a consistent signal."

"Thank you," I replied, a little overwhelmed by the ease of it all.

I stood for a moment, taking it in.

A tall man walked past us carrying a worn copy of *Shogun*. There was something familiar about him, a well-known athlete maybe. He took a seat on a sofa near the kitchen and opened his book. An elegant middle-aged woman sat alone at a table nearby, reading a magazine with a coffee cup at her elbow. I imagined both were guests staying there. I wondered if they had already met Josef and had their portraits taken — or if, like me, they were still waiting for him to appear. Even with Larissa's hospitality, his absence hung in the air. There was no sight of Josef or even any mention of him. And though I told myself to be patient, an urgency crept in at the edges. I wasn't entirely sure what I needed from him anymore, but I knew meeting him still mattered to me immensely.

I sank into a low, generous sofa, laptop warm against my knees, papers scattered across the table next to me — notes from early conversations with Liam, fragments of research, thoughts not yet formed but already stirring with promise.

I began shaping notes for the *Woven Histories* project plan, moving between documents and webpages, searching for insights, and grounding truths that might guide our future visits to the Indigenous communities we hoped to work alongside.

I scribbled questions in my notebook — points to raise with Liam, intentions to clarify, goals to reshape. How could we create space for trust to take root, not simply assume its presence? I needed to regain some sense of agency before the project drifted into terrain neither of us had mapped.

Liam had framed our previous visit as a step toward rapport-building. But rapport with whom? He already had connections. I was the newcomer, the one still learning the language of place and presence. And rapport, I realised, could not be summoned from thin air; it had to be cultivated on firm ground. His experience was undeniable, but in that moment, it cast a shadow — one that deepened, rather than dispelled, my doubts.

I closed my eyes briefly, trying to still the noise inside me. There was too much at stake — not only for me but for the people whose stories we hoped to help carry forward. These were not simply narratives; they were inheritances of grief and grace, of memory held across generations. To do justice to them, I needed to step into this role with steadiness and care.

I drafted timelines, outlined workshop themes, and envisioned conversations that might unfold with openness and reciprocity. I pictured the workshops as circles of dialogue — spaces where cultural memory could surface freely, without agenda.

I noted our first destinations. Each place would be holding onto memory — waiting not to be extracted but to be witnessed, honoured and retold with permission and purpose. I resolved that on our next visit I would arrive prepared — with humility and a listening heart. If I were to inhabit this role ethically, it would not be enough to simply show up and take notes. Respect could not remain an abstract ideal — it had to shape every word, every silence and every choice we made. No more tentative presence or passive participation. I would meet each encounter with full attention, and genuine commitment. Or so I told myself.

Across the courtyard, a soft rustling stirred the foliage. Birds darted above in bursts of colour and sound, their ease a reminder that these lands held stories long before I arrived. Their joy was simple and unassuming. I wished mine was too.

*

I stood and stretched; aware I hadn't thought for a moment about Josef's absence. Looking around, the expanse of the house and courtyard enveloped me.

Leaving my belongings, I decided to wander towards Adam's quarters, perhaps hoping he would be home. The scent of damp earth mingled with flowering native plants, drawing me further into this vibrant sanctuary.

As I approached what I thought was Adam's space I hesitated at the threshold, struck by how the expansive glass walls folded back effortlessly, creating a smooth connection between indoors and out.

Peering inside, I was met with a kaleidoscope for the senses, almost a gallery space designed for art and sound. Various musical instruments were precisely displayed — guitars, violins and other un-nameable stringed instruments. The sight was enchanting; it felt like stepping into an artist's dreamscape where creativity thrived unrestrained. Art pieces were spaced sparingly on walls and easels. A series of photographs captured fleeting moments — expressions of joy, sorrow, resilience — all echoing stories that resonated.

I stepped further over the threshold, drawn in by my curiosity. I was completely absorbed in this creative haven; it was infused with a sense of life and possibility that both excited and unsettled me.

"You found me then." Adam appeared on the veranda behind me.

Heat rushed to my cheeks. I hadn't meant to intrude quite so blatantly into his sanctuary, yet here I stood, trespassing without a second thought. It wasn't his calm demeanour that left me feeling exposed; it was my uncertainty creeping in again.

Speech eluded me as he approached, but instead of retreating into awkwardness, I found myself relaxing under the gentleness of his gaze.

"Would you like a drink?" he asked, as though he had known me for ages.

"Herbal tea would be lovely," I replied, surprised by how at ease his presence made me feel.

He turned towards his kitchen area.

"You must be curious about how all this came to be," he said over his shoulder. "The house, the life here."

"I am," I admitted, following him further into the heart of his space. "It's extraordinary."

As he moved about preparing the tea and some herbal leaves, I studied him — his hands deftly arranging cups as if every motion was imbued with purpose.

"Josef and I…" Adam paused briefly, weighing his words. "We met during a rather difficult time in both our lives. He needed grounding and I needed some recovery time."

"And then you built this?" I gestured around us, aware of the inane way my hand was wafting in no particular direction.

A soft glimmer appeared in his expressive eyes. "It evolved slowly."

As he poured hot water over the herbs, anticipation stirred within me at the mention of Josef's name. Maybe meeting him wasn't what I wanted after all.

"I'd love to show you around," Adam continued casually. "If Josef is here, maybe you'll introduce yourself."

A swell of trepidation welled up inside me. Part of me yearned to stay rooted in the sanctuary of Adam, rather than confront the shadow of Josef's haunting legacy.

I sipped the tea and settled into one of the low chairs on the veranda, watching him move about with ease. For a moment, I felt suspended in time.

"What do you do for a living?" I asked, my curiosity bubbling up.

He smiled softly as if my question had caught him off guard.

"Ah, well... I suppose you could say I'm a jack of all trades." His voice held a casual lilt that belied the impressive tapestry of his life.

"Jack of all trades?" I pressed. "What does that even mean?"

He leaned back against the railing, his posture relaxed yet thoughtful.

"I do some space and building design," he said with an air of modesty that felt almost disarming. "Some architectural projects here and there — mostly smaller scale stuff — renovations or community spaces." He waved a hand dismissively as if these achievements were mere side notes to a more important story.

"And then there's music," Adam said, his tone shifting, his face lighting up. "I play professionally in a Baroque quartet. A lot of what we do is rooted in Bach — or inspired by him — but we also explore cross-cultural elements and integrate them into the Baroque framework."

"Baroque?" I tilted my head. "That sounds fascinating but, how do you even begin to do that?"

"Well, for example, we played in Kyoto last month. That performance blended traditional Baroque with a Japanese instrument called a shakuhachi, which is a traditional type of bamboo flute. It has a haunting, breathy, and meditative sound. We're always looking to expand the repertoire and reimagine it. Sometimes we play on period instruments, using historically informed techniques. Other times, we experiment more — pulling in unexpected sounds and ideas. So, there's a lot of range in what we do."

"You must travel often? Performing I mean."

I couldn't help but picture grand concert halls and captivated audiences.

"Yes," he replied as if it was simply another day at the office. "But I try to spend at least half the year here in Broome."

"And why here? What makes this place home for you?"

He glanced around the verdant courtyard before meeting my gaze again.

"The community," he stated plainly. "These people... they're family." I absorbed his words as they lingered between us.

"I love creating art too," he added almost shyly, as though admitting something personal and intimate.

"What kind?" My interest piqued further; his humility had left me wanting to know more about this multi-faceted man before me.

"Mostly mixed media pieces," he said thoughtfully, glancing towards a few canvases leaning against one wall — striking combinations of colour and texture that evoked emotion without needing explicit explanation.

"I draw inspiration from this land, the colours, textures... the stories embedded within it."

"That's beautiful," I remarked.

"Thank you," he replied quietly.

Our conversation drifted; each word we exchanged felt rich with meaning yet effortless. There was an understated flow to Adam's life — a brilliance hidden beneath layers of modesty that captivated me even more than his achievements alone.

"But what about the travel, do you mind doing so much of it?" I queried again after another sip of tea, feeling emboldened by our dialogue.

"I do quite a bit around the world for various projects or concerts," he answered matter-of-factly but added with an air of sincerity, "but when I'm away too long... well, it doesn't feel right."

"Broome has its own magic," I said self-consciously, quickly realising I hadn't been in the town long enough to form an authentic sense of it for myself.

He nodded in agreement and something deeper shimmered within his expression.

"So, this is where your heart lies?" I asked gently.

"Absolutely," Adam affirmed simply yet wholeheartedly. "Come, let me show you around."

He led me through a wide doorway into the deeper part of his home — a space that felt less like a building and more like something alive. Light poured in from unseen windows, catching the grain of the polished wood floors and softening the contours of the walls.

His friend Lukas had designed the glasswork and lighting. Eighteen years on, their vision had matured into something remarkable: it had always been their intention to build a home that didn't only hold light but seemed to breathe it.

We stepped out onto the veranda where Adam described the courtyard. It hadn't been created for show. It was a habitat, purposeful and responsive, drawing in insects and birds. Grevilleas and bottlebrushes for the honeyeaters; small, rare eucalypts offering shelter and shade. Paperbarks that rustle in the breeze, their bark peeling like old parchment. Native grasses that sway gently, inviting finches and other small wild birds.

We walked the timber paths that wove in and out of the plantings and water features, and Adam moved among them with ease.

He named each species: revealing the depths of attention, care and a devotion that had been invested in the place. He spoke of the birds who visited: the delicate flit of Double-barred and Zebra Finches, the sociable racket of Grey-crowned Babblers, and the quick, fanning elegance of the Willie Wagtails. His favourites were the Rainbow Bee-eaters that created small bursts of colour as they darted after insects.

I remarked on the gentle hum of the place, and how everything seemed in conversation. Adam smiled and mentioned the cockatoos — unruly, loud, impossible to ignore. We laughed. He gestured toward the heart of the courtyard, where the communal space had been left open for gatherings: a clearing surrounded by life, shaped by intention rather than ornament.

When I asked where the idea had come from, he spoke of communal courtyards in various cultures — especially African traditions — spaces that hold people in relation to one another and to the earth.

"Enveloping community," I muttered, unsure what I meant.

He nodded. This wasn't simply about aesthetics. It was about intimacy — between people, species, and the land. And reciprocity.

Standing there, I felt a subtle pull, a recognition of a connection forming, deepening into something more like yearning.

As we walked along the veranda, Adam paused beside one of the guest rooms.

"Come in," he said, sliding back the folding glass with a practised ease.

Like Adam's living space, the entire room opened out to the courtyard, its boundaries defined only by the soft geometry of clay pots and a small sculpture. Nothing obstructed the line of sight.

Inside, the room was unobtrusive and spare. A wide, low-slung futon-style bed sat close to the creamy stone floor, its pale, fine-grained wooden frame wrapped around the base of four squat stone boulders, acting as legs. No fixings were visible — no bolts or glue — only the craftsmanship of perfectly joined materials, the warm ash wood curving over the cool grey-blue stone as though the bed had grown from the land itself. It was striking, though not in a way that drew attention to itself. A quiet magnificence.

"Where on earth did you find this beautiful bed?" I asked.

"I didn't," Adam replied. "We commissioned them from a master craftsperson in Sydney, based on sketches Josef and I worked on when he was still in his exile. Seven were made. One for each room."

We moved out onto the veranda, and I sized up the other suites. Each opened differently — some with broad glass panels, others with narrower thresholds — none were identical. Each held its own character.

"There was a lot of thought given to the rooms," Adam said. "We wanted to avoid any institutional feeling, the sterility of hotels. We intend to allow for solitude, but not isolation and to offer the possibility of encounter with one another."

I said nothing. Instead, I let my attention drift: to a handwoven throw across a bed; to a carefully curated shelf of books with cracked spines and folded corners; and a charcoal sketch pinned to the wall, unsigned, tender. Human traces, carefully unpolished.

"Everyone who stays here comes alone," Adam said as we stepped into another room. "And whether they know it or not, they come looking for something."

He spoke without judgment. "Sometimes they're aware of what it is. Sometimes not. Sometimes they're drawn by the myth of Josef or the idea of being seen in a portrait."

"That doesn't annoy you?" I asked. I felt a flicker of irritation rising behind my eyes, sniffing an imagined air of pomposity.

"Not at all," he said, as we lowered ourselves into a pair of teak chairs that sat neatly between the rooms.

"People who travel alone — regardless of why — are exposed to themselves differently. Their usual scaffolding isn't there. They arrive with their intentions, conscious or otherwise, but what they often meet is something they weren't expecting."

"In other words, they come with baggage."

"Of course," he said, not unkindly. "Most are curious. Some are simply lost. Very few arrive in crisis. But nearly everyone, in one way or another, ends up confronting a version of themselves they hadn't yet met. Their blind spots. Their patterns. How they hold others at arm's length or draw them in for the wrong reasons. And why wouldn't they? The world doesn't train us for self-awareness."

"So this is a retreat?" I said, sceptically. "And you and Josef are what — accidental therapists?"

He laughed. "Call it what you like. But no, that was never the intention. We built what we needed — for ourselves. Not a fortress to hide in, but a place open enough to let others in. That was the point. Not to protect ourselves from the world, but to live more truthfully within it."

"But it *isn't* entirely open, is it?" I said. "You only accept solo travellers. You charge them to stay. And you insist they sit for a portrait. That's not nothing. It's intimate. And it's transgressive, if you ask me."

Adam looked at me carefully, his tone even.

"I think you may be confusing boundaries with conditions. Yes, there are structures. But they're not about control. We don't ask people to be anything other than who they are. They can be wounded, arrogant, self-absorbed — it makes no difference. Most people with difficult traits are charming anyway, at least on the surface."

He paused.

"We don't tolerate destructive behaviour — violence, aggression, persistent intoxication — but that's rare. People who come all this way on their own have a sense they want to make something of the experience. Whether they admit it or not. And once they're here, with no one to reflect them back to themselves but the isolation of this small town, the sea, the expanses of desert, and Josef's lens, they start to see."

"And Josef captures that?"

"Sometimes. Sometimes not. It depends on the guest. And on him."

I didn't understand but felt I might be beginning to.

Adam, for his part, seemed to sense my unease, my flickers of resistance. If he was irritated, he didn't show it. Or he simply didn't mind.

He told me about a famous Danish poet who'd stayed for a month, who'd said little but enjoyed the company of Josef and the other guests. He spent his days walking in the courtyard, sitting with Josef, absorbing the light. When he left, he abandoned a notebook in his room. Only three pages had been used — he hadn't written any poems.

Adam led me along the veranda toward Josef's studio at the far end of the house. A high, vaulted ceiling rose above us, and the broad glass panels folded back so the outside seemed to pour in, effortlessly becoming part of the room.

"I think I can hear him out on the platform," Adam said, his voice low beside me.

We paused at the veranda railing, leaning out slightly to look across the courtyard. I tilted my head, listening for any sign of Josef, though I wasn't entirely sure what I expected to hear. What I wanted now, more than anything, was to stay beside Adam a little longer. There was something unguarded about the way he stood there, the ease with which he seemed to belong to this place. I turned to him, hesitant but unable to keep the question to myself any longer.

"Have you ever been married? Or... are you seeing someone?"

A flicker of surprise crossed his face — so slight it might have gone unnoticed.

"Relationships have never really been a priority," he said evenly.

I wasn't sure how to respond. I felt a strange mix of relief and disappointment, as though I'd been hoping for a particular answer without quite knowing what it was. Part of me had assumed there was something mutual between us. But maybe I'd misread him, or maybe I was only beginning to see what lay beneath the surface of my longing.

We began walking toward the courtyard community area. The silence between us shifted slightly, not strained, but changed. A subtle awkwardness had crept in, and I couldn't tell whether it was mine alone or shared. As we moved, I watched Adam from the corner of my eye. He seemed utterly at ease, his steps light, measured. There was a constant grace to the way he moved through this place.

And there I was, beside him, feeling unsure of where I stood. The unmistakable attraction I felt unfolded alongside uncertainty. Our conversations all seemed to hint at something more complex than friendship, but whatever lived behind Adam's steady kindness remained out of reach.

*

We found Josef seated across from the tall man I'd seen earlier whose presence radiated an ease that was almost theatrical in its composure. Long limbs folded loosely, he leaned forward, studying the chessboard between them with the focused calm of someone accustomed to performance under pressure.

Josef looked up with an expression that was steady and unsettling in its kindness. I had been bracing myself for arrogance — for the brittle posturing of a man too long admired. But there was none. Only a calm, measured welcome that made me more nervous than if he'd been aloof.

"Elizabeth, I'm very pleased to meet you. Welcome."

His attention lingered. Not in a way that suggested judgment but more as if he were reading a map drawn across my face. I wondered, uncomfortably, what Liam had told him. The idea of being discussed unsettled me more than I cared to admit.

"Meet Wainwright Jackson. A fellow American"

The long-limbed man rose slightly from his chair in acknowledgement. Wainwright was, in fact, the legendary power forward and recently retired NBA star with the Los Angeles Lakers. His face, familiar now, seemed impossibly out of place here, in this sun-worn outpost at the edge of nowhere. What on earth was he doing here? His presence struck a discordant note, yet he looked utterly at home, as though this remote corner of the world had always been part of his terrain.

Wainwright nodded, his smile understated, familiar as if we were old acquaintances and not two people from opposite ends of the cultural map. I offered a murmured greeting, acutely aware of the sweat down my spine and the ink smudged on my fingers. I felt dishevelled and faintly ridiculous in their presence.

Josef extended an invitation to supper with a gracious calm clarity. I accepted too quickly, then flinched inwardly, realising how unprepared I felt for any social grace. I mumbled something about needing to clean up, immediately regretting the admission. He was unbothered. He made no performance of politeness to put me at ease, and thankfully that steadied me.

"Great," said Adam. "Let me keep showing you around, we can pick up here again later."

I followed him, feeling out of place, carrying the detritus of all the half-formed theories about Josef I'd brought with me. I glanced back at the two men who remained absorbed in their game. In the waning light, they looked at ease, using a language with each other I was only beginning to learn.

On the veranda we passed the middle-aged woman I had noticed earlier, now ensconced in her guest suite, reading Pride and Prejudice. I envied her calm immersion, contrasting sharply with my inner disarray.

"Hello Julie," Adam said softly, his voice a comforting murmur.

"Oh, hi Adam," she replied, with a relaxed ease that I longed for but couldn't quite grasp.

How did they manage such an effortless connection?

*

Julie Harwood arrived in Sydney in 1981 with a backpack, a copy of Lonely Planet Australia, and a vague plan to work in hospitality until her travel funds ran out. She had recently finished a degree in English Literature at the University of East Anglia, and Australia was her reward to herself before settling back in England.

But things changed when she met a life insurance salesman called Rick Munro in a pub in The Rocks. He was charming, confident, a few years older, with a tan, an imported convertible, and a voice like a game show host. They married within a year and moved to Elsternwick, a quiet suburb in Melbourne's south, close to the beach and not far from the CBD. It was suburban, leafy, and safe — a good place to raise their three children.

For over two decades, Julie's life was defined by mothering, raising community funds, and dutifully navigating Rick's boisterous family gatherings. She volunteered at the school canteen, hosted dinner parties, and tried not to resent how her ambitions had faded into the background. Occasionally she taught creative writing at the local adult learning centre, but it always felt like a hobby, not a vocation.

By 2006, with her eldest daughter married, her middle child in postgraduate law school in Canberra, and her youngest Alex off at Edith Cowan University in Perth studying marine biology, the house had gone eerily quiet. Rick, still selling insurance, had become more of a housemate than a partner. Their conversations had narrowed to household logistics and occasional arguments about money or the television volume.

One morning, as she stood in the ensuite in her robe, staring at her own reflection, Julie realised that she hadn't truly wanted anything in a very long time. The feeling frightened her. She started an online dating profile, had a brief affair with a widowed architect named Barry from Brunswick — who turned out to be more interested in his dog than her — and in a moment that felt like watching herself from the outside, she packed a suitcase and left.

She told friends she was "taking a break." Told Rick she "needed to find something."

The truth was, she didn't know what she was looking for.

In June 2008, visiting Alex in Perth, she impulsively booked a flight to Broome — somewhere she'd always meant to visit. It felt exotic and remote. She arrived at The Stopover with a hard-shell suitcase, linen trousers that creased instantly in the heat, and a blow-dried bob that began to wilt in the first ten minutes.

Broome life was alien to her, and she felt out of place — fellow outsiders in the town seemed to be mostly rich Perth suburbanites, backpackers, drifters, artists, and an endless trail of retired grey nomads in battered hats and 4WD caravans. But something about the vast sky, the red dust, the casualness of it all, gave her a sense of something other than Elsternwick. For the first time in years, nobody expected anything of her. She wasn't a wife, a mother, or a dutiful neighbour. She was just Julie.

It was in The Stopover she truly discovered the meaning of 'something other'. It was very much 'other' than Elsternwick and most definitely 'other' than Barry and his dog. She had intended to stay three or four nights. Then she just stayed. She hadn't believed such a place could exist and welcome her so freely and without judgment. One day she started sketching in a notebook she bought at the local market, and she just carried on, sketching and reading and enjoying the connections and community amidst the shelter of The Stopover.

*

An hour or so later, having cleaned up and changed my clothing, I began the walk from Liam's house back to The Stopover. I didn't know what to do with myself. Not with my body, not with my face nor with my voice, or the thoughts that wouldn't settle.

I'd always known how to be in the world. Or I thought I had. My degrees, my published work, the way I had learned to speak with precision, to argue, to defend. They had made me someone. Not only to others, but to myself. There was structure, clarity and direction. Even when I found my birth mother and the rage that came with it, I used it. I turned it into something productive — something with shape and outcome.

But now, everything felt fluid and unsound. I was asking myself questions I didn't know how to answer, questions I wasn't used to asking. Who am I, here, without the scaffolding? What am I trying to prove, and to whom?

I wasn't used to feeling unsure. I wasn't used to feeling anything that didn't have a clear reason or use. I had put on the dress, which was nothing special, but slightly nicer than needed. I hadn't worn it for myself. I didn't know what I wanted Adam to see, or if I even wanted him to see me at all. I felt exposed. Not by the dress — but by everything underneath it. My skin, my choices, my arrival here, my reactions to this place. My sudden awareness of myself as a woman rapidly approaching forty, alone and unsteady.

It wasn't about being attracted to him. It was that he had seen through something — or around it. I felt seen by him to the extent that I felt exposed. Naked. And because of this, I didn't understand how to simply be me in his presence.

The project, Woven Histories, sounded solid — particularly when I spoke about it and I could describe it with clarity. But the urgency behind it had shifted. I wasn't sure if I was here for the work anymore. Or if I was using this work as a foil to distract from the fragility of my emotional infrastructure.

There was no safety in any of it now.

Everything I thought I knew about myself felt upended. I couldn't hear the voice I trusted, the one that would usually push me forward, and tell me what mattered. What had once been conviction now felt like noise.

By the time I reached the driveway of The Stopover, I knew something had altered. Whatever had protected me, all these years, wasn't holding in the same way. And I didn't know if I wanted it to.

The building came into view slowly. Low-lit, it had an incongruous presence. From a distance it looked almost like a mirage, too carefully tended, too calm. Nowhere else on the street, or indeed the town, looked like it.

I had arrived in Broome expecting the house to have been overhyped, a fantasy dressed up as authenticity. I had come ready to critique it, to keep myself detached and above it.

In truth, I was drawn into it. I didn't understand this place. It unsettled me. It didn't fit any of the frameworks I'd brought with me. It had no strategic purpose, no outcome I could analyse.

And Josef Batten was supposed to be a ghost, a curiosity to be deconstructed. I hadn't expected to feel anything real about him. Certainly not admiration. I'd half-convinced myself I would find the usual components for me to deconstruct — self-mythology and sentimentality, fragments for me to unpick and reframe. But in the brief moment I had met him there was something else — care, vision, humanity. And it felt honest.

And that, too, was a description of Adam.

I wasn't prepared for him. Not for the way he looked, though that was disarming enough, but for how effortlessly he pulled me out of the posture I'd worn for so long. I didn't know it was possible to be so exposed without being humiliated. And still, I didn't know what he wanted. If he wanted anything at all — if this was simply who he was: someone who made others feel seen and then walked away untouched.

But something in me wanted to be seen. Not professionally or through my work, not even through the story of my origins, the one I'd learned to tell with a careful mix of intimacy and distance. I wanted to be seen by him.

That realisation made my stomach tighten, not with desire but altogether something more desperate.

Was that what this was? Was I waiting to be rescued?

The thought felt shameful, but I couldn't shake it. I didn't think of myself that way. I'd never allowed myself to need anyone and yet here I was, walking toward a place I hadn't meant to like, shaped by a man I hadn't meant to notice, with a growing awareness of how tired I was of holding everything together.

I was tired of being a version of myself who always knew what she was doing. And I was terrified of what I might become without her.

*

The front door to The Stopover was wide open, swinging gently as if someone had recently stepped through, which felt like an invitation, though still I hesitated. Not because I thought I shouldn't enter, but because I no longer trusted myself to know what was appropriate.

The hallway was cool and still, lit by the last of the daylight slipping in through high windows. I moved past a series of paintings. They were exquisite, and I wanted to linger, to know who had painted them.

But then I heard the music. A violin being played in the courtyard. It pulled me forward before I had time to think, through the wide entrance hall, and out onto the veranda. The air was heavier there, warm, scented faintly with eucalyptus and soil.

It wasn't Bach and the tune was unfamiliar, perhaps Irish. Unmistakably Gaelic. It should have moved faster, like a reel, but it didn't. He — Adam, I presumed — was playing slowly, holding it with care. He let the melody breathe, stretching certain notes just past their expected length allowing something fragile and deeply human to emerge. I'd never heard Gaelic music played this way, with such interiority and restraint.

I didn't want to move. I stood there on the veranda, and for a long moment, I forgot to brace myself. I simply listened to the presence of it.

Eventually, I stepped onto the wooden path into the communal space, walking slowly, uncertain how to enter, not wanting to break the spell. Adam's playing continued to reach across the space — peaceful, open, unhurried.

When I saw him my heart skipped a beat.

He stood a little to one side, absorbed, his movements precise and unshowy. There was no audience or presentation. Only him and the sound.

A middle-aged man nearby sat cross-legged, a pair of bongos on his knees. He followed Adam's lead with soft, shaped rhythms and inserted perfectly timed single beats that felt more breathed than played, not attempting to draw attention.

Josef sat in a low chair across the space, a glass in hand, his posture at ease. Nearby, Liam scribbled in a notebook, lost in thought.

Two older women were on a sofa near the kitchen, bodies turned slightly toward each other. One traced small circles on the other's back as they spoke with Wainwright Jackson, who sat off to the side, holding a drink, relaxed but watchful.

Julie was close by, sitting alone, sipping from a short glass. Larissa moved at the kitchen counter, arranging food without drawing attention to herself.

No one looked up. There was no welcome, no effort to make space. They were already in it, settled and absorbed, as though the place had shaped itself around them.

I hesitated, not sure whether I belonged. I didn't want to interrupt what I didn't yet understand.

Josef caught my eye. He raised a hand slightly, a small gesture of recognition.

"Welcome again," he said, his voice lifting above the music, his smile warm and open.

"Can I get you something to drink?" He gestured toward the kitchen. "We've got a well-stocked bar. Or Marguerite makes a wicked cocktail if you're feeling brave."

I nodded toward his glass. "I'll have what you're drinking."

"Angostura and bitters. My favourite."

He stood, and we walked over to the kitchen area together. I was aware of everything — my step, my breath, how I stood beside him. None of it felt casual.

He prepared the drink slowly, without fuss and, as he passed it to me, he paused and asked, gently:

"Where do you feel most yourself these days?"

The question landed hard. Not abrupt — but knowing. As though he'd seen straight through me and understood exactly how I was holding myself in the space.

There was no pressure in his voice. No demand. But I couldn't speak. Not because I didn't want to, but because I realised I didn't know the answer.

Before I had time to respond, the music shifted.

Adam's playing abruptly picked up pace, his bow moving with a new urgency. The delicate phrasing gave way to something more animated — reels, unmistakably — and the bongo player responded in kind, coaxing out an undercurrent that was taut, alive. The rhythm lifted and caught fire.

It was celebratory, yet still tender — never brash or showy. Every note felt placed with care, even as the speed built. There was nothing discordant in it, nothing jarring. Somehow, this too felt like part of the atmosphere, part of what the space could hold.

I became aware of the others again. Faces brightened. Julie laughed out loud and began clapping along, the beat finding its way into her palms and her body.

The two older women leapt up with the ease of people who had danced together a thousand times. They caught hands, making stars and wheels as they moved in wide, joyful circles across the platform, their steps sure-footed and exuberant. They were cackling, their whoops echoing through the courtyard, unselfconscious and full of delight.

The tempo surged again. Adam was playing flat-out now, his whole body in motion. There was something almost athletic in it — the physicality of the playing, the bow flying across the strings, his fingers a blur. But he wasn't lost in the music. He was inside it, his expression focused, fierce, but still deeply present. It was impossible not to be swept into it.

Wainwright had started tapping his foot. Larissa wiped her hands and joined in the clapping, and someone let out a high whistle that spiralled into laughter. Liam had stopped writing.

I stood completely still next to Josef.

Part of me wanted to step back into the shadows, to watch it all from the edge. But another part of me wanted to move. Not perform, not even participate exactly, but to belong.

I glanced at Josef. He hadn't looked away from the music, but I felt his presence beside me. I felt confounded by him and embarrassed at myself. A sudden rush of warmth for this man whom I had spent so long positioning as an adversary passed through me. I had arrived in Broome with my judgements sharpened, built carefully over years, laid brick by brick from fragments of stories told and not told. I had made him into something I could hold at a distance — analyse, critique and then dismiss.

But none of that armour made sense here. Not with the way he had greeted me, gently and without awkwardness. Not with how he'd asked that question — so simple, so precise — that it had gone straight to the part of me I tried to hide. And not with the way he was standing next to me now, entirely at ease in the world, giving his attention freely, without needing to take anything back. He hadn't tried to win me over.

I had imagined I'd feel something closer to triumph, or at least satisfaction, at being here — seeing him, having the upper hand. But I didn't feel victorious — I felt exposed, and strangely grateful.

I looked at his profile, the line of his jaw, the way his fingers curved lightly around his glass, his foot tapping to the music. There was a softness in him I hadn't expected. And in that moment, I didn't want to interrogate it or prove it false. I wanted to let it be real.

I took a sip of the drink he'd made me, the bitterness sharp and grounding. The music was still flying, Adam, moving like he was chasing something only he could see. The older women were breathless now, leaning into one another, laughing. Julie had crossed to them and joined in, unselfconscious. The whole courtyard was moving — light and alive.

And there I was, standing in the middle of it, beside a man I realised I didn't know, and whom I no longer wanted to fight.

When the music came to a close, a soft hush settled over the courtyard, everyone collecting their breath. Conversations stirred again — light, easy — but Josef remained beside me. He didn't rush or make any large gesture, he simply turned slightly and said,

"Come, I'd like to introduce you."

He guided me gently through the space, his presence calm but attentive, and began with the two older women, Marguerite and Talia, who were still standing close together, flushed and laughing softly, their hands brushing as they spoke. Marguerite carried a certain charge, yet nothing about her felt performative. She leaned into her partner Talia with an ease that spoke of a long-held deep affection. Talia's eyes met mine with an open, steady light. She smiled without needing to say anything, and somehow I felt included.

Leaning against the low railing was Kai, the bongo player. His hair was wild, his shirt half-unbuttoned, his grin quick and unaffected. When Josef said my name, Kai looked directly at me, gave a nod, and said, "Glad you're here," like he meant it. There was something grounded about him, unforced. He wasn't trying to charm me — he simply was himself.

Wainwright Jackson was a tall, composed African American who carried his presence with a stillness. His movements were minimal, but when he turned to greet me, I felt his attention land fully. His nod was slight, his smile unassuming, but I felt its depth.

Julie looked up as we approached, her expression soft, a little curious.

Larissa was in motion, everywhere at once, bringing glasses to the sink, laughing with Kai, and touching Talia's shoulder briefly in passing. When she looked up and saw me, she gave a small wave.

"You made it," she said like she'd been hoping I would.

Each introduction was simple, and no one asked too much or held on too long. It was easy. For most of my life, I had understood safety as distance — control and containment, particularly when it came to strangers.

I was still unsure of myself, but not entirely outside of it all. Not entirely 'other'.

I watched Adam move into the kitchen — an easy transition from musician to cook. He slipped on an apron; the fabric frayed at the edges and began sorting through the array of vegetables Larissa had laid out.

The kitchen hummed with energy as they worked together. It felt like an extension of the music we'd shared, the notes now translating into flavours. Nearby, the table waited for supper, surrounded by ten exquisitely carved chairs. The warmth of the jarrah timber glowed in the fading light, and I imagined the many evenings it had witnessed, the stories exchanged, and the laughter shared.

Julie flitted about, checking each of the Chinese lanterns strung between the trees and along the veranda with their sun-faded colours, purposefully tapping bulbs until they flickered back to life, and lighting tealights in mismatched jars. Though everything already seemed in place, she still adjusted a napkin here and turned a glass there — small gestures of domesticity.

It occurred to me then that this was where Adam and Josef held court each evening with a loose constellation of locals, travellers, and artists drifting in and out, and that this evening was simply one like many others.

The day's heat still clung stubbornly to the wooden platform beneath my feet, but dusk began to cool the air. The scent of frangipani mingled with salt on the breeze, touching my senses with something both foreign and familiar. This moment felt like a homecoming — I wßas both an observer and participant in an array of diverse people, loosely sewn together by music, food, and the exchange of stories.

The table pulsed with life — voices overlapping, laughter rising and falling like the tide. At its heart were Marguerite and Talia, their rum cocktails fuelling a joyful chaos that was impossible not to catch. Their stories tumbled out, each more improbable than the last, told with sweeping gestures and bursts of laughter.

Across from them, Wainwright and Josef shared a quieter conversation. They sat close, trading low remarks and sidelong glances that spoke of a shared understanding. Neither drank, but the ease between them was unmistakable — dry humour flickering away in their conversation. I wanted to be near that warmth.

Julie, Larissa, and Liam were deep in discussion about the South Australian Riesling they shared. I watched from the edges, glass in hand. The Angostura's dark liquid shimmered in the candlelight, untouched.

Marguerite caught my eye.

"You haven't tried one of these," she said, grinning as she held up her cocktail. "You're missing out."

I hesitated for a second too long, and she was already reaching across the table, sliding a glass toward me.

"Just a sip," she added, the corners of her eyes crinkling.

The first taste was sharp and unfamiliar, sweet at the back, with lime and something smoky threading through the rum. I wasn't sure I liked it. But I didn't dislike it either. I took another sip. And then another.

Marguerite raised her glass in silent approval. "Good, right?" she said.

Later, she passed me a second, this one garnished with mint. I didn't hesitate. The laughter around the table had become a music in itself, loose and rhythmic. I felt something inside me ease, like a knot unthreading gently rather than snapping.

Adam moved through it all with assured, steady rhythm. He laid platters down the table — garlicky prawns, grilled vegetables, a salad dotted with mango and herbs. He refilled glasses with a subtle attentiveness, slipping into conversations without ever dominating them.

It struck me again — his grace, his ease. The perfection of him was beginning to feel almost implausible, arousing a flicker of suspicion, even as it drew me in. Alluring. Intoxicating. Impossible to look away.

As we lingered over the last of the food and plates began to clear, I realised I'd started to feel different — not drunk, or dizzy, but… lighter. The haughty silence I usually carried had lifted a little, and my laugh, when it came, felt like mine. Not a performance, or a defence. The flush from the cocktail lingered, but it wasn't the alcohol alone that had softened me. It was the ease around the table, the shared glances and unspoken familiarity. It was the permission to show up as I was. For the first time since I'd arrived in Broome, I didn't feel like a stranger.

*

Then the temperature changed — just as the laughter rose and fell around the table in a raucous tide of camaraderie, Marguerite's voice rang out, rich and vibrant, as she launched into one of her Pommy jokes.

"How do you know when a planeload of Poms has arrived at Sydney airport?"

"I don't know," said Julie in a perfect English accent, "how do you know when a planeload of Poms has landed at Sydney Airport?"

"When the engines are switched off, you can still hear the whining!"

Julie collapsed with laughter, her head thrown back, utterly taken by it, but my stomach twisted into knots. The joke landed like a slap — too familiar, too tired, steeped in the kind of stereotype I'd spent years unpacking. Each layer held the weight of old wounds dressed up as humour.

I tried to mask my reaction, but the horror must have flickered across my face. Talia caught my eye.

"Has it offended you?" she asked lightly, her tone teasing but her gaze direct.

I opened my mouth, but no words came. The table's energy shifted; the spotlight turned, unwanted, toward me. Heat flushed my cheeks, a blend of indignation and embarrassment washing through me.

Marguerite leaned in, unfazed. "Don't drown in your own pie..." she said with a wink.

"She means piety," Talia added, giving Marguerite's wrist a playful squeeze before they both dissolved into cackles.

I stayed still, breath shallow, caught in the liminal space between guest and outsider. They didn't mean harm — I could see that. But good intentions didn't blunt the edge. The laughter felt like a ripple over something deeper. To them, it was harmless banter. To me, it was the echo of a world that reduced people like my mother — and me — to caricature.

"Alright then," Marguerite said, undeterred, "Did you hear the one about the lifesaver who went up to the surfy chick on Bondi Beach and said, 'Hello darlin', do you wanna fuck?'"

My heart sank as she delivered the punchline — "I didn't... but I do now, you smooth talkin' bastard!" — loud, bawdy, and unmistakably laced with racial innuendo.

They all erupted into fits of laughter.

"Stereotyping isn't funny," I said, louder than I'd meant to as they quietened down. The words landed like a stone dropped in water.

An awkward silence followed — short, but dense. Something flickered in Marguerite's expression, though she masked it quickly with a shrug and a half-smile.

Liam piped up out of the silence with a comic's timing:

"I don't know... how do you make an Irishman burn his ear?"

Julie leaned in, eyes bright. "Go on, then. How?"

"Phone him up while he's ironing."

Laughter erupted once again — easier this time, as if the moment had been reset. But it didn't reach me. I sat still, my fingers tracing the rim of my glass. The levity felt remote, the sound of it muffled, like waves crashing from far away.

Josef met my gaze across the table. He said nothing, but there was something steady in his expression — an anchor in the swirl.

Beside me, Adam placed a dish of mango sorbet on the table, his hand brushing mine briefly.

"It's fresh," he said gently, "from the tree behind the house."

I nodded, grateful for the distraction — and the electricity of his touch.

As the conversation surged again I leaned back and let the evening move around me. I wasn't here to correct them, or to condemn them. But I also couldn't laugh along.

I took more sips of Marguerite's cocktail — citrusy and spiced — and felt it settle and spread inside me. Maybe belonging wasn't about fitting in but staying in the fold and holding your shape when the shit happens.

*

I needed to get away — from the laughter, the churn in my chest and the sharp sense that I no longer belonged to the moment. I stood, murmured something vague, and walked silently down one of the wooden paths leading away from the table. No one stopped me. The sound of them, still talking and laughing, drifted behind me.

The veranda gave me space. A few low chairs and a small table sat off to one side, and I let myself sink into one, low and loose-limbed. The chair tilted a little under me, and I let it. I needed to recalibrate, to settle the storm I hadn't meant to stir. I felt self-conscious again.

Their laughter continued in the distance, and I closed my eyes and let the air cool my skin. Why was I always the one to carry so much weight into a room? Why did I need to be so damn serious?

I heard footsteps and Adam appeared; hands tucked casually in his jeans.

"Mind if I sit?"

I shook my head. "No, not at all."

He sat opposite me, one leg stretched out, watching me with interest.

"You alright?" he asked.

There was no pressure in his voice, only presence. I nodded, not quite trusting myself to say more. He didn't push. Instead, he started talking, lightly, about the mango tree behind the house, the frogs that came out when the rain hit the ground just right, and the screech of flying foxes at dusk. Nothing important. Everything important.

Something in me began to loosen again.

I watched the way his lips moved, the ease in his face, how he seemed both grounded and elsewhere. He had a stillness in his presence that draws you in.

Was it the cocktails still warming me, or something else?

He said something that made me laugh. It wasn't a huge thing, but it felt real, and there was something in his face when I laughed. Or maybe I imagined it. I wasn't sure. The way he was leaning forward, the way his arm rested near mine — there was a pull there. I felt it but couldn't tell if it went both ways.

After a while I said, "I should get home. It's been a long day, and I've got a mountain of things waiting for me tomorrow."

We stood. He stepped close — not too close, enough to hold the moment between us.

"Goodnight," I said.

"Goodnight," he replied, his voice soft, almost intimate.

I stepped toward him and wrapped my arms around him, instinctively. He held me in return, tender, warm and present. And I felt it — his body against mine, the strength of him and it felt... right.

I pulled back a little to look at him. His eyes met mine. And in that breath between thoughts, I leaned in and kissed him.

But he moved, slightly, just enough to stop it. He stepped aside and gently took my hands, both of his around mine.

"I'm not that way inclined," he said gently.

I blinked. "What do you mean?"

"I mean," he said, "I'm inclined towards men."

The words landed softly, but they hit hard. My face burned. My chest tightened.

"I didn't know," I said, too quickly. "I had no idea."

"I know," he said, still kind. Too kind.

But I couldn't stay. I pulled my hands back and turned away. I walked along the veranda and into the entrance hall, and out, fast before I could feel anything more. I didn't look back.

18. A Mausoleum To Silence

In the weeks and months that followed, The Stopover became a peaceful refuge for me; familiar, steady, and gently alive. I returned often by day to work within the peace of the courtyard. And evenings unfolded differently: conversations shifting with the light, laughter echoing into the courtyard or the hush of shared silences under the stars.

A strange jumble of people came and went with a fluidity that mirrored my own restlessness, and Josef built a warm understated connection with all of them and made their portraits.

Yet amid the comings and goings, Julie remained. She stayed on as a guest until, one afternoon, without ceremony or expectation, she asked Adam if she could help around the place. It seemed a modest request but marked a turning point.

Something changed in Julie then. She rented a small house for herself nearby and found her footing, not in a dramatic transformation, but through the routines of being useful — of being needed. She worked beside Larissa, whose energy crackled through the place. But Julie brought something else — a calming steadiness. She arranged table flowers and tended the gardens with considered care and handled the admin with a focus that often went unnoticed but was never unappreciated. She moved through the house with an ease that suggested not only comfort, but belonging.

I watched all this unfold with a distant admiration. Julie had arrived in Broome, like so many of us, looking for something she couldn't quite articulate. And in The Stopover, she found a space where she didn't have to name it. She found herself by living simply as herself.

Our friendship grew slowly, naturally. On the surface, we made an unlikely pair — her simple openness, my guarded interior life. But Julie's kindness didn't require explanation. It was the kind that held space rather than filled it. She was bright, thoughtful and well-read, but she wore her knowledge lightly. In Broome, she didn't have to perform or prove anything. She could simply be Julie.

And that was what made her such an anchor for me.

The work I'd come to do — gathering the threads of forgotten or fractured histories — was substantial, often lonely. The project demanded so much: long periods away in the field, tangled interviews, sleepless nights sifting through the layers of memory and trauma. Some days, it felt as though I were walking barefoot through the past, every step stirring something raw.

But The Stopover offered something else. The opportunity to pause and recalibrate. And in Julie's presence, I found the stillness I hadn't known I needed. Evenings with her were unforced — we might talk softly about the day, or we might say nothing at all. The silences weren't awkward. They gave me space to breathe.

Over time, I found myself looking forward to those hours more than I expected. They became a lifeline, grounding me when the rest of life felt too abstract, or too much. In those moments I felt closer to peace than I ever had.

Liam noticed it, too. Our working relationship deepened — what had begun as a functional collaboration became something more intuitive. There was trust now, an ease between us. In the field, his insights often led me to places I hadn't considered. He didn't try to rescue me from the weight of the work, but he stood beside me in it, and that made all the difference.

And through it all, Julie remained a presence that didn't demand anything from me but somehow offered everything. She reminded me, in her unassuming way, that what we seek isn't always resolution or escape, but simply somewhere to land. Somewhere to feel real.

And so I kept returning. Not only for the place, or the friendliness of its people, but because The Stopover had become part of my own slow unfurling. It held a space for me when I didn't quite know how to hold it for myself.

In those months, beneath its folding glass walls and moonlit garden paths, I began to understand that healing doesn't always come with answers. Sometimes, it arrives through presence — through spaces that allow us to ask our questions without needing to solve them, and in giving myself permission to rest in that ambiguity.

*

Through everything, my relationship with Adam began to evolve. He became like a brother to me — not in some clichéd or sentimental way, but as a grounding presence amid the emotional upheaval I was still learning to navigate.

We often found ourselves deep in conversation about music, a subject I'd never given much thought to before. It began to feel like we were speaking a new language — one that bypassed logic. I had learned piano as a child. The Chandlers had paid for me to study to an advanced level, and I could execute Mozart with textbook precision. But it had always been just that: execution. My playing was efficient, not expressive. I had never understood how to feel the music, let alone convey feeling through it.

Adam, by contrast, seemed to inhabit music. He spoke about it with such intimacy, as if it were not only about sound but a map of human experience. I hadn't known music could speak to the emotional landscape so directly, or that it could help to heal what words alone could not.

One afternoon in the courtyard, he sank onto the sofa beside me, still energised from a recent tour that had taken him through Rome, Venice, and Budapest.

"Have you ever listened to Nick Drake?" he asked, as though it were the most natural question in the world.

I shook my head. "No. I haven't."

His eyes lit up, as if I had given him a gift. "We'll get to him," he said. "But first, Joni Mitchell."

He walked over to the stereo system housed in a bespoke cabinet alongside the kitchen surfaces, handling it as if it were something delicate and beloved. He placed the needle on a record and returned to sit beside me as the opening piano notes of *Court and Spark* drifted into the courtyard. The sound of the piano was clear, spare, and poised, almost architectural. Joni's voice emerged, smoky, elusive, edged with something that felt both wise and wounded.

Adam turned toward me, his voice soft but animated.

"She's not writing about some idealised romance. This is raw and inconvenient — a love that arrives uninvited, carrying all its baggage. The lines about the sleeping roll and the madman's soul? That's a love that doesn't knock — it camps outside your door and brings its volatility with it."

He got up and paused the record.

"This album was her turning point. The moment she moved away from the naked intimacy of *Blue* and stepped into more complex territory — musically and emotionally. *Court and Spark* sounds smooth, but underneath there's tension. Syncopation, unresolved chords, jazz voicings that don't land where you expect them to. She's no longer interested in easy resolution."

He let the needle down again.

"She's always aware of power dynamics," he said. "Even when she's vulnerable, there's a sharpness. She won't romanticise being pursued — she interrogates it. And the melody itself never settles, echoing her ambivalence."

Adam gestured in the air, sketching the architecture of the chords as he spoke.

"These harmonies are too rich for pop, too fluid for folk. It's jazz, but it's also her very own emotional language. She won't offer closure — no repetition, no comforting chorus — only movement."

He let the track run to the end, watching me closely, as if trying to see whether the song had found its place inside me.

"In the end," he said, "*Court and Spark* isn't really about love. It's about resisting it and failing. It's about the aftermath and what lingers in the silence."

I had closed my eyes, letting the music wash over me. His insights pulled something open inside me. For the first time, I could hear beyond the notes and into the emotional architecture hidden in the phrasing, the tension and the dissonance. It was as if he had handed me a key to a language I'd never learned but always longed to speak.

He queued up a Nick Drake song.

"This one's different," he said. "*Northern Sky* is as close as Nick ever got to hope. And even then, it's cautious."

He glanced at me as the song unfolded — a quiet, shimmering confession. Nick's voice floated over the piano and organ, singing of a love that makes the world make sense.

Adam smiled faintly.

"It's about transformation. Not lust or fantasy, but real internal change. Someone enters his life, and the darkness lifts a little. Very few love songs touch that."

He tapped his fingers gently along the armrest, in time with the piano line.

"The rhythm flows like a thought, unhurried, unstructured. No chorus, only a slow unfolding. It's like he's speaking quietly to himself and we're eavesdropping."

He listened for a moment, then lowered the volume so his voice could settle into the quiet.

"Even at his most hopeful, there's a shadow. He wonders if the warmth can last, if someone will stay through the cold seasons, through the worst of him. There's always that fear."

He paused, and added softly, "In his lifetime, Nick Drake barely spoke. He recorded this when he was twenty-two. By twenty-six, he was gone. Withdrawn, unreachable. In 1970, the world didn't know what to do with someone like him — no image, no interviews, no explanations."

He gestured toward the lingering music.

"But here he is, reaching out. It's tentative but filled with longing too. The arrangement lifts him: John Cale's piano and organ playing give it this warm, otherworldly shimmer. There's coldness, but not emptiness. A sense of safety, just out of reach."

Adam continued to look at me intensely.

"To me, this song is a miracle. Not because of what it expresses, but because it made it out of him at all. For once, Nick Drake lets himself imagine a future. Not alone, but in a northern sky with someone else in it."

The way Adam spoke, with such care and precision, felt like he was guiding me gently through the contours of my own emotional life. His voice, the music and the layered meanings all worked on me in ways I hadn't expected.

As we continued to talk about Joni Mitchell and Nick Drake, about the ways their melodies entwined with memory, I began to recognise myself in those songs. Not the longing or the regret, but the hope that music might still help to piece something meaningful together for me.

*

And my relationship with Josef changed too.

He had a way of being present that I hadn't encountered in anyone before — not only attentive but attuned. We would often sit sipping tea together, saying very little.

Sometimes he invited me to play chess — which we did intuitively, slowly. There was no competitiveness to it. It was more like an exchange of tempo — his calm bleeding into mine.

His smile was a constant. Not the strained, performative kind that people wear to cover awkwardness or to manage the discomfort of silence. Nor was it the brittle serenity I'd seen in the faces of men who'd overdosed on New Age retreats and forgotten how to feel anything real. Josef's smile was none of that. It was open and direct — an unguarded expression that connected fully with whatever or whomever was before him. When he looked at me, I felt seen, but not scrutinised.

And when he turned away, the smile didn't vanish. It transferred. His attention shifted fully to the task at hand, his presence concentrated, his expression altering to reflect whatever occupied him. No rush, no dithering.

The Stopover had softened me. Or perhaps it allowed me to soften myself. The sharp edges I'd arrived with — the bracing armour of self-protection, the constant mental calculations about what things meant or where they might lead — had almost completely dissolved. I was no longer held hostage by the tangle of questions and grievances that had accompanied me to Broome, especially those I had long held about Josef. The things that once mattered — what I might confront him with — felt muted now, as though they belonged to someone else.

But one small thing needled at me.

In all the time I had been there, all the hours we had shared together, Josef had never once asked to photograph me.

I had watched the way he worked with others. Always with respect. He didn't impose the camera. He built trust first, lingering in conversations and shared stories. Eventually, at some gently understood moment, he would lead them into his studio, and they would emerge hours later with the air of someone who had undergone a ritual, not a portrait session. I had seen the glow in people's faces when they described the experience of being photographed. It was rarely about vanity; it was about being held in view with care. The invitation to see yourself anew.

But with me, there was nothing.

He never asked. Never even alluded to it.

At first, I told myself it was because he thought I wouldn't want it, that I wasn't ready, that I might say no, but as time passed and I watched him offer the invitation to others it began to feel like an omission. Not cruel, but a distance between us, nonetheless.

I considered asking him about it more than once. The words would begin to form in my mind when we sat playing chess or listening to the evening birds settle into the trees. I would imagine myself saying lightly, "Why haven't you ever asked to photograph me, Josef?" But I worried it would sound vain, or worse — wounded. And I didn't want to risk disrupting the ease we had built, the gentleness of our companionship.

One afternoon, as we sat together in the half-shade, sipping tea with the chess board between us, I noticed that he had stopped watching the pieces and was looking at me. Not in the way that signalled a move or a question.

I looked back. Held his gaze.

And it felt — for the briefest instant — as though he saw something he might ask to record.

But he didn't say anything. And neither did I. We sat there, the game between us unfinished.

*

Weeks later, sometime before dusk, when I'd been working for hours at a table in the communal area, immersed in a trance-like process of writing up my research findings, I went and searched out Josef as I often did on such days.

It had been a quiet day with very few people interrupting my flow and I was aware Josef had been working with a subject in his studio since morning and as I walked along the veranda he was sitting outside his studio, feet crossed, a cup of tea resting beside him.

I approached without needing to say anything. He looked up, and his smile appeared, steady and genuine. He gestured to the seat beside him.

Idly, I asked, "Did you ever go to America?"

I already knew the answer would be an affirmative, but something in me decided I wanted to ask him about it anyway.

"Yes," he said after a moment. "Many times."

I turned toward him.

"I photographed the civil rights marches. Selma. Montgomery. A few others. It was between trips to Vietnam and Africa."

The mention of Vietnam landed in my chest.

I kept my face still, but something inside me had braced. He didn't look at me, and I wondered if he'd noticed.

"Was that…" I began, then faltered. "Was it hard to leave that work behind?"

He shook his head gently. "That life was… another skin. One that has shed itself."

His voice was soft, but not vague. He spoke with steady clarity.

"I used to carry it all. The images, the stories and the grief. But not anymore," he said simply.

I nodded, unsure if I truly understood, but feeling the truth of it anyway.

"So you've never felt pulled back into that type of work again?" I asked.

Now he looked at me, and the smile was there, but it had shifted. It hadn't vanished — only softened and deepened.

"No," he said. "Not once."

We sat there a while longer, the air cooling and the sky darkening by degrees. He reached for his tea. I could hear frogs starting up by the pond.

I didn't ask anything else.

I leaned back in my chair, feeling the weight of his words settle in the air between us. Josef had shifted from guarded to open, recounting how he and Adam had painstakingly sifted through his archive.

"We went through each photograph," he explained, his voice steady. "Every frame contained fragments of stories that needed to be acknowledged and understood…" he added quietly, "…By me."

He paused, gazing into the distance as if peering into those memories.

"We reconstructed narratives that were lost."

His calmness surprised me. There was no hint of the turmoil I'd expected; only a man who had faced his ghosts and emerged unshackled.

"I can't say it was easy," he continued, "but peeling back those layers allowed me to live."

I found myself nodding along. His words could have been used to describe my own work with Liam and the communities we were engaging with.

"That sounds remarkably similar to what we're doing with the Elders," I said, my voice soft but confident.

"We're cracking open stories that have long been silenced, giving them space to verbalise and share their truths on their own terms."

Josef met my gaze then, his eyes narrowing slightly as if weighing my words against something deeper.

"It's about reclamation," I added. "We're enabling people to own their histories rather than letting them be dictated by outsiders."

He leaned forward slightly; his brow furrowed with a searching discomfort.

"I don't mean to be difficult," he said. "But it raises questions for me."

I nodded, encouraging him to continue.

"You've said the purpose of this work is to enable the Elders to speak for themselves. To reclaim their stories from the grip of outsiders. To own their history on their terms."

"Yes," I said, quietly. "That's exactly it."

He paused, his eyes never leaving mine.

"Then help me understand something. Why is it that an associate professor from Stanford is leading this research? Why isn't it fully in the hands of the communities themselves?"

There was no malice in his tone — only a sincere, disquieted curiosity.

"Isn't there a contradiction in that? Hypocrisy even? You speak of decolonising the archive, but doesn't the structure of the project — its funding, its authorship, even its framing — risk reinforcing the very imbalance it claims to challenge?"

I felt the question land — not unfairly, but deeply. He wasn't wrong. And I didn't want to pretend otherwise.

"You're right to ask," I said. "It's something I've asked myself more than once. And others have too."

I paused, steadying my voice.

"When I began, I thought I could simply facilitate — create the space, bring resources, listen. But I quickly realised it's not so simple. I come with a prestigious foreign university behind me. With grant money. With assumptions I'm still learning to see."

Josef watched me and listened.

"I'm not trying to speak for anyone. I'm trying to step back and let the Elders guide the work. But yes — the structure still carries the imprint of institutions like Stanford. I'm part of that, and I can't pretend I'm not."

I took a breath.

"I suppose the best I can do is remain aware of the contradiction. Keep naming it. Keep asking who holds the power and where the story is being told. And when I need to, step aside."

I looked at him, not sure if what I'd said was enough, knowing only that it was true.

"This isn't clean work," I added. "But I believe it matters. And I believe it's worth doing, even imperfectly."

"And you feel it's working?"

"Slowly but surely," I replied, feeling a surge of passion for the work. "Each session reveals something profound — a story emerges from pain, laughter cuts through sorrow. It's all connected — but the real test will come in the writing up of the research."

The conversation flowed from there; we exchanged insights about trauma and healing as though we were both seasoned guides on parallel journeys. I mentioned how much I had followed his career since my undergraduate days, citing how many of his photographs had appeared in the critical theory modules I'd taken.

"They became vital texts for understanding representation and ethics in conflict zones," I said, keeping my voice even while sidestepping any personal implications.

Josef smiled faintly at this acknowledgment, but I noticed something flicker behind it — an understanding that stretched beyond academia into realms we both shared yet could never fully articulate.

For a moment, as the dusk deepened around our little sanctuary on the veranda, silence enveloped us again. Eventually, we began speaking about the past — his, mostly — and the conversation, unforced, circled toward his archive. I'd often wondered where he kept it, or whether it lived solely with his agent in Paris. None of it was on display. Not in the communal space, nor in the studio. It was as if he had chosen to live only forward, refusing the gravitational pull of his history.

"Do you ever look at them now?" I asked. "The photographs, I mean."

He was sitting back in his chair, legs stretched in front of him, a soft breeze lifting the edge of his shirt. He glanced at me, considering.

"Sometimes," he said. "Not often."

"And where are they?" I hesitated. "I mean — I'm fascinated. Your archive… I've often wondered."

He smiled but didn't answer. Instead, he stood slowly, smoothed his shirt, and said, simply, "Come."

I followed him without a word. Something in his tone — light yet charged with intent — made me feel we were crossing an invisible threshold.

We stepped into his studio where the last of the afternoon sunlight had angled across the floor. On the far side, beyond a wall of books, he led me to a plain door I hadn't noticed before. It looked like it might conceal a storage cupboard or fuse box.

He opened it, and we stepped into the darkroom. I had imagined a cramped, utilitarian space, but it was expansive, cool, lit only by the soft glow of safe lights. The faint scent of chemicals lingered, and the air hummed with precision. Everything was clean, ordered, exact.

We crossed the room, and he paused at another door that was unmarked and nondescript. He unlocked it, pushed it open, and stood aside.

It was like stepping into another world.

A natural ambient light filtered down from high clerestory windows. The room was cool and unexpectedly vast. I drew breath. This was no studio or storeroom. It was something else entirely. A sanctuary. Maybe a museum. Or a library.

In the centre stood low shelves and a long table with Anglepoise desk lamps. It was carefully arranged with archive boxes, notebooks, loose prints, and bundles of letters tied with string. One wall was lined with rows of black boxes, each chronologically labelled — coded with the years marked in white ink. A lifetime sequenced and stored. On another wall a more fragile history: the glass plate negatives of Mo Batten, Josef's adopted father. Logged, preserved, cared for. A hidden visual record of the residents of early-to-mid-20th century Leederville.

And in one corner — unexpected, almost domestic, was a king-sized bed. Unmade, as if he'd risen only moments before. A ceramic mug sat beside it, half-full. The faint scent of sandalwood hung in the air.

I turned slowly, absorbing the layers of meaning in the space. This wasn't either a library or a museum. It was a soul-space. An unobtrusive repository of a life lived deeply and with intention.

"Does anyone else know about this?" I asked, softly.

"Only Adam," he said. "And now you. You're the only other person who's entered this space in the eighteen years since I've lived here."

I blinked. "Eighteen years?"

He nodded. "No one else."

Why me? I didn't ask, but the question lingered.

He said nothing. He moved deeper into the room, fingers grazing the spine of a notebook, his presence absorbed into the space — as though I hadn't merely entered his archive, but had been allowed, for a moment, to glimpse something far more private: the man himself. Not the one from the courtyard or the dinner table or even the studio, but the man he kept tranquilly and carefully in here.

*

I took a seat at the long table. After a moment, I asked a question that had lingered in my mind since we stepped into this hidden realm.

"Have you ever been married, Josef? Or in a relationship?"

He smiled, a little wistfully, his eyes narrowing as he considered. "And what's the intention behind that question?"

"It seems to me," I said slowly, choosing my words with care, "that you've lived much of your life in such deep solitude. This place... it feels less like a workspace and more like a mausoleum to silence."

His gaze drifted toward the shelves and returned to mine.

"A mausoleum," he repeated softly.

"Exactly," I said. "I wonder if anyone ever stirred your heart. It feels important. I don't know why."

A pause stretched between us, quiet but weighted. I saw him measuring something within, some threshold he wasn't sure whether to cross.

"I had a connection once," he said at last. "Her name was Cathy."

I leaned forward instinctively. There was something in the way he said her name — something fragile.

"She was… light," he said after a pause, his voice warm, but edged with something quieter beneath. "Very young. Very beautiful. We shared an understanding — one that needed no explaining."

A smile touched his mouth, distant and almost tender. His eyes seemed to be watching something unfold far behind him.

"What happened?" I asked gently.

"We were swept up in each other," he said. "Into the type of intensity it's easy to disappear inside."

He looked away, as if he could still feel her presence, or the ache of her absence.

"But life has its own gravity," he said. "Reality arrives, sooner or later. And it doesn't always ask permission."

"Was it painful?"

"Yes," he said, without hesitation. "But what we shared mattered, and it stayed with me."

I let his scant words settle between us and found myself trying to piece together how these fragments fitted with the man I saw before me.

My curiosity stirred once more.

"What was Cathy like?" I asked softly. "Describe her to me."

Josef paused and walked slowly toward the shelves. With deliberate care, he pulled out a black archive box labelled *JB1967.3* and placed it down on the table.

Inside, a stack of photographs lay preserved in clear acetate sleeves. He sifted through the top layers gently, his fingers moving with tenderness in the way he handled them.

"Cathy was… ethereal," he said, as he drew out five images from the depths of the box.

He laid them side by side on the table and stepped back, allowing me space to look.

Cathy was ethereal. As I gazed at the photographs an unexpected tightness rose in my chest. There was no artifice in her. Each image held something raw, luminous, and deeply intimate — more than portraiture. They were documentary evidence of something once fiercely alive. In her eyes I saw vulnerability, strength, even mischief. And in the way he'd framed her I could sense the depths of their connection.

I felt like an intruder privy to something sacred and fleeting — a glimpse into the depths of Josef's heart. He was allowing me to witness a love both fierce and tender. It wasn't only Cathy he had let me see, it was something far more guarded — the part of himself that still carried her.

19. A Certain Kind of Fury

As I write this now, in 2014, I'm finding it hard to explain what happened next. It was one of the most significant conversations of my life — one I wasn't sure how to begin — and having it was the main reason I had chosen Broome as my base for the Woven Histories project.

Everything had led up to this moment.

"Josef," I said calmly. "Could I… see the photographs from 1968?"

Whatever tenderness had been between us a moment before seemed to slip away. His face changed — no longer soft or reflective, but more still and guarded. He looked at me for a long moment.

He carefully placed the photographs of Cathy back into their box, returned it to the shelf and brought down another labelled *JB1968.1*.

He set it on the table between us and opened the lid. Right on top, there it was, famously titled, *Rescued from the Ashes*.

"Please," I said, barely above a whisper. "Take it out."

He lifted the photograph carefully, almost without breathing, and laid it down in front of us.

I looked at it — really looked. The blood. The torn clothing. The young woman. Two soldiers beside her. The wreckage behind them.

"What's happening in this photograph?" I asked, my voice low, unsteady.

Josef held my gaze for a moment and turned back to the image.

"It's..." he began but paused. "It was taken after the My Lai Massacre. An atrocity I can't begin to describe, committed by American troops."

"No!" I said firmly, "What's *literally* happening in the photograph? Describe it to me."

He looked at me, sharply, quizzically.

"This woman — she's being led away to safety... I think. The soldiers beside her... they're doing what they can to help her." He glanced up at me. "In the background, you can see the extent of the atrocity and what's left of the village."

My chest felt tight. "Thank you," I said.

I didn't know what to say next, or how to say it. My heart thumped, and I could feel the colour rise in my face. My throat closed.

Josef was still watching me.

"Elizabeth," he said gently. "Are you alright? What is it?"

I looked at him, trying to find the words. Then they came out, uneven, shaking.

"One of those soldiers is my father..." I said, "... and I don't know which one."

Josef blinked. His brow furrowed slightly. "What do you mean?"

I swallowed hard. "The woman in the photograph... she's my mother."

His expression didn't change right away. He was trying to make sense of what I'd said.

"Do I need to explain it to you?" I asked almost sharply.

He looked down at the photograph again, and back at me.

"You mean... they raped her?" he said, barely above a whisper.

"Yes." The tears came, sudden and uncontrollable. "I'm the result of that."

I broke then, and he reached out instinctively. I didn't resist. I let myself fall into his arms, and he held me.

*

I eventually pulled back from Josef. My cheeks were wet, and I could feel the heaviness of the moment settling over us like a dark shroud.

"I'm exhausted," I said softly. "Can we lie down?"

The dusk had wrapped around us, cloaking the room in shadows as the ambient light from the clerestory windows faded.

We lay on his bed in stillness, my head resting on his shoulder.

"I never imagined…" Josef began, his voice barely above a whisper. "I didn't know …"

I felt him tense beside me, grappling with the enormity of it all. The implications were colossal; he had documented a moment in history and, in 1968, chosen a caption and some accompanying text to describe it without fully understanding or knowing its repercussions.

"It's not only your photograph anymore," I murmured into his side. "It's her story. It's always been her story."

His breath hitched slightly as he processed that truth. "And you're saying she's… alive?"

"Yes," I replied, pulling back to meet his gaze again. "I found her seven years ago — my mother is alive."

His expression shifted from disbelief to something softer, more compassionate.

"You've spoken to her?"

"Yes," I said. "She verified everything... everything I needed to know."

"Elizabeth," he said softly. "What does this mean for you? For your work? For your mother?"

"I can't ignore how intertwined our stories are — that's why I'm here, with you... now." A wave of exhaustion washed over me as I spoke; my mind spun with thoughts and emotions that needed to be untangled carefully.

Josef turned slightly toward me, his eyes searching mine as if trying to gauge my resolve amidst my fragility.

"You understand what this means for the photograph, for Rescued from the Ashes, don't you? Its legitimacy will shift; people will see it differently now."

"Yes. People need to see it differently now." The truth tasted bitter on my tongue. "This image has been viewed as an emblem of hope for so long — representing both suffering and survival — but it has been misappropriated in many ways."

"What do you intend to do?" His voice was steady but filled with concern.

"We have to return the story to her," I said. "Not only in footnotes or acknowledgements, but in real ways. Through public work, through platforms that centre her voice. She deserves that."

"Is she willing to speak?" Josef asked calmly.

"I don't know," I said. "It's hers to decide. But if she does — if she wants to — we have to be ready to listen."

He drew a long, slow breath.

"I'll support you. In whatever way I can."

I reached for his hand, lacing my fingers through his. His touch was steady. Outside, the last light was fading, and darkness had swept across the room, into a quiet that felt both protective and expectant.

"We. You and I. We need to repatriate her story," I said firmly, the words emerging with more clarity than I'd expected. "Not only in academic circles but publicly — through exhibitions or talks or anything that can bring her story back into focus."

"Is that possible?" he asked cautiously, the uncertainty in his voice betraying how much he too, wanted to believe it could be.

"It must be possible," I said, feeling a current of resolve beginning to rise in me, cutting through the day's fatigue. "If we want to honour what happened — if we want to honour her — it must be told through her voice."

I paused, then added, "I keep thinking about Migrant Mother — one of the most iconic photographs of the twentieth century. But it took decades for Florence Thompson's children to get people to see her as a person who is more than that image. She was turned into a symbol of struggle — of poverty, of resilience — but she was also erased. Her real name, her real story — it was lost in the image."

I looked across at Josef's face and saw the thought land.

"I've often admired that photograph," he said slowly. "There's something haunting in it, something elemental. Dorothea Lange captured... something timeless."

He took a very long pause and for a moment I thought he was sleeping, but then he said with a sigh.

"I never thought about what it cost Florence. I never thought about what it must've meant for her — to be turned into a symbol like that. To have no say in it."

I nodded. "And I don't want that to happen to my mother. I don't want her remembered as an anonymous figure of pity or endurance. I want her remembered as a woman — with a name, a life, a voice."

He looked at me again, and I could feel something shifting between us. A deepening of purpose.

"You're right," he said. "We must make sure she's not reduced to an image. I don't want that either. Not for her. Not for you."

A stillness settled between us, but it wasn't empty. It held something shared; something forged in the mutual understanding of what needed to be done.

This time, when I spoke, my voice was steadier.

"She deserves better than to be remembered through someone else's lens. She deserves her name, her story and her dignity."

Josef squeezed my hand. "Then let's begin," he said. "Let's give her all of that — and more."

We held onto each other a little tighter as if anchoring ourselves against what lay ahead — a labyrinthine path full of heartache and healing that demanded sensitivity and nuance.

"Together?" Josef asked gently.

"Yes. Together."

As dusk turned deeper around us, I closed my eyes, nestled against the warmth of Josef's torso, and fell into a deep sleep.

*

I first saw the photograph titled *Migrant Mother* when I was eighteen in the Stanford University library.

At that time, what I saw was a handsome dignified woman — Florence Owens Thompson — with worry carved deep into her face, children clinging to her shoulders, baby in her lap. I stared at it for ages and there was something deeply unsettling and unresolved about it. Not only the hardship it showed, but what was left out of the frame — what the photograph wasn't telling us.

Dorothea Lange took the photograph in 1936, at a migrant workers' camp in Nipomo, California. Florence was thirty-two, stranded with seven children, broke and hungry after the pea crop failed. Lange was working for the U.S. Government's Resettlement Administration and drove past the scene in her car. Further up the road she instinctively stopped and turned back. She spoke to Florence briefly and took six exposures on her large-format Graflex Super D camera arranging her and the children around her for maximum impact. The final shot she took — the one we all know — became an iconic symbol overnight.

It's often held up as a masterpiece, a depiction of maternal strength in crisis. But it's as powerful as it's also deeply problematic. Florence never permitted the image to be published, and she didn't even know it had been. She received no money or credit — she was not even named.

For the rest of her life, she was known only as the *Migrant Mother*, a symbol of misery rather than a person in her own right. She later said the photograph embarrassed her, that people saw her as a "poor woman" rather than someone who had fought to keep her family alive.

That's what troubles me — the way photography, even at its most compassionate, can strip someone of their voice. It turns them into a message. And once you're a message, you're no longer allowed to be messy, complicated, or real.

Florence went on to work in canneries, fields, kitchens — anywhere that paid. She stayed poor. In the 1970s and '80s, feminist scholars began to look again at the photograph, asking who gets seen and who gets erased. By then, Florence was older, sick, and still struggling. She died in 1983, and it was left to her children to set the record straight — to name her, to tell the full story and remind the world that their mother was more than a face of the Great Depression.

I often look at the photo. It's brilliant, but also an uncomfortable reminder that even the most famous image can betray the person in it.

My mother's story has parallels with Florence's. What moved me most, in the end, wasn't the photograph itself, it was Florence Thompson's daughter, Norma Rydlewski. A woman who, decades after Migrant Mother had established its iconic profile, stood and said:

"No. That was my mother. Let me tell you who she really was."

Norma's reframing of her mother's role helped challenge simplistic narratives of female suffering in American visual culture.

She didn't have a platform, not in the conventional sense. But she had clarity and a certain kind of fury. She refused to let her mother be remembered only as a symbol of suffering. She spoke of a woman who worked her hands raw to feed her children, who hated pity, who never asked to be frozen in a moment of despair and turned into an icon. A woman who was proud, capable and alive with contradictions.

Norma challenged the story that had been told about her family, without their permission, and without compensation or so much as a follow-up call. She didn't speak like a scholar, but what she said had more weight than a dozen academic essays on documentary ethics. She reminded people that photography, for all its beauty and power, can take something from its subject — even as it gives something to the world.

It was Norma who asked the question I've never stopped thinking about: At what cost do we make symbols of other people's pain? And who gets to decide what a life is worth — before or after it's turned into an image?

She didn't shout or seek revenge — she simply insisted that her mother's full humanity be seen. That's what stays with me: the daughter, not the image; and the truth, not the myth.

Norma was my inspiration.

*

Quang Ngai Province, Vietnam, 2001

I remember the smell — wet earth, petrol, and something faintly floral clinging to the trees. I was sitting in the front seat of a battered minibus rattling south through Quang Ngai, clutching my notebook. It was hot and close, and I was nauseous both from the stench of the petrol and from the weight of what I might find.

I had come armed with her name. It was Nguyễn Thi Thu.

A retired archivist at the war museum in Da Nang had scribbled her address on the back of a lecture handout along with a map and said, "She may not want to see you. You must be prepared."

The village was quiet — a cluster of low, tin-roofed homes near a pond, children playing with old tyres, a woman washing clothes at a tap. A man, barefoot and kind-faced, walked me to the edge of the village and pointed to a yellow house shaded by a tall papaya tree.

"She lives there," he said simply.

I stood for a long time before knocking. When the door opened, I saw a woman in her early fifties, slim, upright, wiping her hands on a cloth. Her eyes stopped me cold.

"Xin chào," I said softly.

She tilted her head slightly. Her expression was wary but not unkind.

I reached into my bag and pulled out a small plastic sleeve. Inside was a print of Rescued from the Ashes together with a small, faded photograph of a young Vietnamese woman holding a baby. I handed them to her.

She took them with both hands. Her thumb gently brushed the faded photograph.

"Trời oi," she whispered. "It's me."

My throat tightened and my knees felt weak.

"I think... that's me." I pointed to the baby, then faltered. "I think I'm your daughter. I was born in 1969. Taken to America. Through an orphanage in Da Nang."

Her face was still as she looked at me — not at my clothes or my skin or my hair, but into me as if searching for something that had haunted her for years. She reached forward and touched my cheek with the back of her hand.

"My daughter," she said, in Vietnamese. I understood.

She pulled me into her arms, and I crumpled against her. I had cried when I was handed my adoption papers six months before, but not like this. I sobbed in the way I'd never allowed myself to, not even in private.

There, in her arms, I cried like a child. Her child.

We sat on mats beneath a slow-turning fan. A neighbour came to translate. She spoke gently, pausing often as my mother unspooled fragments of her story.

She had been nineteen when her entire family had been brutally slaughtered by Charlie Company — her parents, her brothers, a niece. She had survived by hiding beneath a collapsed hut, half-conscious.

By the time Josef arrived, with a different unit several hours later, she had already been pulled from the wreckage by two soldiers — men who hadn't taken part in the killings but were sent in as reinforcements. One of them had tried to help her walk. The other stayed behind, watchful. They were the ones in the photograph.

She never learned their names.

Afterwards, at a temporary U.S. medical station, she was examined and treated. Her face darkened as she described what happened next. The men who had helped her out of the village visited the hospital tent. They offered her food, water, and a blanket. She had nothing, so she accepted. That night, they didn't ask. And she didn't scream.

She became pregnant. She was moved to Da Nang. When the baby came in January 1969, a girl — she was forced to give her up.

"I called you Mai," she said, tears streaking her face. "Because apricot blossoms bloom even in the cold."

We spoke long into the night. Her voice reminded me of water moving over stone. Even when I couldn't understand the words, I felt the shape of them in my chest.

In the days that followed, she introduced me to her other children — my half-brothers, Hoang and Duy, and my sister, Linh, who was seventeen and wore jeans and a T-shirt with an English band on the front. Linh gave me a silk scarf she had painted herself. "For your new life," she said.

Their father had been a schoolteacher. He died in 1995. When I told them I had been raised in America and had come searching for a woman I only knew from a photograph, they listened without judgment.

One afternoon, I sat with our mother and her neighbour beneath the papaya tree.

"Why didn't you keep me?" I asked her softly. It was an academic question but one I needed to ask.

"You would have become "bui dời"", she replied. "No choices."

She looked away for a long time.

"Because I couldn't keep you safe. I let you go so that you might live."

I had carried out in-depth research into what happened to babies like me after the war — the so-called Amerasians who stayed behind in Vietnam. We were branded bui dời, "dust of life," and treated like stains on the nation's honour. Visibly different, and essentially unwanted. Many were denied schooling, turned away from jobs, abandoned by families, or left to survive on the streets. We were reminders of a war no one wanted to remember, of foreign soldiers and shame. Some made it out through the Amerasian Homecoming Act, but many more were left behind to live in the shadow of a country that never accepted them. I was one of the lucky ones — but even luck carries its own weight.

I travelled back to Da Nang with Linh's scarf around my shoulders. I have carried my birth mother with me ever since. Always. And, with the Chandlers' blessing, I have visited her each year and provided as much support to my birth family as I can.

*

It had been a long-awaited reckoning with Josef.

From childhood, I had known that I was sent from Vietnam when I was one. For the Chandlers it was a whispered truth rather than an overt fact. They had loved me, but there was always an unspoken acknowledgement of another life, of my family left behind.

As I grew older, pieces of the puzzle began to fall into place. The fragmented stories of Amerasian children, the tales of war and abandonment — I absorbed them all. By the time I was eighteen, I had a comprehensive understanding of what it meant to be an Amerasian child and then an adult in post-war Vietnam.

My sense of justice compelled me to delve deeper into these narratives, and I took that drive into my studies at Stanford University; to explore the true stories of every type of people whose lives were irrevocably altered by conflict and violence.

And among these stories, one photograph stood out as an ever-present reminder — *Rescued from the Ashes*. An image that had become iconic, representing a flicker of hope amid unspeakable atrocity.

Yet, for me, that photograph represented something far more complex. It became a symbol of erasure — a moment frozen in time that failed to capture the true horror.

Over four hours on March 16th, 1968, U.S. troops murdered between 347 and 504 unarmed civilians in My Lai. Women were raped before being killed; babies, children and the elderly were slaughtered without mercy. The lack of precision in the numbers killed reflects not only the chaos and horror of the massacre itself but a collusion, involving denial, suppression, and incomplete record-keeping by those responsible. Bodies were often mutilated, burned, or buried in mass graves. Some victims were tossed into irrigation ditches or wells, making recovery and counting difficult. The U.S. military initially made no effort to count or identify victims. In fact, they tried to cover up the massacre.

Rescued from the Ashes did not provide justice for those murdered people. It didn't even begin to tell their story. And it certainly didn't tell the true story of Nguyễn Thi Thu — my mother.

For years, I had grappled with this image. The woman at its centre was more than a subject to me.

I had long known that my mother had survived My Lai, but the personal significance of this particular photograph was something I stumbled upon unexpectedly. During my years of research, I had come across numerous images and testimonies from that horrific day. It was during an archival deep dive, poring over records and photographs, that I relooked at *Rescued from the Ashes*. One day it dawned on me like a calling. The recognition was immediate and visceral. The woman in the photograph bore an uncanny resemblance to the only image I had ever seen of my birth mother: a small, worn photograph that had been handed to the Chandlers when I was adopted. Such gestures were rare at the time — Vietnamese adoptees were seldom given any clues about their origins. But someone at the orphanage in Da Lang, moved by compassion or by the photograph's significance, had gone to the trouble of capturing an image of Nguyễn holding me shortly after my birth. They ensured that the picture travelled with me to America.

My gut feeling urged me to investigate further. The verification process was arduous. I reached out to survivors, historians, and even forensic experts to piece together the fragments of the woman in the photo's history.

In 2000 I received my adoption papers, and her name was revealed to me.

Rescued from the Ashes, once an abstract representation of war's brutality, now held a deeply personal significance.

Meeting Josef Batten had not been what I expected. The man behind the camera was not a monster but a deeply flawed human carrying his burdens. In confronting him, I sought not only answers but also a form of reconciliation.

He didn't defend his actions nor justify his presence in My Lai on that day. Instead, he listened as I spoke about my mother's life after the massacre — how she had survived by sheer willpower but would never escape the horrifying shadows cast by that day. The photograph had stripped her of her narrative, turning her into an emblem rather than allowing her to own her story and be a representative of truth.

That day with Josef marked both an end and a beginning — a reckoning not only with him but also with myself; acknowledging all that drove me here: love for my mother; a need for justice; and a desire for the truth to be told beyond those images — frozen in time and sold for money as pictures on a page.

20. Reframing The Ashes

In the days that followed, Josef and I began working together to ensure that Nguyễn Thi Thu's story — and those of countless others — would be told with the dignity and truthfulness they deserved. It wasn't enough to change history or undo what had been done — but it was a start towards justice.

I found myself increasingly drawn to The Stopover. The initial shock of our reckoning lingered sensitively in the air between us. We were treading through uncharted waters, and we navigated its undercurrents with care.

As a result, Josef, despite his seventy-eight years and the vigour that still defined him, seemed altered, more tentative in his movements. The robust man I had come to know appeared slightly hunched now, as though the truths we were unearthing together had begun to settle across the top of his back. We spent long afternoons in the courtyard, sheltered beneath the filtered light of overhanging branches, with the hum of cicadas and the rustle of leaves creating a cocoon of calm.

The photograph — *Rescued from the Ashes* — was retrieved from its archive box. We placed it on the table between us to remind us of how charged it was with fresh significance. We spoke with growing clarity about what should happen next.

"The image needs a new context," said Josef.

The silence that followed was soon broken by Julie, who had joined us taking her usual seat with the ease of someone who had begun to feel at home in our circle. She didn't hesitate.

"The title has to change," she said simply. "And it needs to include her name. That's what they should have done with Migrant Mother. They should have changed the title a long time ago!"

We knew she was right.

Nguyễn Thi Thu was never *rescued*. She was exploited, violently assaulted and abandoned. The current title — clinical, passive, depersonalised — was now intolerable. It had once served to universalise the image, to place it among a canon of war photography unmoored from identity. But we could no longer accept that erasure.

Nguyễn was not only a symbol or an emblem of suffering — she was also a person, with a name, a story, and a daughter who had carried the impact of her silence. Reframing the photograph was no longer a question of ethics or legacy — it had to become an act of restoration.

And of love.

That afternoon, Josef called Anne Delacourt at *Agence Frontière* and explained everything that had occurred — the truth about my mother and our intention to reposition the image, this time on our terms. He placed the call on speaker so that I could be part of the conversation, and I listened as he described the emotional weight of the revelation and our commitment to handling it with care.

Anne had, by 2008, transformed *Agence Frontière* into one of the most respected digital photography archives in Europe and she was known not only for her curatorial insight but for her commitment to ethical storytelling. Her reaction, though subdued, was filled with respect and recognition. She understood the gravity of what was unfolding.

From that moment, the tone of our conversations shifted. We were no longer reacting — we were planning. The photograph would be repositioned, its caption rewritten, and its context expanded. But we also understood that the moment the story became public, it would no longer belong only to us. The media would swarm, headlines would simplify, and the image might be co-opted to serve narratives that ran counter to our intent. We had to be ready.

We resolved, together, that nothing would be released until a full public relations project plan was in place. Josef and I, with Anne's guidance, would build a digital archive — not only of this photograph, but of Nguyễn's story, the wider historical context, and the realities of lives lived in the shadow of atrocity. This would be our platform, and from it, we would speak with one voice. We would not let others define the message for us. We would own it.

Julie, ever intuitive, offered her help without needing to be asked. She wanted to support me — practically, emotionally and logistically.

"This gives me something to work towards," she said, and I could hear a renewed purpose in her voice.

Those first few days unfolded with a sacred tenderness, imbued with the unmistakable sense that something irreversible had begun. Between Josef and me, too, something shifted. An enhanced friendship emerged — measured and respectful, but real, nonetheless, imbued with a rare and exquisite tenderness that deepened with each conversation.

One evening, as the light slid gold across the courtyard and the air turned thick with the scent of jasmine, Josef turned to me with an offer that took me by surprise.

"Would you consider moving into one of the guest suites? No need to pay." he gently asked.

I was touched by the gesture. The Stopover had become my sanctuary too; a space suspended from the usual noise of the world.

"I would love that," I replied, pausing as a flicker of boldness rose in me. "But I have one condition."

Josef raised an eyebrow, his eyes steady on mine.

"You must take my portrait," I said. "You've never asked."

He looked at me — truly looked — his gaze sharp and soft and something unspoken and unmistakable emerged between us.

*

It became clear to me, almost without decision, that the work of reframing Nguyễn Thi Thu's story could not — and should not — be rushed. There was no urgency now, no pressing need to act. I had done what I came to do: I had stood before the man who took the photograph, and the outcome was something I could never have foreseen — that Josef would become, unexpectedly, one of the most significant people in my life.

What mattered now was not momentum but care. This was a responsibility that extended beyond my own reckoning, beyond the impulse to set things right on my terms. It belonged to more than me.

Liam and I had spoken. He understood the weight of it, but he also reminded me — with empathic clarity — that *Woven Histories* was entering a crucial phase and the work unfolding in Broome was gathering meaning. Each field trip, and each story entrusted to us, brought the project more fully into focus. That was where my attention belonged.

My mother's story would remain, still and present, but it was not mine to tell alone. Whatever shape it might take — whatever language we might one day find for it — would require her voice, her permission and her presence. Nothing should move forward until I had sat with her, in Vietnam, and asked what she wanted.

For now, it was enough to carry that intention lightly. One thing at a time.

Having moved out of Liam's annexe, my outlook had shifted, and The Stopover felt alive, its light a reflection of my burgeoning spirit.

Relationships flourished in this nurturing environment; Adam stood as my steady anchor, his calm presence grounding me when the tides of emotion surged.

With Julie, our companionship deepened. Julie, in simply being Julie, taught me humility and the joy of being free and alive. She'd done her job of raising her children and had liberated herself. Now she was living for Julie, and I was a beneficiary of her laughter and joy. She found herself becoming ever more curious about my work; it became a source of fascination for her, and she wanted to be a part of it. She began joining Liam and me on our field trips, as an unofficial assistant, and our laughter together on our long trips into the bush was intertwined with deep conversations about art, life, and healing.

With Josef, I could hardly believe how our dynamic had transformed since I arrived in Broome. No longer did I see him solely as the man behind the camera; we became companions in a shared journey of discovery. Our intimate dialogues unfolded layers I don't think either of us had ever intended to share — thoughts on loss, resilience, and memory entwined with vulnerability and strength. We would drift into conversations on the veranda, find solace in the communal courtyard, or take extensive strolls together along Cable Beach.

Despite our age difference, our affection for each other was borne out of an equal exchange of knowledge and understanding that brought us closer together. With our delicate intimacy, we both learned more about navigating the past while finding comfort in the present.

Josef's private sanctuary became my refuge too — a space he still shared only with me, a world within a world. We would regularly retreat, surrounded by his archive, the weight of his career heavy in the air. Together we explored other photographs that might invite scrutiny — ones that deserved to be reevaluated, reframed, and ownership restored to their subjects.

It was less a task and more an obsession, ignited by a shared desire for understanding and repatriation for the subjects and their context.

We read aloud to each other — fragments of theory and criticism, ideas that challenged and unsettled. For Josef, it became more than an academic exercise; it transformed into a burning necessity — to honour those captured in his lens, not as objects of history, but as people still deserving of care.

We often found ourselves emotionally drained, collapsing onto his bed together — there was a comfort for us both in lying there, side by side, enveloped in each other's presence and music became part of our ritual. Glenn Gould's *Goldberg Variations* often graced the air around us, his intricate piano weaving melodies that mirrored our evolving connection. In those unhurried hours, something occurred between us. Not quite romantic love, but a tenderness that surprised me — innocent, and entirely real — a closeness I hadn't anticipated.

*

When I'd agreed to move into The Stopover, I'd made it a half-serious condition that he photograph me, and yet weeks passed, and nothing was said. We shared everything else so easily and openly, that I began to believe he simply didn't want to and told myself it didn't matter — but it did.

When it happened, it was almost without ceremony. He looked at me one afternoon when I'd finished my work — a loose cotton dress hanging from my frame, bare feet dusty from the veranda, only a slick of mascara to my eyes, and said,

"Let's go in."

I followed him into his studio, a space I knew well, having watched others pass through it, and I'd seen the delicate alchemy of his process. But being the subject was something else entirely.

He began with the Hasselblad, his square-format film camera fitted with an 80mm lens. He moved with a fluency that belied his advanced years. It was a dance of instinct and control; he circled, shifted, stepped back and leaned in, always searching. His movements reminded me of Cartier-Bresson in his pursuit of the decisive moment. I stayed neutral, my expression open but unguarded and without performance.

To start he positioned me in from of the background of a white roll, but we didn't stay with it and we moved around the room. Josef usually abandoned anything that might cloud the frame, and he believed in paring back so all that remained was the space between the photographer and the person, but on this occasion, he allowed elements of his studio to seep into the frame, mostly in blurred outline behind or beside me.

Afterwards, he swapped the camera to Mo Batten's ancient 10x8 plate camera on a large static wooden tripod. With this camera he moved slowly with deliberate care and precision and delicately motioned me into his frame. The shift in his process was palpable. With the Hasselblad, he hunted moments. With the large format, he waited for something else to settle in — it was more a meditative process of detecting presence and spirit. In his silence he asked me not to perform, but to surrender, which I willingly did.

Being photographed by Josef was unlike anything I had experienced. Most portrait photography is about vanity and image, but Josef's felt closer to listening. It felt exhilarating, intimate, and strange. I didn't feel I'd been beautified, I felt recognised. I didn't feel arranged by him but allowed to simply be me.

When the prints were ready, I saw myself in a way I never had. The Hasselblad images caught flashes of myself I barely recognised. There were half-smiles, authentic in their stillness, and there was a clarity and authenticity to them that I had rarely seen. I had always felt so self-conscious in front of a camera, but in these photographs none of this showed through.

The 10x8 portrait he selected felt less like a photograph and more abstract, charged with an almost alchemical quality — conjured rather than captured. In the darkroom, unexpected textures had emerged, soft halos and ghosted edges, the chemicals offering qualities of their own. The result reminded me of a burnished mirror, the kind where the silvering slips with age, leaving patches of reflection and opacity — less a likeness, instead something more elemental. Perhaps Josef had reached for spirit instead of surface and I appeared not as a fixed self, but as a shifting presence — part memory and part possibility.

*

The lightness I had felt beneath Josef's gaze lingered long after the cameras were put away. It settled in me, a contentment that softened the edges of things. In his presence, I felt entirely present — recognised in ways that asked nothing of me but to simply be me. There was a gentleness in that seeing, and it encouraged a tender settled space within me.

Later, we lay together on his bed, as we often did, side by side, music drifting through the air, our breathing aligned more by comfort than intent. There was no moment of decision; nothing planned or expected. It simply unfolded between us — a physical intimacy neither of us had sought, but neither resisted either.

What happened was not born of need or desire in any conventional sense. It was a deep human recognition expressing itself in touch, in closeness, and a trust we had built slowly and unknowingly. There was no rush or heat, it was a profound sense of arrival.

We didn't feel the need to speak of it afterwards. The moment had spoken for us, and we understood what it meant.

Over the weeks that followed — and it was only weeks — those moments returned, unannounced. There wasn't a pattern to them, or any escalation or retreat. We would simply find ourselves once again physically drawn together.

There were no gestures of seduction, no flirtation. Only presence and trust — an understanding that didn't need words. We weren't becoming lovers in any traditional sense — we weren't becoming anything really. We were simply in it, together, held in those pockets of time when touch felt like language, and our physical closeness asked nothing more than to simply be allowed.

And then, just as naturally we stopped.

There was no tension, no shift in the air and there was no sorrow. We continued to lay together, side by side on the bed still holding each other and speaking with the same unguarded ease. But whatever had passed between us during those weeks had shifted. The tenderness remained, but it no longer asked to be expressed through our bodies. There was no loss in it, only an understanding that this, too, was part of the shape we made together.

*

In the quiet of New Year's Day 2009, as the courtyard filled with guests and a celebratory lunch gathered pace, I found myself unable to join the mood. I was seven weeks pregnant, and everything in me felt raw. I was overwhelmed by emotion, disoriented by the weight of what I now carried.

Julie had finished setting the tables — she had a gift for making things beautiful. When she was done, I asked her to sit with me on the veranda outside my guest suite. I made tea and, without much ceremony, I told her.

She took the news in with quiet kindliness, the questions — how, when, who — hanging between us without pressure.

What mattered was this: I had wanted a child all my life. Even when I'd convinced myself I could live without through the four uneasy years with Tyler McCoy, who either couldn't or wouldn't step into that future with me. But the longing never left — it was part of who I was, and what I'd always carried.

Julie listened. She didn't try to soothe or fix anything. She simply held the space, steady and kind, letting the truth of it all settle.

When I said Josef's name, she understood. I explained that I hadn't told him yet because I needed confirmation from the antenatal clinic that everything was okay first — there was too much in a delicate balance at The Stopover to be considered.

Julie didn't press, and I was quietly grateful. Her presence offered steady comfort — the assurance that, whatever lay ahead, I wouldn't be facing it entirely alone.

Three weeks later, she accompanied me to Broome General Hospital for an ultrasound. I hadn't expected the experience to feel so calm, almost peaceful. Morning sickness had taken its toll and was a persistent inconvenience, impossible to completely hide, but that morning, I felt steadier.

Thankfully, the scan clarified that everything was as it should be. As I lay there watching the screen, a sense of reassurance warmed me from the inside out and I felt something close to joy.

Afterwards, Julie and I spoke briefly — about Josef, and whether to involve Adam and maybe speak with him first. We concluded that I now simply needed to go and tell the child's father.

Back at The Stopover, the courtyard buzzed faintly with late afternoon life, and I paused for a moment, taking it in, steadying myself before I went to find him.

He was tidying his darkroom with the door ajar, and the overhead lights on full exposing the room in a way that felt stark and alien. Usually, our passage through the darkroom to his archive and sanctuary was guided by the dim red of the safelights. I felt a nervous jangle as I approached him.

"Josef, there's something I need to tell you." My hands suggesting we move into his sanctuary.

The kindness in his eyes and smile made me feel everything would be alright. The door was already unlocked, and we stood opposite each other. I had already decided that I should not preface anything and simply come out and tell him.

"Josef," I said looking directly into his eyes, "I'm pregnant."

After a brief look of confusion, he paused, looked directly at me, smiled and simply said, "Elizabeth, if you are happy about it, I am overjoyed."

A few tears of joy rolled down my cheeks as he stood and took me in his arms and held me. He needed no confirmation that it was his baby — it was not something that seemed to matter to him. The only thing that seemed to matter was that I was happy and for that, I will always be truly grateful to this extraordinary yet unknowable man.

*

The following days felt lighter, and I was buoyed with the joy of knowing I would become a mother. Remarkably, from the moment I told Josef, the nausea that had plagued me seemed to lift. I felt well, more alive than I had in years, and ready to meet the world with renewed energy.

By then, the wet season had fully taken hold, making it impossible to carry out the remaining field trips without risking becoming stranded somewhere even more remote than Broome. Liam and I both agreed that, given my condition, it would be best to postpone any further travel into the Kimberley until the rains eased, and the tracks became passable again.

I continued with some of the writing and research, but my thoughts returned, insistently, to *Rescued from the Ashes* and my desire to rebalance it. After discussing it with Julie, we agreed that the time had come for me to travel to Vietnam to speak directly with my mother.

Adam and Josef both supported the plan on the condition I would minimise all risks: travel only by air-conditioned car and ensure that Julie would be by my side throughout. Julie was delighted by the prospect, and my gratitude for her in my life seemed to grow by the day.

I had let my mother know in advance we would be coming and in the second week of February, we left Broome on a mid-morning flight to Perth. Julie handled everything — tickets, bags, accommodation and what I should eat.

The following day we flew business class to Singapore. I slept comfortably for most of the flight, drinking ginger tea and keeping my legs up like the midwife told me. In Singapore, we stayed two nights near the Botanic Gardens, and I walked a little under the trees, but we mostly stayed inside.

From there, we flew to Da Nang in a small plane that bumped its way through thick clouds. A driver was waiting with our names on a sign. We drove south in his large black Hyundai in silence, past rice fields and narrow houses, mopeds and schoolchildren. I kept my hand on my belly the whole way, not sure if I was holding on or letting go.

In the small town close to my mother's village, we stayed in an air-conditioned hotel which was basic but comfortable and the driver took a separate room nearby.

The following morning, we drove to see her in the tiny rural settlement tucked between the paddies and the hills — where the roads narrowed to single tracks and modernity felt a long way off. The air was thick with heat and the slow rhythm of daily life. Chickens scratched in the dust, and the scent of boiled rice lingered in the still air.

Nguyễn Thi Thu greeted me with a smile that held all her usual warmth. This was my eighth visit to her community, and we were familiar with each other in ways that didn't require words. This time though, she held my hand for a long moment — she could sense without articulating it that I had something important to tell her.

Julie and I were offered tea, and we sat cross-legged on a woven mat in the sparse, shaded front room of her home. The walls were bare save for a faded calendar and a small family altar — a tranquil space filled with a sense of humility.

Beside us sat Anh, her neighbour who had often assisted us with translation. She was kind and unobtrusive, careful not to insert herself into the conversation, only to bridge it gently. I had rehearsed what I wanted to say, and yet the words faltered the moment I tried to speak them. How do you ask someone to reopen a wound they have taken decades to bury?

Still, I tried.

I told her that I had now confronted Josef Batten with the truth of what had happened to her; that I felt it was time for the truth of her story to be told. I said the photograph, *Rescued from the Ashes,* had shaped the lives of many, mine included, but that its power came at a cost. Her anonymity had always felt like an omission, a silence where the truth should have been. I asked her what she wanted now. How she wished her story to be told… if at all.

Nguyễn Thi Thu listened without interruption. When I finished, she sat still for a while, her hands resting in her lap. When she began to speak, her voice was steady, words slow and clear.

Anh translated softly, letting each sentence settle before continuing.

She said she was glad I had told him, knowing he knew what had happened to her was a blessing. But as for the rest, she had no wish to revisit it. What had happened belonged to another time, one she had learned to live beyond. Her life now — simple, quiet, unremarkable to the outside world — was enough for her.

The photograph, she said, was not her story anymore and it alone, was not the only truth. Reclaiming it would not return anything to her. It would only bring people and questions and judgment. She did not want her village to whisper, or for outsiders to descend on them. She did not want to be anyone's symbol.

I absorbed her words with a growing weight in my chest. I had thought, or hoped, I was coming to offer something — restoration, perhaps. But she was telling me that what I carried was a need of my own, not hers.

Then I told her I was pregnant.

Anh's eyes flickered slightly, and she translated the words with a softness. I told my mother the truth — that the father was Josef, the man who had taken the photograph. There was a moment of stillness in the room, and I saw something shift in my mother's face. Shock, even horror. Her lips parted slightly, then closed again and her gaze dropped to the floor.

I hurried to explain that he was not the man I had imagined growing up — that he was gentle and kind, and that he had carried the burden of the image too, that he had given me so much — not only love, but space, and trust, and healing.

She looked at me again, searching my face for something, and though she said nothing, I sensed a softening. Not acceptance, but a willingness to let the moment pass without judgment. Julie reached over and placed her hand lightly on my arm. That simple gesture helped me steady myself and to see that Nguyễn Thi Thu's refusal was not a denial, but a wisdom.

It wasn't my place to extract anything from her. Not her story, nor her pain — not even her name.

We left shortly before sunset and that night, I lay awake amidst the quiet hum of the air conditioning, an embroidered cloth my mother had given me folded beside my bed. I recognised that for my mother truth doesn't always need to be spoken to be honoured, and how sometimes, dignity lies in silence, not exposure.

In the morning, we returned to say our farewells. She gave me a small bundle of herbs from her garden, pressed into my hand without words. I held her for a long moment, promising I would bring her grandchild with me next time to meet her. She smiled and hugged me again.

*

Somewhere over the Timor Sea, with Julie asleep beside me and the drone of the plane engines soft in my ears, I found myself sink-ing into a stillness. Outside the window, clouds moved in quiet waves across the darkening sky. Inside, something had shifted.

For as long as I could remember, I had needed answers — to name things and fix what had been broken, to bring light into every shadow. I'd called it justice — my work, my cause, my conviction. But the truth of it was it had also been about me and about my own need to make the world make sense — to assign blame, to right wrongs, to speak when others had been silenced.

I saw, with a clarity that made me ache, how I had projected that need onto my mother, asking her to unearth a past she had no wish to revisit. I could see how I had expected Josef to carry not only his guilt but my demands for redemption. And how, in some way, I had turned society itself into an adversary — an indifferent structure I must confront, reshape and outwit.

That militancy had defined me — the sharp, almost aggressive hunger for truth. I'd been praised for it — respected even — but I could see now, how it had come at a considerable cost.

Despite all my degrees and my carefully cultivated understanding of trauma, power, and history, I had failed to grasp something very simple. That truth is not fixed, and it doesn't sit waiting at the end of some noble inquiry, shining and clean.

Josef had said it once, after a long conversation in which I'd tried to press him for an answer he didn't want to give.

"Truth," he said, "is a moveable feast. It changes with time, with light, and with who's sitting at the table."

I had smiled, not really taking it in, but I understood now. What we believe to be true may not always remain so. And what someone else carries as truth may have no place in our own crusade.

My mother's truth was silence. A life rebuilt around peace, not pain. Josef's was ambiguous, shaped by memory, regret, and the burden of a single frame. And mine? Well, mine was still forming, somewhere between defiance and surrender, between justice and grace.

I looked down at my hands resting on my belly. Perhaps the only truth I needed now was the one within me. This child. This moment. This breath.

21. Jimmy

Thomas Josef Batten Chandler was born at 10:27am on Thursday 12 August 2009, in Josef's king-sized bed in his hidden sanctuary at The Stopover. He weighed a healthy three and a half kilos, and I had been in labour for little more than two hours. We had anticipated him being born at Broome General, but I went into labour so fast we had no time to get there. Instead, the midwife came to us.

The sanctuary was alive that morning with sunlight streaming through the clerestory windows, just in time to celebrate this new beginning. Each contraction brought me closer to the moment I had dreamed of and feared. Adam and Julie were standing nearby; their faces lit with awe and joy.

When Thomas emerged his first cries pierced the hushed room. At that instant, Josef let out a yelp — a raw, involuntary cry from his gut, mingling joy and grief in equal measure. The sound was startling, a primal note that seemed to echo the glorious magnitude and wonder of a new life.

The midwife placed Thomas against my chest, and I looked down at his tiny form feeling an overwhelming sense of completeness wash over me. He seemed so fragile — his little fingers curling instinctively around mine. Josef stood by my side watching our son with an expression of wonderment and a new sense of responsibility.

Adam began capturing the moments in photographs from across the room, and the midwife took some photos of us all together and I felt Julie's hand rest on my shoulder. Now, when I look at those images, they can still move me to tears. Snapshots that contain something rare — a sense of a community shaped by trust and care, and the kind of love and understanding that rarely needs to be spoken but is deeply felt.

*

The arrival of Thomas changed the dynamic of life at The Stopover. Our son transformed the space with his presence, turning our carefully crafted sanctuary into something even more vital.

He was not simply our child, but a living embodiment of what we had become as a community — something treasured and nurtured by all who found themselves drawn to the peace of the courtyard.

In those early months, I watched Josef's transformation deepen further. The man who had spent decades documenting other people's stories now found himself irrevocably part of one. He would carry Thomas against his chest for hours, whispering stories into his tiny ear — not the stories of the war that had haunted him, but tales of light and beauty.

Our local community flourished around us. Marguerite and Talia took on the roles of exuberant, slightly wild aunts who had missed out on children of their own and were now compensating in magnificent waves. Talia would arrive with tiny handmade shirts sewn from fabrics she'd collected on her travels, while Marguerite taught Thomas to recognise birds before he could even speak, holding him up to the courtyard sky and naming each creature that passed overhead.

Adam gave Thomas music. He would sing Scottish lullabies from his childhood, play quiet pieces beside the cot, choosing melodies that would lull him to sleep — the quiet rise and fall of the piano in Arvo Pärt's *Spiegel im Spiegel*, or *Bach's Cello Suite No. 1* played so softly it merged with the rustling trees in the courtyard. Thomas would drift off with his tiny fingers curled around Adam's thumb, his breathing synchronising with the rhythm.

Liam and I continued to work together to complete *Woven Histories*, with Thomas alongside us. We had slowed the project down, understanding that the additional year or so it would take to complete was not only a necessity for my role as a mother but that it would deepen the quality of our research and give us more time to soften some of the sharp edges of our findings. Liam would often take Thomas while I conducted interviews, carrying him in a traditional sling and speaking to him in his indigenous language, teaching him words I couldn't pronounce.

Life felt calmer, less urgent. The rage that had driven me across oceans to confront Josef had transformed into a profound contentment that had seeped into my bones.

Other people entered our evening circles, each bringing something they could contribute. Adam brought Miriam, the local solicitor, back into the fold. She was a woman in her late fifties by then, with an extraordinary spirit and intellect who had never married. They had begun singing together, engaging in choral music that traversed a spectrum of genres and styles, even including Gregorian chants. Sometimes Adam would accompany her solo chants with his saxophone, which created a rare ethereal sound. The courtyard hummed, a rich oasis of both peace and intellectual stimulation for all who entered it.

In early April 2010, Adam's mother Maggie arrived at The Stopover for an extended stay. She was an extraordinarily youthful woman in her late sixties who exuded warmth, intellect, and a steely earthiness. Meeting her and seeing her engage with Thomas, I understood why Adam had become the man he was. I was in awe of her strength and beauty, and she became a solid foundation at the heart of our community during the six months she stayed with us.

The trail of visitors to The Stopover was relentless, yet somehow each person who crossed the threshold — whether for days or weeks — seemed to dissolve into the fabric of our shared existence without disruption. The courtyard possessed magic, an alchemy that transformed strangers into family before they'd even unpacked their bags.

Whatever identities they'd constructed in the outside world, the armour they wore to protect themselves, they seemed to shed at the front door like unnecessary clothing. I watched this metamorphosis time and again. A visiting photographer from Berlin arrived with her portfolio and credentials clutched like shields; by evening, she sat barefoot in the courtyard, laughing with Talia over mangoes and gin. A novelist from Melbourne entered with careful distance in his eyes; three days later, I found him cross-legged beside Adam's keyboard, discussing Bach's mathematical precision with the abandon of old friends.

Josef orchestrated these transformations without seeming to try. His presence provided room for people to unfurl. He asked questions that peeled away pretence and offered silences that invited truth. And Thomas enhanced this gift.

In the portrait sessions, Thomas became an unexpected catalyst. Placed in his rocker chair at the edge of Josef's studio, he'd observe with bright, curious eyes, occasionally punctuating the silence with delighted gurgles. I noticed how subjects would glance at him between poses, their faces softening imperceptibly. Something about his unguarded presence, his absolute lack of judgment or expectation, allowed people to shed their self-consciousness.

A Singaporean diplomat, stiff and formal in his first minutes, melted into a smile when Thomas reached for his glasses. A grieving widow from Sydney, who'd barely spoken since her arrival, found herself telling Thomas stories about her husband as Josef's camera captured the moment her face transformed with memory and love.

"It's extraordinary," Josef whispered to me one evening as we watched Thomas sleep. "He creates a bridge I never could. People seem to look at him and remember what matters."

I understood what he meant. Thomas had become an anchor for the community that had formed around us, a living reminder of hope. In his presence, people remembered their vulnerability and seemed to become, for a little while, their truest selves.

*

Perhaps our most memorable visitor was the superstar American pop princess, a notorious diva who graced The Stopover shortly after Maggie's arrival. She had shot to fame in the early 1980s, her wealth rivalled only by her reputation for being as difficult as she was talented. I never expected someone of her stature and notoriety to arrive at our quiet haven. Only Larissa had been informed of her impending visit, and she was sworn to secrecy.

She landed by private jet at Broome's tiny airport, flanked by a formidable entourage. Men were stationed in hired vehicles outside on Darnley Street watching the house like hawks. Yet, when she strolled through the front door on her own carrying only a weekend bag, it was as though she knew she needed to enter without fanfare.

Initially, Josef was nowhere to be found. As I caught sight of her wandering alone into the courtyard, I recognised her immediately. Larissa greeted her with the same warmth she extended to every guest and provided a drink before disappearing to fetch Josef.

She looked around, settled herself onto a low bench and began chatting easily with a few other guests who were blissfully unaware of who sat among them. From my distance, curiosity prickled my skin. This woman whom I would have prepared myself to dislike seemed remarkably ordinary — almost plain.

Eventually, Josef appeared with Thomas strapped to his chest. As he greeted her she lit up with genuine warmth upon seeing our son. Leaning closer to Thomas, cooing and smiling without an ounce of artifice — it was unexpected and disarming.

In the following days, she melded into our community life. Julie engaged her openly about how much she had enjoyed the music that formed the soundtrack to family holidays. Adam spoke at length with her about their shared love for music and soon enough they were busking together — her guitar harmonising beautifully with his fiddle. Marguerite and Talia were unguarded and raucous with her; they took liberties with their humour that had me anxiously praying they wouldn't say something incendiary enough for her to storm off in a diva-like huff. Yet there she was — this larger-than-life figure laughing among us, plucking notes alongside my son's surrogate uncle in our remote courtyard wedged between desert and sea on the far edge of that vast continent.

All my prejudices told me I should dislike her. Every story I'd heard detailed her arrogance and entitlement, yet here was proof of something else; she felt like one of us, and astonishingly, I liked her.

For the duration of her stay, she remained within The Stopover's walls except for one afternoon when, after a portrait shoot, she asked Josef to photograph her on the beach. He agreed and asked if I'd like to accompany them with Thomas — a proposition that delighted her, so we all climbed into her security detail's car and drove out to a quiet part of Cable Beach.

In the afternoon sun, she looked natural and unadorned, wearing a cream silk dress that wafted and splayed in the breeze. As we walked, I handed Thomas to her, and Josef asked her to hold still. In that instant, he captured her with Thomas cradled in one arm, her posture radiating an extraordinary serenity. It was a decisive moment — everything aligned. The photograph would become iconic, not of a princess or diva, but of a warm, compassionate woman in her fifties.

*

One sun-warmed afternoon in September 2010, Josef, Adam, Liam and I had fallen into one of those easy, open conversations in the courtyard that tended to unfold only when there was no agenda, or any pressing need to be somewhere else.

Josef, in his usual way, took his time before speaking. Gently, he said he'd been thinking about the future, his work, The Stopover, and what might happen after he was gone. Age was catching up with him, and despite being the father of a lively one-year-old, he was beginning to consider how to shape what he would leave behind.

He spoke with openness. He had no fixed agenda, he said, only the beginnings of an idea he hoped we might help him refine. He wanted to propose the establishment of a trust — something that could protect The Stopover as a place of welcome and exchange and preserve the integrity of his photographic archive. He was not interested in its preservation as a monument to himself, but as a space that might carry forward the values that had grown around The Stopover.

It was clear he had thought about it deeply, but he didn't present it as a finished plan. Instead, he invited us to collaborate: to develop a constitution, to agree its principles and shape its vision. He wanted us — me, Adam and Liam — to develop this with him, and eventually without him.

For a very long time, Josef and I had discussed the questions of authorship and the narrative that surrounded *Rescued from the Ashes*, and the many other images whose meanings had shifted with time. We had both come to believe that stories, like photographs, could be distorted as easily as revealed, and that truth required not only courage but care.

Our shared past, and the presence of our son, meant we could no longer see things only in terms of justice or exposure. We had responsibilities now to the living, to the legacy, and the complexity of it all. We had agreed, without ceremony, that my birth mother would never be named in any public account. She had not asked for any of this. Our story, in whatever shape we chose to tell it, would be told with restraint and care.

Liam, when we had first begun to speak of this, had said simply, "The truth isn't always served by revelation." and that phrase stayed with us. It allowed us to step back from the impulse to tell everything.

So, when Josef shared his thoughts of a Trust that would be not only rooted in the idea of truth but also in respect, resistance, and creative freedom, it felt like the natural next step. The vision was generous and far-reaching: to offer residencies and forums for those whose voices too often went unheard — Indigenous artists, war survivors, postcolonial thinkers, young people pushed to the margins. Josef's archive would be preserved with respect for cultural protocols, ensuring that communities connected to the work, and the people and places in the photographs could, if they wished, guide how they are used and interpreted.

We agreed, there in the courtyard, not in a formal vote but in an unspoken way that it wasn't simply about safeguarding the past. It was about shaping and offering a future — and it would begin, with the principal aim of listening rather than telling.

*

Through the long, rain-soaked summer of 2010 and into early 2011, several things happened that would forever alter the shape of our lives at The Stopover.

There was the formal establishment of *The Josef Batten Trust*, and the making of a film that would tell the story of Josef's legacy, The Stopover and all our lives into a satisfying and sustainable narrative.

By January, Miriam Finch had worked tirelessly with us all and a formal constitution for the Trust had taken shape: a document built not only from legal clauses but our shared values and a future we were willing to commit to. In February, the ownership of The Stopover was transferred to it, and we became a registered charity. Josef, Liam, Adam, and I became the initial primary trustees — not for symbolic reasons, but because it made sense that we should carry the responsibility of its future together.

Anne Delacourt, now semi-retired, joined us as an additional trustee soon after. She brought with her a network of contacts and a sharp sense of how stories moved through the world. Her brief was to establish connections and open the kinds of doors that might allow our work to reach people who needed it. I appreciated her carefulness, and how she approached each conversation like a long game, rarely rushing, always listening.

We launched the charity quietly, steering clear of excessive fanfare or celebration. Instead of announcing it to the world with a bang, we wanted to ease the concept into public consciousness — slowly transitioning our visitors from curious tourists attracted merely by Josef's portrait work to supporters who understood and aligned with our vision.

However, it was an initial press release Anne had published that reignited interest in Josef's story. Twenty years on from a previous enquiry they'd made, the producers of Nine Network's *60 Minutes Australia* came knocking again — this time with a proposal for a dedicated programme focusing on his life as a portrait photographer and his new family and the story surrounding it. The prospect stirred mixed feelings within me.

When Anne phoned Josef about their enquiry, I could sense tension crackling in the air. We all recognised how delicate this situation was; while we were eager to share Josef's journey, we also feared how it might be framed. Would they focus solely on sensationalism? Would they exploit the past rather than honouring it?

It was Anne who eventually broke through our spiral of doubt when she suggested the alternative of reaching out to her contacts at the BBC in London — commissioners for arts and culture who might appreciate what we were trying to achieve at The Stopover. She envisioned submitting an outline for a film that could bolster our mission without compromising its integrity.

The BBC moved swiftly after Anne made contact. In March 2011, ideas flowed freely between us and their team during a Skype meeting. When the conversation concluded I believed a film could be made that aligned with what we were trying to build.

As the rains thinned out and the gentler days of the dry season set in, the film began to take shape with the careful attention of a team that knew how to listen.

From the outset, the BBC producers approached the project with restraint and depth. In June they arrived at The Stopover — not only filming but observing, allowing the rhythms of the place to speak for themselves. It was fronted by a well-known arts presenter who held it together with gravitas. He was masterful at asking the right questions, leaving space for silences, and allowing Josef the dignity of context, whilst still injecting subtle humour in all the right places. He interviewed us gently, without intrusion, and captured what could not have been scripted.

One warm evening in late September, when the edit was assembled, we all watched it for the first time together, projected onto Josef's studio wall. There was no sentimentality, no sensationalism. Instead, the film revealed the arc of Josef's life through the lens of his work and his relationships — not only the iconic images of war and the Broome portraits, but the stories beneath them: the ethical tensions, the silences in the frame, the lives on the margins.

There were scenes of Broome's red earth and the sea beyond it, of visitors coming and going, of Liam and Adam sorting through contact sheets, of Josef speaking, slowly and deliberately about his psychological transformation and the dawning of his sense of responsibility.

The film did not try to resolve what could not be resolved. It offered no neat redemption, only a careful laying down of what had happened: the trauma of war, the betrayal of institutions, the shadows that had been cast by secrets. Yet through it all, the message that emerged was one of resilience. Josef spoke not only of what had been taken, but of what had been given — how the act of staying in one place, of building something honest and shared, could itself be a form of justice.

When the documentary aired in the UK in November 2011 on BBC Two, it was also broadcast in Australia on SBS. The response was immediate and deeply affirming. Reviews in both countries praised its sensitivity and visual elegance. Viewers described it as "a portrait of conscience" and "a meditation on memory, art, and accountability." Critics noted how it resisted the easy arc of revelation, choosing instead to dwell in ambiguity and complexity.

For all of us, it was moving to see it unfold — not as a monument, but as a living conversation. The film did more than tell Josef's story, it reflected the values The Stopover had been built around: truth with care, art with ethics, legacy without self-glorification. And in doing so, it carried the message further than we could have imagined.

*

It was not only the establishment of the Trust and the making of the film that changed all our lives in 2011; it was the arrival of someone who, in his quiet and unintended way, overturned everything.

In May, while we juggled meetings and arrangements for the film, a man in his early forties appeared at The Stopover. Jimmy Fielding-Holland — a name that would soon become as familiar to us as our own — brought with him an aura of British formality. His polished brogue shoes gleamed in the sunlight, paired with a freshly laundered open-necked shirt and perfectly pressed trousers. He stood out amidst our more casual attire, as if from another planet.

At first, we suspected he might be with the BBC, perhaps an early arrival from their team checking us out or something. The way he carried himself — confident yet unassuming — gave me pause. But his charm quickly disarmed any apprehensions I harboured. He seemed interested in our work and approached each conversation with warmth.

Julie took an instant liking to him. They were quickly deep in conversation, and it struck me how she almost enveloped him in a maternal embrace, drawing him into our circle as if he belonged there all along. Her nurturing spirit sought to ease his evident discomfort; it was clear he was not accustomed to this way of life.

As the days turned into a week, I watched Jimmy begin to navigate The Stopover with an ease that belied his stiff exterior. He engaged with everyone — some visiting Elders, Liam, Adam — listening intently as they shared stories that had shaped their lives and community.

But there was something else underneath his charming façade; I could sense a yearning within him. He revealed snippets about his past, how he had an adoptive father and how his mother had shielded him from much turmoil.

Josef gave Jimmy something rare — a quiet, unconditional acceptance that softened the tension I had noticed settling around him. It was unspoken but palpable.

Early one morning shortly after dawn, I was following Thomas, by now a determined little toddler, along the veranda, when I came upon them in Josef's studio. The glass screen was folded open as it most often was, the light low and diffuse. There was a stillness to the space as if something delicate had begun to take shape.

Josef was setting up his plate camera, that beautiful, clumsy old machine with its heavy tripod and leather bellows. I paused in the doorway, keeping an eye on Thomas as he navigated a low step. Inside, Jimmy stood beside Josef, his curiosity apparent, the mood between them quiet but charged with mutual respect.

He asked about the camera — the hood, the ground glass, the upside-down image. I watched as Josef guided him through the ritual of looking. Jimmy slipped under the black cloth and emerged slowly, visibly altered, eyes wide.

"Extraordinary," he said softly. "How do you know what you're capturing when you can't even see it straight?"

Josef's reply came gently, almost without thinking — something about trusting the frame, about learning to feel where the edges fall. He demonstrated the card mount he sometimes used to visualise a shot. Their conversation unfolded in fragments, questions answered with more questions, but something between them had begun to settle and grow.

That afternoon, we went to Cable Beach together. Josef walked with his camera slung over his shoulder, Jimmy beside him still in his pressed trousers and polished shoes. He looked and felt incongruous and out of place. Thomas and I stood at a distance, watching them on the shoreline, and between us, the sea light flickered across the wet sand.

Josef began making some portraits moving with practised ease. I watched the way he observed Jimmy, searching for what lay behind the surface. Jimmy's smile gave way to something more uncertain. He leaned in and handed something to Josef, the sound of the sea and the breeze stopped me from hearing, but whatever he said, it reached Josef. I saw it in the set of his shoulders as he looked at his hands.

I saw Josef step back. His face collapsed inward. Tears slid down his cheeks before the sobs came, heavy and I could see him shaking as though in disbelief.

Later, when they returned to The Stopover, Adam was waiting for them in the drive. No words were exchanged. He simply moved towards Josef and placed a hand on his back as they walked inside together.

None of us spoke much that evening. The atmosphere of The Stopover had changed. We sat close but apart, each one of us sensing the enormity of what had passed without knowing its full impact. Josef stayed quiet, his grief folding in on himself before he retreated alone to his studio.

*

James Fielding-Holland was born in October 1968 in a small hospital in Canterbury, seven months after his mother, Cathy Holland, had abandoned her short-lived career as a model in London and returned to her parent's modest house in Folkestone.

She was barely twenty and crushed by the shock of pregnancy from her affair with Josef Batten, a man she'd loved deeply — a world-renowned war photographer who vanished into Vietnam before she could tell him she was carrying his child. At the hospital, the nurses barely concealed their bitter judgment of her. There was no father on the birth certificate and no explanation.

James' early childhood was shaped by the women who called him Jimmy. He lived with his mother at his grandparent's tiny, terraced house until he was three. Later Cathy married Keith Fielding, a surveyor with a decent income and a steadiness she must have found reassuring. Keith adopted Jimmy and raised him as his own and they didn't have any other children together. Cathy did what was expected, and they made a comfortable home in Canterbury.

There was no secret about his adoption. Cathy told him plainly and without sentiment. His birth father, she said, had been a photographer who covered wars. That was about it. The name Josef Batten wasn't spoken often, but Jimmy knew it. How could he not? Josef was famous — his books lined shelves in university libraries, his images circulated in art galleries, and his name was cited in academic journals and photojournalism courses. Later, there were a few radio interviews on YouTube and plenty of online articles to be researched. Although his reputation was legendary, Jimmy never sought him out or imagined writing him a letter or knocking on his door. The idea of meeting him felt unnecessary for a very long time. Josef was more a figure of history than of family.

Jimmy had always preferred the order of things. He boarded at Dulwich College, where he was a mediocre cricketer, and he took law at Bristol University, before climbing through the ranks of a city firm. A bachelor by inclination, he found comfort in work and routines, in the clarity of contracts and deadlines. There had been flings and a few tentative efforts at something more, but he was never quite available. His time and his focus had always belonged elsewhere.

When Cathy and Keith amicably divorced, Jimmy wasn't surprised. They'd lived parallel lives for years. Cathy, always spirited, tried to reinvent herself and took a course in Florence where she fell for an Italian artist. It turned out he was more invested in himself than in her. When she came home, disappointed but not defeated, something shifted between them. Their conversations deepened. Cathy, needing to unburden herself, began speaking more about the past and Josef.

She told Jimmy how much she had loved Josef. How she had never stopped loving him, or at least the memory of him. She had wanted him to be part of her life, but by the time she understood how deeply she felt about him, it was already too late, Josef had gone to Vietnam. There, she knew he had seen things no one should have to witness and there had been no way to reach across the widening gulf between their lives.

Jimmy already knew about Brian, who had seemed to be a regular part of his life when he was young, long after Cathy had met Keith. He was always around, helpful, handy, eager to please and hoping Cathy would come to love him again.

Brian was still in love with her when he had searched her out in London and it happened to coincide with the moment she discovered she was pregnant with Josef's child. Cathy had been young, unprepared and she hadn't known how to hold the enormity of love and loss and pregnancy all at once. Assisted by Brian, she fled London in a panicked state of confusion.

After Josef, Brian hadn't been Cathy's lover, he'd been a crutch, a stand-in while she navigated her parent's fury and the loss of her modelling career — as well as the man she loved.

Jimmy couldn't stop thinking about it. He started re-reading the articles and watching the clips again. He read the clipping of *The Sunday Times* article that had spurred Brian to search Cathy out — the one with the famous photograph of his beautiful young mother. And he found himself drawn to Josef's work differently — not as history, but as the work of a man he now wanted to recognise as his father. He already knew about The Stopover and Broome — he'd read about it and seen the portraits and photographs of this extraordinary oasis. He told himself there would come a time.

Eventually, he decided to take a sabbatical and travel to Australia. As a man for whom preparation was a prerequisite of his work, he was remarkably unprepared for the otherness of Broome. He left London without a solid plan or any appropriate clothing, only with the knowledge he wanted to meet his father.

The night before he spoke to Josef, he found Adam in the courtyard watching the stars and he told him why he was there and what he was about to do. Adam didn't seem surprised.

He simply said, "Tell him. I'll be there."

The following day, on the beach, Jimmy handed Josef a small photo of Cathy that Josef had taken of her in 1967. She was laughing, mid-sentence in a London park, her hair catching the light. He told him she was his mother. Other than that small gesture he didn't dramatise it.

He simply said, "You are my father, and my mother loved you."

Amidst his sobs, Josef replied that she had never left his heart.

And Jimmy saw it on the beach; how much it cost Josef to hear those words. Not because he doubted them, but because they unravelled something he'd carried for decades — the belief that Cathy had loved someone else. That he'd been abandoned.

So, Jimmy found himself at The Stopover surrounded by people he hadn't expected to care for, in a place that felt oddly like home. He had a younger brother, and the knowledge took time to settle in. In his understated, polite, and unemotional way, Jimmy had unintentionally upended, not only Josef's, but all their lives. He wasn't sure what came next other than he needed to stay a little longer.

*

That evening, after Jimmy told him the truth on the beach, Josef joined us in the courtyard for a while. We sat with him quietly. The shock moved between us like weather — it was palpable, shifting and unspoken. Without ceremony, he got up and walked off, withdrawing to his hidden sanctuary, the place so few of us had ever seen inside.

He stayed there for three days and no one, except Adam saw him.

Adam delayed a flight he had booked to New York without discussion. He didn't try to speak to Josef or intervene. He simply remained close by, enough to know that Josef was okay.

He knew Josef well enough to understand that silence and distance were what he needed most.

Josef had carried the memory of Cathy for decades. Fixed in his mind for all that time was that moment in Folkestone, the boy at her side and the kiss she had initiated. He hadn't needed words, he'd seen what he believed to be the truth: that she had chosen someone else. That she'd moved on and it had settled in him as a fact.

And now Jimmy's revelation. It had unravelled something more that was buried and long held. For over twenty years, Josef had lived in relative peace at The Stopover. The people, the life they shared and the rhythm of the seasons, had given him an existence that asked little and offered much. He had grown into himself and accepted who he was and what he had left behind. But now his mind turned inwards, heavy with the weight of what he hadn't known.

He waited, as he always had, for the turbulence to pass.

*

Jimmy stayed on at The Stopover and no one asked how long for. He didn't know himself.

Josef emerged from his sanctuary and the smile quickly returned. It was less spontaneous, but it was genuine, and soon enough he was available to us again in that open, unmistakably Josef way.

But in the following months, there was a change in him; it was subtle, but we all noticed it. The vitality that had defined him, the sharpness in his eyes and the quickness in his step had begun to fade. It was nothing dramatic, but there was a subtle slowing down. His gait had shifted, and he tired more easily. Watching him with Thomas on the veranda, I noticed how he steadied himself more often and how the playfulness came in shorter bursts.

But he never stopped.

His bond with Jimmy deepened quickly. There was no awkwardness between them, no sense of having missed the years they could never recover. They met one another as they were now, and that seemed to be enough.

Jimmy, for all his composure and careful speech, softened in Josef's company. He took to carrying his camera bags, holding reflectors and loading film. There was something almost boyish in his enthusiasm for it and a quiet pride. They spent many hours together in the darkroom, Josef transferring his knowledge and skills onto his son.

And it was easy to see that Josef found in Jimmy, not only a son, but a companion. In the early evenings, the three of them, Josef, Jimmy, and Thomas, would walk down to Cable Beach to watch the camels trail along the tide line. It became a ritual, unspoken and simple. Josef with his camera, Jimmy holding Thomas's hand. And when they returned, they would take it in turns to read Thomas a story and settle him for sleep.

Something in those walks allowed Josef to lean into his role as a father, in a way that was both belated and entirely present. With Thomas, he was soft and patient. With Jimmy, there was laughter, teasing, and the ease of shared time.

Jimmy changed, too. His Englishness and the public-school air of formality he'd arrived with, the polished shoes, the preppy collared shirts and the slight stiffness that seemed part of his posture, all began to dissolve. He stopped wearing long trousers and his signature brogues. It took him around three months, but one day he turned up to breakfast in the courtyard in a T-shirt and shorts, with bare legs and sandy flip-flops. He smiled sheepishly as if acknowledging that something had shifted for good.

He was still thoughtful and articulate, reserved in some ways — but the reserve no longer held him apart. He was funny and easy to be with. He helped in the kitchen, played cards with the guests, swam in the mornings, and took to calling flip-flops "thongs" like the rest of us, albeit with a smirk.

He didn't talk much about London. He'd left the city on a sabbatical, unsure of what he was looking for. And somewhere in the slow, quiet days at The Stopover, he had begun to find it. He adored his brother. Loved his father. And, as the months passed, it became clear he didn't want to leave — and I didn't want him to either.

*

Early one morning, after Jimmy had been at The Stopover for about four months, he and Josef were sitting side by side on the veranda outside his studio when Jimmy's mobile rang. He looked at the screen and hesitated before answering, rose and walked a few paces away. The shift in his voice and the way his back stiffened told Josef it was Cathy.

Josef didn't turn his head. He was listening without trying to listen.

He heard footsteps nearby and Jimmy held out the phone and said without expression,

"She wants to speak to you."

Josef didn't move at first. If he'd been given time to think, he might have refused — not out of bitterness or pride, but because some moments were easier not faced. But the moment was already happening, and it was too late to step away.

He took the phone.

"Hello?"

There was a silence. Then a breath.

"Josef," Cathy said.

Her voice was lower than he remembered, careful, measured.

"I didn't think I'd ever speak to you again," she said. "I didn't know if you'd want to."

He didn't answer right away. He didn't know what he wanted. He looked out across the courtyard, watching the light shift on the leaves.

"I didn't understand," he said.

Neither of them rushed to fill the silence that followed.

"I didn't understand either," she said. "I didn't know what I was doing. I panicked. I think I wanted to hurt you — or prove something. Brian wasn't what you thought."

"I know that now," Josef said. "Jimmy told me."

There was a pause. Cathy spoke again.

"I didn't choose Brian. I didn't know how to hold on to you. Or maybe I thought I didn't deserve to."

They talked for nearly half an hour. After the initial awkwardness passed, something easier settled between them. They spoke about their lives now, how they filled their days. There was no nostalgia or sentimentality — only two people adjusting to a new truth.

Toward the end, she said, "Thank you for letting him in."

"I didn't," Josef said. "He let himself in. But I'm glad he did."

She didn't reply. There was nothing more to add.

"I don't know what this means," Cathy said quietly. "I'm not asking for anything. I… wanted to hear your voice."

He nodded, though she couldn't see him.

"I'm glad we've spoken at last," he said.

They left it there. No promises or plans to meet, only the sound of two people who had once mattered to each other sharing an imperfect understanding.

Josef handed the phone to Jimmy without a word and stared out at the changing light across the courtyard.

*

Over the following year, through the wet season and into the slow, tentative return of the dry, Jimmy stayed with us. He renewed his visa without complication, settling quietly into the pattern of our lives. For a time, we became something that resembled an extended, unorthodox family — loosely formed but deeply connected.

Our work on *Woven Histories* reached its quiet conclusion. The paper was sent for peer review, and the intensity that had defined those months gradually gave way to something steadier and less consuming.

Liam, Adam, and I turned our attention to The Josef Batten Trust. We worked slowly, shaping it with care, designing and planning for The Stopover to become its anchor. Josef gave us his blessing. What energy he had left was given, almost entirely, to his sons.

I watched the shift unfold in him. His camera was still at hand, but it no longer led him. There was less urgency in the way he moved, less hunger to capture anything. His attention had narrowed in the best possible way and focused now on the two sons who, despite everything, had come to him late but not too late.

With Jimmy, the dynamic seemed to form naturally. There was no need to define roles. He became Thomas's older brother without hesitation or effort — tender, intuitive, and often, gently fatherly. I watched him hoist Thomas onto his shoulders, kneel to meet his gaze, and turn each question into a small, shared discovery. He was attentive without overstepping, and responsive without expectation. And slowly, my affection for him continued to deepen in its intensity.

But it wasn't only the way he was with Thomas. It was how he was with all of us. He was present, available, kind and never imposing. He was always attuned and the formality he'd arrived with had fallen away. The shoes and shirts were gone, and he wore sun-softened T-shirts now, shorts and the same pair of battered flip-flops every day. He moved differently, with a looseness that suggested he felt comfortable in his own body.

Josef noticed the change too. I believe he understood what was happening between Jimmy and me long before I had words for it. There was no awkwardness between us, only a quiet recognition. What was forming wasn't dramatic, and it didn't ask for permission. It was subtle and slow and made visible only by the way we all began to move around each other — gently, with care. What grew between us did so in the spaces where we simply showed up, day after day.

Still, I felt the need to speak to Adam. I wanted to be sure I wasn't misreading things, that I was treading with the care the situation deserved. He listened in his usual way — attentively, without judgement — and told me that Josef already knew. He'd seen it happen, and his only wish was for our happiness. Mine, Jimmy's and Thomas's.

Not long after that conversation, Jimmy began sharing my bed. There was no discussion and no announcement. We didn't hide it, and nothing changed outwardly in the way we moved through the day. It was unspoken and without ceremony, something that had quietly become true.

*

The pressure from Stanford University had been building for months, but by early 2012 it could no longer be deferred. The letters from the Dean's office had grown more pointed, the calls from my department chair more frequent. My research leave, though sanctioned and well-documented, had been extended too many times. The university wanted me back and while no one said it outright, the message was clear: if I wanted to maintain my standing and move toward promotion, I needed to return.

It wasn't simply a question of reappearing on campus. Returning meant stepping back into a world governed by deadlines, grant applications, and committee meetings. It meant preparing lectures, advising students, and securing the next publication. It meant proving, all over again, that I was still serious and still relevant.

I had tenure, yes, but that was a foundation, not a refuge. If I wanted to become a full professor and leave any a legacy in the field, I couldn't simply disappear into motherhood and a project in a remote corner of northern Australia. I had already stretched the rules as far as they would go and the expectation now was that I would recommit.

And yet everything in me resisted the idea of leaving.

The Stopover had become more than a temporary station; it had become a life — our life. Thomas had never known anything else, and his days were shaped by ocean air and red dirt, by the freedom of being surrounded by people who adored him. And Jimmy and I had evolved into something steady and sustaining. We lived together, not in name, but in practice. There was no dramatic shift, no formal start, only the slow accumulation of trust and care and affection until it became impossible to imagine a day without him.

But the deepest weight and the real complication was Josef.

His presence had changed over the past year. He was still himself, still wry and perceptive and watchful, but there were signs: a certain weariness in his movements, longer pauses in conversation and a frailty he tried to disguise. He spent more time alone and he stopped taking his camera out. And while he never asked, I knew he relied on us more than he admitted.

Leaving would mean pulling up the roots we had laid down. Not for me and Thomas, but for Jimmy, who had begun to find something of himself here.

The thought of abandoning Josef — because that's how it felt — was unbearable and yet, the call of responsibility was insistent. I knew I couldn't avoid it forever. Something would have to give.

It was Adam who saw it clearly. He was the one who named what I couldn't, and he told me I had to go, that Stanford wasn't a betrayal of what we'd built, but the next phase of what I could contribute. That The Stopover would go on without me for a while, and that Josef would not be alone.

"I'll be here," Adam said. "He'll have me. He'll always have me."

That was the moment something shifted. With Adam's reassurance came the clarity I'd been waiting for. The guilt didn't vanish, but the paralysis eased. I could go, and trust that what mattered here would hold. That the love we had invested into this place would outlast our physical presence.

As for Jimmy, there were no ultimatums or dramatic declarations. After long conversations, half-finished thoughts, and quiet recognitions, the understanding came. He would come with me, to San Francisco and Stanford and into the unknown. It was a choice we made together.

And so, the plan emerged and in August 2012, we left Broome, The Stopover and our makeshift family.

*

The night before we left, I couldn't sleep.

Thomas and Jimmy were in our suite, and I wrapped a blanket around my shoulders and sat in the courtyard, beneath the tilted bowl of stars, listening to the breath of the house — its murmurs and nocturnal sighs, the shift of wood and the rustle of palms.

At some point, I moved from the chair to the long low sofas near the kitchen and watched the silhouettes of moths flickering at the edges of light, the sky darkening still before it began to brighten.

I was not alone. Josef had wheeled his bed into the courtyard, as he often did. He didn't see me. Or if he did, he said nothing. The smooth, burnished frame of the cot glided almost soundlessly across the boards, the mosquito netting suspended like a ghostly sail above him. He always positioned the bed with care, just so, to face the sky. He would lie there in stillness for hours, charting the slow arc of constellations, asking the questions he never stopped asking — those impossible questions with no fixed answers. I know this because we discussed it often.

He said it was in the pre-dawn silence before the shrieks and chatter of the birds began, that he seemed most at peace. It was in this silence that the house felt most alive to him: each breath, each footfall, each subtle creak and click a thread in the web of his awareness. In those hours, he could listen to the house breathe and feel, once again, the fragile bliss of simply being alive.

Before the first mutterings of dawn, I watched him stir. With the same slow care he always showed, he drew back the netting, unclicked the brakes, and guided the bed across the platform — wheels gliding like silk over velvet — back along a wooden path to his studio where he tucked it away amongst the shelves, where it vanished almost entirely as if it had never left.

The studio was his refuge. It was much more than a room, it was the essence of him — vaulted and open, edged with books and drawings and the quiet order of a life constructed entirely on his terms. It opened to the courtyard on one side and to the far garden on the other. The glass walls were folded back, letting the morning air drift through. I remained still, hidden from view, watching the last of the night fade into the blue hush of dawn.

He boiled the kettle, poured tea, and sat at his desk with his back to the veranda, waiting. He knew the ritual.

And sure enough, not long after, Thomas appeared. Barefoot, breath held, body coiled with anticipation, he crept along the boards, trying desperately to be invisible, to surprise Josef. It was a performance they played out every morning.

Josef waited until Thomas was within reach before spinning in his chair with a whispered shout, feigning alarm.

"WAaaah!"

Thomas shrieked and clutched at his chest, "No! Not 'gain, Josef!"

Whispering, giggling and mimicking, he pressed his small finger to his lips to hush him.

Josef did the same, smiling, and pulled him close.

Thomas curled into his lap, warm and wriggling, and kissed his stubbled cheek. Then came the story.

"Camels went to beach," Thomas announced, milk dribbling from the side of his mouth.

"How many camels Thomas?"

He held up his fingers, slowly and seriously, "This many." He paused. "One gone."

"Gone? What happened?"

"Pirates eat it," he said, with exaggerated gravity. "Get 'nother one 'morrow."

The same lines, told with the same conviction, every morning. But this morning, something was different. When Josef set him down, Thomas's mood shifted. His face clouded. He didn't understand the day was different, but some part of him felt it. Josef knelt to meet him at eye level and took his shoulders gently.

"What's wrong, little man?" he said.

Thomas stared and, without warning, he smacked Josef on the shoulder with his small, furious hand.

He ran — blindly, head down, arms swinging — around the veranda, feet pounding against the timber. It wasn't loud enough to wake the guests, but it was enough to tell us what words couldn't. He was three. He didn't know why he felt this way. He just did.

Josef stood at the doorway, unmoving, watching the blur of motion and frustration streak past, again and again. Each time Thomas rounded the corner, Josef's face softened a little more.

And finally, Thomas flung himself at Josef's legs and clung onto them. Josef bent, gathered him up, and held him close. He rested his chin on that warm, tousled head and looked out toward the courtyard where I sat, still watching.

I saw something wordless and deep pass between them, a primal love, beyond explanation or understanding. Josef carried him gently along the veranda, towards our room. Thomas's hand was still clenched around his shirt.

As they drew near, I rose to meet them. We didn't speak.

The sun had begun to rise. It was morning now and a few hours later we left for the airport and though my body was taken thousands of miles away, part of me — part of all of us — remained there, in the house that breathed like a living thing, and in the courtyard where the birds would always be singing.

Epilogue

Adam Laidlaw, London, 2025

Josef Batten died on the 9th of April 2013. He knew he was ill long before he told any of us.

In many ways, Josef's departure marked the end of an era, yet it ignited a flame in the heart of The Josef Batten Trust that burns brighter today than I ever thought possible.

The world we inhabit now, so laden with uncertainties, feels alien to the one he knew. In 2025, we navigate a landscape warped by the idea of there being post-truth ideologies and we live in a world dominated by divisive narratives. Conspiracy theories are predominant; and images and information swirl in an endless stream, distorted by algorithms designed to manipulate rather than enlighten.

As I write this on a rainy London afternoon, Rumi's words resonate with me:

Out beyond ideas of wrongdoing and rightdoing
there is a field
I'll meet you there

What does it mean to truly understand one another when our language can only convey fragments? In this field beyond judgment lies our shared humanity — a vast expanse where we can listen without bias or preconception.

Undoubtedly, the world today remains too full of talk and noise that masks genuine connection — a chaotic hum drowning out cries for understanding.

When I learned Josef was dying, the world outside The Stopover blurred into insignificance. I cancelled all my appointments and performances, and my focus narrowed to simply being with him in those final weeks.

Josef spent his last days in the wooden cot on wheels, positioned out on the platform beneath a canvas of stars and shifting clouds. Maggie, Marguerite, and Talia drifted in and out like guardian spirits, providing practical assistance amidst the inevitable sorrow.

A week before he passed Elizabeth arrived with Thomas and Jimmy. Cathy asked if she could see him; her desire felt raw yet sincere and Josef was moved to tears. When she flew over, their meeting was poignant — a dance of emotions between two souls who had cared deeply for one another. It was beautiful to witness how love could bridge years of silence.

As Josef faded further into the realms of pain relief administered by palliative nurses, he turned to me one evening with a glimmer of lucidity igniting his weary eyes.

"Record my voice," he said softly as if uttering an incantation against oblivion.

I set up my phone beside him and pressed record and for days we spoke about everything and nothing.

We also listened to music together; much of it filled the air with the echoes of joy and memory that seemed to define our relationship. Those weeks bore a bittersweet beauty — we navigated each day through laughter mingled with tears.

For days I found solace sleeping in a chair beside him in the courtyard where the stillness enveloped us as if even time itself had paused for a heartbeat longer and stretched the possibilities of life a little further.

When Josef took his last breath, surrounded by those who loved him dearly, I felt an overwhelming sense of peace settle upon us all — he had found his way home.

The Josef Batten Trust

The Josef Batten Trust was set up in 2010 at The Stopover in Broome, Western Australia. It also has offices in London and San Francisco. The Trust is a charity that supports truth-telling, cultural protection and creative reconciliation. Inspired by Josef Batten's life and work, it keeps The Stopover as a place for ethical witnessing, rest and respectful conversation.

The Trust aims to encourage honest truth-telling, creative responses to injustice, and storytelling that includes many voices. It works to amplify people who are often unheard — especially Indigenous communities, survivors of conflict, post-colonial scholars and emerging artists from marginalised backgrounds — by offering residencies, forums and mentorship. The Trust also looks after Josef Batten's photographic archive, making sure its use follows cultural protocols and that materials are repatriated or interpreted in ways led by communities.

The founding trustees are Liam Karri, Elizabeth Chandler and Adam Laidlaw. They bring Indigenous governance, academic expertise and personal care of Josef's legacy. The trustees have the sole power to appoint future trustees, so the Trust's founding values — truth, inclusion and respect for land and story — are protected.

Core programmes:

Cultural preservation: Protecting The Stopover and nearby land under Traditional Owner guidance and embedding Indigenous knowledge in the Trust's work.

Residencies & retreats: Giving time and space to people working where art, trauma and reconciliation meet.

Archives & memory work: Preserving and cataloguing Josef's work and working with communities on ethical exhibitions and repatriation.

Youth engagement: Partnering with schools and cultural groups to teach visual literacy, storytelling and history to underrepresented young people.

The Josef Batten Forum: An annual gathering on topics such as ethical seeing, memory and the role of silence and story in healing.

The Stopover is owned and held by the Trust to protect it as a public cultural space. Adam Laidlaw and Elizabeth Chandler continue to have access. Guided by honesty, art and the practice of slowing down, the Josef Batten Trust offers a straightforward model of care and creative peacebuilding in a time of divided stories.

INDEX OF MUSIC

Search and follow the Spotify Playlist:
"The Many Truths of Josef Batten"

The Green Green Grass of Home | Tom Jones	102, 222
Suzanne | Leonard Cohen:	108, 109
Road | Pink Moon, Nick Drake	110
Sarasate: Zigeunerweisen Op. 20 | Itzhac Perlman	123, 126
In a Landscape | John Cage	123, 126
Foreshadowed | *The Pearl,* Harold Budd, Brian Eno	123, 126
Astral Weeks | Van Morrison	123, 126
In A Silent Way | Miles Davis	123, 127
Köln January 24 1975 Part I | Keith Jarrett	124, 127
Born Under Punches | Talking Heads	124
Bach Volin Concerto in E Major: I. Allegro | Stern	174
Violin Concerto no.2 in D minor op.22 | Wieniawski	126
Tabula Rasa: I. Ludus. — Live | Arvo Pärt, Kremer	126, 161
Comes a Time | Neil Young	126, 157, 161, 214, 221
May You Never | *Solid Air,* John Martyn	160, 161
Fire and Rain | James Taylor	160, 161
Court and Spark | Joni Mitchell	291, 292
'Cello Song | Five Leaves Left, Nick Drake	160
One Love/People Get Ready | Bob Marley & The Wailers	167, 168
Secret O' Life | *JT,* James Taylor	221
Kathy's Song — Live | Simon & Garfunkel	222
Take Me Home Country Roads | John Denver	223

A Song For You | Carpenters	163, 222
Top of the World | Carpenters	163, 166, 222
I Shot The Sheriff | Bob Marley & The Wailers	168
Satie: 6 Gnossienne | E Satie, Anne Queffélec	172
As | Stevie Wonder	178
Another Star | Stevie Wonder	180
Für Alina — Extended Version | A Pärt, A Malter	180
A Song For You | Leon Russell	222
Islands In the Stream | Dolly Parton, Kenny Rogers	223
Violin Partita No. 2 in D Minor | JS Bach, H Hahn	253
The Sailor's Bonnet — Live | The Gloaming	276
Northern Sky | Nick Drake	292
Goldberg Variations Aria | JS Bach, G Gould	323
Spiegel im Spiegel | Arvo Pärt	336
Cello Suite No. 1 in G Major | JS Bach, Yo-Yo Ma	336

THANK YOU

Jeffrey Wilkinson, Claire-Louise John,
Simon Gravatt, Cosima Worth, Anna Ralph.

Special thanks to Cordelia Hampton-John
for your, love, encouragement and support.

Thank you for reading
The Many Truths of Josef Batten.

This is my first novel — a story I carried with me for over twenty years until it grew into something I knew I had to share.

As a reader, your thoughts matter to me. If you enjoyed the book, I would be grateful if you could **leave a review** on Amazon or Goodreads.com.

Your words will help others discover the story too.

You can find out more about my work at
johnworth.co.uk, on Substack **@johnworth01**
or on Instagram **@johnworth.artist**.

With warmest thanks,

John Worth